Courting the Country Preacher

4 STORIES OF & FALLING IN LOVE FAITH, HOPE...

Courting the Country Preacher

4 STORIES OF FAITH, HOPE... & FALLING IN LOVE

ANGELA K COUCH, CAROLYN MILLER, NAOMI MUSCH, KARI TRUMBO

BARBOUR
PUBLISHING

The Mountie's Rival ©2024 by Angela K Couch
Convincing the Circuit Preacher ©2024 by Carolyn Miller
The Angel and the Sky Pilot ©2024 by Naomi Musch
Mail-Order Minister ©2024 by Kari Trumbo

Print ISBN 978-1-63609-976-7
Adobe Digital Edition (.epub) 978-1-63609-977-4

All scripture quotations, unless otherwise noted, are taken from the King James Version of the Bible.

This book is a work of fiction. Names, characters, places, and incidents are either products of the author's imagination or used fictitiously. Any similarity to actual people, organizations, and/or events is purely coincidental.

Cover image © Kirk DouPonce, DogEared Design

Published by Barbour Books, an imprint of Barbour Publishing, Inc., 1810 Barbour Drive, Uhrichsville, Ohio 44683, www.barbourbooks.com

Our mission is to inspire the world with the life-changing message of the Bible.

Member of the
Evangelical Christian
Publishers Association

Printed in the United States of America.

The Mountie's Rival

BY ANGELA K COUCH

DEDICATION:

To my husband—thank you for your example of kindness.

ACKNOWLEDGMENTS:

I have been blessed with a wonderful family and community who have made this book possible. A huge thanks to my husband whose support is invaluable and to my kids who put up with me during the two crazy months of putting this story onto paper. To my hubby and others who took the time to read through my rough work so readers don't have to. To my editors at Barbour who believed in me and helped bring this story to life. To God, who fills in where I lack and gave me the story to write.

CHAPTER 1

Rowley, Alberta, Canada, 1907

Fear was a sensation Jonathan Burton was familiar with. Fear of making a fool of himself. Fear of failing. Fear of not being good enough. Fear of forever living in his brother's shadow. Each of these threatened to crush him as he stood for the first time in the pulpit of the small rural church and faced his new congregation, which included a man in a scarlet coat. The North-West Mounted Police constable had the nerve to grin as he sauntered up the aisle to find a place in one of the front pews. He drew his flat-brimmed Stetson from his head and hooked it on his knee, that blasted grin never leaving his face.

Jonathan couldn't smile if he'd wanted to. Not with his heart threatening to choke him. Why hadn't Mother said something to him when he'd told her that Rowley, Alberta, would be his new home? Unless this was her doing. Jonathan forced a breath. Yes, that made more sense—Mother must have told David of Jonathan's new position, and he was simply visiting.

Forcing his gaze away from his brother, Jonathan looked over the rest of his congregation. Not a huge group—no more than fifty people, including young children and babies—but they were his. His sheep.

A large pair of bright eyes caught his, staring up with expectation and something more. Probably the same something that caused the woman to lean forward while her hands clutched her Bible.

Hope.

He wished he had more confidence he'd not disappoint her or anyone else—himself included.

Jonathan cleared his throat. "Good morning, brothers and sisters. For those who don't know, my name is Jonathan Burton, and I will be your new pastor." After so much work and study to get here, he could smile about that. "Before we get into my message for you today, I have been asked to extend an invitation for the community to meet after church. A picnic lunch has been organized by Mr. and Mrs. Matkin. It should give us the opportunity to visit and come to know one another better." He couldn't help but glance back to the woman with golden hair pulled up in a loose bun and a shyness in the way she held herself. "I look forward to meeting each and every one of you." But especially her.

Time to get to what he'd come here to say, the sermon he had written and rewritten at least a dozen times. "Every *one*. Each individual and his or her needs must be our focus. As in these parables Jesus gave His disciples." He continued, reading from the book of Luke about the lost sheep that strayed from the ninety and nine, followed by the lost coin and the rejoicing of the widow when she found it. "And then there was a son, beloved of a father, despite his flaws. The important thing to remember about the prodigal son is—"

A gunshot pierced the air, as loud as though fired from just outside. Shouts rang out. David jerked to his feet, but before anyone could move the door burst open and a man raced inside the church. "Constable!" he hollered, though the man he sought stood within feet of him and stuck out like a sore thumb with the brightness of his coat. "Arthur's drunk again! Near took off Matt's arm. We're needing the doc too."

As though that was explanation enough, David, along with half the congregation on his heels, flowed from the church like tomato ketchup from the bottom of a jar. Men stepped over and around their families, and women called for their older children to remain behind. Some heeded, while others scampered off with the crowd. What a disaster. A full five minutes passed before the room was quiet enough for Jonathan to hear himself think, but the attention of his diminished flock ping-ponged from him to the disruption on the street.

"I hope that is not a regular event on the Sabbath," Jonathan finally managed with a weak chuckle. He looked over the few who remained, which did not include the woman with the pretty eyes, and felt his chest deflate. What was the point of trying to continue his sermon? Instead of hunting down the *one*, he was left trying to gather back the twenty-five to thirty. And that didn't count those who were truly lost and hadn't made it into the front door to begin with! Was he up for such a task?

"For today, let's give those stories some thought." And give the devil his due. "How can we extend fellowship and the hand of help to those who are astray? I hope you invite your neighbors to the picnic this afternoon." Hopefully then he could make a better impression on the community. Unfortunately, he saw no recourse but to forfeit this round to his brother.

The chipping paint fell away under the touch of her fingertips as she pressed against the side of the church. Voices faded toward the back of the building where an open field and playground buzzed with activity. April Harvey's stomach churned. Maybe she should simply spend her afternoon alone at the top of the grain elevator as she often did when not harvesttime. Or at home. The small, framed house—little more than a shack for the care given its construction—would be quiet for the foreseeable future, what with Pa in jail.

April's face grew hot as she recalled the look on the new pastor's face. He'd turned quite red with his exasperation, poor man. All the more reason she should stay away from this gathering.

April sighed. She really shouldn't fault folks for their opinions of her or the way they looked her way, accusation in their eyes. She had grown used to them believing she was somehow responsible for her pa's actions. And perhaps she was, in some way. Pastor Jensen seemed to think so, always handing out suggestions on what more she could do to help Pa.

She'd failed him. In more ways than most folks knew.

"Miss Harvey, what are you doing to the paint?"

April jerked to where Miss Maddie stood with raised brows and felt a trickle of relief that someone else hadn't found her. "Just wondering how much longer folks will pretend the church only has a front."

The elderly woman laughed. "When Mr. Matkin volunteered enough paint to freshen up the church, I guess he decided only what is seen counts."

April gave a rueful smile. "Reminds me of what it says in the Bible about painted sepulchres."

Miss Maddie's mouth dropped open. "Oh, child! What an unkind comparison." Then her expression softened, and she winked. "Though I suppose sometimes it seems as though some put on a perfect display while not truly changing who they are on the inside."

It was April's turn to grimace. Did that apply to her as well?

She tried so hard to pretend, to place a smile on her face when around others, while anger and fear reigned within. The Bible spoke strongly against both.

Miss Maddie seemed unaware of April's distress or desire to remain unseen. She slipped her arm through April's, pulling her toward the noisy gathering. "Come along, dear. No reason to hide back here."

"I wasn't hiding," April protested, though that was exactly what she'd been doing. Hiding. Always hiding, even from her true feelings.

Miss Maddie didn't argue but led April forward while going on about how nice she looked in her blue frock and how it brought out the color of her eyes. April felt some of the tension ease from her shoulders. Her blue eyes and honey-toned tresses were her inheritance from her mother who had immigrated from Germany as a child. April wished that was what people saw when they looked at her—someone like her mother, as kind and genuine a person as ever existed. Maybe then they could forget her connection to the man locked behind bars because his temper and the whiskey had yet again gotten the better of him.

"Welcome, Maddie." Mrs. Johnson greeted her sister with hardly a glance at April. "I wondered what was taking you so long."

"I was visiting with April. I quite enjoy her humor, you know."

Mrs. Johnson's face tightened. "I wasn't aware."

April wasn't either. She'd been quite serious in all her comments.

"Yes, I do find her quite a delight." She smiled at April with such warmth, April's breathing eased.

"That is all well and good, but..." Mrs. Johnson cast another sidelong look at April before looping her arm through her sister's and leading her away with the newest gossip abuzz in April's ears though she remained behind. Alone, despite being in the middle of the crowd. Folks glanced her way. Many whispered behind their hands or in their neighbor's ears. Few ever said anything out loud.

A smile will chase hurts, like a swatter does flies.

Mama seemed to believe the saying, and April had repeated the words over and over until it became simply *Smile until hurts fly.*

And so she did. Shoulders back and smile in place, she took in the large gathering. . .while slinking again to the outskirts where she belonged.

From her vantage point, she could see the new pastor nodding vigorously while Mrs. Matkin introduced him to the Henrys, a family who farmed a few miles west of town, neighboring the Matkins' quite extensive spread. The Matkins' oldest daughter, Bethany, looked up with her large brown eyes and flashing lashes. Though only seventeen, the young woman filled out her dress better then April ever had. Thankfully, Brother Burton's smile was merely polite—which made it easier for April to keep her own.

Burton. She hadn't thought much on his name in church that morning when he was introduced, but the local Mountie was a Burton as well. Was it possible the two were related?

No. They were simply too different. Where the preacher was tall and lanky, the Mountie was a few inches shorter and had a solid build. They both had dark brown hair, but the shade was common enough. Facial features were completely different, except for maybe the shape of their noses. She'd have to see them together to be sure.

As though summoned by her thoughts, Constable Burton appeared in the crowd and made a beeline for the preacher. April moved a step to the right to get a better view of the two of them together. On actual inspection, perhaps they did share some similar features through the eyes and the shape of their ears, of all things. Perhaps they were related after all. Cousins, perhaps? She moved closer, edging into the crowd. Curiosity was a gnawing hunger at times.

April snatched a soft roll from the table as she passed, and she nibbled one pinch at a time, trying to act casual in her approach. Others stood with filled plates, visiting. Her stomach pinched, a reminder that she'd gone without breakfast that morning. Maybe she should have also taken the time to fill a plate—but then she would miss the Mountie's greeting which accompanied a full bear hug. He pounded the preacher on the back and even messed his hair. The poor preacher flushed and attempted to tame his molested locks, shooting the Mountie a glare. Strange. The one appeared much happier at the meeting then the other, though perhaps the pastor simply disliked his hair being out of order. He seemed very particular about his clothes as well. Each item fit to perfection and was neatly groomed. She would have to take extra care with his laundry.

"You've met my brother." The Mountie's voice boomed, as though the announcement was meant for more than those in the immediate area.

April stopped short and almost laughed out loud. She had not expected that close of a relation. She couldn't help but want to learn more about this preacher whose smile was just as practiced as hers.

CHAPTER 2

Why hadn't she simply asked him? April berated herself and her shortsightedness at avoiding a conversation with the new preacher while she'd had the chance at the picnic yesterday. But Monday was now here, and she stood in the early morning chill, trying to decide if she should knock and speak with him now about the arrangement or wait until he left and assume nothing had changed. The parsonage would still need to be cleaned. What did it matter that a new preacher resided there?

Except that her arrangement had been with the previous preacher. What if this one decided he didn't care to have the daughter of the local drunk in his home?

"I need that money."

Not a reminder she required. Not only did the little she earn help feed her and Pa between the employment he found, but if she made any less, she wouldn't have the extra coins to squirrel away for her escape from this place.

No, she needed to keep this position despite Pa and what this new preacher thought of her. Better not to give him a chance to change the arrangement. She would continue as she always did, and the preacher would see how well she did her work and have no reason not to pay her.

Hinges creaked on the storm door, and the man in question strode from his new home. April shuffled deeper behind the lilacs so as not to be seen, but she could hear his footsteps heading toward the church. She had been afraid he would not keep the same schedule as Pastor Jensen, but it seemed she'd worried for nothing. She should have until noon to fix lunch and clean the small house until every surface shined.

April's feet were a little lighter as she hurried up the short walk and inside. Not much had changed since she'd left a week earlier, but that was not surprising, since the house had remained empty until last Friday. Plus, the man was a bachelor, unlike the last preacher, who was a widower with three older children. She frowned at the thought. Perhaps Pastor Burton would not require as much from her—would the man make any mess?

Some of her fears eased as she stepped into his bedroom where clothes hung over the back of a chair and three days' worth of socks were piled on the floor. The quilts were bunched in the middle of the bed, and a glass half full of water sat on the small table beside an open Bible. That was strange. Pastor Jensen always took his Bible with him to the church for his morning study.

April set about straightening up the room, putting anything that required laundering near the door to be taken home to be washed this afternoon.

She shook out the quilts before folding them to the bottom of the bed so the sheets could air out for long-lasting freshness. Something small and hard flew from the quilts and struck the floor with a *ping*. What on earth? April crouched and scoured the area, catching sight of a small, surprisingly round stone just under the corner of the bed. She reached to grab it, but as she released the corner of the quilt, it swung down and struck the pebble, sending it deeper under the bed. She lowered to her stomach and shifted until she could see the stone near the center. She wiggled forward, stretching out her hand, pushing herself under the bed. Just a little farther...

"Excuse me?"

April cracked her head against the bottom of the bed frame. "Ouch!"

Hands clamped around her ankles and drew her out. Sunlight flashed in her eyes, blocked partially by a tall form and glowering face. Maybe glowering wasn't the right word, but the preacher didn't appear very happy with her presence under his bed.

"What are you doing?"

"What...?" It took her a moment to remember her mission. She opened her hand to reveal the prize. "I was getting this."

"You broke into my bedroom to steal one of my rocks?"

"No!" April shoved the stone into his hand. "I don't even like rocks. And I would never take anything that wasn't mine."

"Then what are you doing in my house?" He sounded more confused than angry.

"I clean. I'm cleaning." April straightened her apron and tried to appear at least half put together. "I am your housekeeper."

His dark brows arched. "I have a housekeeper?"

Her heart dropped. If he hadn't been told about her, he would probably resist the extra expense. "Yes. Pastor Jensen began the arrangement, and I assure you I am well worth it. I come three times a week and prepare lunch on those days, so you needn't trek to the diner or boardinghouse. I keep the house clean, along with any dishes and laundry." She motioned to the pile behind her.

"That all sounds wonderful, Miss..."

It probably would have helped if she'd found the nerve to introduce herself yesterday, but then everyone standing near might have felt the need to inform the new preacher of her relationship with the man who had disrupted his sermon that morning, and she couldn't risk that even now. "Folks around here just call me April. No need to be formal in such a small town."

"Then you can call me Jonathan, I suppose, April." Her name rolled off his tongue so prettily, she almost didn't hate it. When most said her name, they might as well be mentioning the month, but he made it sound like a real name—actually addressing her instead of just speaking at her. "I have no doubt you do a wonderful job, but—"

"Please." She hated to beg, but the thought of losing her position broke sweat along her brow and down her spine.

"I just don't—"

"It doesn't have to be a great expense. I will do the same work for half the amount. But I need—"

"You're not letting me finish."

"I just—"

"I am simply trying to say, I don't believe this is the appropriate place for a conversation."

"But I…" Heat rushed into April's face, and she pressed her palms to her cheeks. "Of course." Discussing employment in a parson's bedroom. What a disaster! She scooped up his clothes and rushed past him. After dumping the clothes into a basket in the kitchen, she returned for the one sock that had slipped her hold. Laundry tucked away, she filled the kettle and put it on the stove then stoked the fire—though, goodness, the house was already far too warm. Not that anyone would even want tea or coffee. She simply needed something to do while she allowed her embarrassment to shift from the flames in her cheeks to the sick feeling in the pit of her stomach.

Jonathan tried to keep his smile in check but was not entirely successful. Thankfully, Miss April With-No-Surname kept her attention focused elsewhere. He'd hate for her to think he was mocking her or laughing at her expense, but in truth, after getting past the surprise of finding her feet poking out from under his bed when he'd returned from the outhouse, he couldn't be happier with his luck. Or was this a miracle? He'd noticed her yesterday in church and at the picnic but had been unable to meet her, much to his disappointment.

"I do hope you will forget all this." She waved her hand toward the bedroom. "I hate to imagine what you must think of me."

"A simple misunderstanding, just as you said." But he had no intention of ever forgetting how pretty she looked when her cheeks flushed with color—or any of the past ten minutes, really. Far too entertaining.

"Yes, a misunderstanding," she repeated, pulling a teacup from the cupboard. "Do you prefer tea or coffee?"

"I am fine with either. So long as you join me."

Her eyes, large and blue, flashed in his direction.

"It sounds as though we have things to discuss. You will join me, won't you?"

April looked undecided between him, the kettle, and the door, almost giving him the impression that she might make a run for it. Then, finally, she nodded and pulled a second teacup from the cupboard along with the teapot.

Jonathan smiled more freely as he found a seat at the table and relaxed. He'd gladly sit and watch her flit around his kitchen with both grace and precision, but that was probably not the best activity for a new preacher with finding a wife on his mind. Or maybe it *was*. Already he was drawn to the woman without any understanding of whether she would make a good partner or promote his standing in the community. "You said you worked for Parson Jensen before I arrived?"

"Yes." She placed the teapot on the table and set out the cups and a plate of biscuits he hadn't seen until now. She must have brought them with her. "I came here a couple of hours on Monday, Wednesday, and Friday mornings while he prepared his sermon and studied at the church. Like I said, I clean, do laundry, and prepare a fresh midday meal the days I am here."

"And how much was that service?"

She rattled off the numbers, watching his reaction closely. "But seeing as you are single, while he had three children, I can work for less."

"Nonsense. I'm sure I will be no cleaner or less hungry than the Jensens. Though I hadn't planned on studying at the church. I've always found the table a comfortable location, and strong coffee helps me think."

"Perhaps, but. . ." Again, her face flushed red. This time the color crept over her ears. "But you are an unmarried man, and folks might not be comfortable with me coming and going with you in residence. If they know you are at the church, there can be no wagging of tongues."

"Uh, yes, wagging tongues."

A smile twitched at the corner of her mouth. "Our small town is well known for such."

"Is it?" He tapped the table as though considering that while his actual subject of consideration watched from beside the stove. Now that humor had entered their conversation, light sparked in her eyes, making them even more vibrant than before. "Would a sermon about the woman taken in adultery be in order? 'He that is without sin among you,' and all that?"

April grimaced. "Might be a little too blunt for them."

He chuckled. "A simple 'love thy neighbour' sermon, then?"

Her smile became more genuine, lighting her face. "Loving

one's neighbor can never go amiss."

Jonathan nodded though she wouldn't see it, her focus on pouring their tea. Of course, some neighbors were easier to love than others, and Miss April With-Last-Name-Unknown would probably be one of the easiest.

CHAPTER 3

Jonathan remained at the table long after April left, though his tea sat cold and his Bible remained in the bedroom. All he had was the chunk of agate she'd pulled from under his bed and the promise that she would return tomorrow so he had time to vacate the premises for the morning. The only downside to their arrangement. He'd much rather continue their conversation.

Jonathan huffed out a laugh. He'd not been overly excited about this rural location when he'd received his assignment—seeing as Rowley was smack-dab in the middle of nowhere—and less so when he'd found out his brother was here as well, but suddenly he wanted to grin about it all.

A knock sounded at the door, and Jonathan shot to his feet. Was it possible April had forgotten something? She hadn't been gone long, but already he wanted to see her again. He swung the door wide—

His smile fled at the sight of the red uniform. "David?"

His brother clapped him on the shoulder while pushing into the house. His boots pounded across the wood floor. "Impressive, Jonny." He poked his head into the main bedroom. "Much better than the cot they give me across from the cell. Nothing worse than trying to sleep when you have a snoring drunk locked up."

The tension eased a smidgen from Jonathan's spine. David was right. He had a whole house with a bedroom to spare—house enough for a family. While his brother slept at the North-West Mounted Police post down the street. "It's all right," he said with a shrug.

David just smiled as though it didn't matter and moved to the table, taking the seat April had graced not a half hour earlier. Jonathan would have traded his brother for the former without hesitation. David didn't seem to notice his unease, instead toying with the piece of agate Jonathan had left on the table. "I see you still collect rocks." His tone was almost dismissive and carried tones of laughter.

Jonathan took the stone and shoved it into his pocket. It might appear like an ordinary rock, but with some work and polish it would appear almost gemlike. "What can I do for you?"

David grinned up at him like he had at the church. "Isn't this the best? You and I in the same town. I've hardly seen you for the past three years. Now it can almost be like old times."

Jonathan frowned. "I doubt stealing sheets from someone's laundry line and making a barn look haunted is an appropriate activity for the town's preacher or constable."

David winked. "That's what would make it so great. No one would suspect us."

"And even if they did, who would take us to task?" Jonathan almost smiled.

"Exactly!" David laughed out loud.

Jonathan wished he could feel as lighthearted about the arrangement. They were grown men now, after all. But something gnawed at his peace, leaving him unsettled. He was the town's pastor, and that should be enough—but somehow, he would end up in his brother's shadow again. David was too vibrant and full of energy. The scarlet of his coat suited him well, while the black of Jonathan's displayed the differences in their personalities far too aptly. Differences that would leave Jonathan again on the outside and underappreciated.

"What has you looking so glum?" David questioned, his brow furrowing. "I thought you would be glad to see me."

"Of course I am," he lied. No, it wasn't a lie. As a preacher he taught against such things and would try to live his life as an example. He was glad to see his brother. He simply wasn't glad David was staying in town. "I have a lot on my mind, and plate for that matter. I need to get settled in and start working on my sermon for next week." One he'd hopefully have a chance to finish.

"Ah, I understand. And I have reports to write. And lunch to arrange for Arthur." David narrowed his eyes as though considering something. "You should come by and have a talk with Arthur. He's a good enough fellow, but most days he could be counted as 'the one' you were talking about Sunday."

Jonathan raised a brow, not quite following. "The one?"

"Yeah, the one who's gone astray, that we need to find and bring back to the fold, like Jesus taught. When the shepherd left the ninety-nine."

"Ah, the parable of the lost sheep." It was Jonathan's duty to extend a hand of fellowship and help to those struggling and suffering and lost. "I guess it would serve my purposes—I mean, God's purposes—to meet Mr. Arthur and see how we can help him. What is he locked up for?"

"Disrupting your sermon," David said with a wink, back on his feet.

Understanding dawned. "I thought he shot someone."

David frowned. "An unfortunate accident, as far as I can tell. Arthur's temper does get short when he's drunk, and he and Matt got in a bit of a tussle. Does complicate my first week here." He waved it off as though it would sort itself out. "Come, I'll show you my place now. That should improve your gratitude for your many blessings." He chuckled and led the way.

Jonathan grabbed his jacket and hat and trailed his brother out the door and down the street past the bank and the barber-shop and then across to the local newspaper office. Beside the latter, a diner emitted a glorious aroma and the reminder that he'd had neither breakfast nor lunch and would have to return later. The biscuits that Miss April provided hadn't done quite enough to satisfy a day's worth of hunger. Finally, David paused and fished a key out of his pocket. Jonathan gave the town one last look before glancing heavenward. A dark form caught his eye, perched high on the roof of the huge grain elevator beside the railway track.

What on earth. . . ?

The lock clicked. "Jonny?"

Jonathan glanced at his brother then back at the elevators, but the person was gone. Could he have imagined it? How could someone have gotten up there?

Jonathan pushed it from his mind as David motioned him into the dimly lit room that held a desk and cot in one corner and a small cell with another cot in the other. Snoring filled the entire room. Cozy indeed.

"Wake up, Arthur," David called to the man asleep in the cell. "Brought you a visitor."

The stocky man snorted and sputtered as he blinked his eyes open and sat up. "She finally came, the ungrateful. . ." His dark eyes widened as he focused on Jonathan. "You ain't her," he grumbled.

"This here is the new preacher." David leaned against the barred wall. "And my brother, so don't give him any of your attitude."

"Your brother, eh?"

And just like that Jonathan was shoved into place. It didn't matter what he did or said to his own credit, he would always be seen as *David's brother*.

Thoughts tumbling around in her head too quickly to fully grasp, April skirted around town, a route that would keep her from being seen as she stole to her hiding place. The tall red building stood out with offered solitude. With harvest still months away, the grain elevator sat mostly abandoned alongside the railway tracks. She slipped through the lower door and began the climb upward, the narrow wooden ladder solid as she scaled one story, then two, then three. High above the town, above even the tallest trees. Almost to the clouds.

There was only a small, very dusty window she'd liked to look down from, but one winter day she discovered the small door on the highest wall that opened onto the steep roof. She wasn't sure about its purpose, except perhaps to make roof repairs easier, but she hadn't been able to stop herself from opening it for a clear view of everything below. She perched in the opening and looked down over the town. She had at first been afraid she'd be spotted and get in trouble for trespassing, but she soon learned that few people looked up.

The flat plains stretched for miles in every direction, green with life. Though apple trees had lost their blossoms, a few lilacs still clung to their purple-pink flowers. She could almost smell their sweet fragrance from here, though it was probably just her imagination. To the east a herd of red cows grazed lazily—not so very different from the town below, folks moving about but no one in a rush.

Mrs. Bailey stood in her backyard, bent over a tub of laundry, while her two youngest chased each other toward a large elm. The elder—no more than four—hung himself over the swing and pushed off with his feet. All was well until he swung back and crashed into his two-year-old sister. The child wailed, though barely more than a hint of a cry at this distance, and Mrs. Bailey left her laundry to crouch and open her arms. She seemed to do better on the days her four older children were in school, but she looked especially tired today. Her shoulders hung, as did her limp bun. She was probably exhausted with her current pregnancy. April could only imagine what it was like trying to keep up with a household of children—and yet she still craved the opportunity for a home and family of her own.

A movement behind the schoolhouse caught April's eyes, and she shifted her attention. "Don't do it," she whispered, though she wished she could shout it out. Charlie Kent was at it again, a young woman by the hand as he led her to the bushes behind the schoolhouse. With the children in classes, the location provided seclusion, being on the edge of town and behind the teacher's living quarters.

Wait...

April leaned forward, peering harder. The girl was blond, not the brunette Charlie had lured there not a week ago. The cad! Even now he drew the young woman to him, cupping her face and kissing her right on the lips! It had to be Helen Johnson. What April wouldn't do for a rock about the size of the pastor's pebble. The first time she'd seen Charlie behind the school was with the schoolmarm herself, a sweet young woman with light auburn hair. April knew such a liaison could cost the woman her position, so she kept her mouth shut, but this was really too much. Charlie should be ashamed of himself.

A dog barked, and April looked to the north where Mr. Allard's collie, Juniper, yapped at a passerby—which led her to look to Mr. Fredricks' backyard. His garden was already twice as tall and lush as anyone else's in town, but that plot of soil was his pride and joy and what supported him and his wife through the long winters. He did struggle to maintain it against the weeds, though, and they grew alongside many of his rows.

In the distance the train whistled its approach from the south—the one direction blocked from her view. It was time for her to abandon her perch and finish the parson's laundry that waited for her at home. She filled her lungs one last time and began to pull back inside when the scarlet coat came into view on Main Street, a man in a trim black coat on the Mountie's heels.

April's muscles tensed. They were headed to the jail where her pa sat. Soon the new preacher would know—if his brother hadn't told him already. She'd be lucky to keep her job, and yet that wasn't what sat heaviest in her chest.

Abruptly, his head tipped upward, and he looked right at her. Her breath froze while her heart raced. She'd never been spotted before. What must he think of her now? What if he told someone?

April scampered inside and pulled the door closed. Her hands trembled, so she waited a moment before risking the downward climb. Her heart sank with each rung she lowered herself.

CHAPTER 4

The first rays of dawn slanted through the open window, providing a soft glow for April to dress. She was used to not lighting a lamp as Pa was often hungover in the morning and hated to be disturbed. Though today it wouldn't have mattered, as the house was hers alone. She didn't feel the least bit lonely—just guilty for enjoying this sense of peace.

"You are not in the wrong," she reminded herself, yet the feeling of guilt persisted. How could she feel relief that Pa was still in jail and she didn't have to deal with him? What sort of daughter was she?

"A tired one," she answered herself. She was tired of judging his moods, of trying to keep him happy or avoid him altogether. Wasn't that why she squirreled away every dollar she could, waiting and longing for her escape from this shack?

April pushed such thoughts aside as she buttoned her blouse and brushed out her braid, taking extra care with her preparations for the day. She never concerned herself with breakfast, so she took her basket and stepped into the cool morning air to gather the clothes off the line. She should have done so the evening before, but she'd fallen asleep reading her Bible.

Thankfully, the clothes seemed unaffected by her neglect. She folded the preacher's shirts, followed by a pair of pants and then some towels and sundries. She hurried with the last, her mind on what their meeting this morning might be like. Because she hadn't finished her work Monday, they had agreed she should come back today instead of waiting until Wednesday, so at least she didn't have to agonize until tomorrow.

April couldn't have eaten breakfast if she tried.

The sun was well above the horizon by the time she had the laundry pressed. She tucked a jar of raspberry preserves into the basket and sent a prayer heavenward. Perhaps the sugary fruit would sweeten the preacher's disposition toward her and he'd not be so repulsed by her familial connections or dangerous escapades to the top of grain elevators.

She nodded at Mr. Fredricks as she passed where he worked in his garden. He frowned and watched her out of the corner of his eyes. Juniper offered a happier greeting, and she paused to slip him one of yesterday's biscuits as she often did. It was important for a person to have at least one friend.

The others she walked past were too busy with morning preparations to give her much heed, so she picked up her pace. Might as well get it over with.

The preacher sat on his front stoop, cup of coffee in hand, Bible balanced on his knee. She braced herself, but he smiled as she approached.

"Good morning, Miss April."

"Morning." She couldn't help the apprehension from pulling the word taut.

His eyes narrowed. "Is something wrong?"

Apparently, nothing, though she wasn't sure how that was possible. "I didn't expect you out here when you should be relaxing at your kitchen table, enjoying your morning coffee."

Or at the church as he'd agreed to.

Pastor. . .*Jonathan*—it was going to take some time to become accustomed to that informality—shrugged. "I've been enjoying the fresh air. I wasn't sure when you would arrive." The smallest hint of red climbed into his cheeks. Was he embarrassed? About waiting for her? The next thought hit with even more power, and she felt warmth climb into her own cheeks. He'd waited for her instead of simply taking his coffee and Bible to the church. As though he'd wanted to see her. . .

April shooed the thought from her head. That couldn't be right. Not after visiting with her pa yesterday or spying her atop the grain elevator. Unless her father hadn't said anything and he hadn't recognized her from such a distance. A funny-sounding laugh bubbled up from her chest, and her breathing relaxed.

His head tipped to the side, and he gave her a questioning look.

"I'm sorry." Though she didn't know what she was apologizing for. "I should take this laundry inside and get to work."

Jonathan stood, towering over her since he was two steps higher than her. Though instead of feeling intimidated, a sense of security and peace settled through her. He was nothing like her pa, and there was a goodness, a kindness, that emanated from him.

"And I'll head to the church to continue my studying." His smile stretched across his face, and his eyes twinkled. "I'll try to keep out from underfoot."

She nodded and slipped past him, though she wished he would stay. As she entered the kitchen and set the basket of laundry on the table, the longing grew. She could easily imagine him sitting as he had yesterday at the table with his coffee while she prepared him breakfast and straightened the house. They would laugh and joke about the goings-on in town, and he would share thoughts on what he was studying, perhaps asking her thoughts on his upcoming sermon.

"You really are daft, girl," April chided herself. Of course he would never ask for her advice on a sermon. He was the trained theologian while she was…nothing. She had just enough schooling to read and write. Why would a learned man pay any attention to a woman who had to sound out the words she read in the Bible and didn't understand the meaning of a good number of them?

Mood sufficiently doused, April hurried through the morning's tasks, though she made sure each was done to perfection. She would give Pastor Burton no reason to regret keeping her on.

It took a while before she relaxed enough to hum while she worked, and longer still before she dared voice the words of a favorite song. Mama always insisted music made the work pass so much quicker. Soon, she was arranging the preacher's lunch on the table and setting a tray overtop to hold the warmth. She'd pause at the church to make sure he didn't stay away too long.

Not that she had ever offered Pastor Jensen the same courtesy.

It wasn't a long walk, but April was surprised at how quickly her nerves strung tight. She slipped in through the front door and paused in the small foyer, the melodic sound of a piano filling the chapel. She inched forward, not wanting to disturb whoever played—she would rather not be seen by anyone besides Jonathan. But he was the one bent over the piano, fingers leaping across the keys.

April leaned into the wall, folding her arms across her chest while the music poured into her, filling up every empty part with something truly beautiful, though tinged with a feeling she didn't understand. Her vision blurred, and then warmth cascaded down her cheeks. She listened, not sure if she was being put together or torn apart.

A loud chord sounded with finality upon the piano, and

April jerked away from the wall to look at the man rising from his seat. She blinked her eyes clear and swiped at her cheeks. No, she couldn't face him now that she was a blubbering mess. She backed into the foyer and made her escape.

Jonathan pressed the final chord before sparing a glance at the clock. Almost noon. He shook his hands loose and stood from the piano. A moment later the door at the front of the church banged closed, and he twisted to see who had come. The room remained empty, but a figure darted across the windows as though the devil rode their coattails—or was it skirt hem?

"April?" He shook his head. What would have brought her to see him, or the bigger question, why would she have come only to flee?

Not able to guess the reason, Jonathan pulled on his jacket and headed home. Maybe he had mistaken the visitor's identity and she would still be there. But when he arrived, the house was quiet, though it smelled a bit like heaven—if savory beef stew was served in heaven. He found a large bowl hidden under a pan on the table along with fresh bread and creamed butter. A jar of raspberry preserves sat nearby that would transform a slice of bread into dessert. He'd not let her labor go to waste.

Tasted a bit like heaven too.

He was only a couple bites in before someone rapped on the door. Just as it had the day before, his heart kicked up its pace with visions of opening the door to April. Again, he was disappointed. Three older women stood with arms full.

"Good afternoon, Parson," Mrs. Matkin sang out. "We are with the Rowley Benevolent Society and wanted to welcome you properly."

"The picnic Sunday was a hearty welcome." Jonathan tried

to smile but mostly wished he could close the door and get back to his lunch.

"Nonsense." Miss Maddie, as she had been introduced to him, set a warm loaf of bread wrapped in brown paper into his hands. "Since you're a bachelor, we feel it our duty to see you are properly looked after."

He wasn't sure how to take that but offered a nod of thanks. The bread did smell wonderful but only served to remind him of the two warm biscuits he had just slathered with butter and balanced on the edge of his bowl. They were likely quite saturated with the thick gravy by now.

The third woman, Mrs. Johnson, spoke with a strange sort of gleam in her eyes—enough to remind Jonathan of being introduced to her eighteen-year-old daughter. "We also understand that as a young, *unmarried* parson, a home-cooked dinner cannot go amiss, so we insist you come to our house this evening for dinner."

"And *our* house tomorrow evening," Mrs. Matkin inserted.

"Oh. . . Thank you." Jonathan's smile was becoming harder to maintain. The butter would be fully melted now as well and starting to soak in. His mouth watered at the thought. "That sounds wonderful."

They chatted on, offering directions to their homes and instructions on when to arrive. Then continued rambling about some of the ills of the community and where he should focus his attention. All the while, Jonathan's thoughts wandered to April. He wondered about her family and their situation. That would be one dinner invitation he would look forward to.

"You have more at stake than our last pastor, being unmarried." Mrs. Matkin's chastisement brought Jonathan's head up. "Your reputation is much more fragile than Pastor Jensen's, since he was a widower with three half-grown children at home."

"Quite right," Mrs. Johnson agreed. "The best thing for you is to find a wife." She nodded knowingly. "That would keep your reputation safe and give you more credibility with the community."

"Never mind negate the need for a housekeeper," Mrs. Matkin squawked.

Jonathan stiffened.

"Stop pushing the man." Miss Maddie rolled her eyes—presumably at the other women. "And there is nothing untoward about April Harvey working here. She's a respectable girl."

"But young and unmarried," huffed Mrs. Johnson at the same time Mrs. Matkin muttered, "Questionable."

Mrs. Johnson continued. "I heard that someone has been stealing from the Fredricks' yard. Tools. Vegetables. Why, only yesterday a handful of young carrots were uprooted and hauled off."

"April would never do such a thing," Maddie protested. Jonathan grew fonder of the woman with each comment she made.

"It would be easy enough for her, what with the Harveys' hovel being right behind the Fredricks' home. We thought it was that good-for-nothing father of hers, but he's—"

"Oh, stop with your gossip." Miss Maddie shoved a basket of muffins into Jonathan's hands and waved him back into his house. "The good parson has no need of listening to you slander a good girl's name."

"Well, I—"

Mrs. Matkin took up the rant. "Pastor Burton should be aware of whom he associates with and what effects it could have on his standing here."

Jonathan raised himself to his full six feet two inches. "Excuse me, ladies. While I appreciate your concern, the lunch Miss Harvey fixed me is growing cold, and I have work to do."

He wanted to chastise them for their words against April but was too new to the community and did not know enough about her. Instead, he nodded to the women, thanked them for their generosity, and retreated into his house. Unfortunately for Mrs. Johnson and her daughter, their words had only given him more desire to get to know Miss April Harvey.

CHAPTER 5

The next morning, April stopped short at the sight of the pastor again seated on his front steps, coffee mug cupped in both hands. This time a second mug sat beside him, steam swirling in the crisp morning air. He smiled and stood, scooping up the second mug as he did so.

"For me?"

He nodded and motioned for her to sit. "I wasn't sure how you like your coffee, or if you even like it. Last time we drank tea. I added cream."

"I'm sure it's fine." April took a sip to appease him, and the hot liquid burned her mouth. "Ouch!" She took some quick breaths to try to cool her hurting tongue.

"Not enough cream?"

"Just. . .a little. . .warm, still."

"I should have added more cream." He started to stand. "And sugar. Some people like sugar."

"No. I—just cream. And this is fine. I'll give it more time to cool." Which meant she would not be able to gulp it down and shorten this awkward meeting. "It's good. Thank you." She slanted a glance at him. What now? Were they simply to sit and visit until their coffee cooled enough to drink? Did he truly plan to remain with her all that while? She was supposed to be working, not loitering with her employer.

"It's a beautiful morning," Jonathan said easily. He took a sip.

Casual conversation. She could probably manage that. "It is."

"I like being out of doors instead of hiding away. We have such long winters, it's a shame to waste a day when the sun is shining."

"It is." She tried a small sip, but not enough time had passed to drink comfortably.

Though there was nothing untoward about sitting in each other's company for a few minutes, she was grateful that lilac bushes concealed them from the view of the community.

"Any headway with Sunday's sermon?" She blew on the hot liquid.

"I don't know. I'm leaning toward tying in the parable of the ten virgins."

"You seem to enjoy parables."

"Some people learn better through stories." He shrugged. "I understand why Jesus used them so often. Simplified His teachings."

"Yet His teachings weren't that complicated, were they?" She smiled.

He chuckled. Somehow just listening to the deep, throaty sound gave her the sensation of being tickled on the inside. "No, they really were quite simple. Yet still lots of folks struggle to understand, never mind live according to them."

"Love God and love your neighbor." She peered at him over the top of her mug, far too aware of how well his nose fit his face and how his eyes twinkled when he spoke of Jesus. "Do you have a favorite parable?"

"Do you?" Jonathan countered with a half smile.

"I asked you first."

"That's easy. The good shepherd and the lost sheep."

"I have a feeling you'll make a good shepherd."

He shook his head. "I struggle to reach the ninety-nine, never mind the one. I met with a fellow over at the jail briefly, and I'm pretty sure he hated me by the end of our conversation."

April's heart fell. "One known fact about sheep is their stupidity."

A full laugh broke from Jonathan's chest. "Speaking of the real ones out in the field, or of those who fill the pews every Sunday but don't seem to listen?"

"The woolly counterparts, of course." She couldn't keep the sarcasm from her voice.

"You have much experience with sheep?"

She shook her head.

"Me neither. I feel like it shouldn't be so hard to reach them. Like you said, love God and your neighbor. Is that so hard?"

"It can be." She tried to keep her smile in place, to pretend she jested, but she had lived on the outskirts of the community for too long. The simple command was probably a lot to ask of the people of Rowley.

"Rowley seems like a nice enough town."

"It is." April spoke too quickly, and now he watched her closely. Unfortunately, her coffee was still too hot to gulp down.

"Have you always lived here?"

"We moved here when I was ten."

"From?"

"From Calgary." Why did he have to keep prying?

"What brought about that change?"

She signed in resignation. "My mother passed away, and my pa was looking for a new start." An escape, really. Away from the memories of their former life and their loss. But with April along, he could never fully escape. Except into a bottle.

"Do you wish you lived elsewhere? You don't look very happy."

April straightened and forced a smile. "No, I like Rowley well enough. As long as I keep to myself." She clamped her mouth shut, immediately regretting giving her thoughts a voice.

His head tipped forward, and he appeared far too contemplative. Silence hung between them, increasing the discomfort of the moment. "I don't know if it will help," he finally said, "but someone once told me that kindness is key."

Try harder to encourage your father. More love. More keeping a peaceful home. That was the advice the last preacher gave as well. Her efforts hadn't affected her own pa, so what good would it do against a whole community?

"I'm sorry. I should save my preaching for Sunday and for those who actually need it." He said the words gently, but she still felt condemned.

"I should get busy."

"It can wait." Jonathan watched her as though trying to peer past her pretenses, as though seeing exactly who she was and how much she lacked.

April took a large gulp of her coffee only to choke on the bitter liquid. She sputtered a cough.

"Are you all right?" His words were said kindly, but his hand moved quickly toward her, and instinct overpowered logic. She flinched away. His hand, gripping a clean handkerchief, froze midair. His eyes widened just enough to reveal his shift of thoughts. He knew.

Heat rushed into April's face, and she shoved to her feet. "Thank you for the coffee. I do need to get a start on the day though." She slipped into the house and prayed he wouldn't follow.

Jonathan remained on the stoop, considering what had transpired, what had gone wrong. She'd ducked away from him as though she expected him to strike her. What on earth? It was everything he could do to remain in place while his mind followed her inside. He wasn't ready for their conversation to be at an end—despite the disaster it had been. Or perhaps, *because* of that. He wanted to make amends, to end on a happier note...and to do more than scratch the surface of who that woman was.

But logic prevailed. She had fled him for a reason, and he needed to respect her wishes. He downed the last of his coffee, left the cup on the top step, and then picked up his Bible and started the short walk to the church.

The building was far too silent, allowing for his thoughts to dwell on Miss April Harvey and everything he knew about her. Not much, really. She was an unmarried young woman with blue eyes and a stubborn tilt to her jaw. She was industrious and proficient at what she put her hand to. And a good cook. He smiled at that as he lit a lamp near the piano. Not that he required extra light to see his hymnal. A new song already itched to be released from the tips of his fingers. He set the Bible aside, though he should be studying for his sermon on Sunday.

He shrugged away the thought. It was only Wednesday. He still had time to consider a topic and prepare something. Besides, music helped him think.

He pressed the first chord and then heard footsteps at the front of the church. Though tempted to keep playing and ignore the visitor, he was too new a pastor to neglect his flock. He sighed and stood. "Good morning," he said as he turned. "What can I..." He frowned.

"What can you do for me?" His brother grinned at him. The

red coat hugged tight across his chest, and his hands braced on his hips like he owned the world.

"Hi." The greeting came out flatter than it should have, but, really, how could Jonathan make his own mark on the world with his brother hovering over him constantly? It was as bad as when they'd been kids.

"Don't look so happy to see me," David teased, his smile never leaving his face.

"Sorry, I was hoping for a quiet morning to get some work done."

David's brows arched high. "What work is that?" He smirked.

"Never mind." His brother probably didn't consider anything Jonathan did as consequential, so there was no point in pressing the matter. Jonathan raked his fingers through his hair and started toward the front of the chapel. "What did you want?"

"Arthur has agreed to meet with you."

"He has?" After the apparent animosity during their first meeting, this was the last thing Jonathan expected.

"Yeah. I convinced him it would look good if his case went to trial."

"Ah, trial. So that's why he's still hanging out with you?"

"Yeah, but it might take a while until they work him into the schedule—his case isn't that important to anyone. So we'll probably be roommates for a while." David groaned. "The man snores like he's cutting logs." His eyes suddenly brightened, and his smile returned. "Hey, you have an extra room in that house of yours."

No, no, no. . . Jonathan wanted to shout his protest, but it clung to the back of his throat. What excuse did he have for denying his brother a comfortable bed and a decent night's sleep—especially after spouting the importance of service and doing good to others? But all he could think about was David turning that grin on April when she came to clean on Friday. She'd have no reason to look at Jonathan after that. "On one condition."

"Anything."

"I need the house quiet in the morning." He didn't need to say why, did he? "By nine o'clock every morning, I need you gone."

CHAPTER 6

There is power in forgiveness, Arthur." Jonathan leaned forward in his chair, wishing there was some way to make his words penetrate the thick skull of the man across from him, but two weeks of trying only seemed to set the man more against him.

"I haven't done wrong to anyone who didn't deserve it."

"What about Matt Larson?" David called from his desk across the room. "You shot a man. A young man with a family dependent upon him."

Arthur pushed to his feet and jabbed a finger in David's direction. "That was an accident. And he didn't die. I'm not planning to shoot someone while I'm sober, and I've been sitting weeks in this box. What're you holding me for?"

Jonathan leaned back but resisted the urge to cover his ears while Arthur bellowed.

David stood and sauntered over, thumbs hooked on the thick leather belt that also held his holstered pistol. "You shot a man. We're just waiting to hear when you go before a judge."

"It's not like I killed him."

"Near enough. Took a chunk out of his arm so he's unable to work. It's not a matter to be shrugged off."

A long string of curses brought Jonathan to his feet. His words were being wasted here, and he had other visits to make—one long overdue. He nodded to Arthur and his brother while they continued their argument, and then he slipped out the door. The sun hit his eyes, and he set his hat back on his head. David had already given him directions to the farmhouse about a mile out of town where Matt Larson lived with his wife and several children. Jonathan had met Mrs. Larson and the children at church, but Matt hadn't been in years according to several older ladies who had felt the need to fill in details.

East of town was the Rowley cemetery, and Jonathan thanked God he hadn't been asked to officiate at a funeral his first few days in town. The small cabin he sought was easy enough to find, and he had to smile at the children playing. Someone had redirected water from the pump in the middle of the yard, digging a shallow ditch which now served as a stream that flowed down into a three-foot-round lake. A toddler stood in the middle while a four- or five-year-old girl yelled for him to get out of the way.

"Hello there."

The girl glanced up, and her eyes widened. Without a reply, she took off toward the house, yelling, "Mama, the preacher's here!"

When she disappeared inside, Jonathan looked at the toddler. Didn't seem right leaving the child unattended. While he was old enough to walk, his cheeks had the full appearance of an infant. "How are you, little fellow?"

In answer, the child plopped down in the middle of the "lake," a swoosh of muddy water overflowing the banks as it was forced to move for him. Still, no one exited the house.

"Should we go find your Mama?"

The boy slapped the water, and mud sprayed up in every direction, including his face. A squeal of surprise turned to a cry of pain as the mud ran into his eyes.

There was nothing for it. Jonathan reached into the puddle and plucked the child into his arms. Small, muddy hands grabbed hold of his clean neckcloth, and the boy buried his face in it. By the time Jonathan made it to the house, the front of his shirt and jacket were soaked, but the child had stopped crying.

Mrs. Larson met him at the door. Her face immediately turned the shade of a beet. "I'm so sorry, Parson. Here, let me take Matthew."

Jonathan kept his hold on the child. "No use the both of us getting muddy. Do you have a towel?"

"Of course." She hurried to a heaping basket of laundry and retrieved a towel that looked almost as dirty as the boy. She took him from Jonathan, wrapped him up, and hugged him to her. Her eyes widened. "He's done ruined your fine shirt."

Jonathan had to agree but kept his expression relaxed. "I'm sure it will be fine." Though he hated putting the extra work on April. The white of his neckcloth was probably a lost cause. "I came to ask about your husband. How is his recovery?"

Mrs. Larson gave a weary sigh. "Well enough, I suppose. He's—" She glanced at the bedroom door. "Why don't you step in and see him. I'm sure a visit is just what he needs."

She gave a tight smile and ducked out of the house with the children.

Though with a sense of foreboding, Jonathan moved to the bedroom. A man in his midtwenties sat propped up in bed. He wore no shirt, his right shoulder and upper arm bandaged. His eyes widened. "Where did Joanna go?"

"Your son was in need of cleaning, so she's seeing to him," Jonathan said easily. He sat on the nearby chair so he wouldn't tower over the man. "You have a fine son."

"He's all right. What happened to your clothes? I thought

preachers liked to stay clean and presentable."

Jonathan smiled. "I'm not above getting my hands dirty for a good cause."

Matt's eyes narrowed. "What is it you're after, preacher? I don't aim to start coming to church anytime soon, so you're wasting your breath if you are trying to evangelize me. Sure, I was raised by a God-fearing woman and believe in God and all, but I got no time for the backbiting biddies in town. My wife might put up with all that, but she's more of a saint than I am."

Jonathan sat for a moment. The focus at the seminary had been learning the words and how to share them with a congregation or how to succor the individual. But neither Arthur nor Matt wanted to hear just words.

"Thanks for coming out, all the same. I know it means something to Joanna."

Jonathan nodded and pushed to his feet.

"Don't take it personally. I got enough on my plate with things falling apart around me and being laid up. Doc says not to even think about lifting or moving about too much for another week."

"What needs to be done?" Jonathan heard himself say. "I have some time."

The man just stared as though he didn't understand.

Kindness is key. Wasn't that what he had spouted off to April weeks ago? Maybe it was time to start preaching by example. "I have a couple of hours this afternoon, and I grew up on a farm. Tell me what needs doing." Jonathan tugged his arms free from his jacket. He wouldn't worry about his shirt, as it was already plenty dirty.

"Chopping and hauling wood is the most vital. Joanna's been managing, but it's not easy on her."

Jonathan nodded his understanding and headed out to the

yard where the young wife leaned against the pump, watching the children play in the puddle. She was surprised at his request for the axe but hurried to show him the dwindling woodpile and several larger logs in need of chopping into manageable pieces.

The sun was hugging the horizon before he left the farm, leaving a replenished wood stack, a clean barn, and a mended fence, feeling that he had actually done some good with his day.

April stared at the shirt, her hands holding it over the washbasin. The dirt didn't just sit on the surface of the cloth, waiting to be washed away. It had soaked into the fibers, leaving deep stains. How in the world had the neat and immaculately dressed preacher managed to soak his shirt in both dirt and sweat—and a little manure by the smell of it?

Maybe it was his brother's shirt. That made a little more sense.

No, the shirt would be too tight across the torso for the Mountie. And she'd never seen Constable Burton sport a white neckcloth.

April plunged the shirt into the water and set it to the washboard, though even the extra effort would probably be insufficient. Usually throwing his clothes in a basin with a minute or so of plunging was enough to leave them clean. While she worked, her mind conjured explanations for the extra dirt. Maybe he tripped and fell in a puddle. Unlikely, since it hadn't rained in almost two weeks. A mudslinging fight with. . . She couldn't imagine anyone in this town who'd engage in such an activity, though the image of it made her chuckle.

She continued with the washing and quickly noticed all his clothes were not quite as clean as usual. What had that man been up to?

By the time she had the laundry hung, curiosity nagged. April headed to the grain elevator and perched herself in the small door where she could see the goings-on of the town. It was well past noon, so the pastor was probably making visits. She scanned the town, not spotting him right away. Mr. Fredricks was in his garden as usual, but those weeds still appeared to be getting the better of him. Mr. Allard, the stationmaster, sat alone on the bench at the station's platform, scratching his dog's head. Probably waiting for the next train though it wasn't due for hours.

Mrs. Bailey's yard buzzed with activity. School had let out a short time earlier, and children were in and out of the house, up and down the large tree in the backyard—yet no one seemed aware of their exhausted mother pausing to catch her breath and lay a hand to her swollen abdomen. How she would keep up with yet another young'un, April couldn't imagine.

One after another, April watched her neighbors hurry about their business, unaware that anyone watched. Finally, April could no longer sit still. She climbed slowly down the ladder, her heart pinching, thoughts churning. They didn't deserve anything from her. They had judged her and shunned her.

Kindness is key.

Those words had been her bane since Jonathan had spoken them, but she couldn't chase them from her thoughts. Mrs. Maddie was kind, and Mr. Allard had hired her to clean the station and his home twice a week, but few others had extended much by way of fellowship.

Kindness is key.

Sounded like something her mother would say.

April trekked behind the school and back toward her home. She set her hand to push open the crooked gate when the upper hinge broke. She gritted her teeth and shoved the gate so the lower hinge broke too. Easier to have done with the thing.

"I'd hate to ever be the focus of your ire."

April startled and spun to the tall man with a black coat, slouch hat, and lopsided smile.

"I'm just coming from Fredricks'," Jonathan said easily. "They have quite the garden."

"They do." She stepped so the broken gate would be less obvious.

Jonathan brushed his hands across his slacks, and she noticed the dirt under his nails.

"You were helping in the garden?"

He shrugged. "A little weeding. That place needs an army to keep up with it."

"Huh. It's strange I didn't see you—"

He gave her an inquisitive look.

"When I walked past there." Not technically a lie. She'd never admit to seeking him out from her hiding place.

"Ah." He looked past her to the decrepit shack. "This is where you live?"

She again wished she could lie but forced a nod.

"Need a hand with that gate?"

The man was far too perceptive—and didn't wait for an answer before stepping around her and pulling the gate out of the tall grass. She watched as he set it in place and fiddled with the hinges.

"Not much I can do right now unless you have tools and replacement hinges, but I'll come back later and fix them."

"You don't have to do that." April wanted to shoo him away from the mess that was her life.

Jonathan smiled at her, and any arguments fell by the wayside. "It'd be my pleasure."

Her heart gave a thump, and she felt herself nod. Even as

he took his leave and strode back toward the parsonage, she couldn't chase the feeling away. No wonder kindness was key—to unlocking a whole myriad of pent-up emotions. She wasn't sure if she wanted to laugh or cry.

CHAPTER 7

The next Monday, April set the basket of laundry at the door and glanced again at the clock on the kitchen wall. Still far too early to leave, but her own house was clean, and even with the quiet of Pa's absence, the peace was superficial. Too much pain. Too many memories. She abandoned her basket and slipped outside where breath came easier. She hadn't realized how oppressive it felt just being in that house.

The gate swung easily on new hinges, aiding her escape, and she couldn't help but smile. Her walk led her inevitably to the grain elevator, where she slipped out of sight and climbed high. Seated in the small doorway, she looked down at the small town. Her gaze snagged on the red uniform standing just outside of the jail, a tray in hand—probably breakfast for Pa. She should pay him a visit like a dutiful daughter. It had been three weeks, and yet she hadn't been able to bring herself to go.

April hugged herself. She still had no desire to face the wrath that would no doubt be the result of her neglect. But was it better to confront him now, while he was behind bars, or when he finally came home?

She shivered at the thought.

Unless she wasn't there.

April only savored the idea for a couple of minutes before burying it under another bucketful of shame. How could she abandon him while he was in jail and facing so much uncertainty? And who would keep the house until he came back? No, she needed to wait.

The Mountie reappeared and headed toward his horse. Even he couldn't stand more than a few minutes of being with her pa.

Pushing the air from her lungs, she shifted her focus. Mrs. Bailey was already out, ready to collect laundry off the line—including bedding a child had likely soiled. She seemed puzzled to see it all neatly folded in the basket.

The schoolhouse's windows glistened with cleanliness.

Mr. Fredricks' garden looked less like a jungle.

April's smile grew. Then slipped away. She leaned out a little farther, gripping the doorway for support. "That little rascal," she murmured, watching as young George Johnson scurried from the Fredricks' yard with a fistful of greenery in his hand. Young carrots, probably. A snack for his walk to school?

Mr. Allard's dog, Juniper, yapped as he chased a fox out past the railway station into a northern pasture. Hopefully, he would run the rogue to ground and save the Johnsons from losing any more chickens.

Farther north, a herd of cows moved along the railway track. She squinted, leaning forward just a little. It was true. Mr. Matkin's cows were on the railway track. Most of them were content to graze the lush grass on either side, but some stood directly on the rails.

Where the fields met the sky, a train appeared, a thin trail of smoke like a beacon trailing above it. April pulled herself back through the door and dropped down the ladder as quickly as she could safely manage, a difficult task with her skirts trying to tangle her feet. She fumbled one of the rungs and dropped the last several feet to the ground. She pushed herself upright and sprinted from the building, not caring about the large door flapping behind her.

The train was still miles away, maybe five minutes from the herd. It was possible they would see the cows and slow enough to clear the track, but there was a rack on the front of the engine for a reason, and it would be a shame for the Matkins to lose some of their cows.

She cringed at the grisly thought and quickened her speed despite the burning of her lungs. The station was the closest, so she raced to the window. Mr. Allard stood at the counter, probably preparing for the arrival of the train.

"Cows!" she shouted at him.

He looked at her as if she were mad.

"On the tracks." She gasped for a breath.

His eyes widened, and he jogged to the door, joining her on the small platform. He spun, coming to a halt at the sight of Constable Burton rounding the corner on his horse.

"Constable!" April jumped from the platform and ran to him. "The Matkins' cows are on the tracks. And the train—"

He needed no further urging to spur his horse to the north and race up the tracks. He whooped and hollered for the cows to move. One was especially stubborn, and it took a hard whack on the rear with the constable's reins before she sauntered off the tracks. The train rumbled by, thankfully slower than before. The engineer leaned out his window to give the Mountie a wave. April watched, her heart gradually slowing to a more regular beat.

As the engine's whistle announced its approach, April slipped away. No need to stick around. She retraced her steps back to her house and collected the laundry before heading toward the parsonage. Her steps felt lighter the closer she came to her destination. Walking past the lilacs to where the small pale yellow house sat was almost like walking into a different world, and a weight lifted from her chest.

Jonathan smiled up at her from the top step, and she felt a sigh slip from her. "Good morning," he said.

"Yes, it is," she agreed. She set the laundry basket inside the door and then joined him, taking the proffered mug. He'd figured out how she liked her coffee and always seemed to have it just the right temperature to sip when she arrived. "Thank you."

His eyes smiled as well. "You are very welcome. How was your weekend?"

"Uneventful. Which is the way I like them." She took a warm sip. "I did listen to a moving sermon on Sunday about the dangers of complacency in our lives. The preacher beautifully tied in the parable of the ten virgins."

"Clever," Jonathan said. "Though you probably give him too much praise. I happen to know he took weeks writing that one."

She shook her head. "I have enjoyed every sermon I've heard him preach."

"All three of them."

She tried to keep her face passive but felt the pull of her lips. "Three and a half."

He chuckled and set his empty mug aside. He'd likely been half done before she'd even arrived.

"This morning was eventful, however. Your brother saved a herd of cows from the train."

Jonathan's brows twitched upward. "Did he?"

"Yes, it was quite fantastic. Matkin's cows had gotten onto the tracks, and your brother was able to chase them off just before the train ran headlong into them. They didn't seem to have any inclination to move on their own. It was a miracle he was right where he was needed." She felt a little breathless at the memory of her race against time and watching it all unfold.

"My brother really is something, isn't he?" His tone contradicted his words.

"Does that bother you?"

Jonathan shrugged.

"I imagined you two were close. Especially since he is now living with you."

"We're close enough." A low grunt sounded in the back of his throat. "Too close, if anything."

"What do you mean?"

He waved her off. "Nothing."

"Obviously not nothing," she whispered, not finding the courage to voice what she really wanted to say. "You don't have to tell me anything." Something seemed to be gnawing at him, but it was not her place to pry. The last thing she wanted was to upset him.

His lungs emptied in a loud gush. "It's just, I came out here, into the middle of nowhere, with the hopes of building a life on my *own*, of having something of my own. But there he is, already running the town, and now he's in my house. It's been this way my whole life, since the day we were born."

Wait… April tried to grasp what he had just said. "You're twins?"

Jonathan groaned. "What sort of pastor am I, complaining about my own brother, my twin, no less. I shouldn't have said anything. Forget—"

"Don't apologize." She loved that he trusted her with his feelings. "I know that simply because someone is family doesn't mean living with them is easy."

It was Jonathan's turn to look intrigued, and April shrank back. She was the one who should keep her mouth closed. But it was too late. Jonathan was already saying, "You sound as though you have experience."

April downed the last of her coffee in three gulps and gathered up both mugs to take inside and wash. "I should get to work."

He caught her arm as she stood and held her in place until she glanced down at him. "You can talk to me, April." His mouth twitched a smile. "I'm your pastor, after all. It's my job to listen and help however I can."

For some reason that didn't make her feel better. She didn't want to be a part of his job, his duty. She wanted him to listen because she meant something more to him. "Thanks," she muttered, and pulled away. Thankfully, he didn't follow. Instead, he picked up his Bible and headed toward the church.

April hurried with putting the clean laundry away and tidying the house after the two bachelors—twins. Though they really didn't look it. April couldn't imagine what it would be like to have someone to share everything with, a sibling. Her little brother was a toddler when he passed away. She didn't allow herself to consider how different life might have been if he'd lived to tease her mercilessly or play pranks on her or sit and talk long after bedtime about their hopes and dreams.

April leaned her hands against the table and braced herself against a wave of despair. "What dreams?"

CHAPTER 8

Jonathan approached Sundays with mixed emotions. While he kept busy the rest of the week serving his congregation in a myriad of ways—including mucking out old Mr. Carlson's barn last Wednesday—the Sabbath was when he truly felt like he was earning his keep and contributing to the community. Yet he wasn't sure he'd ever not feel sick with nerves as he stood before the townsfolk and laid his humble offerings before them. All the study and education in the world did not make one a great orator. Even Moses had Aaron to speak for him.

David grinned up at Jonathan, but Jonathan couldn't tell if his brother was trying to encourage or mock. That was the worst of it. He was still trying to find his footing as a wet-behind-the-ears preacher, and constantly questioning if the community was comparing him to his twin didn't help—especially as he'd probably be found wanting.

Jonathan fumbled a couple of his words and forced his brain to focus on his congregation and their needs. He'd already lost the attention of half of them, including most of the children and for sure Mr. Fredricks, who was snoring in the third row. At least April watched with rapt attention.

Some of the tension eased from between Jonathan's shoulders despite wanting to impress her. He already knew her well enough to know that even if he quoted Paul's words and gave the credit to Samuel, she might tease him for it but would not think less of him.

He relaxed into his sermon and noticed more eyes centered on him as he spoke. By the end, he felt comfortable greeting the families as they took their leave. Some even thanked him for his words. April merely smiled as she passed, but the kind gleam in her eyes promised commentary on the morrow. That was worth looking forward to.

Feminine laughter drew Jonathan's gaze from April to where Helen Johnson stood next to David, gazing up with her large dark eyes. His stomach soured. She'd never showed even a smidgen of interest when Jonathan joined her family for dinner. Not that he was interested in her, but salt stung when rubbed in old wounds. April glanced at the couple as she passed, and Jonathan's heart gave a start. She wasn't interested in David too, was she? Girls had always found him more attractive, even before he'd donned the scarlet uniform, and now he gathered the fairer sex like flies to a big pile of...

Jonathan amended his very un-preacher-like thought. He filled his lungs and forced his focus on the next family desiring his attention. The Matkins stood impatiently, though their oldest daughter was already on her way to join Helen and David. Mrs. Matkin's foot tapped an unsteady rhythm. "I suppose it is good the Johnson girl has shifted her attention to the Constable Burton. Better than that Kent boy."

Jonathan felt heat curl over his ears. Hopefully they couldn't guess his thoughts on the matter.

"We've been quite satisfied with Constable Burton's service in the community," Mrs. Matkin commented.

Jonathan nodded, glancing back at his brother, who had paused his own conversation and ignored the two women bidding for his attention to spare a glance at April's retreating form. More uncharitable thoughts reared their ugly heads.

"—so grateful to him for saving our herd. I trust our Bethany wishes to pass along our thanks. Mr. Matkin has hired several men to replace the old fence along the railway track, so it never happens again. What a disaster that would have been!"

"I imagine so." Jonathan shook Mr. Matkin's hand as the couple continued on with their youngest son on their heels complaining about not being allowed to play at the lake with his friends just because it was Sunday. Jonathan looked over the citizens of Rowley and the surrounding area and tried to ignore the uneasiness in his gut. Why did he feel like an impostor?

Jonathan couldn't manage a proper greeting as his brother approached with his usual smile in place.

"Ready to head home?"

Home. Because they even shared that again. It was like stepping back into their childhood, when Jonathan hadn't really had anything to call his own. Not even clothes. He'd tried to take care of his clothes, which just meant his lasted longer and David would steal them when his own fell to rags. They had each gotten a brand-new pair of boots one birthday—the first new boots either of them had ever owned. Two weeks later Jonathan couldn't find his. He discovered later that David had borrowed them to muck out the stalls in the barn so he wouldn't get his own dirty. He'd left them outside because they'd been covered in manure, and they'd gotten chewed to scraps by the dogs.

Now David was in his house, eating his food, borrowing his socks. As a man who had given his life to teaching others to love their neighbor, one would think Jonathan could set the example by loving his own, literal brother. But at the moment, he just didn't feel it.

April made her way from the church, not socializing as the rest of the community lingered. Not that she didn't want to be part of their well-wishing and light conversation, but experience taught her to keep walking. They didn't want her there. Why beat a dead horse?

The constable caught her eye before she'd made her getaway, a question in his gaze. They needed to talk—she knew they did, despite her putting it off. She could well imagine all the complaints Pa had levied against her. But hopefully the new Mountie would not believe everything he heard—or pass it on to his brother.

"It doesn't matter to him," she said aloud. Jonathan didn't seem to mind who her pa was. He hadn't said a thing about it. "It doesn't matter."

"What doesn't?" Miss Maddie asked, coming alongside her, a large hat ornamented with an impressive array of feathers on her head.

"Nothing. Just talking to myself."

"About that fine-looking Mountie?" Miss Maddie's smile tipped to one side. "Or his preacher brother?"

April couldn't keep the warmth from rushing to her cheeks—no doubt betraying her feelings. "While we are on the subject of fine-looking men," she countered, "I thought Mr. Allard looked well today. Do you suspect he's been putting more effort into his wardrobe since you took him the hot cross buns at Easter?"

Miss Maddie's face took on her own hint of scarlet hue, and April smiled in triumph.

"I suspected as much."

"Nonsense. We're too old to get lost in romance like a girl your age ought. Besides, Orvil Allard doesn't love anything better than that mutt of his. Speaking of which, have you seen him—Juniper, I mean. Overheard Mr. Allard asking about. Seems he's run off."

"Juniper runs off and does his own thing all the time. Why should Mr. Allard be so distressed this time?"

Miss Maddie shrugged and then fixed how her lace shawl set over her shoulders. "Juniper has been missing for over two days now. Have you seen anything from up there on your perch?"

April froze. "What?"

Maddie gave her a knowing look. "You think you've gone completely unnoticed? Mind you, for the most part, I don't think anyone else sees you up there, but. . ." She tapped April's shoulder for emphasis. "I have a love of all things avian."

"Avi. . .what?"

"Birds. I watch birds. I have books and books if you ever wish to expand your own knowledge in that area. My daddy was one of the foremost experts on the local birds and started his own text with sketches and descriptions, even migration habits. It has been my dream to finish it for him."

"Ah." April wasn't sure of what more to say, so she nodded.

"The point is, I imagine you see a lot from up there."

"I do. But I haven't seen Juniper for days. Last I saw, he was chasing ol' Mr. Fox out in the Matkins' north fields."

"The day the cows got out?" Her smile appeared quite smirk-like.

April sighed. "I get the feeling I don't see near as much as you do."

The older woman laughed. The lines around her eyes and mouth deepened, yet they only made her more lovely.

"I wonder if Juniper ran into trouble chasing the fox. It might be worth a look."

"Will you tell Mr. Allard?" Miss Maddie asked.

April glanced back up the street to the church. "You know, it's probably a wild-goose chase, and I could use a walk. I'll wander that direction and let him know if I see anything."

Miss Maddie smiled. "You are an angel, April. You really are."

April shook her head and started away. As she'd made her practice, she bypassed the NWMP office and headed home. Once there, she collected a shawl as well as a sturdier pair of shoes and wrapped a couple slices of buttered bread in a hand-kerchief so she could enjoy a small picnic.

The mid-June air was perfect—not too hot despite the sun high overhead warming her shoulders. April took the back streets to the school and then followed the railway track north past the station. Jonathan stood on the edge of the platform as she approached. "Going dog hunting, I hear."

April gaped. Miss Maddie must have told him and asked him to accompany her. He would have had to come straight from the church to beat her here. "Just going on a walk."

"Ah." He smiled. "Can I offer you some company?"

Yes, she wanted to shout, but she supplied a nod instead. She really should decline. It might hurt his standing in the community to be seen alone with her. Their discreet morning conversations were bad enough. But instead of heeding logic, she paused long enough for him to come alongside her and then matched pace.

"I wanted to ask what you thought of my sermon today," he said after they had crossed into a field.

He sought her opinion? April bit her bottom lip. She was hardly a scholar like he was. "I've always enjoyed the parable of the pearl of great price. The idea of finding something so precious, and then willing to give up everything else. . ."

"You've never felt that?"

April glanced at him, and her heart froze with the realization that her feelings for this man were developing into something she could treasure with such devotion. But just as with her mother and brother, Jonathan Burton was probably not meant to stay in her life forever. "Not for anything I've been able to keep."

It wasn't *technically* a lie.

CHAPTER 9

Jonathan watched as April's shoulders slumped and she quickened her pace. He lengthened his stride to keep up. "But that parable isn't really about finding treasure," she threw over her shoulder, "but the gospel, like you said in your sermon. And I have that. I have my faith and treasure it above everything else. No matter what others might believe about me."

He caught up but wasn't sure what to say. He hated the thought that anyone would say anything bad about April Harvey, but he'd heard enough whispers in the weeks he'd been there. Regardless of the rumors, he'd come to know her. She was intelligent and kind and enjoyable to talk to. He loved her subtle humor and how her eyes twinkled with mischief now and again. She was also quite pretty, in his opinion.

April huffed out a breath, but probably not because she was winded from walking so fast. "Please don't believe everything you hear about me."

"Unless it's good?" he tried to jest.

She glanced at him. "Especially not then." Her mouth twitched a smile. Finally, she slowed a little and surveyed their surroundings—flat, boring prairie—then angled in an eastwardly direction.

"You think you know where he went?"

"I've seen him chasing a big old fox who's been terrorizing Rowley's chickens for the past month. The fox always heads off in this direction, so it makes sense his den is somewhere over yonder."

Made sense. "You seem very observant about things in the community."

She shrugged.

"Maybe you can help me. I feel I need to do more for folks around here, but I've been fumbling around trying to decide who to reach out to."

"From what I've seen, you've been doing plenty." April caught a tall blade of grass between her fingers and broke it off as they passed. It snapped easily, and she fiddled with it while she walked.

"I try to be of use. But any direction would be a boon."

April nodded but didn't answer right away. She seemed to be considering, and he couldn't help but watch her as she did. He hadn't noticed before, but she appeared lighter, *brighter* even, than when they had first met. And happier. She smiled more. "Mrs. Bailey has been overwhelmed with the care of her children. She is pregnant with number seven, and I think keeping up with the house and so many young ones wears on her. Her husband travels for work and is gone for long stretches at a time."

Jonathan opened his mouth to comment, but April hardly paused.

"The Matkins put on a good show of prosperity, but I fear they may be struggling in that area. They have the land and a small herd, but from what I've seen, they have been selling off furniture and such outside the community in hopes no one finds out. I only mention it so you don't put them in a position that might strain them financially or cause embarrassment."

"Good to know. But—"

"And Mr. Allard. He's lonely. He has Juniper and the folks who come and go from the station, but he lives in the back alone and has no one else. He often walks out, carrying on conversations with his dog as though he were a person. I think he would enjoy a friendly visit now and again."

"Of course."

"And Charlie Kent is generally a good enough fellow. He helps his mother out on their small farm, but his pa died when he was young, so he could use a good example of how to treat a woman properly—or maybe a good talking-to. He's always sneaking girls behind the school, as it can be quite private back there, and..." She shook her head. "I'm sure you understand the workings of a young man's mind better than I, but he stands to hurt more than just reputations and hearts if he continues on his present path."

Jonathan could only stare as she continued on with the speed and directness of a river, explaining person after person and the struggles she saw. The question he couldn't let go of was, how she could possibly know so much about those around her? He'd never heard such a detailed list, or such compassion as she spoke of the people of Rowley.

Kindness is key.

And that was what he heard in her voice. Kindness.

Jonathan felt a grin spread across his face. He now knew how to move forward. Thanks to this beautiful, kindhearted woman. He could only imagine what a boon it would be to have her at his side...as his wife.

The thought sent a bolt of excitement through him, along with a dozen images, scenes of more than just conversations over a cup of coffee on the front steps, but also over breakfast or while washing dishes together. He could easily picture a home of laughter and teasing, and of service. He could imagine taking her in his arms, brushing a strand of hair from her luminescent eyes. Pressing his mouth to hers.

April glanced up at him, brows raised, lips pursed. She really did have pretty lips. What would they feel like? He'd never kissed a woman before—but then again, he'd never found someone he was so drawn to before.

"Have you not met Miss Maddie, yet?"

"What?" He had no clue how much of the conversation he'd missed as he daydreamed. "No, I've met her."

She arched a brow at him while her eyes narrowed. "Is something wrong?"

Jonathan shook his head. "I'm just amazed how well you know the community, and on a level so few ever do—never mind want to."

A pretty blush rose into her cheeks, and she looked away. "The only reason I'm saying anything is because you asked. And you're their parson. If anyone can help them..."

"I will try."

April glanced back with a gentle smile. "I know you will."

Again, he found himself quickening his pace to catch up with her. He scanned the terrain and was surprised to see a small lake ahead, the blue of the water breaking up the shades of green fields and pastures surrounding it. A thin stand of trees stretched along the southern shore.

"I didn't realize there was a lake so close to town."

"It's not much of one, but it collects a lot of wildlife."

A handful of deer had stood almost invisible until they jumped from their resting place and bounded across the field.

"As I was saying."

"I will never argue the fact that you are very observant."

She glanced over and grinned. And again, he had the urge to kiss that pretty mouth of hers.

April's feet felt glued in place as Jonathan stepped to her, his gaze again dropping to her lips. Was it possible he was thinking of. . . No, he couldn't be. But there was that look in his eyes again, one she'd seen with more frequency over the past week or so during their morning coffee. She wet her lips and then questioned the motion. Would it give her own thoughts away? Licking one's lips was natural enough—this part of Alberta was dry, and her skin, including her lips, was prone to chapping. Surely he wouldn't think anything of it. Or did she want him to?

Did she want him to kiss her?

Nervousness skittered through April as she explored the thought. A kiss. Should be simple enough. She'd seen other young folks do it often, so what harm could there be?

The thought gave her pause and tightened her chest. She'd seen others lose friendships, even become enemies, after a kiss.

"April. . ."

Oh, how she loved how he said her name. She loved so much about this man. But he was a parson. He really shouldn't be kissing. . .

The thought fled as he moved nearer and the warmth of his breath cascaded across her skin. Her heart pounded, and she felt herself lean forward, stretching upward onto her toes. His hands cupped her shoulders as his gaze shifted to her eyes and searched them, peering right down into her soul.

A dog barked then gave a long whimpering whine.

April staggered back a step. "The— Mr. Allard's dog." She turned, not letting herself look at Jonathan or judge his expression. Was he disappointed she'd withdrawn? His feet crunched over the rocky soil behind her, following yet again. "Juniper?"

A whiny bark called to her from the willows along the southern shore of the small lake, and she quickened her pace. It was too late to consider what could have been if she hadn't pulled away. Or to determine whether or not it was for the best.

It took a few minutes wading through dead reedlike grass to finally locate Juniper, who whimpered and whined but wasn't able to stand due to the steel trap clamped on one of his front paws.

"I wonder if someone was trying to trap Mr. Fox." April knelt beside Juniper and rubbed his head. "His den is probably here somewhere."

"Poor fellow." Jonathan joined her. "Can you hold his head to keep him from biting me while I release the trap?"

She clamped her arms around the dog's neck while cooing encouragement to the animal. A sudden yelp, and the dog almost jerked free from her hold, but he only had kisses for them as Jonathan tossed the trap aside.

"I think he's been here for a while." Jonathan motioned to the festering wound. "Let's get him home."

April pulled her picnic lunch from her bag and knelt beside the dog, her knee meeting something hard. She rocked back and shifted off the fist-sized stone and its spiraling edges. She grabbed it and went to throw it, but Jonathan caught her wrist.

"Wait. Let me see that."

She dutifully dropped the rock into his palm and returned her attention to the hungry dog. He gobbled the bread down in moments and searched her hand for more. "Sorry, boy." April glanced at Jonathan, who was still examining the stone. "What is it?"

"Ammonite. It's a fossil." He shoved the rock into his pocket and threw her a smile. "Just wait until I clean it up." Taking the handkerchief from her hand, Jonathan wrapped Juniper's wound before lifting the dog onto his shoulders for their hike home.

As he pushed to his feet, April couldn't help but smile at the image. "You know who you remind me of?"

He glanced back, one brow arched. "Who?"

"The good shepherd, bringing home the lost sheep on his shoulders."

Jonathan chuckled. "Strange-looking sheep."

"They come in all shapes and sizes." She followed close behind him, not ready for a conversation about lost sheep or men...or a discussion about what had almost happened between them only moments ago.

CHAPTER 10

Lost sheep and men. April couldn't put it off any longer—couldn't live with the shame. All afternoon since she'd left Jonathan to deliver Juniper back to Mr. Allard, guilt had pestered her, giving no peace of mind. She had kept herself busy, helping where she could in the rest of the community while avoiding her own pa. But the inevitable would have to be faced eventually, and that eventuality was eating her up slowly. So, here she stood, pacing outside the NWMP post, trying to work up the nerve to go inside.

The door swung open, and April jumped, swinging around to see Constable Burton watching her. He slipped outside and closed the door behind him. "Miss Harvey?" He kept his voice low, probably knowing her pa's reaction if he was aware that she stood within earshot.

"How is he?" April knew the answer, but it seemed proper to ask.

"As happy about life as a hornet whose nest got plowed, but otherwise fine. We're waiting to hear back from Judge Beazer in Calgary on the timing of his trial."

"So he'll be going to court?"

The constable nodded, and April couldn't help but notice all the ways he resembled Jonathan—little things like his eyes and the way his rueful smile slanted while a small dimple appeared in his chin. "Should be soon. Knowing the judge and the circumstances of the shooting, there probably won't be much jail time. More likely a hefty fine."

April couldn't help but cringe. Pa never saved money. He drank it away as quickly as it came in, leaving little even for food. What sort of daughter was she if she left her pa in jail? But if she was able to help him, would she have any savings left?

"Were you wanting to see him?"

It was her turn to give a doleful smile. "I should."

Compassion filled the constable's eyes, making him resemble his brother all the more. "You don't have to."

"Don't I? I can well imagine how angry he is that I've waited so long." She sighed. "I have to face him sooner or later." Putting it off didn't help her nerves.

The constable nodded and opened the door so she could step into the building. The shouting started before her eyes adjusted to the dim lighting. She flinched, though the bars would keep him from laying a hand on her.

Jonathan sipped the now-cool tea as he listened once again to how his brother saved the train and Matkin's cows. Mr. Allard spared no detail, rambling on at the speed of a ground squirrel dodging between burrows. After they had properly treated Juniper's leg and settled the dog in the small living quarters in the back of the railway station, Mr. Allard insisted he stay for tea. With April's words in mind, Jonathan agreed, but a short visit had turned into over an hour of listening to story after story of life on the prairie, including the finding of huge, fossilized bones only miles to the south.

A description of the *Albertosaurus,* so named only two years earlier, and the other local finds were interesting enough, but when Allard started an even more in-depth description of how David had arrived in time to save the cows from certain death, Jonathan began working out the best way to take his leave.

"'Course, I don't think anyone would have seen them in time if not for Miss Harvey."

Jonathan's head snapped up. "What was that?"

"April Harvey was the one who spotted the cows out on the track. Came running over here like the devil was on her heels. Guess she's the real hero."

"Interesting." She really *did* notice everything going on in this town.

"She's a real peculiar one, she is. I see her all the time, sitting up at the top of the grain elevator, like an angel looking down over Rowley."

"That's how she does it." That must have been who Jonathan saw that day on his way to the jail with his brother—Rowley's own guardian angel.

"What's that?" the old-timer queried, leaning forward.

"Miss Harvey seems very aware of what goes on in this town, what people need."

"I reckon she would at that." Mr. Allard nodded before pushing to his feet and moving to refill Jonathan's cup. A minute earlier he would have declined and insisted he needed to leave, but what else did this man know about April that would shed more light on why she shied away from speaking about her family and her past?

"Has Miss Harvey lived in Rowley long?"

The man scratched his head while he thought. "Maybe ten or so years now. She was just a girl when they arrived. She and her Pa moved into the old Jensen place on the south side along

Railway Avenue. She finished her schooling here and then took up working odd jobs for whoever needed laundry or mending. Does mine Fridays plus some tidying up around the place."

Jonathan glanced around the small parlor and into the kitchen and could immediately see her hand, though it was also obvious from the pile of dishes in the sink that she hadn't been there for several days. Before Jonathan was able to ask more, Juniper yipped from where he rested under the table, and Mr. Allard bent to pass him a cookie. Then he started talking about the Jensen family, who had built the cabin April now lived in. Seemed they had too many children to contain in the small house, and Mrs. Jensen finally demanded they move to a larger house in a larger town closer to her family. Jonathan never managed to circle the conversation back to April, though he sat there for most of another hour before giving up and excusing himself.

Again, April was right in her observations. Mr. Allard needed someone in his life to listen to his stories, and maybe clean up after him a bit more.

Jonathan's heart was full as he stepped into the warm late-afternoon sun. It was near dinner hour, and he would be expected at the Laytons' by six for the meal, but it was April he itched to see again. Had it been only a couple of hours since she'd left him at the station to assist Mr. Allard with his dog? Jonathan glanced up at the elevator that towered over the town. He didn't like the thought of her so dangerously high and wondered why she made a habit of climbing up there. Maybe he would ask her tomorrow when she joined him for coffee.

Tomorrow morning had never felt so distant.

The mumble of voices farther up the street drew Jonathan from his musings. He couldn't hear what was being said but saw his brother in uniform standing very close to a woman, his hands on her shoulders. The Johnson girl, perhaps?

Despite his desire to see someone else standing there, Jonathan recognized the pale blue dress and the honey-colored hair hanging in a braid from under a straw bonnet. His stomach clenched as though someone had rammed it with a fist. What was April doing with his brother, and standing so ridiculously close?

Get your hands off her.

The words resounded in his head as though he had shouted them, but his jaw remained clamped as he watched from a distance. David stooped to gaze fully into April's eyes. He was saying something, but his voice was too low. Hadn't Jonathan stood like that only hours ago while considering a kiss? So help him, if his brother so much as leaned another inch, he'd—

He'd what? Storm over and throw a punch in David's face? That hadn't gone so well for him the last time he tried it in their youth. David had always been the more athletic one. And it wasn't like Jonathan had any claim over April or her affections, as much as he wished it.

April was the one who leaned forward, falling into David's arms, which wrapped around her possessively.

That was that. Jonathan forced himself to turn away, retreating the direction he had come then circling the long way around to his home. He sank to the front stoop where he had shared a dozen conversations with April while they sipped coffee. Why hadn't he seen it earlier? No wonder she'd turned away when he tried to kiss her. Obviously, Jonathan couldn't rival his brother's looks or charisma. David had always drawn in the women and had broken plenty of hearts. What were his intentions with April? Was he simply playing with her? Did it matter? She'd obviously chosen him over Jonathan.

He'd lost again. But it had never hurt so bad.

CHAPTER 11

April folded the last of the diaper cloths and placed the basket under the wide elm in case the gray morning gave way to moisture before Mrs. Bailey got to them. She smiled as she passed the Fredricks' yard. The garden appeared almost free from the weeds that had infested it, which would give the rows of vegetables room to truly flourish. She'd also talked to Constable Burton about the veggie poacher, and he'd agreed to have a word with young George Johnson, which would probably be enough to deter the youth from making off with what was not his.

As hard as April tried to keep her thoughts distracted, each step she took toward the parsonage sent a jolt of nerves through her. Jonathan almost kissed her yesterday. Would he have if she'd not pulled away? Would she be able to sit calmly with him this morning and talk about dogs and his sermon without replaying that moment over and over in her head as she had most of the night?

If she could go back in time, she probably would have stayed in his embrace instead of fleeing.

April hugged her shawl tighter and quickened her pace, anticipation battling her nervousness. Jonathan was the kind of man to be patient and not fickle with his attention. He wouldn't toy with her or use her. He wouldn't have considered kissing her if he didn't have real feelings for her—as incredible as that was.

Was she brave enough to return those feelings? Sure, she felt them—she felt drawn to him like no other. But she couldn't explain the conflicting urge to hide away, to keep on her current path, one she knew. She could well imagine how angry Pa would be. Her, falling for the preacher, abandoning him while she went off and took care of another man. Living her own life...

A shiver shifted through her, though she wasn't sure if it was from hope or fear.

April took a breath and started past the lilac hedge. The flowers had long since faded to brown, and dark green leaves were now the prominent feature. The steps of the parsonage sat abandoned but for a lone coffee mug. She glanced around, but there was no other sign of him. She picked the mug up from the step and held it close, but the heat had faded, leaving the dark liquid cold.

Her chest constricted, though she chided herself for the reaction. A knock on the door went unanswered. The house was as abandoned as the front step. Loneliness seeped into her bones as she poured the cold coffee down the kitchen sink. Was he avoiding her?

"Don't be silly," April chided herself. He could have been called away for any number of reasons. Illness, death, spiritual direction, or someone simply needing a listening ear.

Like her.

April worked quietly and quickly to tidy each room, though by the looks of things neither brother had been home much the past few days. Several dishes sat on the counter, some laundry lay over the backs of chairs. Socks were piled near the foot of both brothers' beds. She smiled while gathering them into her basket, but her smile soon slipped away again as the emptiness of the house pressed over her.

Someone knocked on the front door.

April jolted upright, not sure whether to answer it or pretend no one was there. Was it possible Jonathan had returned but wanted to keep things proper and not be alone with her in the house without a chaperone? She set the basket on the bed and started to the door, wiping her palms on her apron, not sure when they had started sweating. She opened the door to Mrs. Matkin and felt her heart drop to her shoes.

The woman pierced her with a glare and folded her arms across her chest. "I assume Pastor Burton and his brother are away."

April's stomach squirmed uneasily. Mrs. Matkin seemed confident, which meant she hadn't come to see either of them. "Of course. I'm just finishing here."

"I wish you were," the woman murmured, pushing her way into the house. She looked around as though scrutinizing April's work.

"Is there something you wanted? Jon—Pastor Burton is probably at the church." *Please go there and leave me alone.*

"What I want is for you to keep your distance from the pastor. You have already turned his head, and it's no good. No good at all. He needs a strong woman of faith and good standing in the community."

April felt the words like a slap across her face.

"Helen Johnson or even my Bethany would be much better suited to be a pastor's wife."

Both young women who had allowed themselves to be kissed passionately behind the schoolhouse? Both who had already shamelessly flirted with the Mountie? Those girls would be better suited then she? April held her tongue. Putting someone else down would not raise her standing.

"I can't believe you've been allowed to stay on here while your father is in jail. I heard he'll stand trial in Calgary. He drunkenly endangered lives. The man's a brute."

April couldn't argue, but she wanted to defend her own merits. Only, did she have any? Was she not somewhat responsible for her pa's behavior, for his need to bury himself alive in a jug of liquor, for the anger that never gave him rest?

"Do your work here, if you must, but mind my words and stay away from the parson, or your every misdeed will be shouted from the rooftops and you'll no longer be welcomed in this town." The woman shot her one last haughty glower before turning and slamming the door behind her.

April sank against the wall. Her hands trembled.

Good-for-nothing child. This is all your fault. Get out of my sight. You've ruined everything. Ungrateful. Worthless. Weak. Stop crying!

But April couldn't help the tears as she sank to the floor.

Jonathan sat in the basement of the church, a single candle doing little to dispel the darkness. But that suited his mood. Above him was a brightly lit chapel, the afternoon sun streaming through large windows. But here he hid in shadows, hardly enough light to read his Bible. Not that he'd had much success. This morning, he had found himself turning through the pages of First Samuel, the stories of David and the lesser known— lesser in every way, really—Jonathan. David Burton had been born first, even if only by minutes, and he needed a friend. Who better than a Jonathan.

A deep breath did little but settle the sense of resignation in his gut. He couldn't compete with David, had never been able to. Not in looks, or humor, or the ability to woo women, obviously. Jonathan gritted his teeth and shoved to his feet. Enough pitying himself and his situation. He had a choice, and it would not be to remain in this town, forever in his brother's shadow, watching him romancing April. Bible gripped, he blew out the candle and started up the stairs, climbing toward the sunlight and the determination not to remain in Rowley a day longer than he had to.

His small desk held paper and pens, and he scribbled a brief request—that a replacement be found for the town of Rowley and a new assignment be granted him. He didn't care how it made him look, or that others might think him weak or fickle for not being successful in his first parish. It had been a disaster from the beginning, as soon as David walked into the church that first Sunday. Jonathan shoved the letter in an envelope and headed for the door, faltering at the sight of a hunched form seated in one of the pews.

"Pastor."

Jonathan slowed and pushed the letter into his pocket. "What can I do for you, Mr. Allard?"

The man smiled up at him, the wrinkles deepening at the corners of his eyes. "Just wanted to come over and let you know Juniper is doing much better today. Up and walking, though with quite the hop to his step. Figure a couple more days he'll be right as rain."

"Glad to hear it." Jonathan offered a smile he didn't feel. He took another step, hoping it would encourage the older man to join him in his departure from the church.

Mr. Allard leaned back in the pew, getting comfortable. "You know, I'm real grateful for you and Miss April finding Juniper for me. I don't know where I'd be without that dog."

Jonathan merely nodded. He'd been thanked enough yesterday, and besides, April was the one who found him.

"You and Miss April were real kind searching for him."

Maybe, but Jonathan didn't feel very kind at the moment. He should sit and visit with the man, have some charity toward his situation, but right now he just wanted to escape. "It was nothing. I was merely—"

"Must admit it's got me to thinking, all last night. The thought kept pestering me. Didn't hardly get a wink of sleep."

"I'm sorry. But—"

"What are your thoughts on matrimony?"

Jonathan's jaw dropped along with his train of thought. "I—"

"I married my Lucy back when I was not older than nineteen. Loved her since we were young'uns. Had her by my side for thirty-seven years before the good Lord took her. Raised eight children, buried three. Now they're off living their lives and here I am, dependent on a dog to keep me company. Didn't realize how dependent I'd gotten on an animal until he went missing for more than a day. But aren't I too old? Is it silly for a man of my years looking at taking a new bride? And what about my Lucy? Won't she feel betrayed, watching from heaven while I make a fool of myself with another woman? She was the jealous kind, you know."

Mr. Allard huffed out a breath, allowing Jonathan a moment to respond. He did so, not knowing when the next one would come. "How long has it been since your wife passed?"

"Over fifteen years now. She was around to raise the children and then slipped away. Can't imagine loving another woman like I loved her, but it would be nice to have someone else in the house, someone to talk to in the evenings and whatnot."

"I doubt your late wife would want you to be lonely,"

"You think she wouldn't mind sharing me for a while?"

"I think maybe when we get to heaven, our priorities might shift a little." The weight of the letter in his pocket seemed to increase exponentially. He was supposed to be a man of God, a man who had a more eternal and heavenly mindset. Why was he letting such mortal angst derail him?

"Maybe that's right. Seems like it would be." The man grinned and pushed to his feet. "I'm glad I walked over. I looked at the clock and realized I had a whole two hours before the next train and wondered why not come over here and get your advice. Usually, I don't put much stock in what fellows as young as my own boys have to say, but after our talk yesterday, I figured maybe it would be different, since you're a man of the cloth, as they say. I figure I was right."

Mr. Allard kept on chattering away for another half hour at least before he looked at his pocket watch and realized he needed to be back at the station. From the boardwalk at the front of the church, Jonathan watched him go and considered the letter in his pocket. He could see the NWMP post from where he stood, though thankfully his brother was not in sight. Mr. Allard was wrong. Jonathan had no more wisdom than any other fellow out there, and no more ability to forgive or overcome hurt. He was just a man. And there was only so much a man could take.

CHAPTER 12

April didn't know what to pray for. That Pa be acquitted and allowed home, or for him to be held responsible for his foolishness and the harm caused to another man. Today, a hundred miles away, that would be decided. She scrubbed the floors of the train station with vigor, though sweat already dropped from her brow. She just couldn't push the unease of uncertainty away, or the guilt for not doing more for him. Piled on top of those feelings was lingering hurt and disappointment.

April groaned. Not that she had expected or hoped for anything to develop between her and Jonathan, but the steps of the parsonage had looked so very empty for the past week. Not even a cup of coffee had awaited her after the first morning.

Her knuckles grated against the wood floor, and she gave a yelp. A bit of skin had been peeled back, but not enough to draw blood. She let out her breath and shoved the scrub brush into the pail. Enough of this. The floor was sufficiently clean, and the chore did little to alleviate her anxiousness.

Besides, Mama always said that lies were bad but lies to oneself were the worst. April had begun to hope Jonathan would see her as someone special, someone worth loving—and not just as a neighbor, though that was all well and good. Truth be told, she was already well on the way to falling in love with him.

She picked up the pail, hauled it out back, and dumped the water on the flowers planted along the wall. She believed Mr. Allard's late wife had planted them, but little had been done to maintain them since her death over fifteen years earlier. April took a couple of minutes to pull weeds, though that wasn't one of her duties.

"There you are," Mr. Allard huffed as he came around the corner of the building. "A telegram just arrived for you."

"For me?" Fear mingled with anticipation as she reached for the thin strip of paper.

YOUR FATHER SENTENCED TO YEAR IN JAIL OR HUNDRED DOLLAR FINE *Stop* ON MY WAY TO ROWLEY *STOP* CONSTABLE BURTON.

A hundred dollars. Her stomach dropped and churned. The amount was a small fortune. She glanced at Mr. Allard, who stood watching her, his expression somber. He obviously knew what the telegram said, but what he didn't know was that she had that sum—or near to it.

"I–I'll finish later," April managed, before turning away and making her way home.

Home? What a laugh. This shack had never been home. Had never even *felt* like a home. It was a prison, and she hated it.

April knelt and pried up the floorboard where she hid her leather money pouch. She wasn't sure exactly how much was there after years of saving every cent that came into her possession, all in the hopes of one day escaping this place.

"April?"

She jerked around to Miss Maddie, who stood in the open doorway, and quickly replaced the floorboard. "What are you doing here?" She'd always been kind but had never set foot in this house before now.

Miss Maddie walked into the room as though nothing was out of the ordinary. "Mr. Allard told me you looked unwell when you left."

"Why would he go to you?"

Miss Maddie glanced away, her face infused with pink. "I was with him when he received the telegram."

"You were *with* him?"

"It's not wholly unusual for an engaged couple to spend whatever time they can together."

April's jaw sagged. "How didn't I see that?" She'd known of the interest on Miss Maddie's side, but hadn't seen anything of actual courting or—

"We've kept things secret for some time now. And you've been a little distracted." Miss Maddie smiled gently. "I think you've distracted our new parson as well."

April wanted to laugh, but it hurt too much. "That's where you're wrong." He'd been effectively avoiding her for most of two weeks. It felt so much longer than that.

"But I'm not wrong about the fact you have been saving every penny you earn so you can leave, and yet you are still here, am I?"

"I never had enough." April tucked the heavy leather purse into her apron pocket along with the telegram.

"Balderdash. You are very industrious. The only thing holding you here is you. You've had plenty saved and could have left at any point, but you haven't worked up the nerve, or are too stuck on your sense of responsibility. You are not responsible for him."

"He's my pa." She felt herself shrink back, tucking inside herself. If her own pa couldn't love her, how could she expect any man to?

"He doesn't deserve anything from you."

Her purse hung heavy in her pocket. Indecision swirled

within, mingling with shame and guilt for even considering abandoning her pa. But she left it unspoken. Miss Maddie couldn't begin to understand. "I need to finish up my work before I go." She had no choice but to travel to Calgary. And how could she not give what she had for his freedom? What sort of daughter would leave her pa in jail when she had the power to set him free?

What about your *freedom?*

She shoved the thought aside. As a Christian, she was supposed to forgive.

Yet there was no peace in that thought.

"April. You know I'll help you, however I can. April?"

April ignored Miss Maddie's call. She slipped outside and started walking. She wasn't really paying attention to which direction she went until she stood in front of the church. Should she seek advice from her pastor?

This time a laugh broke from her throat, and she shook her head. He had been happily keeping his distance. Possibly for this very reason. Because she was the daughter of a drunk. Because she was broken too.

She fled, past the houses and even the grain elevator. She was tired of trying to fix everyone else's problems, as though that could aid her in escaping her own.

Jonathan watched as April turned on her heel and hurried from the church. His shoulders slumped. He had hoped for a moment that she would come in, that she had wanted to see him, that she missed him as much as he missed her.

He moved to the piano but couldn't bring himself to play. The music in his head was more suited for a melodrama on the stage than the hallowed walls of a church. He plucked a key or two before standing again and trying to find solace in his Bible. He would be happy if David finally decided to settle down. Perhaps then the other available women in town would stop gawking David's way and give him a fair shot.

He groaned and flipped the Bible closed. If David would choose anyone but April, he'd be ecstatic for his brother. The worst would be if he simply toyed with her heart and then broke it. Even if she changed her mind and decided Jonathan was an acceptable replacement, he would always wonder if he was simply that—a stand-in for his brother.

The door tapped closed, and Jonathan swung to see who disturbed his misery. David was pulling the hat from his head as he hurried up the aisle. "Have you seen April?"

Jonathan gawked at his brother. That was what David needed to ask him? That was why he'd come here?

"She wasn't at the parsonage. Isn't this the day she cleans?"

"Only first thing in the morning. In the afternoons she's at the station." How wasn't David more aware of her schedule? He should tell David the direction she'd headed, but the words choked him. "I can't help you," Jonathan growled, though he'd intended to speak without emotion.

David's head tipped to one side, and his hat shifted to his other hand. "What has you upset? What happened?"

You. You happened. "Nothing. I have a lot on my mind." He cleared the gruffness from his voice. "I received word that I will be moving to Coleman. A church there has requested a minister."

"Coleman? That's awfully close to that deadly landslide a few years back. I was there right after it happened. Not sure I'd trust any of those mountains."

"The Frank Slide?" According to the map Jonathan had been studying, a few miles separated the two towns. Besides, he'd been curious to see the damage done, and mountains—even crumbling ones—were much prettier than the bald prairie. "I'm not worried."

"But you just got here," David complained. "After all I did to get posted here. It's been so perfect and—"

Jonathan felt his jaw slacken. "You *asked* to get posted here? I thought it was a coincidence."

David laughed. "It would have had to be a miracle."

It *definitely* hadn't been that. "Why? Why would you do that? Go live *your* life." *Leave me alone!* He clenched his jaw and bit off the last part of the thought. David had ruined everything. Again.

David arched a brow at him, probably detecting the growing anger Jonathan was trying so hard to keep from his voice. "This *is* my life, and I've loved the past weeks of being in the same town—"

"The same house."

"What's eating at you, Jonny? What has you madder than a kicked hornet's nest?"

"You." The word broke free like a curse word but couldn't be taken back. Jonathan wasn't sure he would, even if he was able. There was a scripture about the truth setting you free. While he was pretty sure this wasn't how it was supposed to be applied, he planned to run with it for once.

CHAPTER 13

"Me? What did I do?"

Jonathan sucked a breath. "Where do I even start?"

David stiffened but didn't budge. "Why don't you start by telling me what you're really thinking?"

"Because that wouldn't be a very pastor-like thing for me to do," he muttered.

"Come on. It's me. We used to share everything."

"We still do, it seems. And I'm tired of it."

"Fine, I'll move out of the parsonage. Is that what this is about? You could have asked me to go at any time."

"It's not that. Not entirely."

"Then what is it? It's not as though I steal your clothes anymore. You're so tall and slim, they would hardly fit me anyhow," David joked.

For some reason it struck more like an insult. "As if you would want my clothes anyways." They were plain and ordinary—just what one expected a preacher to wear.

David's eyes narrowed. "What's going on, Jonny?"

"I hate that name."

David stared, and it was all Jonathan could do not to shrink back like he always did. "Why? I've always called you that."

"So did everyone else when I was five. It makes me feel like a kid, like you don't take me seriously. Which you probably don't. Does anyone?"

"You're the town's preacher. I'm pretty sure everyone takes you very seriously." He paused for a breath. "But this isn't just about names either, is it?"

"No. I'm tired of trying to compete with you, of always falling short. I'm sick of coming in second in everything we do." Thoughts of April sat like a rock in his chest. "I wanted someplace to be me, without you taking all the attention. Why would a woman even look my way if you're within fifty miles?" Jonathan finally allowed himself to turn away. He collected his Bible from where he'd left it and tucked the book under his arm.

"Where are you going?"

"Coleman." Somewhere his brother wouldn't follow. Somewhere he could get away from thoughts of April.

Unfortunately, David did follow. All the way back to the parsonage. The front door slapped closed behind his brother and they were again alone in the same building. Jonathan retreated to his bedroom, but his brother followed him there too.

"Can't you leave me alone?"

"No. I'm still trying to figure you out. And maybe I need to apologize. I should have asked if you minded me coming to Rowley before I took the posting. I was excited. I missed you and thought it would be fun living in the same town again."

Jonathan sank to the edge of his bed, guilt pressing him deep into the mattress. He should be glad to have his brother nearby. He should be more giving and forgiving and. . .and. . .

"I'll go." A half a laugh sounded in David's throat. "Guess I need to pack my things anyways if a new parson is going to be showing up. I'm assuming they're sending a replacement."

Jonathan nodded.

David turned away.

"I'm sorry. I just can't keep up with you, and I'm tired of falling short of the great King David."

"What, like in the Bible?" David leaned into the doorframe. "David was the son of a shepherd. He wasn't much more than that himself for a lot of the story. Jonathan was the son of a king."

"And then Jonathan was slaughtered with his fallen father, and David became king. No one remembers Jonathan, and if they do, it's only because he was David's faithful friend."

"Even when his father tried to turn him against David. He was the best friend David ever had." The lilt of David's voice held too much sincerity.

Jonathan shook his head. "Not that David needed him. He could slay giants on his own, after all. After Jonathan's death, David continued on just fine—better even, because he took the throne."

"I'm sure David missed him."

Jonathan sighed, shaking his head at their ridiculous conversation. "But he'll get along all right. He'll keep slaying giants and wooing women, and after a while he'll forget."

"We're not talking about the Bible story anymore."

"Hopefully, I won't meet such a tragic end, but our story isn't so different. So go find April like you were trying to. Just don't hurt her."

"I think the damage has already been done. But I do need to talk to her, let her know what options there are."

"What do you mean?" Jonathan shot to his feet. "What options?" *What damage?*

"With her father, Arthur. You know Arthur. His trial was this morning. He's facing a hefty fine or time behind bars."

Jonathan's wheels were still churning through the information.

"Arthur is April's father?"

David stared at him. "How did you not know that? April's here half the week—I know that's the reason you always want me gone early. So I won't interrupt your romantic rendezvous on the front porch."

Anger surged through Jonathan. "Not that I had any chance with her. Not with you sabotaging me at every turn."

"What are you talking about?"

"I'm talking about the fact that you knew I was pursuing April and yet stood right in my way."

David's eyes widened. "I did no such thing."

"What a laugh! I saw you take her into your arms. The whole town could see you staking your claim."

David sank back. "I never. . . Wait, on the street, more than a week ago? Just before I took Arthur to Calgary?"

Jonathan nodded, folding his arms across his chest. Not that he wanted a confession from his brother. He merely didn't know why David would deny it.

"Did you also see her tears? Did you see how upset she was from the verbal assault her father had just rained down on her?"

Jonathan continued to deflate. "What?"

"Her father isn't the nicest drunk, but he's worse sober. Why do you think I wanted to stay here at the parsonage so badly? I have no designs on April Harvey, Jonathan. I could see from the start how much you liked her, and she seemed to share the interest."

Jonathan sank back onto the edge of the bed. How had he been so mistaken, so confused? He'd been avoiding April for no reason other than what he'd conjured in his head?

"You know what the best part is," David said softly from his side of the room, his words tinged with bitterness. "I've spent my life feeling exactly the same way. Everyone always asked me why I wasn't more like you. More mature. A harder worker. Kinder. That's why I left home as soon as I could to join the Mounties. I was tired of trying to measure up to you."

Jonathan looked at his brother, recognizing the hurt in his eyes—the same hurt that had stared back at him so many times in the mirror.

"I set out to prove myself to me and everyone else. To show them that I could do something worthwhile with my life too. 'Course, when I heard you were coming out to Rowley as a bona fide preacher man, I knew I still wouldn't quite measure up. But it didn't seem to matter anymore. Till you arrived and I couldn't even keep the peace on the streets of Rowley long enough for you to finish your first sermon. That was pretty embarrassing for me. And the way folks gathered to meet you that first Sunday, throwing you your own picnic and all. Trust me, that's not the greeting Mounties get."

"David. . ."

"David might have become king, but it was only because Jonathan helped him stay alive. And we all know how much King David messed up later on. But Jonathan? I can't think of one negative thing the Bible has to say about him." David shoved his hat on his head and turned from the room. A few moments later the front door clicked closed.

Jonathan remained in place while his world shifted under his feet.

CHAPTER 14

The house was clean, everything in its place. A hearty stew just the way he liked was simmering over the fire. What else, what else, what else. Pa hadn't been home for over a month. Had she missed anything? His pipe. Cleaned and on the small table beside his chair. She hadn't enough money to buy fresh tobacco, but he couldn't fault her for that. She'd given every last cent, even borrowing her next month's wages from Mr. Allard, to pay for his freedom and the train ride home.

"It was the right thing to do," she reminded herself. She was bringing the lost sheep home.

Heavy boots trod up to the front door, and April's shoulders tensed. Her head spiked with pain from the building tension. A knock sounded, and she leaped into action. Had she forgotten and locked the latch? Why else would he knock? He hated it when the door was locked and was probably getting angrier by the second.

"Good evening, April."

April rolled back on her heels. "Jonathan? I mean, Pastor Burton." She wasn't sure which he preferred now. "What—what can I do for you? Why are you here?"

He glanced past her. "Your father isn't home yet?"

Disappointment nearly flattened her. Of course, he'd come because of her father. "No. I heard the train, so he should be here any moment."

"Good." He looked at her so intently her heart sped. "I was hoping—"

"What's this?" Pa's voice roared from behind Jonathan, who was slow to step aside. "A man leaves awhile and some young whippersnapper thinks he can swoop in an' steal away his daughter? She ain't for you, boy."

Jonathan stiffened as he faced her father. April's face might easily burst into flame for the heat surging to it. "Pa, this is Pastor Burton. I believe it's you he came to see."

Pa shoved past and stomped into the house. "Even worse. I ain't in the mood to be sermonized to after what I been through." He glared at Jonathan. "Save your preachin' till Sunday."

Instead of leaving as he should, Jonathan's gaze focused on April. What looked like concern lined his brow.

April stepped to the door to shield Jonathan from Pa and his growing wrath. He was in a fine mood tonight and that would only compound every minute he was kept away from a warm meal and his pipe. "You should go. He'll be better tomorrow," she said to him in a low voice.

"What are you whispering about to that preacher, April? You conspirin' with him to save my soul or something? Well, save your breath and hit the road, Preacher. I have no more use for you than I do for that Mountie brother of yours." He shoved April aside and slammed the door in Jonathan's face.

April took a slow breath, considering retreating as well. She could find somewhere else to sleep tonight and come back tomorrow when things were a little more settled. But no, Pa wouldn't take well to abandonment after he'd been gone for so long. That would only make him angrier.

April skirted around him, silently praying that Jonathan was starting for home. "Why don't you sit down, Pa, and I'll get your stew dished up. It's all ready for you."

"Stew?" Pa huffed, though he moved to the table. "Is that the best a man gets after what I've been through?"

You brought it on yourself. "I was a little short on funds." She couldn't curb the edge in her voice. She'd given up everything for him, and he was going to complain about the meal she'd spent the past hour making just how he liked it? She crossed to the fireplace and swung the pot away from the hot coals. Other than for cooking, the fire was hardly needed this time of year, and the room was quite stifling.

"Don't you get snappish at me, girl. After how many years I've fed you and kept a roof over your head, I expect more gratitude. You owe me!"

April hugged herself, fighting down the urge to scream back at him.

"Where'd you come up with all that money, girl? A hundred dollars don't just magically appear. I was told you sent it with the Mountie."

"I worked for it," she whispered.

"Speak up. How am I supposed to hear you when you're mumbling?"

"I worked for it. For years."

"You've been holding out on me." The words came as a low growl, warning her that his anger was growing.

April felt herself shrink back. She'd grown accustomed to more freedom and security in her home while he'd been gone, and it pinched to force herself into the mold of who she'd once been.

"You could have bailed me out weeks ago, girl." His voice was low and threatening.

"No. No one mentioned anything about bail."

"I could have been free. I didn't have to be locked in that hole for over a month!"

She retreated another step. "I didn't know anything about the bail. No one told me."

"You didn't come askin'.." A string of curses spewed from Pa like the stew from the pot as it hit the floor. Hot gravy bit at her ankles as she tried to leap out of the way, but he already had hold of her arm. She braced for the impact she knew would follow. His open palm slashed across her face. She knew better than to cry out but couldn't help it. She'd been able to avoid his wrath or to manage it for so long, but she was out of practice and patience. Flashes of memory from when she was younger strung every muscle in her body taut, preparing her for what more was coming. He'd gripped her other arm and dragged her around to face him when a gust of cool air rushed against her skin.

"Let her go," Jonathan roared, and April dared a glance at the lunging preacher, who grabbed at her pa's sleeve. Pa turned, swinging, and the first fist met Jonathan's jaw. The younger man hardly flinched as he shoved his opponent back. "April, get out."

April lunged for the door. Pa tried to grab her again, only to be cut short when Jonathan tackled him.

"You can't take my daughter!"

April hesitated as Pa fought Jonathan's grasp that was already failing. Her pa was a shorter man, but stockier. Would the lean preacher hold any hope of walking away without substantial damage? This was all her fault.

"Get David," he shouted at her.

She bolted into the night air even as she heard Pa's roar. A moment later there was a crash, but she couldn't look back. She ran.

Jonathan had never wrestled a bear, but it was probably a lot like this. Arthur was shorter than him by most of a foot, but even a month locked away hadn't stolen his muscle mass. Jonathan could only imagine the strength the man had in his prime—which thankfully he was far past. Too many times Jonathan caught a fist with his face or side. After the first hook to his ribs, he tackled Arthur to the floor. They collided with the rough planks at the same time, their sides striking hard. Pain spiked up Jonathan's arm and through his shoulder. Before he could catch his breath, Arthur rolled over on him, pinning him.

Jonathan brought his knee into Arthur's back, and he gave a yelp. His hold loosened, and Jonathan took the opportunity to roll, offsetting the other man's balance. For a few minutes it was hard to tell who was up and what was down as they tussled for positions.

"Stop right there and raise your hands, Arthur."

Jonathan had never been so relieved to hear his brother's voice. He relaxed into the floor while the weight of a man lifted from his chest, replaced moments later by the feathery touch of a concerned woman.

"Oh, Jonathan, are you all right?"

As tempting as it was to lie there awhile longer, Arthur was still grumbling and throwing every insult and curse under the sun at his daughter. Jonathan pushed to his feet and pulled April close as though he could somehow shield her from the monster. "Let's get you away from here." He led April around her father and into the evening air.

"You ungrateful—"

"Are *you* all right?" Jonathan asked April, trying to override her father's crude words.

"I will be." They stood out of the way when David led Arthur out and toward the jail. Again.

Jonathan glanced at April and saw the concern in her expression, as though she still worried about the man who had just accosted her—he couldn't call him her father. What true father would intentionally harm his child? Both men were out of sight before Jonathan realized he still held April. His body felt like he'd been run down by at least one cow if not a full stampede. April shivered in his arms.

It wasn't cold, but his reaction was the same. "Let's get you inside." He glanced back at the house and shook his head. He couldn't leave her there alone. But he couldn't take her to the parsonage either. "Is there anywhere else you can go?"

A minute passed before she nodded. "Miss Maddie's."

"Good." He kept hold of her arm but let her lead the way across town—a whole two and a half blocks—to a small but charming cottage. No other word seemed to fit whitewashed walls and decorative shutters so well.

The stone walk to her front door was narrow, so Jonathan took up the trail behind April but reached around to knock on the door. The usually cheery woman's expression quickly turned to shock at the sight of them, and she hurried them into her petite kitchen with a cabinet and table painted egg-yolk yellow. An eye-searing color, but at least April would be in good hands here. Thanking Miss Maddie and nodding to April, Jonathan started to leave. April needed attention and someone to talk to. As loathe as he was to leave her, he'd just get in the way.

"Where are you going, Parson?" Miss Maddie demanded.

"Home to clean up."

"I don't believe that for a moment. You'll fall into bed and stain your bedsheets." She motioned for him to sit at the table while she moved to the stove to put a kettle on. "Do you two want to explain exactly why our pastor is a bloody mess?" She sighed. "Or should I take one guess?"

"One guess would probably be sufficient," April murmured, her voice barely above a whisper.

"You paid his fine, didn't you, child?" Miss Maddie shook her head. She stepped closer and touched the tip of April's chin where shades of red had begun to mingle with purples. Jonathan shoved to his feet.

"He hit you?"

April waved him away, shrinking back, though the tiny kitchen didn't allow her to go far. "It would have been worse if you hadn't come."

"I shouldn't have left to begin with. He was angry, but I didn't think he would hit you."

She shrugged as though it didn't matter. Her acceptance stoked his anger. Was this how her father usually treated her? The man should be horsewhipped. If Jonathan had any say in the matter, Arthur Harvey would never be allowed to lay another finger on his daughter.

CHAPTER 15

"Where are you going?"

April pulled on her shoes and glanced back at Miss Maddie. "I have work this morning." She wouldn't say it was at the parsonage or how nervous she was at the possibility of seeing Jonathan in the light of day.

"Very well. So long as you don't plan on going home."

No, not after David had come last night to speak with her. They had agreed that keeping her father overnight would be sufficient—or at least she had convinced him to not hold him longer or press charges. She'd already given too much for his freedom to let him throw it away within twelve hours.

"I should send over some more of that salve for the preacher's face."

April bit her lip but paused to wait as Miss Maddie fetched a little jar of green salve that smelled of tree sap. More than just the jar was pressed into her hand. April stared down at the small wad of banknotes. "I can't take this."

"'Course you can. Nothing would make me happier than for you to buy yourself something pretty." Miss Maddie held her gaze, her own turning somber. "But at least so you know you have options."

"But I—"

Maddie shook her head and waved April out the door. "You tell that man of yours to take it easy. He only has a couple of days to mend before he has to go back to sermonizing." She shook her head, though she chuckled. "I can only imagine what folks will have to say about him looking so much like the man found beaten on the road to Jericho."

Unease skittered through April. With everything else to consider, she hadn't thought on what folks might think when they saw their bruised preacher. "You don't think they'll be upset with him, do you?"

"Don't you worry your pretty little head about that. Off with you."

April complied but couldn't help but worry. Especially when she stepped past the thick green lilac hedge and saw the damage in the light of day. Purple and blue bruises spread across Jonathan's jaw and circled one of his eyes. His lip was split and still swollen.

"You look horrible."

Jonathan paused his pacing in front of the steps and faced her fully. "Not quite the greeting I was hoping for," he grumbled, though his mouth twitched upward.

"I'm sorry." April stepped closer so she'd be less visible to passersby. "I'm sorry for what Pa did. I haven't seen him that angry in years." Probably because she'd learned to gauge his shift in moods and knew when to slip away.

"But he is prone to anger. David told me as much." Jonathan stepped to her and slowly reached out to brush a finger over her bruised cheek. "He's hit you before, hasn't he?"

April wished she could lean into Jonathan's touch, but it was too fleeting. "It doesn't matter."

"Of course it matters." Jonathan's brows pushed together. "Why didn't you tell me? I've met with Arthur several times, tried to speak to him, and yet I only find out yesterday that he's your father?" His voice sharpened.

April pulled back a step. This was exactly what she had feared. But why had he withdrawn from her earlier if he had only just found out who she was? Either way, it was evident that any tenderness and kindness he'd shown her was due to his being a minister and nothing more. She'd get on with what she came here to do. April charged past him, trying to ignore the two coffee mugs sitting side by side on the top step and the hope that gesture threatened to resurrect.

"April, stop." Jonathan followed her inside and caught her arm. "Look at me." He gently drew her around and touched her chin, tipping her face toward him. His gaze locked on her sore jaw and the bruise she hadn't been able to hide.

April bit her lower lip. "I'm fine."

"No, you're not—this is not fine."

"It's not your problem. All will be well as soon as he's gotten some rest and blown off some steam." A few drinks might help him settle in this case. "It was my fault he was upset."

"No." Jonathan dropped his hand to her shoulder. "There is nothing you could do that warrants him lifting a hand to you." The muscles in his jaw worked as though he had a lot more he wished to say. Finally, he muttered, "He should stay locked away."

Part of her wished he would, but. . ."What good would come of that?" Her voice cracked while moisture obscured her vision.

"What do you mean what good? You—"

"We're supposed to help him back to the fold, to rescue him. He's not a bad man. He's angry and hurt. I hurt him. I lied about the money I had hidden. I just found out I could have posted bail weeks ago and didn't. Of course he was angry."

"That is still no excuse for what he did to you. It was your money, wasn't it?"

April shrugged. "I was living in his house. And he's my pa. Besides, I'm the reason he's so miserable. He wasn't always this way."

"I find that hard to believe."

April couldn't look up, couldn't meet Jonathan's eyes. He would see through her, see all her flaws and everything she hated about herself. Her shoulders curled forward while she slunk back a step. Withdrawing from his touch. "I killed my mother and little brother." April stared at nothing, hearing her pa's accusations echo in her brain. It was her fault. Her fault. Her fault.

Jonathan watched as the woman before him, one he had once considered strong and indomitable, seemed to shrink before him. Her body curled in on itself, and the color drained from her face.

"I brought smallpox into our home. I made them ill. My mother slaved away trying to make me well, she didn't sleep, hardly ate. So, when she caught it. . ."

"She was weakened and died." Jonathan stepped toward her, but she shrank farther away. "Do you hear what you are saying, April? You could have died too. Your father should be happy he didn't lose you, not take their deaths out on you."

"But I—"

"You purposefully caught the smallpox and spread it to your family?"

She glanced up, eyes widening.

"It's not your fault. None of this is." He stepped forward again, cupping her shoulders in the warmth of his large hands.

"And it's not your responsibility to rescue him."

"But—" Her voice squeaked.

"You are not the shepherd in this story, April. It's not your job to save your father." He stepped to her, and this time she stood still. New understanding lit his mind. "You're the lost sheep."

"No. I'm not lost." She shook her head and tried to pull away, but he held her fast. "I've accepted Jesus. I try to live as I ought. I don't need rescuing."

"You are one of the most devout women I know, April. I don't question your heart. But you are backed into a cave with a wolf. You're not *safe* in the fold."

It was as though his words punctured her already-crumbling dam, and tears streamed down her cheeks while a sob broke from her throat.

"You can't stay there anymore. You have to leave. Or he does."

The slightest nod offered hope. She was listening. He wanted to pull her into an embrace and kiss away every hurt and fear, but they stood alone in the parsonage, the door open behind him. Anyone could look in and imagine whatever they wished. He wanted to protect her, not throw her into the path of gossip. Nor did he wish to lose his position. . . The one he had already offered to another.

What a mess.

"April. Why don't you take some time here. Don't worry about cleaning today. Rest. Have some coffee." He motioned to the abandoned mugs, though something fresh was probably in order. "I need to speak with David and take care of other business."

"Of course." A flicker of the strength he had seen so often in her showed in her glistening eyes.

"We'll figure this out." He tried for an encouraging smile, though it probably fell short. He needed to know if April would be safe in town despite her father, write the new preacher before he started his journey to Rowley, and figure out how to convince April to allow him to protect her as only a husband could.

April dumped the cold coffee in the sink, watching the dark liquid swirl out of sight. She rinsed the mugs and set them on a cloth to dry and then walked through the house. Jonathan had told her not to worry about cleaning, but she couldn't help going through the motions. If only one last time.

You need to leave.

Jonathan's words haunted, but they rang with truth. She'd put it off far too long already.

She ran her hand over the assortment of rocks on Jonathan's bedside table. Oh, how she wished things were different. That she could stay here, in this house, that he would come back and tell her that he cared about her as a woman, not just one of his lost sheep.

A tear trickled down her cheek, and she picked up the now-polished fossil they had found together. Shades of the rainbow wrapped around it like a corkscrew. Would he miss it if she kept it? Would he miss her?

April straightened the beds and folded back the quilts before escaping from the parsonage. Her feet carried her to the grain elevator. From high above, the train seemed so small as it approached the town. It rolled to a stop, and people buzzed around on the platform like busy bees preparing for their journey. Tomorrow, that would be her. She'd prepare tonight and somehow find the money needed for a ticket. She hardly cared how far she made it or what awaited her there. Miss Maddie had already offered help. Employment could be found. She was a hard worker. Like Jonathan said, she'd figure it out.

A flash of red drew her attention to the scarlet uniform in

front of the diner. A man in a dark coat stood nearby, gathering some attention, by the looks of it. Folks gathered around the brothers like turkey vultures around a ground squirrel. She was ruining Jonathan's life, just as she had her father's. The longer she stayed, the more harm would be done. Somehow, she had to be on that train when it left, but how? She didn't dare go home to gather her things. It would be like entering a wolf den with the whole pack of them sitting there waiting for her. No. She would have to start over with only the few dollars Miss Maddie had given her this morning. There was no time for goodbyes.

CHAPTER 16

The wolves were circling, looking for blood.

Probably an exaggeration, but that was what it felt like as the folks of Rowley crowded around Jonathan, throwing questions out faster than he could collect them—never mind manage an answer.

"Settle down!" David roared too close to Jonathan's ear. "Stop talking and let the parson explain."

Either folks had a healthy respect for the uniform, or they actually wanted an explanation. With ringing in his ears—thanks to David—Jonathan faced what appeared far too much like a judge and jury. The judge, Mrs. Matkin, of course, had pushed to the front and stood with arms folded, toes tapping. The jury flanked her, mostly women, who wanted to know why their preacher looked like he'd been fighting. Why Arthur Harvey was back in town and free as a lark—that question was aimed more at David. And why a new preacher had arrived on the train.

"I asked Parson Jones to visit Rowley to see if the community would be a good fit for him and for the town," Jonathan started. "But he and I have several things to discuss before a final decision is made." Especially as Jonathan suddenly had second thoughts about leaving at all. He wanted time to explore his new relationship with his brother now that it seemed they were on more equal footing. But most of all, he wanted to be with April. "As for my appearance, may I turn your minds back to the stories of the shepherd boy, David, who slew a bear and a wolf in the protection of his flock. I was merely rescuing a lamb."

"It's that Miss Harvey," Mrs. Fredricks complained. "She's gone and turned your head. It's as plain as day."

"Why, she isn't much better than that Pa of hers," Mrs. Matkin continued. "Keeps to herself too much to not be up to some mischief."

"Especially with her cleaning the parson's house like she's been doing." Mrs. Johnson picked up the rant. "An unattached woman has no right to be picking up after and fixing meals for an unmarried man in his own home. It isn't proper."

"Hogwash." Miss Maddie pushed into the verbal foray. "April Harvey is as good a Christian woman as anyone here."

"Then who was out behind the schoolhouse a couple weeks back with Charlie Kent?" Mrs. Matkin demanded.

"You saw her with your own eyes?" Miss Maddie questioned before Jonathan had a chance.

"Maybe not, but one of my boys told me about it," Mrs. Matkin protested.

Jonathan shook his head, not believing it of her. "I'm sure Miss Harvey would guard herself more carefully than that."

"She's been stealing from us," Mrs. Fredricks inserted. "Right from our garden."

"Only your weeds," David replied. "She let me know it was George Johnson making off with your vegetables, and I've already had a talk with him. He and I planned to come over this afternoon to speak with you."

"Well, I—" Mrs. Fredricks stepped back, her bluster stolen.

"April Harvey has been folding my laundry and fixing things around the place when she thinks I'm not looking," Mrs. Bailey spoke up, pushing herself forward, a toddler on her hip.

"Saw her out one morning scrubbing the schoolhouse windows as well," Mr. Allard added with a smile. Beside him stood a portly fellow Jonathan had not seen before. Pastor Jones, no doubt. Time was short.

"If you want the truth," Jonathan said, "April Harvey watches over this town like its own guardian angel, doing good where she sees it needs doing. And what's more, I intend to court her properly and hope to someday make her my wife."

Several of his audience gasped, while Mr. Allard pushed forward. "Then you best get moving, young man. She bought a ticket for that train that will be leaving shortly. I was just showing Mr. Jones here where to find you."

Jonathan hardly cared about Mr. Jones or the discussion he should be having with him or anyone else. He glanced at his brother, who offered an encouraging nod, and then pushed past Mr. Allard and the rest of the crowd, grateful Rowley was as small as it was. Minutes saw him to the station, where folks were climbing aboard the passenger car. He didn't see April among them, so he boarded as well, trying to refrain from shoving people out of his way. One larger lady took a particularly long time finding her seat and allowing him past.

April's eyes widened as soon as she saw him, but instead of standing to greet him as he'd hoped, she shrank deeper into her seat. "What are you doing here?"

"Coming after the one."

April had no choice but to scoot over as Jonathan plopped beside her. Her heart fluttered against her ribs, but she tried to tamp down any hope. As flattering as it was that he cared enough to come after her, this was not where he needed to be right now. "Your flock is out there, Parson. I don't belong with them."

He frowned. "That isn't true, but it's not the point I came to argue."

She stared at her hands clasped on her lap, wanting to look at him but not trusting herself. "What point is that?"

He set his hand over hers, warm and strong. "You belong with me."

Air fled her lungs, but she managed to shake her head. "What about the town, everyone else in Rowley?"

"They'll be in good hands. Pastor Jones has years more experience than I do and will be a better fit for the town, if that is what you want. It's not like I've abandoned *my* flock." He smiled. "I'm merely in pursuit of the one who fled."

"I'm not the *one*," she grumbled. Though she couldn't argue that she was fleeing.

"April, darling." He reached for her hand. "We are all *the one*. You. Me. Everyone. We all fall short, we all go astray, we all need rescuing from time to time." His voice lowered, growing husky. "I need as much grace and help as anyone. If you want..." He trailed off.

The sincerity in his eyes was unarming. She squeezed his hand. "What do you mean, if I want?"

He started to speak but paused when the train's whistle announced its imminent departure.

"You need to get off the train." April glanced up and down the aisle. Everyone was settling into their seats.

"Only if you get off with me. Otherwise, I'm coming with you."

She stared. "You can't leave." But did he really mean that? "You have no luggage. Your books. Your rocks. Even your Bible."

"David can ship them to me without much difficulty." He looked her up and down. "You don't appear much more prepared than I do."

April shrugged. "There isn't much for me here." It wasn't worth facing the wolf again. She slipped her hand into her pocket for the polished fossil. "I have this."

He chuckled. "I knew it from that first day I saw your feet sticking out from under my bed. You're quite the thief."

"I found it, I would have you remember." She glanced from the rock to the man, wishing she could keep both but not quite believing it was possible. "And maybe I wanted something to remember you by." Though she sounded pathetic saying it out loud. Even to her own ears, her voice sounded hollow with defeat. There was so much more she wished she had the courage to say. She wished she could tell him exactly what it meant to her that he'd come after her, that he wanted her. She wanted to believe that he would hear her. Maybe he would? Maybe he had really meant what he said. Her heart thudded painfully, but hope had taken root there, and those roots were stretching deeper than any of the weeds she'd pulled in Mr. Fredricks' garden.

"April, I—"

The train lurched forward, jostling as it began rolling along the tracks.

Jonathan laughed. "I guess that decides that."

"But—do you even have a ticket?" Oh, what a mess. What a perfect, confusing, hope-filled mess.

"I—"

The steward approached, his glare focused on Jonathan. "You Pastor Burton?"

Jonathan straightened and nodded, though he seemed surprised. "I am."

"The stationmaster asked me to hand you this." He extended a ticket marked with the same destination as April's.

Jonathan thanked the man then smiled back at April. "God works in mysterious ways."

She couldn't help but arch a brow at him. "Mr. Allard and Miss Maddie are less mysterious and more incorrigible."

"I'll take my miracles however they come." He settled into the seat and took her hand. "And it appears we now have a couple hours to decide what happens next."

She leaned on his shoulder and allowed herself to breathe—and to believe. "All right, Preacher, tell me what you have in mind."

EPILOGUE

April stood outside the church, nervousness skittering through her. She gripped the tiny summer daisies, not sure if they would survive the next hour—or even the next ten minutes for that matter. Then the door of the small church opened, allowing music to wash over her while David grinned and offered his arm.

"Thank you," she managed, grateful for the soothing sound of the piano and something solid to steady her. She clung to the flowers and the memory of Jonathan's gentle encouragement and words of love over the past two months.

"You look beautiful," David said, though she hardly heard him as they began their walk. "Jonathan is a lucky man."

She was the one who felt lucky—or *blessed*. When they reached Coleman, she had been introduced as his fiancée and put up in the local boardinghouse. His mother had arrived a week ago and had taken to fussing over April as though she were her own daughter. Even now tears threatened at the outpouring of love the woman had given so freely.

Then David came last night with news that Pa had settled back into his old life of working when sober and drinking when he had two coins to rub together, and uncertainties returned.

What would the good folks of Coleman think of her if they knew?

April shook the thought from her head. Pa's decisions did not define her.

David's shoulder brushed hers as he whispered in her ear. "Look up."

April hadn't realized she'd been staring at the floor, another habit she worked to break. It was strange to see another pastor standing where Jonathan preached each Sunday. Even the place one would expect the groom remained empty.

"Almost there."

She could hear the grin in David's voice, and she shifted her gaze to where Jonathan sat at the piano, having insisted a wedding needed music and that he was the only one who could adequately provide it. As they neared the front, the music concluded, and Jonathan stood to meet her. The warmth in his eyes drew her in.

David delivered her to his brother and stepped away, but she was hardly aware of his departure. Jonathan's hand wrapped hers, and his smile anchored her.

I love you.

He'd told her so many times over the past few weeks that she could almost believe it.

You are strong. You are beautiful. You are intelligent. You are good. You are Mine.

The last seemed to come from somewhere within her. Though she imagined Jonathan felt the same way in this moment, this time it was as though someone else whispered the words into her thoughts, bringing a measure of restoration to her heart. She took a healing breath as she clung to the truth—she had a Father in heaven who loved her and claimed her.

"Brothers and sisters, we are gathered together to witness

the joining of these two souls in holy matrimony." The pastor continued, but April only heard half of what was said while she repeated the words in her head, words that brought life. She spoke as required and compelled herself to breathe through the ceremony until Jonathan slipped a small gold band onto her finger, a small stone cut and polished to gleam like a gem but with tones of swirling reds and blues.

"The agate you tried to steal from me that first day," he whispered in her ear as his hand cupped her face.

"I didn't—"

Jonathan drew her to him, his mouth still wearing a smile as he pressed a kiss to her lips. She smiled in return. He was the real thief.

HISTORICAL NOTE

A couple of summers ago, I had the opportunity to visit a small "ghost town" in rural Alberta, Canada. Once a busy little farming community, Rowley remains a charming historical site that was fun to explore. With the towering grain elevators alongside the railway, a one-room schoolhouse with tiny quarters for the schoolteacher in the back, and a quaint church with ridiculously steep stairs down to its basement, Rowley captured my imagination and begged for a story to be told. While the characters in this story are all fictional, the town itself remains a little gem in the middle of nowhere.

To keep from freezing in the great white north, **Angela K Couch** cuddles under quilts with her laptop. Winning short story contests, being a semifinalist in ACFW's Genesis Contest, and being a finalist in the 2016 International Digital Awards also helped warm her up. As a passionate believer in Christ, her faith permeates the stories she tells. Her martial arts training, experience with horses, and appreciation for good romance sneak in as well. When not writing, she stays fit (and toasty warm) by chasing after five munchkins.

Convincing the Circuit Preacher

BY CAROLYN MILLER

CHAPTER 1

Picton, New South Wales,
Australia
1863

The sigh of the creek's she-oaks stole past the opened church windows, the cold sandstone walls threatening to send a teeth-chattering shiver up her spine, but Dorothea Maclean's gaze refused to budge from the visiting preacher. Reverend Carter had introduced Mr. Jonas Hamill as his replacement for when he took leave, and while she had suspected that Reverend Carter had been young once, she was fairly certain he had never looked quite like Mr. Hamill.

Mahogany-toned hair flopped across a broad forehead, while Mr. Hamill's dark eyes implored from the pulpit, his hand on his Bible, his heart in his voice. There was something rather appealing about a young man who was passionate for the things of God, whose wit stirred as much as his voice did. Reverend Carter loved the Lord, but his long graying beard and grave demeanor seemed to place him at least a decade older than Mr. Hamill. Perhaps that was a result of carrying the responsibility of this church. Her focus slid to the reverend's wife, Sarah, balancing their young son Edward in her lap. Or the strain of a young, hopeful family who had suffered loss in recent years.

Mother nudged Thea's side with a gentle press of her elbow, her demeanor such that nobody would be any the wiser. Thea returned her attention to the front, her shoulders easing as she focused on the handsome man still pleading for the congregation to put all their trust in the Lord.

A pang of shame at being distracted by the circuit preacher's handsome appearance was quickly followed by a fresh stirring to listen and truly attend to his sermon.

Mr. Hamill tapped the Bible again. ". . .which is why we know this book forever remains a place where the disciple can find instruction, the heedless can find warning, the weary, inspiration—"

Thea straightened, his words seeding faith in her soul.

"—the fainthearted, courage, and the sorrowful, comfort."

His voice cracked, and he paused, an expression crossing his features that drew her heartstrings tight.

"And it remains a place where peace with God can always be found for those who are searching. So whatever your circumstances, remember, you can always trust God and trust His promises found in His Word. Now, let us pray."

She closed her eyes and bent her head, but it was more than a pious posture. Some might regard the eldest Miss Maclean as little more than the frivolous eldest daughter of one of the town's leading families, but she longed for more than to make a good match matrimonially. She had often felt a tug to deeper things and had many times discussed elements of faith and purpose with her former governess, Miss Brady. It was Miss Brady's influence that had seen Thea own a faith that was less about lip service and more about trying to follow the commands Mr. Hamill had pointed out in today's sermon.

"And help us to trust You, and lead us into Your plans and purposes. In the name of Jesus Christ, amen."

"Amen," Thea echoed, opening her eyes to see her younger sister hide something in her skirts.

She nudged Eliza just as Mother had done her, subtly pointing to the hidden object and lifting her eyebrows.

Eliza peered up with an aggrieved expression and sighed, then drew out a tiny furred creature, which elicited Thea's high-pitched yelp.

"Dorothea!" her mother reproved.

She straightened, willing the heat in her cheeks to fade as she glanced at the front to where both Reverend Carter and Mr. Hamill studied her. Uneasiness rolled through her stomach, but she willed her lips up in the small smile Mother deemed appropriate for Sunday services. Ladylike, interested, friendly, yet also cool and calm. It wouldn't do to appear too much of the tomboy that she had once been, and that the younger Maclean daughter most definitely was still. And it definitely wouldn't do to admit she'd been startled by the baby possum Eliza had hidden in her reticule. Eliza's love for all creatures great and small had caused more than one fracas between the Maclean women.

The service concluded with a rousing hymn played above them on the balcony by the violin, cello, and flutina. The reverend and the guest preacher walked swiftly down the carpeted aisle to the small stone-flagged porch and outside where they would shake hands with the congregants. They were followed by Sarah Carter and her small children, then the prominent families of the district: the Antills, Harpers, Cowpers, and Cavanaghs, along with Dorothea's.

The cedar pews were close to full with the less wealthy or land endowed, who waited as the Macleans shuffled to the center aisle before turning right near the stone baptismal. One of the tall lancet windows spilled sunlight on Thea's face. She caught Anthony Cavanagh's smile and ducked her head. There was no reason to give that young man ideas. Father would never countenance him as a future son-in-law, no matter how desperate Mother felt about Thea's unwed state. The Cavanaghs might possess the delightfully named Fairy Hills property, just east of the township, but Anthony was known to frequent the local hotels and be fond of gambling, two vices that crossed him off the list of eligibility as far as Father was concerned. That, and the family name was not quite what he envisioned for his daughter, or so he had said many a time.

By now they were passing through the arched porch, and she could hear Father's response as Reverend Carter shook his hand and introduced him to Mr. Hamill. Then it was Mother's turn. Now it was hers.

Dorothea's chin lifted, her smile stretching into genuine as the reverend introduced her to Mr. Hamill. She reached out, and he clasped her gloved hand.

Her heartbeat hitched. Up close he was even more handsome. His eyes were a very dark blue, but they held glints of light, which sparkled in the morning sunshine. "Miss Maclean."

Her chest fluttered at his deep voice, and she had the greatest temptation to curtsy, except he wasn't royalty, and she knew her father would likely have a fit if she curtsied to someone he'd declared a disappointment, with none of the glow attached to those of greater means.

Father had been thrilled to learn of the Antills' connections to Governor Macquarie and that the reverend's wife, Sarah, was the granddaughter of Samuel Marsden, the colony's chaplain until his death. He'd often declared it was only a matter of time before the Maclean name would be brought into such hallowed circles. Yet neither Mrs. Jessie Antill nor Sarah Carter possessed the airs and graces Father believed should be attached to such esteemed families. And Thea couldn't help but notice that despite Father's wealth and best efforts, the Macleans seemed destined to forever sit outside the exclusive circle of local society. Mr. Hamill's lack of known connections, and his mysterious past, meant he was no different.

But her father's objections to the visiting preacher fell heedless, as something within Thea refused to let go of Mr. Hamill's hand. It was as if her fingers, her very being, recognized something in this man, something she couldn't articulate, but which drew her to him in a way she'd never felt drawn to a man before. She clasped his hand a little tighter. His head tilted slightly, his eyes widening, as a furrow grooved his forehead.

"Dorothea."

She ignored her mother's whisper and smiled at him. "I enjoyed your sermon very much."

He inclined his head. "Thank you."

Reverend Carter cleared his throat. "And this is the younger Maclean daughter, Eliza."

Mr. Hamill's gaze fell to Eliza. He released Dorothea's hand, and she instantly felt the loss of his warm touch and attention. She glanced at her sister, the undeserving recipient of Mr. Hamill's consideration, who did not seem to care a whit for the handsomeness of the man who gently shook her hand. Eliza's bag fell to the ground. She gasped and instantly released his hand and swooped to collect it, her face now screwed into a scowl. "I hope you haven't hurt him."

Mr. Hamill blinked. "I beg your pardon?"

Her sister drew apart the sewn satin ribbons of her small bag then gave an audible sigh.

"Eliza," Dorothea warned in a whisper. Surely she wouldn't.

Not in church. Well, outside of church, but it counted nonetheless. Mother would never forgive them, would blame Dorothea for Eliza's scapegrace ways as she had so many times before.

But Eliza, headstrong as ever, paid decorum no mind as she held up the small furry creature from before, which drew Mother's gasp, Mr. Hamill's rumbly chuckle, and fresh heat to Dorothea's cheeks.

Reverend Carter coughed. He loudly drew Mr. Hamill's attention to the next in the queue. But even as Mr. Hamill nodded, his glance met Eliza's then lifted to Dorothea in an expression that could only be counted as conspiratorial. His lips curved, releasing a dimple in one cheek, as the startled look of before was replaced with the glorious sight of his smile.

Her heart trembled afresh in recognition, with the strangest sense that this man, this God-loving, good-natured man, was somehow meant to be part of God's plan for her life. As his attention quickly returned to Reverend Carter and the next family waiting to greet him, she knew that she would need to convince her parents—and Mr. Hamill—of this as soon as possible.

"We look forward to seeing you shortly."

Jonas bowed his head as Jessie Antill smiled and was handed up into the carriage being driven by her husband.

"An invitation to the Antills is an honor indeed," James Carter murmured as Jonas joined the remaining congregation members in watching the well-dressed couple drive away.

"You will find them the preeminent family of this district," Sarah Carter said. "The major was an aide-de-camp to Governor Macquarie, and a friend to his wife."

Jonas swallowed. "I did not realize he was a major."

"His father was the major."

James nodded. "Major Antill was very public-minded, a director of the Bank of New South Wales, and also the local police magistrate. It's only natural the Antills would be aware of their duty to the local community."

"Nobody is saying they are unaware. Quite the opposite," Sarah said with a wry glance at Jonas.

He bit back a smile, conscious he needed to stay neutral in what was obviously a debate this married couple had had before. Still, he'd had experience with wealthy landowners who had little time to serve their communities, and he'd much rather spend time with those who cared. And from everything Jonas had gleaned, the major's son, and current police magistrate, was a very busy man with a vast array of interests. Everything from agriculture to establishing a local school and political matters was under his keen eye.

"I am honored to have the opportunity to further the acquaintance," Jonas said as diplomatically as he could.

"I suppose with my absence for several weeks it is to be expected that John Antill would want to get to know you more," James said.

Jonas nodded. He had been asked by those in charge in Sydney to pause his traveling ministry as a circuit preacher and serve in this small village nestled between brooding hills while James and Sarah took some time away with family. He was here to serve as a kind of curate, his duties of preaching and taking services not dissimilar to what he'd done before, when he rode Noble along the lonely, dusty trails that connected scattered villages in a wide realm that took in both mountains and sea.

"I trust you will enjoy your time here," Sarah said.

"Thank you." He might say the words, but he scarcely believed them. This was a mere pause in his life before he returned to his own ministry, where he was truly needed, where he might one day forget. With no ties and only shallow connections, he would never make the mistake of letting his heart get entangled with domestic affairs again. God had given him this new path, and he'd been so grateful for the opportunity to forge past the grief which had swallowed him in those first few weeks. Enjoyment wasn't a concept he could trust anymore. Rather, it was something worldly, destined to distract him from the call of God. If he hadn't loved Mary so deeply, he wouldn't have been so devastated at her loss.

The Carters took their children to be cared for at their home, Oak Villa, where Jonas had arrived yesterday, and Jonas soon followed on Noble, passing the tall chimney of the steam mill positioned beside Stonequarry Creek.

A short time later they were all ensconced in a cart, bouncing along the rutted dirt track on their way to the Antill homestead known as Jarvisfield. They passed the George Hotel, with its two-storied rival situated opposite. The horses' hooves clomped across the wooden bridge and past the general store, followed by the butcher's, the post office, another public house, and a motley array of other buildings. All were deemed necessary for a town bustling with self-importance as the major stopping post for travelers before the Great Southern Road wound south to Goulburn and beyond. The extension of the railway, which had necessitated the building of a new station, due for completion soon, made Jonas wonder how long the many coaching inns and associated blacksmiths and wheelwrights might exist.

The road led northeast, winding around the base of a tall broad hill known to have several vaults on it. The family graves of the Antill family, so James had said, and more evidence of the importance of the family he was about to dine with. Such seemed like something his father had once mentioned about an estate he knew back home in Scotland.

Soon they passed the stone pillars that marked the entry to the Jarvisfield estate, the collection of buildings and imported elms and oaks showing the genteel leanings of the Antill family. James had mentioned their connection with the colony's fifth governor, and that Major Henry had gone so far as to name their son after Macquarie and their estate after Jane Jarvis, Macquarie's first wife. His stomach tightened as he wondered just what he should expect.

"Thank you for joining us for our meal," Jessie Antill said, gesturing for Jonas to take his seat next to her at the oak dining table.

"Thank you for having me."

She smiled at Jonas, and the nerves eating at him slowly ebbed away. Mrs. Antill was good-humored and quick to smile, unlike her husband, who seemed cast in a more serious frame. Likely that derived from bearing the preeminent family name in the district and all the weighty responsibility of being the local police magistrate. Word had it that several bushrangers had been seen not too far south in recent days.

The meal was soon served, and the conversation shifted to the matter of the new homestead John Antill was building. Their host cleared his throat. "William Weaver is an architect who is making a name for himself. Once the house is finished, it will have arched landing windows set with colored glass, all situated around a courtyard." He gestured to the surroundings. "This house is adequate, and certainly a great improvement on the slab house my father built fifty years ago. But we look forward to moving to something more suitable for our family."

Family. A word Jonas scarcely dared think about. Not anymore. Not with his parents gone, severing all connection to Scotland. Not when—*no.* He would not think on her. He sipped from his water glass, willing the memories away.

A peek at his hostess saw her looking curiously at him. Quickly now, he needed to get the focus off family and onto something far more innocuous. "I believe I saw another building beyond the trees."

"Ah, yes. Oliver Whiting runs that as an inn. He used to be a convict and worked as a servant here for some time."

"It's good to see a man breaking away from his past," Jonas said. The man might have been sent to the colonies for a crime, but Jonas had learned that many of those cast off from English shores had simply been struggling to keep their families fed. The crime of stealing a loaf of bread had resulted in many a boy sentenced to hard labor on the other side of the world, never to see his family again. He winced. There was that word again.

"Mr. Hamill? Is something not to your liking?" Jessie Antill asked.

"I have not eaten so well in an age." He heard how that sounded and quickly glanced at Sarah. "Not since I last dined with you, that is."

Laughter rippled from his hostess. "A nice attempt to save yourself, Mr. Hamill. What say you, Mrs. Carter, do you forgive the young man for such a faux pas?"

"Of course." Sarah's smile at Jonas showed she held no offense.

"We'll put it down to the fact he is not wed, shall we?" the irrepressible Mrs. Antill continued.

Jonas stilled, glancing at where his bare ring finger mocked him. He had felt like a traitor to take off the ring Mary had placed there four years ago. It seemed so strange that she'd now been gone for the same amount of time as he'd known her. Three years. Three achingly long years.

After a quick look at Jonas, Sarah hastily put a question to their host, diverting attention from the awkwardness. Clearly

Mrs. Antill had not been informed of the personal circumstances surrounding the new church minister. But, awkward as it could be, in some ways he was grateful, as he hadn't wanted the gossip from the city to chase him out here.

Mrs. Antill studied him as the others continued their conversation then said in a quiet voice, "I fear I have overstepped. Forgive me."

He shook his head. "There is nothing to forgive. I—" He cleared his throat. "I am not married, that is true."

"Well, you need not remain that way, should you wish. I couldn't help but notice the way a certain young lady regarded you this morning."

His skin prickled. Oh, he knew exactly whom she meant. Miss Maclean. Dorothea. His mother's name. He'd first noticed her during his preaching, then her startled cry at the service's end. How could he not notice someone who shared similar fair features to his lost Mary? But it was only when she'd spoken to him outside and smiled up at him and held his hand that he'd realized she was dangerous. For there was such sweetness in her countenance, such vivacity in her sparkling green eyes, that he knew he needed to stay away. He would not let his heart succumb again to a woman's charms. That way danger lay.

Conscious his hostess still awaited an answer, he said, "I have no interest in taking another wife."

"Another? Oh! Pardon me." Mrs. Antill regarded him with sympathy. "I am sorry. I did not know. The loss of a loved one makes it very hard to move on," she added softly. "My father-in-law grieved the death of his daughter Margaret and spent many an hour visiting her grave."

He nodded but could not answer.

"Well, perhaps it is uncharitable of me to say this, but you may wish to make your position clear. Mr. Maclean is never backward in issuing invitations to Glendalough, so it won't be long until you're invited to dine there, I'm sure."

"I am not averse to easing the burden of my hosts by partaking elsewhere on occasion. But anything more than a meal is simply not of interest to me."

"Ah, but who can say what the Lord has in store for those who trust in Him?"

A reluctant chuckle pushed out, even as he toyed with her subtle challenge. Marry again? Never. God would not want him to seek a wife. And certainly not one who laughed in church and held a man's gaze—and hand—longer than polite society deemed respectable. Even if she was the prettiest lass he'd seen since—

No. He could never desecrate Mary's memory by comparison with an inferior creature. He refocused on his meal as the conversation swirled around him, but guilt drew queasiness in his stomach, keeping him from eating another bite. Mrs. Antill might mean well, but clearly she did not understand he was no catch. Far from it. For who could ever want the man who had failed to save his wife and newborn son from a catastrophic fire?

CHAPTER 2

"Thank you, Miss Larkin."

Miss Eva Larkin nodded and drew Eliza inside the small, square brick building used as a music room. Thea suppressed a smile at Eliza's pleading look before the heavy wooden door closed. After Miss Brady left, Father had insisted that both his daughters continue to study music, deeming it one of the softer graces that marked a young lady. And while Thea enjoyed her lessons almost as much as she did her gardening, Eliza had always preferred her animals to more ladylike pursuits.

The high square bell cot of St Mark's church peeked above some nearby trees, and she wondered if the Carters had left yet. Father had said they were traveling to Sydney this week, now that Mr. Hamill had been introduced to the congregation. She hoped he was of a mind to visit the church members as Reverend Carter was. Perhaps she could encourage Mother that they needed to be neighborly and invite the poor man to dinner. He would likely get lonely staying at the rectory by himself.

A wooden seat positioned under a large eucalypt beckoned, the tree offering shade in today's mild sunshine. Their horse grazed beside the sulky, a small two-wheeled cart that Father deemed suitable for today's excursion to their music lessons. Normally he would demand that the rules of propriety be observed and insist upon a chaperone. But with Mother unwell and no servants able to be spared from their duties, Thea hoped his magnanimous gesture in letting her drive the two miles to town would not meet with any incident to mar this welcome burst of freedom.

She drew in a deep breath, relishing the warmth in the February air. Life here was so different from what her father had experienced back in Scotland, and not just because there seemed to be a more relaxed way with certain social rules and customs. Father always noted the differing seasons and how strange it felt to have summer in February when Scotland would be enduring wintry bleakness. But that was hardly a complaint. Father loved living here. He'd often said this land held a promise, a raw beauty, the old ways being cast off in a manner like this tree, with bark that peeled off in gray strips like a dripping candle, revealing the clean bark beneath tinted gold and pink. She could see a similar parallel in the messages Reverend Carter had given. How faith in God allowed the old life to be cast aside, so that one could live knowing the guilt of one's sins had been stripped away by the forgiveness available to all through the death and resurrection of Jesus Christ.

She closed her eyes, a prayer of thankfulness drifting heavenward, as a magpie sang from the branches above. She was grateful for so many things. Grateful for her family, for the chance to study music, to live in this pretty valley, for the many other blessings in her life. "And Lord, I'd be *especially* grateful if You could please bring Mr. Hamill across my path again."

No sooner did her last words escape into the air than a raucous cry came from above, which was swiftly followed by a loud *plop*.

She blinked, her face wrinkling in disgust, as she held out her green-and-white marred glove. Ugh. A quick glance revealed no one around, so she tugged her glove off from the fingertips, taking care not to touch the bird's unwelcome deposit. Thank heavens Mother was not here to witness such a ghastly and most unladylike sight. She'd no doubt complain that it was as bad as the stubborn tiny specks of dirt that forever lay under Thea's nails.

After a careful wipe on the grass—adding green grass stains to the white cotton—she straightened, just as a horse and rider drew near. No.

Mr. Hamill brought his chestnut horse to a standstill. "Miss Maclean."

She dipped her head, thrusting her ungloved hand behind her. "Mr. Hamill."

He studied her, a slight crease in his brow drawing heat to her cheeks. How could she possibly explain this situation? Yes, she'd just prayed to meet him again, but certainly not like this!

"May I inquire whether you are quite well?"

"I'm very well, thank you, sir." Her nerves eased. Perhaps he hadn't seen her, or if he had, had not thought her wiping her glove on the grass so terribly strange. "Thank you for asking."

His frown deepened as his gaze lowered to her skirts then back up again. "I ask because I saw you appeared to be in some distress."

"Oh!" Oh dear. So he *had* seen her after all. "It is nothing." And certainly not anything Mother would think fit for a young lady to discuss with a young man.

"Are you sure?"

The fact that he kept persisting in inquiring about her welfare surely meant he cared. Her heart glowed, drawing her smile. "I truly appreciate your concern, but I am quite well."

She ducked her head, only to spy her floral-printed crinoline adorned with a large spot of residue similar to that decorating her glove. "Ugh!"

How embarrassing! She drew a handkerchief from her reticule but hesitated. The flimsy wisp of cotton and lace Mother deemed appropriate for a young lady was hardly fit to deal with the tears that threatened to escape at this humiliating situation, let alone mopping up a mess of this magnitude.

Awareness grew that he had descended his horse and drawn closer and was now holding out a square of folded cloth. "Please."

She blinked rapidly and glanced up, her watery gaze finding his expression had softened. She sniffed back her emotion—oh, how Miss Brady would despair at her lack of genteel behavior today—and grasped his handkerchief. "Thank you."

After cleaning her gown as best she could, she folded his handkerchief carefully then hesitated again. Would he want it back? She held it out. He shook his head. Fresh chagrin filled her. Of course he wouldn't. What gentleman would? Her chin wobbled, what remained of her composure threatening to slip. Oh, she was childish to take this so much to heart.

"There is no need to cry."

"I'm *not* crying."

His wry lips suggested he disagreed, and frustration mounted. Surely he must think her as vain as any schoolgirl, disappointed over her spoiled dress, when in actual fact she was simply frustrated she was not presenting the calm sophistication worn by the likes of Mrs. Antill or the reverend's wife. Still, the fact that he remained meant all hope was not yet lost. She drew up her chin, dashed a finger under one eye to remove the telltale moisture, and forced up her lips. "See?"

Any trace of his severity from before quite disappeared as he smiled. "I do indeed."

How she wished to have made a better second impression, for a woman could get lost in the depths of his smile. Her shoulders relaxed, and she grew aware that the sounds of imperfect pianoforte playing had ceased from within Miss Larkin's music room.

A moment later, the door opened, and Thea stepped away from him. Heaven forbid anyone accuse them of impropriety by standing too close together.

"Thea?" Eliza called, her footsteps slowing as she skidded to a dusty stop in front of Mr. Hamill. "Oh. It's you."

"Miss Maclean."

Eliza shook her head. "I'm not Miss Maclean. That's Thea there. I'm only Eliza."

"Forgive me, Eliza," he said gravely, his lips curving only slightly. "May I ask after the state of your young possum?"

"Do you mean Henry?"

A dimple quivered in his cheek. "I suppose I do."

"He is quite well, thank you."

Appreciation for his largesse in not teasing her sister drew new warmth. Still, they should not be seen talking to a young man, unchaperoned as they were. Even if he was only the circuit preacher. "Eliza, please don't bother Mr. Hamill. I'm sure he has more important matters to attend to."

His dark blue gaze lifted to Thea then returned to her sister. "On the contrary. I find myself intrigued as to whether we are to expect other small furry creatures at the Sunday service. If so, I think it best I'm prepared."

Eliza's head tilted. "You do not mind? I only brought Henry because he's so little and was missing his mother—our dog, Darcy, hurt her, and I managed to save Henry before he was killed too—and I knew Mother wouldn't want me to, but I couldn't leave him at home by himself. Not with Darcy there."

"Quite right."

"Eliza." Thea placed a hand on her sister's shoulder, but Eliza shrugged it off.

"No, he asked about it, Thea. And I wasn't to know that he'd be far more interesting to listen to than Reverend Carter, was I?"

Thea stole a peek at Mr. Hamill, who seemed to be struggling to suppress a smile. God bless him for overlooking her sister's foibles.

"Besides, it's not right to let such a small creature die, is it?"

A myriad of emotions flickered over his features, the light from before shadowing as he cleared his throat. "Indeed."

The man's obvious pain twisted Thea's heart, drawing new sympathy. "Oh, sir."

He glanced up at her. The distress there dried her mouth, stole her words of comfort. She moistened her lower lip, noting the way his gaze dropped there before instantly veering away.

"Thea." Eliza tugged at her hand. "We need to go back. Henry needs me."

He refocused on her sister. "Your little possum didn't join you on this excursion?"

"Not today." Eliza sighed dramatically. "I brought him once, but Miss Larkin screamed. She is even more chickenhearted than Thea here."

"Eliza!"

"What? It's only right that Mr. Hamill knows. You used to be far more brave and do interesting things, but ever since you put your hair up and started talking about beaux, you've gotten boring."

Thea gasped then tossed a "Please excuse us" at Mr. Hamill as she snatched her sister's arm and drew Eliza to the sulky amid her protests. She didn't dare look at him. She unhooked the horse's reins from the stump and clambered up into the seat, ignoring his offer to help. Fresh frustration heated her chest and cheeks as she slapped the reins and urged the horse away. What must he think of her? Of them? Oh, there was no possible way the most interesting man she had ever encountered would ever want anything to do with them again.

"Ahem."

Jonas spun from watching the exit of the Maclean ladies to face Reverend Carter. "James, I did not see you there."

"Is everything quite all right? You seemed lost in thought."

He willed his cheeks not to flush. He was not a schoolboy in trouble. "I was helping Miss Maclean."

"Hmm." Reverend Carter eyed him. "You need to be careful with that family."

"I beg your pardon?"

"Alexander Maclean might be somewhat new to town, but he is not without influence, especially considering his connections with the new railroad. And I don't think it would help your cause to stir up the interest of his eldest daughter."

Jonas lifted his hands. "As I said to Mrs. Antill just yesterday, I have no desire to wed again."

"You told her you have been married?"

"Miss Maclean?" Jonas realized his mistake as the reverend's face tightened. "Forgive me, I do not know why I said that." He hurried on, conscious the older man's face said he didn't believe him. "I am surprised that Mrs. Antill did not know of my situation."

"We do not like to gossip here."

That would make a first. His experience of church communities showed that few were immune to that particular vice. And he could imagine in this quiet valley there might be many who enjoyed enlivening their days through some stimulating conversation about their neighbors.

"The younger Miss Maclean certainly seems a spirited young thing," he said, aware he needed to throw the focus onto Eliza and away from her older sister.

Reverend Carter smiled. "She is certainly that."

He had no wish to give away Eliza's secrets but was curious whether certain furred creatures had ever been known to attend Sunday services before. "She was telling me of her love for small animals."

"Ah, yes. If she had been born a boy, I'm sure she would have liked to have trained as a veterinarian."

Jonas gathered from that remark that the reverend was not conscious little creatures had sat among the congregants before. "I found her most refreshing."

"Yes. I remember her sister was not dissimilar when they first moved here four years ago, but she soon settled down."

That comment only caused further intrigue about the elder Miss Maclean. Her sister's comments had suggested the same. What had she been like prior to the young lady who had been upset about the unfortunate bird droppings on her clothes? He didn't care to explore why he felt a degree of gladness that she wasn't as missish as she'd appeared before. And precisely how old was she? Her actions suggested she was younger than her at-times poised appearance might suggest. Perhaps a careful question put to Sarah Carter might elicit the truth. Not that he had any intention of showing interest in the young lady. Because he wasn't interested. Not at all.

He steered the conversation away from hazardous waters, instead inviting the reverend to remind him of any last-minute instructions before they effected their departure in the afternoon. The Carters would stay at an inn in Camden tonight, after traversing the dangerous road carved into Razorback Mountain, before traveling the next day to family in Parramatta. He didn't actually need the reverend's instructions, as this wasn't his first time filling this type of role. But it wouldn't hurt to alleviate any perceived concerns the man might have. And it would also help him to stay focused on what truly mattered. Which was the church. Not the young lady with the personality that shimmered like chandeliers dripping with diamonds, capturing light, capturing his attention, whether it be through her tease, upset, or smiles.

But later, when the rectory was finally quiet, the bustle of the family's departure replaced by evening birdsong and other hushed sounds, he couldn't help but picture her, and wonder. Was Mrs. Antill right in assuming the elder Miss Maclean held a particular interest in him? It hadn't seemed that way today. Of course, she had been at a disadvantage, and he couldn't blame her for being embarrassed. He smiled in the darkness. Her little sister hadn't helped matters either.

He wondered what their next encounter would bring.

Jonas finished paying for his groceries, thanked Mr. Cornell, and made his way out to the street, nearly bumping into Mr. Cavanagh, a wealthy landowner whose wife had invited Jonas to join them for a meal. "Forgive me, sir. I did not see you." Jonas tipped his hat to him.

Samuel Cavanagh waved it off. "I believe my wife said you are dining with us tomorrow night."

"I'm looking forward to it." One of the perks of being new in a small town was the many invitations to meals. Perhaps it stemmed from curiosity, or perhaps from genuine hospitality, but he'd often found he rarely needed to cook for himself, which was a good thing, considering his poor domestic skills. He'd been blessed with a wife who refused to let him lift a finger to help in the home.

"You know where we are?"

Jonas nodded. "Fairy Hills. I recall passing the gates last week."

"I am assured it should be a clear night, so no mishap should affect our diners."

"Shall I expect the pleasure of others to join us?"

Mr. Cavanagh nodded. "A few of the other notables of the district. I'm eager to hear what some of them have to say about the railway expansion and how that will affect us."

Jonas felt his heart skip a beat. "I know I am new, but I understood from Reverend Carter that Mr. Maclean has some interest there."

"Oh, indeed he does. Alexander is as canny a Scot as anyone I've met. And he shall certainly be in attendance."

Jonas nodded, willing himself to appear disinterested, his gaze peeling away to where Larkin's tall chimney showed the steam mill was at work. He would not let his base curiosity get the better of him.

"As shall his daughter." Mr. Cavanagh chuckled. "I was under instructions to make sure she attended."

"I beg your pardon?"

"My nephew, Anthony." He jerked a thumb at a tall, strapping young man hoisting large boxes into a cart. "He's had quite a penchant for young Dorothea ever since the Macleans came onto the scene."

Jonas nodded, hoping no speck of disappointment had crept onto his face. Of course he had. Who wouldn't want a young woman of charm and intelligence and spirit? It was only to be expected of any young man in these parts with eyes in his head.

Even if that young man had vowed not to ever let a young woman touch his heart again.

CHAPTER 3

Thea studied herself in the looking glass. The hand-me-down from her mother's bedchamber held a mottled watermark behind the glass, which meant she couldn't see all of her reflection but could still see enough to know whether this gown was suitable for tonight's dinner at Fairy Hills.

When Father had first informed her that the Cavanaghs had especially requested her presence, she'd been dismayed, unsure why he was keen to encourage the connection. But he'd been so caught up in the likelihood of being asked for his insider knowledge concerning the railroads, he had barely listened to her objections. Therefore, she now wore her least appealing gown, the snuff-brown taffeta with a high neck that held no pretensions to elegance despite being imported from America, or so her maiden Aunt Agatha had said when giving Thea the gown at Christmas. That, combined with her fair hair pulled tight into a chignon, with none of the loose soft curls Thea usually preferred, made for rather a severe look. She tilted her head, stretching out a well-covered arm. Why, she almost resembled Aunt Agatha.

She spun to face her sister sitting on the bed, critically

observing as she stroked little Henry. "Well? What do you think?"

"You're not very pretty." Eliza's nose wrinkled as she eyed Thea's ensemble.

"No? Well, then I look the way I should." Anthony would hardly be inclined to talk to her if she looked like a dowd.

Eliza lifted the little possum, who seemed to agree, burrowing away against the light as if he couldn't stand the sight of her either. "But what if Mr. Hamill is there?"

"He is hardly likely to be invited," Thea scoffed. "If Father and Mother think him beneath our notice, then I can't imagine the other families inviting him to their table."

"Perhaps they did not know the Antills invited him on Sunday."

"What?"

Eliza shrugged. "I overheard Mrs. Antill invite him, and Mr. Hamill accept."

"Why didn't you say anything?"

"I didn't know I was supposed to." Eliza's smile held a mischievous quality that instantly put Thea on her guard. "You like him, don't you?"

"Don't be silly."

"You do! I should've realized it before when you held his hand for so long at services. You *like* him. That's why you and he were speaking so long when I was at music lessons the other day." Her eyes widened. "And that's why you don't care what you look like—because you don't think he will be there tonight!"

Thea gritted her teeth. Sometimes she loathed the fact that her sister was so needle-witted. "You are such a child."

"You're the child if you think an ugly gown will stop Anthony Cavanagh from paying you attention."

"What would you know about anything?"

"I know it'll take more than a brown dress to stop him from

chasing you when he thinks you're an heiress."

"That's ridiculous," she snapped, even as a pang convicted her. Father wasn't rich by Sydney standards, but perhaps for some of the settlers here who were land-rich but cash-poor she might be considered a catch. She wondered if Mr. Hamill knew or even cared about her supposed dowry.

"Girls, girls. Why am I hearing the sounds of discord?" Mother entered the room, looking with disfavor at Thea's apparel. "And why are you wearing that? I thought you would wear the silk, seeing it's so warm today."

"I have not had the chance to wear Aunt Agatha's gift and thought this would be a good opportunity."

Her mother's brow wrinkled. But she could hardly admit her elder sister's taste was poor. "Well, it *is* new, I suppose. But if you must wear that then at least arrange your hair in a more becoming way. That style has never suited you."

"That's what I said," Eliza piped from her perch.

"But Mother, it is only our neighbors, and I do not think I need to try to impress them. They've all seen me many times before."

"It never hurts to make an effort, even if it is only for one's neighbors. Besides, you know a woman always feels more comfortable when she is dressed well rather than being the least well-dressed person. Now sit." She gestured to the low stool in front of the dressing table. "I will attend to your hair, although I do not know why you did not ask Susan to help."

"She was busy helping you." As the only maid should be.

"Never mind. Let us do what we can now."

Thea restrained a sigh and resumed her seat, picking the dirt from the garden out of her fingernails. Helping with the gardening might be considered unladylike, but she preferred to feel she was useful. As her mother primped and loosened the waves around Thea's face, the harshness from before was soon replaced by something softer and more elegant. "Thank you, Mother."

"It never hurts to look one's best. You never know who might be in attendance."

"That's what I told her," Eliza said again.

Thea narrowed her eyes at her sister. She had better not say just who she thought might be there.

Eliza's mouth tipped up in a smirk. "In fact, I said that I think Mister—"

"Mother," Thea rushed to interrupt, "do you think we should leave now?" She inched closer to the looking glass, patting her hair. "You have done a splendid job, and I would hate for us to be late. How far is it to Fairy Hills again?"

"It should not take above half an hour."

"Good." She rose abruptly and collected her wrap, refusing to glance at her tiresome little sister. "Then perhaps it's time for us to go."

Thirty minutes later they were rounding the bend in the road where the railway station was near completion.

"It won't be long now," her father proclaimed. His role on the board that had overseen the extension of the railway from Campbelltown to Menangle then a further thirteen miles to Picton meant he was growing in consequence by the day. People liked to ask his opinion of everything from the design of the new Picton train station to the establishment of its new telegraph post, which was already in operation, to how long he thought the extensive railway bridge over the creek might take to build. Thea had seen the plans and thought the design quite beautiful, with its arches of stone evenly spaced across the valley. The viaduct would likely be a scenic drawing card to Picton, especially as this was the first bridge of its type attempted on such a scale in the colony.

The gate with the sign denoting Fairy Hills drew their attention, perched as it was between two gum trees of equal height. Misgiving churned Thea's stomach. While glad to have escaped her sister's unfortunate propensity for blurting out the truth, she held little gladness about attending. And although she would enjoy a change in routine and scenery, she had no comfort in thinking tonight would prove comfortable at all. Mrs. Cavanagh's cook was not known for serving hot meals, the kitchen being in a building apart from the main house to prevent fires, so the meals when served were often lukewarm at best. The invited guests would likely be everyone who ever attended these things, and as the youngest person there, she would be forced to listen to conversation about topics that held little interest as she did her best to evade Anthony Cavanagh's advances. Dodging his "accidental" brushes and conversation laden with innuendo was exhausting. After the last encounter, which Thea had spilled to her sister in a moment of weakness, Eliza had even gone so far as to recommend Thea carry a hatpin in her crocheted reticule to ward off unwelcome advances. One resided in her bag today.

Father turned the carriage into the drive. The homestead of the Cavanagh family was built on a ridge, with views to the south and of the treed juncture where Carriage Creek joined the meandering Nepean River three-quarters of a mile downstream from Stonequarry Creek.

The original cottage was now the central part of the homestead, with symmetrical gabled wings added later. A wide veranda crossed in front, allowing occupants to sit and see the views, and was reached by a steep set of stone steps with roses planted on either side. But if experience was any indication, there would be no sitting outside to take in the views. Instead, they would be inside in the hot parlor, then the dining room, then the parlor again, at least until the gentlemen joined the ladies after their postdinner port and cigars.

A variety of horses and carriages were near the outbuildings, suggesting there would be more than the usual number of guests. Thea's stomach tensed. Would Mr. Hamill make an appearance? The vain part of her hoped not. Not when she had dressed in such an inelegant manner. And not when she had made such a goose of herself the other day with her silly, childish behavior. He must think her a simpleton indeed! If only she could have made a better impression on him. That was twice she had failed now. Twice she had let herself get carried away with actions that were not truly representative of who she was or what she hoped to convey. But. . .no. Her nerves calmed. It was unlikely he would be here.

"Well, my dears, here we are." Father steered their horses to the hitching post, handing the reins to Thea as he clambered down and secured them.

For a man some deemed rich and self-important, Father was not above forgoing the use of a carriage man and driving them himself. She had once wondered aloud about this, and Eliza said she'd heard Father described as a Scot whose hands were too short for his pockets, which Father had laughed at while Mother had been aghast.

"*It's not tightfisted, but frugal,*" Father had declared. "*What is the point of putting on a show and pretending to be wealthier than one is by employing servants one does not need? Wealth doesn't lie that way. Besides, why should I forgo doing the things I enjoy? I enjoy travel, else I would not have left the mother country and come half a world away and be blessed to meet your mother.*"

He assisted Mother down then helped Thea. "You look very nice, Dorothea."

"Thank you." Father had never been known for having a critical eye for women's fashion.

"Just make sure that young Cavanagh does not get any ideas. I have a feeling the reason you are here tonight is because of him."

Her insides tensed again. "I have no inclination for him, Father, you can rest assured."

"Have you an inclination for any other young man?"

She laughed and tucked her hand in his arm. "Of course not."

They ascended the steep steps and waited to be welcomed by their hosts at the front door. A rider pounded up the dusty drive, and she peered over her shoulder. She froze, her palms slicking within her gloves, proving her earlier statement false.

For that newest arrival proved to be none other than Mr. Hamill.

Jonas glanced across the dining table, just in time to see Miss Maclean's gaze lower again. That made the third time tonight she'd avoided his gaze, almost like she was embarrassed from their encounter yesterday. His stomach clenched. How dreadful to think that someone who looked so similar to Mary might fear him.

Around him the conversation about railways had shifted, and Mr. Larkin was being asked again about the future of wheat being grown in the area.

Larkin sighed. "I cannot like the appearance of rust yet again. I fear we are too near the coast for wheat to grow successfully, and this is an industry better served further inland, beyond the Great Dividing Range."

Jonas nodded, although he had little knowledge of such things. Delving into the mysteries of agriculture had never been as important to him as exploring the mysteries of the Bible and how they applied to the human heart.

"What say you, Mr. Hamill? I'm sure on your travels you must have seen more than your share of farms blighted with disease."

He placed his fork and knife on the edge of his plate. "I have no expertise about whether this area can support the wheat industry, but I have seen similar areas succeed with dairying."

His host nodded. "I confess that when my father and brother settled here, it was because the area held some similar characteristics to my native Ireland."

Mr. Maclean's chin dipped. "I thought the hills quite reminded me of Scotland."

"May I ask what part of Scotland you came from, sir?" Jonas asked.

Mr. Maclean glanced at him. "Near Ayrshire."

"My father's family come from near Lanark, not a day's walk away."

"I thought Hamill an Irish name."

"I've been led to believe it has its origins in France."

"Hmm." Mr. Maclean studied him, and Jonas did his best to appear unruffled, concentrating on his tasteless meal. "May I ask about your family, Mr. Hamill?"

"There is not much to tell," he answered. "I was born here, but my parents sailed to New South Wales on the *Lady East*."

"The *Lady East*, you say?"

Jonas nodded.

"I did too. What year?"

"In 1833." A quick peek at Miss Maclean showed she was listening, her eyes not veering from his, even as Anthony Cavanagh tried to get her attention beside her.

"I do believe I must have traveled on the same ship as your parents. Hmph."

Why Jonas had volunteered this information he did not know, as it could not be of any great benefit to be further entwined with the family of the first woman who had stirred his interest since Mary's death. Especially as she obviously had a young suitor, even if she'd barely spared him a glance. Young Cavanagh was probably someone far better suited to her.

The conversation soon shifted back to railways, leaving him free to study the railwayman's daughter and wonder whether he would be freed to have a moment's conversation with her again.

After the meal, the women passed through to the parlor. In a few moments he could hear music being played, and he wondered if Miss Maclean was responsible for the delightful singing. Such wonderings made him less than attentive to the men's conversation and made him glad when Anthony rose and declared he had no taste for cigars tonight and would far prefer to join the ladies.

This drew a collective sound of agreement, and it wasn't much longer before he'd returned to find Miss Maclean seated at the pianoforte with young Mr. Cavanagh turning the pages of her music book. Judging from her small frown, she was not best pleased, which cheered his heart a little, although he knew it was unchristian to be glad at a rival's downfall. He inwardly winced. Why he could even consider the other man a rival when he had no right to claim a woman's affection seemed the epitome of selfishness. He needed to put her out of mind, as quickly as possible. He should leave them to it and escape the burden of staying a minute longer than politeness deemed necessary.

Miss Maclean played the last chord, and he joined the others in applause, his gaze stealing to where she resumed her seat beside her mother. Anthony stood nearby, shooting him a frown.

The evening continued with desultory conversation, but he was growing more impatient to leave. He could not afford to stay, to let his heart care. He was here for only a few weeks, and then he would be back on the road. His life was not suitable for a wife. *He* was not suitable for a wife. He'd proved that.

As soon as an avenue of escape opened, he rose, followed by Mr. Maclean. He had to make his apologies first, to not look like he was leaving because Miss Maclean was.

He moved to Mrs. Cavanagh and bowed slightly. "Thank you, ma'am, for a delightful evening. Forgive me, but I must away."

"We too must depart," Mr. Maclean said.

"But thank you all for your kind invitation."

Mr. Cavanagh nodded. "My nephew will escort you out."

Of course he would. Jonas bid farewell to the other guests, thanked Mr. Cavanagh again, and then found his hat and gloves and riding coat. Traveling dusty roads in evening wear made for a less-than-elegant appearance, so he was thankful that people had not seemed to judge too harshly here.

While young Mr. Cavanagh went to speak to the servant charged with looking after the horses, Jonas joined Miss Maclean and her parents standing on the veranda. The scent of jasmine drifted on the night air, the clear sky of velvety blackness spotted with twinkling stars.

"It is a beautiful evening," Miss Maclean murmured.

"The heavens declare the glory of our Lord," Jonas said.

She glanced quickly at him then ducked her head.

"I trust you enjoyed tonight, Mr. Hamill," her mother said.

"I did." Parts of it, anyway. Like the musical ability of the young woman who stood beside him in the shadows now. "I've enjoyed getting to know more of the local concerns."

"You should dine with us soon," Mr. Maclean said. "I should like to know more about these Scottish connections of yours."

Part of him longed to, and yet another part cautioned he should refrain. But politeness demanded he say, "I would be honored. Thank you."

Before further conversation could continue, Anthony returned leading Noble, while the Macleans' carriage was being wheeled out to them by a servant.

Mrs. Maclean was assisted down the steep steps by her husband, leaving Jonas to escort their daughter. He held out his hand, and she glanced at it then up at him.

"You need not fear. I do not bite."

Her lips rolled inwards as she gently grasped his hand, and they descended to where her father waited, talking with Mr. Cavanagh, who frowned over his guest's shoulder at where Jonas still held her hand.

Jonas released her, and she murmured her gratitude before moving to stand next to her mother. Jonas thanked the servant, giving him a small coin for his trouble, and checked over his horse as Anthony spoke urgently to Miss Maclean while helping her into the carriage.

Her gaze stole to Jonas, and in the flickering lamplight he saw her lips twist in resignation, which drew new protectiveness. He swung onto Noble's broad back and gently nudged him to move beside their carriage. The clear warm skies meant the top was down, and his position meant he drew quite close to Miss Maclean, thus forcing young Mr. Cavanagh to shift away.

"My apologies, sir." Jonas then nodded to the Macleans. "I hope it would not be forward of me to offer my protection, at least until we reach the township."

"Thank you."

Anthony instantly offered to ride with them also, which met with Mr. Maclean's impatient, "There is no need, not when Hamill here has already offered."

"Thank you for a pleasant evening," Jonas said again, which drew a scowl as the young man retreated to the steps, his hands fisted beside him.

Mr. Maclean snapped the reins and began to drive, and Jonas encouraged Noble to move to a trot to the opened gate before rejoining the road to Picton. There really was little need for him to accompany them. The bushrangers that haunted the wilds of the colony tended to roam farther south, in the wild tangled brush of Bargo and beyond. There, escaped convicts known as "bolters" had been known to hide for weeks in caves and thickets, taking advantage of unsuspecting travelers on the highways and robbing them under arms. Picton was not entirely immune from rough characters, although the presence of the local gaol and lockup tended to keep such behaviors restrained. He had been blessed to not encounter any bushrangers in his travels.

Noble trotted on, the sound of his hooves preventing conversation, but Jonas was content to ride and enjoy the cool evening air. Around them, the carriage lamps together with the stars provided enough light to see the road, and he glanced across just in time to see Miss Maclean avert her face. His chest tightened. Had she been watching him?

They soon attained the village, and despite Mr. Maclean's protests, he continued to accompany them through the main street to their homestead not far from Jarvisfield. Only when they reached the gates of Glendalough did he rein in Noble as Alexander Maclean invited him to call upon them soon.

"I would like to know more about a fellow Scotsman, and your gentlemanly actions tonight prove you are not quite what you first appeared."

How magnanimous. "It is always preferable to exceed expectations than the reverse."

He glimpsed Miss Maclean's smile and knew another pang

of internal conflict. He knew he wasn't worthy, that he didn't deserve a young lady's smile. But another part of him, that same part that considered it adventure to travel lonely trails that were more unmarked tracks than roads, dared to wonder if adventure could be found with a woman again.

And later, in the quietude of the rectory, after praying and committing the matter to God, he fell asleep and dreamed of her smile.

CHAPTER 4

Thea placed her booted foot on top of the shovel's blade and pressed down. The shovel dug deep into the brown earth, the dry clumps of dirt needing a good mix of fertilizer and a thorough soaking of rain. She planned to attend to the chicken manure shortly, and judging from those clouds gathering overhead, God looked certain to soon help with the rest. She turned over the dirt then wiped the sweat from her brow, her shoulders aching from this morning's labors.

With Mother out visiting and Father attending another railway meeting, she was at home with Eliza, who was not practicing the pianoforte as she'd promised. But then, Thea could hardly make a fuss, as she was not attending to her needlepoint. Preparing the garden for a winter crop of vegetables had seemed a far better use of her time. This she had done, and now she was replanting a lavender plant which had not thrived in its original spot.

There was something so satisfying about working like this, feeling like she was of use rather than merely decorative. Her limbs might grow sore, but it was a good kind of ache. And by careful positioning of her bonnet to protect her face from the sun, and goose grease that helped soften her hands, Mother remained none the wiser.

Eliza's words last week had challenged Thea into realizing she had grown too complacent, her desire to be seen as ladylike stealing the zest from life. She had always decried those women who sat around and did nothing, so why had she succumbed to such ways? Hence the need to prove herself in this way today. *Some* might think her frail and foolish, but doing this proved she wasn't.

She moved closer to the house and tapped on the window. "Eliza? You should be practicing."

"And you should be sewing," Eliza shot back.

It was fortunate that Susan and Mr. Dillon, their man-of-all-work, were also out today. "I will be doing that as soon as I'm finished here."

A loud sigh met her, but it was soon followed by imperfect scales on the pianoforte, which meant Thea could resume her work.

Darcy lay asleep in the patchy sunlight, and the raucous cries of black cockatoos screeched from the nearby gums. Since moving to the homestead and renaming it after Father's house in Scotland, the front garden had been transformed into a welcome oasis of imported shrubs and flowers including roses, pansies, and petunias, in a series of formal terraces. Hedges lined the garden path, and wisteria grew across the front veranda.

The back garden also boasted a small orchard, with everything from limes and apples to pears and apricots. The plots of cauliflowers, potatoes, cabbages, onions, and strawberries kept Mr. Dillon busy, and Thea liked to help as much as possible. One didn't have the luxury of the cheaper produce found in Sydney, where competition between stockists meant one could find a bargain if one looked hard enough. Here, although Father might have money to afford otherwise, they had learned to care for the gardens and grow what they could.

The sun burned through her thin sleeves as she displaced dirt. Mother had decried the pale spots freckling Thea's skin, giving instruction to apply lemon juice frequently, hence the need to ensure their lemon trees grew well. She bent, her bonnet tipping forward, just as Darcy barked and jumped up from her position.

Her stomach tensed. Surely Mother wasn't back already? She had assured Thea it would be midafternoon before she returned. She quickly finished planting the lavender bush and straightened. Inside, the pianoforte ceased, as if Eliza heard Darcy barking furiously. The sun, temperamental today, had now stolen behind a dark cloud.

"Excuse me."

Thea jumped, her mouth drying, and held the shovel as she slowly turned.

Oh no. How she wished she might not appear quite so dusty. "Good afternoon, Mr. Hamill." She surreptitiously wiped her hands on her apron and, heart sinking, found a smile. After the last few encounters where she'd left him with an unfavorable impression, there could be no doubt about her unladylikeness today.

"You seem hard at work."

She nodded. At least she hadn't been halfway through collecting the chicken manure. "Was there something I can help you with?"

He cleared his throat. "I was passing by and called in the hopes that your father might be available. He mentioned last week I should call, and this has been my first opportunity."

"He is not here," she said flatly. "He is in town."

"Right. Well, never mind."

Easy for him to say. She minded. Just once she would like the chance to appear to advantage and not feel inadequate thanks to bird droppings, sweat, an ugly brown dress, or a possum stealing his attention.

"Well, in that case, I suppose I should leave and let you continue your endeavors. Unless you require assistance?"

Judging from his fine clothes, obviously worn for visiting rather than laboring, that offer was made more from politeness than any genuine desire to help. "Thank you, but no."

He took a step forward. "Please?"

Her breath hitched as something slithered near his feet. She slowly raised the shovel and then, as hard and fast as she could, slammed it into the earth with a loud "No!"

Mr. Hamill sprang away as the snake twisted, its body sliced in two. Her heart raced, and Eliza quickly hurried out.

"Stay back," Thea commanded, checking the snake was truly dead. "Keep ahold of Darcy. I don't want her touching the snake and accidentally getting poisoned."

"Is that a brown snake?" Eliza asked, grasping Darcy's whining figure as the dog tried to lurch forward to investigate.

"It certainly looks like it," Mr. Hamill said.

"It did not strike you?" Thea asked.

"No. It did not have a chance, thanks to your quick thinking."

She used the shovel to gently prod the snake's head. It did not move. "Ugh." Nausea cramped her stomach, the rush of energy rapidly fading so that she suddenly felt lightheaded.

"Here, let me bury it." Mr. Hamill gently took the shovel from her. "It's the least I can do, seeing you have saved my life."

She glanced up at him and saw something she'd never seen in his expression before. Something that, instead of pity or shock, looked a little closer to respect. "Thank you."

"I should be the one thanking you." His eyes shone midnight blue. "I did not see it."

"You're like a heroine," Eliza said. "That was so brave!"

"I barely had time to think," she confessed. Another bout of wooziness clutched her, and she staggered slightly.

Mr. Hamill swung an arm around her waist and steadied her, and her breath caught as she toppled into his chest. His broad and firm, rather nice-smelling chest.

She drew in a deep breath then reluctantly pushed gently away, catching a glimpse of Eliza's wide eyes. Oh dear. Heaven forbid anyone else see their closeness and leap to the wrong conclusions.

"You should sit down," he said softly. "Eliza, I think your heroic sister needs a cup of tea. Do you know how to make that?"

"I'm not a child, Mr. Hamill. Of course I know how to make it."

"Forgive me." He stole a look at Thea, his amused glance suggesting he wasn't offended by Eliza's comment. Or perhaps it was just the echo in what Thea had said to him not so long ago that entertained. At the thought he might indeed think of her as immature and childish as her sister, Thea ducked her head, the tears from that day edging closer as her emotions wobbled.

"I shan't be long," he said. "Eliza, please help your sister. And make sure her tea has lots of honey. Sweetness can be good for shock."

Thea shrugged off her sister's arm and made her way inside as Darcy trotted after Mr. Hamill. She sank down at the dining table while Eliza stirred the coals in the smart kitchen range Father had imported to make life easier for Mother and the servants.

Darcy returned, nuzzling her nose into Thea's knees as she sat in the coolness of the dining chamber. A shiver racked her body. How thankful she was that Darcy hadn't been bitten. She closed her eyes, her face propped in one hand while the other stroked the dog's head and the chaos of moments earlier spun around her head like buzzing flies. Gradually the images faded, the familiar sound of tea preparation providing ease as her heartbeat slowed. Soon Eliza brought in the tea. Thea thanked her and took a grateful sip.

"Miss Maclean?"

Her cup clattered to the table, spilling hot liquid. "Ow!"

"Look what you did!" Eliza complained.

"That was my clumsy fault," Thea said, peeking up to see Mr. Hamill's look of chagrin.

"Forgive me. I should not have just presumed to let myself in, but the door was open, and—"

She reached up and clasped his hand, silencing his speech. He glanced at her hand, then at her, and she slowly unpeeled her fingers. Oh, she might try to be ladylike, but it seemed a failed cause where he was concerned.

"I should go," he said softly.

He probably should. She nodded, humiliation at her brazenness forbidding her to look at him.

"Miss Maclean? Are you sure you are well?" he persisted.

She lifted her chin and forced a smile. "I am very well. I shall return to finish my gardening presently."

His lips twisted as a *pat tap* came on the tin roof. "I suspect the rain may give you other ideas."

"And you," Eliza said. "How are you to get home if it's raining?"

"I have ridden through rain before," he assured her.

A giant boom of thunder rattled the house, sending Eliza to the nearest window. "Look, the gum tree has been hit by lightning!"

Her words dragged Thea from her chair to join her at the window. The tree was now splintered in two, its branches like bony fingers stretching to the dark sky.

The steady drumming of the rain escalated, and she shivered

again, glad for the warmth of Mr. Hamill's presence beside her.

"The rain is getting heavier," Eliza announced.

Thea peeked up, catching the wryness on his face as he looked at her. "Would it inconvenience you greatly if I remained a little longer?" he asked.

"Of course not. You cannot go out in that downpour."

"Where's your horse, Mr. Hamill?" Eliza asked.

"Noble!"

He pivoted, and Thea hurried after him. "Put him in the barn."

"You should not get wet," he objected as she moved to join him.

"I'm hardly going to melt if I get a little damp. Come on."

She crossed the breezeway, designed to keep the house cool in summer, then hurried through the rain to open the barn doors as Mr. Hamill collected his horse from where he'd hitched it to the fence. A few moments later the horse was in a stall, stamping its hooves as it sought to dry itself. "He's a beautiful animal."

He stroked its neck affectionately, and the horse calmed. "Noble has kept me out of trouble more than a few times."

"You make it sound like you are often getting into trouble, sir."

"I have experienced more than some, I suppose."

His features shadowed as she'd noticed before, and she wondered what had happened. Perhaps he might feel comfortable sharing, seeing he was forced to spend time with them.

She gestured to the house. "We best go inside. I'm sure you are needing a cup of tea to warm up with."

"I should not wish to inconvenience you."

"It's no inconvenience."

"I think Noble will prefer me to remain here."

"In the cold and dark? I think you would be far more comfortable inside."

"I should not."

"Why?" She tossed a clump of her damp loosened hair behind her shoulder.

"Because some might question a young man visiting a young woman who is unchaperoned."

She put her hands on her hips. "I didn't think you would be like my Aunt Agatha."

"Excuse me?"

"You didn't come to visit me. You came to see my father and got trapped by a storm. If anyone questions that then they are foolish indeed."

His tweaked lips said he was well aware that practical common sense wouldn't stop some small-minded types from leaping to foolish suppositions.

She shivered. "Well, I'm cold, and I need to return inside to my sister. She can always act as a chaperone. Not that anyone would think a church minister would need one of those." He'd made it obvious he did not find her attractive anyway.

So, heart sinking, she shrugged and departed.

If only she knew. A church minister had to be above reproach. This country might be more lenient in some aspects of social expectations, but in other ways people were less forgiving. He'd encountered more than a few in what counted as upper society who put on airs and graces as if trying to remove themselves from the stain of a convict heritage.

And he had no wish to besmirch Miss Maclean's reputation. Especially when it was obvious that she had no thought for herself. And as fascinating as he found her, he should do nothing to kindle her interest. He was only too conscious of his own unsuitability, and that made him stay here in the barn, keeping Noble company.

Jonas shivered, the pelting rain on the roof getting heavier. He'd experienced summer storms before, but nothing to this magnitude. He stroked Noble's nose, the horse content in the stall. The barn was built of rammed earth, the front section portioned into several spaces for horse accommodation and carriage storage.

He moved to the doors to peer out at the falling rain. Rivulets of mud tracked down the long drive he'd trotted up not an hour earlier. What an eventful space of time this had proved. Saved from certain snakebite then clasping a young woman he admired but could not have too close in that accidental hold. At the memory of her form against him, his skin heated, despite the cold. He'd seen the way young Eliza had stared, and known he could not linger in that embrace. She was hardly the kind of young person one could count on to not blurt out unfortunate truths.

Another thunderous boom rippled overhead, and he hurried back to soothe Noble. Memories flickered of previous excursions in wild weather, when he hadn't been as fortunate to shelter in a solid barn. He'd been on the road in storms and hail and wind, forced to hide under the tall trees known as widow-makers, with dead limbs and branches ready to topple onto any unsuspecting individual below. His heart twisted. How cruelly ironic that he'd been on such a trip, worrying about leaving Mary a widow, when he'd been made a widower.

He exhaled, praying for God to heal the memories, to release him from the past. The rain intensified some more, and moisture slipped under the walls, staining the earth floor dark. Noble was restless, but Jonas wondered how the two young ladies were faring inside. The house seemed sturdy, built of stone, but it must still be frightening. Perhaps he should go across and ensure they were not panicking.

After a last pat for Noble, he picked his way to the barn door as the sheets of rain blanketed the scene in gray. If he'd gone with Miss Maclean when she had first suggested, he could have been warm and almost dry in front of the fire, but instead he'd let pride get in the way again. Sometimes he could almost hear Mary's gentle voice chastising him to be careful about his pride. He swallowed. Then he pushed outside and through the rain to pound on the back door.

The door swiftly opened, and he almost fell in on top of Eliza.

She scuttled out of the way, smirking. "I thought you'd eventually come inside."

He wiped at the moisture trickling off his jacket, glancing up to see Miss Maclean. "I'm sorry for making a mess."

At her smile his heart instantly eased. "I take it you must be ready for that cup of tea?" she asked.

"I came to check you were both all right. . ."

Her smile widened.

". . .but yes, please."

She pointed to a chair already positioned beside the fire, and he took it, relishing the warmth. It was funny how a warm day could turn cold so quickly, but such was often the case with these summer storms. This one seemed to be a little more persistent than most, with the rain appearing to increase its intensity yet again.

After inquiring about his need for milk and sugar, she soon handed him a steaming cup of tea, which he accepted with murmured thanks.

Her attention stole to the window, where rain pattered against the glass. "We've lived here nearly five years now, and I've never seen it rain quite so hard."

"Do you think we'll get another flood like a few years ago?" Eliza asked.

"There was a flood?" he asked.

Miss Maclean nodded. "The village is in a valley with all the hills around, and the creek is narrow in parts, so the water gets quite high rapidly and moves very quickly. And because there was so much rain it didn't have anywhere to go, so there was a flood through Picton. Several feet of floodwaters went through the church."

He half rose from his chair. "I should go check."

She shook her head. "I don't think it will be that bad this time. The ground is so dry, most of the water will soak away."

Her practical perspective eased some of his fears. "What about those who are traveling?"

"Like you were?" Eliza asked with a cheeky grin.

"Then I'm sure they will have found hospitality wherever they could," her sister said.

"Like I have," he said, his gaze slanting to Thea's again.

Her eyes held his, and he noticed the moment wariness dropped away. He'd seen so many different facets to her, and this one, in her home, her hair down, relaxed, was his new favorite. Or maybe the tea held some special elixir designed to make him feel this way.

He dragged his gaze away, noticing that a chessboard had been set up on the table, with some of the pieces already moved. "Did I interrupt your game?"

"Mother thinks it isn't ladylike to play—"

"She'd much rather we play games that are morally improving, like the Mansion of Happiness," Eliza said with a roll of her eyes.

He stifled a chuckle. "I take it that is not your first choice, Eliza."

"Does anyone really think people will become good simply by playing a game?" Eliza demanded.

"I don't think that was its inventor's intention, necessarily."

"I imagine you would enjoy it, seeing you are a church minister, but I think it's rather dull."

"Why, thank you. I think." At Miss Maclean's ripple of amusement, he glanced at her hiding a smile behind her hand. "Do you think me such a boring fellow too?"

"I scarcely know you, so I could not say. Although if you are prone to falling into trouble as you suggested before, I'm sure you cannot be as dull as Eliza believes."

"I don't know if that comment makes me feel any better," he complained.

"*Are* you prone to falling into trouble, Mr. Hamill?" Eliza asked, her head tilted to one side like an inquisitive sparrow. "I hope that you are, for it would make me like you more."

"You do not like me?" he asked, disconcerted.

"I think I do, because you didn't seem too bothered by the fact my possum came to church with me. But I could like you a great deal better if I knew you weren't impossibly good."

"I am very far from impossibly good," he said as gravely as he could.

"See?" She cast a triumphant look at her sister. "It *is* impossible to be good."

"But that doesn't mean we shouldn't try. Is that not correct, Mr. Hamill?"

He swallowed a smile then glanced at the younger sister. "The Bible says there is nobody good, except our Lord Jesus Christ. I'm grateful that our relationship with God isn't based on how good we are. But I think your sister is correct. We can ask God for help with those things that seem difficult, and He can help us make better choices."

Eliza's face screwed up as if she was in deep thought. "Sometimes I don't want to make better choices though."

"I understand." Only too well.

"Hmm. I think you should tell us some stories about how you got into trouble."

"Eliza," her sister protested.

"No, I don't mind sharing."

So, between stirring up the fire and helping Miss Maclean prepare the evening meal, he spent the next few hours doing exactly that. He shared about some of his trail rides, such as when Noble had been spooked by kangaroos and they'd become lost in the bushland until they'd encountered an Aboriginal fellow who had led them to the nearest house. He shared about when as a boy he'd once broken his leg slipping down an icy path while chasing a friend. He shared about how he'd once tripped on a ship and almost fallen overboard, saved only by a length of rope that swung him wildly out across the sea before being brought to safety again. The telling of these and other tales in this cozy environment warmed his heart. It had been a long time since he'd thought of these stories, and while most seemed to highlight his ineptitude, he was grateful to have cause to look back on these episodes and see God's hand in keeping him alive these many years.

"You sound like you have had more than your fair share of trouble, sir."

"But God has been with me all this time." He smiled at Miss Maclean. "It does my heart good to remember that."

"I'm glad."

He could feel the way her sweet understanding wove around his heart, gently cracking at the buttresses placed there since Mary's death. Miss Maclean might be young and impulsive and appear to own some of the qualities of a hoyden, but she had faith, courage, and a good heart. And a most winsome smile.

He ducked his head. He couldn't afford to let her think he was a free man. His heart was still Mary's. And Miss Maclean's parents would hardly look with favor upon a man with no fixed address.

The room filled with a coolness, and he went to check on Noble before returning to the house. The rain had eased by now, and the scent of a meal cooking drew hunger pangs.

His boots were three inches deep in mud by the time he reached the back door again, and he slipped them off, not wanting to spoil the tiled floor.

"Yes, leave them there," Miss Maclean said. Then she looked at his socked feet.

His gaze fell to his socks too, and he winced. "I should darn them but have not had the time." Nor the inclination.

"Would you like me to do that for you?" she asked.

"Thank you, but I know how to do it, I just haven't had the opportunity."

"No time like the present," Eliza announced, looking not at him but at a small creature he strongly suspected was Henry the possum.

The next hour passed as he mended his poor holey socks, and then Miss Maclean served a meal. He found himself both distracted and enchanted by the easy manner the sisters had, the way they seemed to invite him to dare believe this could be something he could partake in again too. The more he was getting to know Miss Maclean, the more estimable qualities he could see. Her sister might dismiss the board game as silly, but he strongly suspected that Miss Maclean's temperament and talents could lead to a mansion of happiness for the man lucky enough to secure her affections.

"Mr. Hamill? Is the meal not to your taste?" she asked him.

"Forgive me, ma'am. I cannot fault your delicious meal."

She smiled. "Now that is not something that requires my forgiveness."

He laughed, the sound surprising him. He'd spent so much time in the past years feeling the weight of responsibility and grief, he'd forgotten that he once had laughed with abandon. It was yet another reason he wished to stay and dine on the joy he sensed lived in this family.

Which was why he was embroiled in the depths of domesticity, playing chess with Miss Maclean, laughing at Henry's antics, when the dog's barking announced a new arrival. A very muddied and clearly exasperated Mr. Maclean entered, followed by his wife, the former demanding to know what Jonas was doing there.

CHAPTER 5

Thea leaned against the window, her ear pressed to the glass, as she prayed neither man would turn and see her. Eavesdropping wasn't mentioned as a sin in the Bible, was it? And she desperately wanted to know the meaning behind Father's black looks that he'd been shooting poor Mr. Hamill ever since he and Mother had returned so unexpectedly.

Awkwardness didn't begin to describe Thea's feelings. After a lovely afternoon spent with Mr. Hamill, when she'd begun to feel so at ease that she dared to tease him, to have her father's presence bring it to a sudden end felt like a shock of cold water on her face. Considering the fact that the rain had made several roads near impassable, hence the late arrival of her parents, one would think they would be sympathetic to his reasons for staying. Instead, her father had hinted none too quietly about Mr. Hamill's departure before escorting him to the back porch where she now strained to hear Father's final words to him.

"Dorothea, you need to come away."

"Yes, Mother." She would. In a minute or two.

Eliza grinned, tiptoed to the other window, and raised it slightly. The rain had ceased, and the evening sounds from outside traveled in.

"I must reiterate my concerns about your behavior," Father said. "I cannot believe you were so foolhardy as to stop here and then stay, unchaperoned, for nearly half the day."

Mr. Hamill's response she could not hear from her position at the window. She peeked over her shoulder. Mother had disappeared to the bedchamber, so she had a moment longer. Eliza, as much as Thea, looked determined to stay.

". . .will not countenance a match between you and my daughter, you understand?"

Thea's breath hitched. What would Mr. Hamill say to this very bold statement? He did not care for her, did he? And yet, there had been those moments today when he'd seemed to gaze upon her with a softer expression, when his smile appeared fuller, and he'd laughed. She loved the sound of his laughter and sensed that he didn't do it nearly often enough.

"I well understand your concerns, sir. You need not worry. I have no thought of her or any other woman in that way."

Her stomach dropped as ice crept across her soul. She had known he did not care. Yet stubborn hope had still leaped at the possibility. Today had been most eye-opening in so many ways, and she was sure to be tired, which doubtless was muddling her emotions. But to think he had no care for her, even after those moments of long gazes, seemed so much worse now than earlier in the day. Now that she thought about it, there was an Old Testament verse which warned of the perils of listening. Emotion balled in her chest.

"I don't think I like Mr. Hamill." Eliza sidled next to her.

"Eliza, why ever do you say that?"

Eliza sniffed, her pointed chin jerking upward. "I do not think it is good when a church minister lies."

"Mr. Hamill has not lied."

"Oh yes he has. He said he didn't like you, when everyone

can tell as plain as day that he likes you very much indeed."

If only that were true. "I think he might appreciate the fact I saved him from the snake, but I don't think he cares in that way."

"You didn't see the way he kept peeking at you when your back was turned when you were making dinner."

"He looked at me?"

Eliza nodded. "His face was exactly like Darcy's when Father gives her a lamb bone."

Her breath caught. "You must be mistaken."

"Is this you fishing for a compliment?"

"No. I just cannot believe it."

"You are the prettiest girl in these parts, and he'd be silly if he didn't notice." Eliza's bright green eyes narrowed. "You like him too, don't you?"

"I find him pleasant company," she allowed.

"Then you should make Father listen."

"You know how stubborn he can be."

Eliza crossed her arms. "He's not the only one, is he?"

Why was it that it was her little sister who could spur her to recall what she once had been?

For Eliza was right. Stubbornness might not be a quality listed in the Mansion of Happiness game, but perseverance was an estimable virtue listed in the Bible. And while her mother's meekness suggested it had skipped her, it was one of those qualities that had seen their father ascend to great heights in the railway world. And a quality present in both of their daughters.

The flood through Picton was all her parents, Susan, and Mr. Dillon could talk about when their servants finally returned late that night, and it remained the chief topic of conversation the following day. Mr. Dillon, a longtime resident of the area, had reported the creek's waters hadn't risen as high as it had in 1860 but had still caused damage, flooding buildings, destroying crops, and even moving some of the cemetery headstones perched precariously next to the creek. She'd hate to think some of the graves might slip away some day.

Some of the local stores had been inundated with water, and the George Hotel beside the river had seen waters fill its cellars and the tiny lockup that had been used until the building of the courthouse and gaol. The suddenness of the summer storm deluge had also seen the Larkin mill affected by floodwater, and Father had wondered aloud whether it would recover, between this latest weather event and the rust-affected wheat. His ill temper the night before was because the flood had affected the building of the viaduct, washing away the bridge's trusses, scaffolding, and frameworks.

But it was hearing that the church had been flooded that pained her the most. Poor Mr. Hamill would likely be cleaning out the mud by himself, and he must be tired and hungry. He might not care for her as she wished, yet her heart sorrowed for him. It was only a few days until the Sunday service, so he'd likely be trying to clean the church as well as write his message for Sunday. He must be so weary. . .

That thought propelled her to ask her mother if she could bake scones, which met with Mother's, "But whatever for?"

"You always say a lady should know the rudiments of cooking, and after preparing a meal the other day, I realized how much I enjoy it." And how much she enjoyed seeing new appreciation in Mr. Hamill's eyes upon realization that she'd cooked it. "And I thought it might be good for some of those poor storekeepers to have a bite of something fresh to sustain their strength in the cleaning up." And if one of those people should happen to be cleaning St Mark's Anglican church, then so be it.

Her mother's eyes softened. "What a wonderful idea. How very thoughtful."

They spent the morning baking, and it was past noon when she finally asked Mother if she could ride to the village, seeing Father had left early that morning to check on the station and viaduct building works.

"But I do not like the state of the roads," Mother protested. "I thought to send Mr. Dillon."

"He probably has more important things to do around here. Besides, if Father made it through, then I'm sure I could as well. And I should go soon, especially now we have made so many scones. I need to distribute them before they get stale."

"Oh, very well. But I do not want you riding. Take the sulky instead. And your sister. She can hold the scones while you travel."

"Thank you, Mother." She glanced at Eliza. "We had better change into clothes best suited for dirty conditions."

A short time later, dressed in stout boots and gowns they never wore outside of the house, they had driven to the top of the small hill near the Jarvisfield estate, where the village lay before them. Thea had to take great care in the descent, as the road was rutted with deep, muddy holes. She had to ensure they did not topple or get stuck, as some of the heavier wagons and carriages had done. Every inch was covered in mud.

"If it's this bad here, how terrible it must be for those closer to the creek," she said.

"I don't mind if the George doesn't reopen," Eliza said.

"Eliza, you can't say that."

"It's always so smelly, and there are fights nearby."

"Yes, but it is a business and someone's livelihood. Imagine how you would feel if Father couldn't work anymore and had no income to buy you food or clothes."

Her sister quieted, likely thinking this over, as they drew into the central part of town. As tempted as Thea was to go straight to the church to check on Mr. Hamill, she'd have to make it seem less obvious that he was her primary reason for this excursion.

They arrived to see the main street's flooded shops being swept out. Great reams of muddy brown water, twigs, and litter filled the road. Various shop contents lay in the sun, hardly recognizable, encased in a thick layer of mud.

"Miss Maclean, Miss Eliza." Mr. Cornell, their usual grocer, greeted them outside his store. "What are you doing here?"

"We thought you might be busy and made some scones for you." Thea held up the basket.

He leaned on his broom. "That would be right handy about now. We've been going nonstop since the early hours. All this food wasted." He shook his head. "It's such a shame."

"I'm so sorry," Thea said.

"Ah, it's not your fault, lass. These things happen." He jerked a thumb at the George across the river. The bridge still stood, tree branches jumbled against the wooden sides. "They had it worse. And over at the church."

She glanced that way, wincing at the mud marring the bottom sandstone bricks. Poor Mr. Hamill.

"That new minister has been over there all day. Works hard as a Trojan, never complaining. I'm betting he'd appreciate your scones more than anyone at the George. If I were you, I'd think it was right Christian of you to go see him." He winked. "He'd likely think two angels had dropped from the sky."

Her cheeks grew hot, but she managed a cool smile, determined to not let the man see her fluster. "Are you sure there is no one else who might need sustenance?"

"Well, seeing as you've got so many, how about you leave a few here before you go to the church?"

"We can leave as many as you think is necessary."

He grinned. "Well, I might like to eat them all, but let's just say you give us a dozen. That should leave enough for the handsome church minister, wouldn't you agree?"

Agree that he was handsome, or that he'd have enough to eat? "If you're sure."

He winked again. "I'm sure he must be due for a rest soon." Mr. Cornell gestured to the church again.

She peered over her shoulder. Mr. Hamill stood outside the church now, in his shirtsleeves, his hands on his hips and what looked to be the weight of the world on his shoulders. Her heart panged.

"Come on, Thea. Let's go," Eliza said.

She nodded, wished Mr. Cornell well, and turned the cart toward the church.

A glance at Eliza showed her grin. "What?"

"This is the real reason you wanted to bake scones, isn't it?"

"I'm sure I don't know what you mean."

Eliza chuckled, and Thea bit back a smile. "It is our Christian duty to help," she said.

Eliza groaned. "Is that why you insisted we wear our oldest clothes?"

"Come on." She slapped the reins and encouraged the horse to trot.

What was he going to do? Well, that was obvious. He was going to have to clean the entire church and get it dry so it was ready for this Sunday's service. But with many of the congregation members attending to their own flooding issues, none were free to help. At least the rectory had been spared the deluge, positioned as it was on the hill.

He rolled his shoulders, trying to ease the knots and kinks, and studied the mess decorating the church courtyard. He'd dragged out several rolls of soggy carpet and some of the smaller furniture that had shifted as the water rushed through. The heavier cedar pews had mostly held their position but still needed to be wiped clean, and the whole area mopped and swept and probably mopped again. It was tempting to ask God for some divine intervention, but he figured that was why God gave him a strong back. And sleep was overrated. He exhaled, movement drawing his attention to the road.

His chest squeezed then released, and he straightened, pushing away his hair and smiling as they drew near. "Good afternoon, ladies. What brings you here?"

"You do," Miss Eliza said with a glance at her sister that looked awfully like a smirk.

"We made scones this morning," Miss Maclean said, "because we knew that many people would have such a lot of work to do, and as members of the church we wanted to help in some way."

"That is most kind of you."

Miss Maclean descended the sulky, tied it to the hitching rail, and then joined Eliza, who was holding a cloth-covered basket that emitted a stomach-tugging scent.

"That smells heavenly," he said. "Give me a moment, and I'll wipe my hands."

"Here." Miss Maclean handed him a square piece of cloth he recognized.

"My handkerchief."

"It's clean, and if you dampen it with water, it should suffice."

She was so thoughtful, knowing he'd be pressed for time, caring in this way.

"Look," Eliza commanded, lifting off the cloth. "We made different sorts. Thea wasn't sure what type you'd like best—"

"Eliza!"

"—so there are some with raisins and some without. I like the plain ones best. With butter. No cream."

His stomach growled in anticipation. "You did not bring cream?" he teased.

"Actually. . ." Miss Maclean pointed to a lower level of the basket, where a small crock of butter sat next to one of cream and a smaller one of what looked like strawberry jam.

He glanced up at her, noting her nearness, the way her smile seemed to echo in her eyes. "Are you an angel?"

Her smile widened as Eliza laughed. "That's exactly what Mr. Cornell said. Not about her, but that you would think that."

Right now he was too hungry, too touched by Miss Maclean's thoughtfulness, to care what anyone thought. "I'm famished," he admitted. "I've been working since dawn and haven't had time to stop and return to the rectory to eat, so this is like manna from heaven."

"Except it will only go stale and not get worms, which is what happened to the Israelites, is it not?"

"You certainly know your Bible, Miss Maclean."

"I had a governess who made sure I read it cover to cover."

His eyebrows rose. He'd been to theological college with men who had not done so. "That is most remarkable."

"It is, but somehow not something I remark upon too often."

He mirrored her smile, enjoying her banter. Her humor lifted his spirits, just as her encouragement did yesterday.

"You'd better eat before the scones get cold," Eliza said.

"Of course. Thank you, ladies."

A few minutes later, having cleaned up as best he could, he joined them on the pew at the back of the church and tucked in. The scones might have cooled a little, but there was still warmth enough that the butter melted into the round puffs of goodness, and it was hard to not appear greedy. But given they were ladies and he wanted to appear a gentleman, he forced himself to eat slower than he might usually. Was there no end to Miss Maclean's talents? Her father might have warned him away, but a man could still appreciate the thoughtfulness of a young woman. Especially, as she put it herself, if she was part of the congregation and thus felt she had a duty to help.

"Which do you prefer, Mr. Hamill? The plain, or the raisins?" Eliza inquired.

"I'm afraid I cannot decide. Especially given the options of spreads, it is too hard to make a definitive decision."

"And one should be definitive about these things if at all possible," Miss Maclean teased.

He smiled at her and once again got caught in the depths of her eyes. They were so pretty, like a cool, green meadow he'd like to lie down and rest in, with the promise of refreshing. . .

He blinked and shook his head, pushing to his feet. "Thank you, ladies. That was a wonderful repast, and truly the tastiest scones I've ever eaten."

"You say that because you're hungry," Eliza said.

"I say that because it's true." His gaze stole to Miss Maclean's again. "Thank you."

"You're very welcome." She rose and placed the basket on the pew. Then, from the other basket, she drew out an apron and tied it around her middle.

"What are you doing?"

"You did not think we came merely to feed you, did you? We're here to help clean up."

"But it is dirty work."

"I think you should know by now that neither of us is afraid to get our hands dirty. And this is far too big a job for one man, is it not? So imagine what can happen when two *ladies* assist you."

"I'll be finished in a quarter of the time."

She smiled. "Just you wait and see."

From their first encounter, he never would have expected Miss Maclean to have the muscles and fortitude she was demonstrating today. She and her sister had turned the cleaning of the church into a type of game, with silly challenges between them to mop out or wipe down certain sections. They had come prepared with another basket of cleaning supplies, which meant he'd not needed to beg or borrow from neighbors who needed such supplies themselves. Their utter thoughtfulness filled his heart with gratitude and made his feelings toward Miss Maclean, whose idea it originally was, even more tender.

Jonas' gaze strayed to her now, her hair falling from its chignon, a streak of mud adorning her cheek, her skirts inches deep in mud. She was laughing at something her sister said, her merriment ringing through the stone building like he imagined angelic laughter to sound. His chest squeezed. He'd never thought a woman so lovely.

Her father might have warned him away, and he knew himself unworthy, but her sweet spirit had stolen past his walls and encouraged his battered heart to dare to dream again. Which wasn't wise. And given the way Miss Maclean's laughing expression grew tender whenever she caught his gaze, it wasn't fair either. For how could a man who had no home dare to dream of her? She might have a tomboy-like streak, but his time at their home yesterday proved she was used to living with the finer things. And a man who truly cared for a woman wouldn't ask her to live without that.

He should not—would not—do anything that might stir up her feelings, so did his best to steer his glances away. He couldn't ignore her, that would be rude, especially when he was indebted to her for both the nourishment and the assistance. But he'd have to show her that this could never work. She was a much-loved rich man's daughter. He was a circuit preacher, of no fixed address.

He squeezed another cloth near the path outside. The sun had lowered behind the hill on the Stargard property, the German man who had served as the colony's first astronomer.

Miss Maclean joined him, her smile eager. "I think we are almost done."

"You and Miss Eliza have worked most industriously."

"In a quarter of the time it might have taken otherwise?"

"Indeed."

Her smile sent a bolt of heat to his chest, and he ducked his gaze. He couldn't allow these feelings between them to grow any more than they already had.

"Mr. Hamill?"

He motioned to the skies. "It's getting late. I'm sure your mother must be missing you."

Her nose wrinkled. "I do not like to leave things when they are almost finished. It's like eating a slice of cake and leaving the last bite."

"A crime indeed."

"See? I knew you would understand."

"But will your mother?" he reminded gently.

A sigh escaped her. "I have no wish to worry her, so I suppose we should go soon. But first, can we please finish cleaning?"

He should say no. He should ensure she left before anyone grew the wiser of just who had helped him today. Not that it should be a concern, with her sister here and the church open for anyone to see that nothing nefarious could take place. But it would be best to go before her father saw them and worried aloud about her unladylike behavior.

"I'm merely concerned about your reputation," he said.

She groaned. "Why does that have to be the hallmark by which a woman is judged? Surely it would be better to judge a person based on their character or good works."

"People judge others by what they see and what they want to see."

"Which is terrible, is it not? Why must people be so small-minded?"

"We all can do so, can't we? It is a good thing God judges the heart."

"Yes." Her shoulders slumped.

"I truly am grateful. I could never have done this without you."

"I'm glad that we could help."

She went inside, and he was set to follow when a rider drew near. His stomach tensed. Oh no. He hurried to the church's great wooden door and murmured, "Your father is here."

Eliza groaned, but Miss Maclean only scrubbed harder.

"Miss Maclean, did you not hear?"

"Oh, I heard," she gritted out. "But I still want to finish."

But there was a time for stubbornness and a time for being wise. And right now they definitely had to be wise. "I think you should come outside now," he said, his words clipped and far more terse than he wished.

She ceased, her gaze straying to him. Then she slowly rose, her cloth in hand, as footsteps behind him said they were too late.

He swiveled to face her frowning father, whose eyes bulged as he surveyed the scene. "What is the meaning of this?"

CHAPTER 6

"And let me remind you that you are not to talk to that young man. Do I make myself clear?"

"Yes, Father," Thea murmured, her head bowed.

It was a good thing God saw the heart and Thea's true intentions, because she had not meant to cause so much trouble. It was perhaps fortunate that her father's initial outburst had occurred at the church in a semipublic setting and that he'd not had the privacy to fully vent his spleen. She'd hoped his anger would have lessened by the time she and Eliza made it home, but that didn't appear to be the case. His upset at the delay in the viaduct, and all that would mean for his reputation, seemed to have fueled his anger about the perceived damage to her own.

"How could you be so foolish?" he'd raged at poor Mother once they'd reached home. "Your daughters were in the church building looking for all intents and purposes like two scullery maids."

"I thought they were merely delivering food to the hungry workers."

Father snorted, grabbing the long-handled mop Thea had taken. "You did not see the cleaning supplies they took with them?"

Mother eyed him steadily. "No. And I do not appreciate being made to feel I'm being reprimanded in this way."

"You are their mother," he snapped.

"And you, as their father, should be thankful to have two daughters who have hearts big enough to care about the church. I cannot believe that at this time you are so petty-minded to speak to us in this way. I dare not think what you said to poor Mr. Hamill."

Thea dared not think on that either. For the past two days she and Eliza had been basically forced to spend time at home, forbidden to leave Glendalough except to attend church today. Father had even murmured something about sending her to Sydney to Mother's sister, to keep an eye on her if she did not behave.

"But how can Aunt Agatha keep an eye on her when her eyesight isn't good?" Eliza had asked.

This unhelpful comment was met with her father's renewed fury, and Thea had done her best to protect her sister and mother by declaring that she would not do anything that would bring shame on her father again.

Hence today, her first real test, when they would attend church and she would pretend to not care about Mr. Hamill.

She was silent on the carriage drive in. Her senses might tingle at the warm air and scent of the eucalypts, but she knew Father would not welcome her conversation. In some ways it would almost be a blessing to be banished to Aunt Agatha's, even though she was fairly sure the woman did not like her. One could not choose one's family, after all.

The bell cot of the church appeared, and they soon descended the carriage and moved inside to their pew. She glanced around. Apart from a slightly damp odor, there was little sign of the flood affecting the church. She peeked at Eliza, who was Henry-less today, not wanting anything to upset their father any further, and squeezed her hand.

Eliza nodded, her smile small. She'd been hurt on Thea's behalf about their father's attitude, and quite supportive of Thea, whispering in their room, "I don't know why he's so angry."

"I think it's because of the new delay to the bridge," Thea had offered. That knowledge allowed her some grace toward her father and kept her heart from shriveling. But still, his words and manner to her hurt.

Mr. Hamill's arrival drew her to sit straighter. Father had insisted that Thea enter the pew first, so her position would be away from the scrutiny of the townsfolk. What he didn't realize was that her seat next to the stone wall meant she was in direct line of sight of Mr. Hamill when he stood in the pulpit. So, because it was the polite thing to do in church, she directed her attention to the front, and feasted on his features.

If only Mr. Hamill could see her as more than a rich man's daughter. If only he could see she was more than someone who cared about her reputation. She had loved their interactions, loved feeling like she had purpose. To think he had been subjected to her father's nasty bout of temper—twice now, in one week—was anathema.

Her heart might beat for him, but he didn't look her way, and the hollowness that caused within chilled her. Emotion clamped her throat, and she lowered her gaze, the very picture of submissive femininity, just as Father seemed to think she ought to possess.

She sang the hymn, the words reminding her that now was the time to focus on God and not herself. And as she went through the rituals of prayers, the songs, and Bible readings, all was well until communion, when she joined her parents at the front and knelt at the wooden communion rail.

Mr. Hamill spoke the ancient words. "The Lord Jesus the same night in which he was betrayed took bread: and when he had given thanks, he brake it, and said, Take, eat: this is my body, which is broken for you: this do in remembrance of me."

He placed a piece of bread in her hand. She ate, then sipped the wine from the silver cup and dared meet his gaze. His haunted gaze. That instantly moved to the next congregation member.

She pressed her lips together and ducked her head, almost missing the step as she returned to her seat, conscious of the scrutiny of eyebrow-raised congregation members who'd obviously heard about her exploits and leaped to wrong assumptions again. Her father's gaze narrowed at her as he waited for her to enter their pew, and she carefully inched past Eliza and took her seat.

This being near Mr. Hamill but knowing he was forbidden was agonizing. Emotion swelled within, begging for release, and she went through the rest of the motions, but she felt itchy with what others around her must be thinking.

The service concluded, and soon it was her family's turn to exit. Eyes followed her, conversations cut off as she moved near. Her name was whispered, and her stomach clenched. Perhaps Father was correct, and this was something she should have thought through more carefully. But she'd only wanted to help. Why couldn't people see her good intentions?

Ahead of them, the Cavanaghs waited, and she caught Anthony's cold glare before he glanced away. Oh. She swallowed. If her one and only admirer could look at her like that, then perhaps Father was correct and her reputation had been ruined. Perhaps going to Sydney for a time would be the best alternative.

But knowing she was being talked about did not mean she needed to act like she was guilty. So she lifted her chin and smiled at her neighbors. Even Mr. Cornell, who she was fairly sure had told Father where they were. He hadn't meant her harm, something he seemed to express as he caught her gaze and offered a wry grimace in response.

She nodded, her lips tweaking to one side, then joined the slow procession behind her mother as they waited to shake Mr. Hamill's hand. She could do this. Shake his hand. Pretend nothing was wrong. Smile and move away. She could even do so without talking to him, as her father had requested.

She passed the wooden seat where they had eaten scones three days ago. They moved to the gray flagstones in the small vestibule with its arched wooden door. Then they were out in the sunlight, and Mr. Hamill was shaking hands as he greeted each parishioner.

"Mr. Maclean."

No response. Father was excellent at keeping a grudge. He quickly moved away.

"Mrs. Maclean."

Mother murmured something Thea couldn't hear. And it was now her turn.

He held out his hand, and she grasped it. "Miss Maclean."

Something about the way he said that, or the way his eyes looked deep into hers, filled with regret and sorrow, drew fresh sadness to her own. She blinked away the moisture, ducking her head, releasing his hand even though she wanted to hold it forever.

He sighed and turned away, then said, "Eliza."

"I enjoyed your sermon very much," Eliza said, at a volume no doubt designed to annoy their father, but which brought an echo of what she'd said to him a mere two weeks ago. Had it truly been such a short amount of time? Thea felt like she'd known the man all her life.

She stood meekly next to her mother as Father joined Mr.

Cowper and Mr. Antill and as Eliza spoke to some friends.

Mother's conversation with Mrs. Harper drew to a close, and she gestured for Thea to precede her to the carriage. "I will see if I can hurry your father along."

Thea moved to the carriage, her gaze stealing back to where Mr. Hamill spoke to Mrs. Larkin. He nodded, and then his gaze lifted, sifting the crowd until it alighted on her. Her smile was involuntary, and he smiled too, before his attention was stolen by Mr. Mulloy, the postmaster.

Her smile faded as she noticed her father had seen their silent exchange, and her heart sank. He would not like that, she was sure.

Anthony Cavanagh drew near, his sneer putting her on her toes. "I heard something rather alarming, Miss Maclean. Is it true that you and your sister were here helping the minister clean the church all day?"

Irritation burned inside. "Why is that alarming?"

"I beg your pardon?"

"I believe you should be begging mine."

He frowned. "You are not making much sense."

"No, you are the one not making much sense. I don't know why this is of any interest to you. I fail to see why it alarmed you and fail to understand why you think it so important to come over here and tell me so."

"It is not something most young ladies around here would do."

She tilted her chin. "Well, I am not most young ladies."

He sniffed and shook his head as he moved away. He had never been able to best her in a game of wits.

But the thought that even Anthony Cavanagh could have the temerity to speak to her about her reputation made her realize just how fraught matters must be. And when she glanced at Mr. Hamill and saw his smile had quite disappeared as several townsfolk spoke to him, she realized how her actions had affected him. His reputation shouldn't be injured because of her impulsiveness.

Her heart tightened and her eyes burned, as emotion ballooned within. And when her father arrived and told her in no uncertain terms that she would be leaving to go to Sydney as soon as arrangements could be made, she was unsurprised and meekly agreed that might be best.

Jonas never imagined that a simple offer of help would descend into a stew of gossip and speculation. He was already feeling the sting of pointed remarks and was praying that Miss Maclean would not be suffering a similar fate. But from the way her admirer had stormed away, it seemed she was not immune. He grieved for her and suspected her father would have yet more harsh things to say. His assessment of Jonas' character the other day had stung him to sleeplessness.

Yes, he'd known not to take advantage of her. But informing her father she was the one who had instigated the assistance seemed destined to make things worse for her. The poor lass didn't need any more umbrage from her father. Anyone could see much of this stemmed from the man's pride and self-importance. Although what could Jonas do when her own mother was not inclined to stand up for her?

Yet even while knowing this, knowing he should leave Miss Maclean well enough alone, another part of him wanted to further explore this connection that sang between them. She was the only woman who had stirred his interest since Mary's death, and he might have an uncertain future, but didn't everyone? Everyone's lives were in God's hands, and only He could truly open doors and lead people on the paths they might desire. A man could plan his course, but only God would direct his steps, or so Solomon, a much wiser man than Jonas, had once said.

He spent the rest of the morning nodding, smiling, and doing his best to let the small-town gossip slip past him. But the more he heard words denigrating Miss Maclean's behavior, the more he wondered if perhaps a better outcome would be for himself to offer his name as protection. And while he doubted her father would agree, perhaps appealing to her mother might soften that lady's heart to his cause. He could give up his circuit-preaching ways and find a parish somewhere that would want a young man. There were bound to be many in the country that the city-preferring clerics wouldn't wish to serve in. Perhaps when his time here finished he could return to the city and find out if such an option was possible. Then he might have something to offer that was more tangible than just his heart. This matter would obviously require much prayer.

He was riding back the next day from a visit to the Antills' when a smart Cobb and Co. coach headed north passed him. He didn't know what it was that made him look up, but he recognized a face that had fast become quite dear. Miss Maclean was leaving?

Half tempted to wheel around and give chase, he instead encouraged Noble to turn in at the Maclean property. He wouldn't be welcomed by her father, but Mr. Maclean might be out, and he could learn from Mrs. Maclean where her daughter was headed—and whether he might ever have a chance.

But when he arrived there was nobody from the family there, save a maid, who let him know in no uncertain terms that he was not welcome, that Mr. Maclean had informed both her and Mr. Dillon that the assistant minister was not to be let onto the premises.

His hopes of winning over Mrs. Maclean dropped even further. "May I inquire if Miss Maclean has left? I thought I saw her on the Sydney-bound stagecoach."

"She left not an hour ago," the servant said with a sniff. "Not that you need to know that, but if it stops you coming around..."

His chest wished to cave in, along with all hope, but he merely dipped his chin, bid her good day, and remounted, turning his horse toward Picton again. Perhaps that was God's answer after all. He'd prayed half the night, and this was the answer.

"But Lord, if it isn't, then please make that plain."

The rest of the week passed with visits to parishioners, learning about people's needs, praying for the sick, taking meals where he could, and drinking many cups of tea. But no accompaniment to a meal tasted as good as certain scones. And no conversation held his interest as much as a certain surprising blond.

He missed Miss Maclean, missed her wit and teasing smile, missed the light in her face and eyes, missed everything about her. Regrets knotted his chest. It seemed ridiculous that he'd known her for such a short time, for the feelings he'd discovered in her absence proved this was deeper than mere friendship. She was so kind and thoughtful, sweet and good-humored. But more than this, he'd felt a deepening bond with her, as if they were connected by their shared faith and viewpoints. She was remarkably well informed about matters of the Bible, and he wished they'd had more opportunity to discuss this—and everything else. His depth of feeling led to an urge to pray for her, to share more deeply with her. He should have talked with her of Mary. Would that have changed her mind about him?

Somehow, he didn't think so. She possessed too much compassion to hold that against him. But now he'd never know, unless God opened up a miraculous door and revealed a way.

How he wished he'd spoken in that moment after the Sunday service and offered the protection of his name in a way that was more than merely to save her reputation. If he'd been more alert to the state of his own heart, he would have laid his case out simply, as he had once done with Mary's father, and then seen if he could find a way to receive her parents' blessing to woo her.

But he had not. So he could not. He could only trust God and hour by hour pray for His protection and blessing to be on her.

The Friday of that week he was attending to his groceries at Mr. Mulloy's store, which doubled as the town's post office. He expected no mail, and so he was surprised when Mr. Mulloy held up a thin missive.

"Something for you, Mr. Hamill."

Was it a letter from her?

The speed his heart leaped to that hope revealed as much as the disappointment when he opened the letter and realized the name at the bottom was not Miss Maclean's but an entirely unknown one.

A solicitor. From Scotland. From a little village called Kirkcudbright. He frowned. Read it. Then dropped the page.

"Mr. Hamill?" Mr. Mulloy asked. "You look like you've seen a ghost."

He felt like he had too. "Forgive me. I've just had some startling news."

"I hope it is good news, sir."

It could be. But it could also be the kind of news that would break his heart in two. "That is yet to be determined."

"I suppose you'll have to trust God with that one, eh?" Mr. Mulloy laughed, and Jonas nodded acknowledgment of his sermon's topic from last week.

"It's good to know someone was paying attention to the sermon."

"Well, it was a toss-up between that and watching how Miss Maclean tried to not look at you."

"I beg your pardon?"

"Your Miss Maclean. She didn't want to let her father see how much she watched you. I saw it all, seated behind them as I was."

Was that true? The past few days he'd questioned everything, worrying over the fact that she had barely looked at him and that even her last smile might have been directed at someone else. He was sorely tempted to get on Noble and ride to Sydney and find her—heaven only knew how he could begin—but instead simply nodded, paid for his groceries, and returned to the rectory, his mind ticking, ticking, ticking.

For if this letter was true, then perhaps God had a different path for him after all.

CHAPTER 7

Aunt Agatha placed her spoon in the bowl, the signal that the meal was done, which hastened Thea's last scoopful of stewed peaches before the maid came and removed their plates. The meal's conclusion meant the day was done and their respective bedchambers beckoned, despite the last gasps of summer sunlight still streaming through the window that looked onto a sparkling Sydney Harbor. Such it had proved these past five days. The evening meal, followed by her aunt's poke at Thea's foolishness, timed no doubt for Thea to ruminate on her folly as she went to sleep.

Staying here was like being in prison. A gilded cage of a prison, with no bars on the windows, but a prison nonetheless. It was quite possible she was going to die of boredom. Aunt Agatha believed that a young woman needed to be protected from anything that might possibly happen during the night, which meant that after an early dinner, Thea was expected to turn out her light and go to sleep. Despite staying in one of Sydney's more appealing suburbs, Thea had barely stepped from the front door. In fact, the biggest treat of her exile here would be to attend tomorrow's Sunday service. At least then she might get the chance to see somebody else's face other than her aunt's wrinkled one.

Conviction clanged. It was uncharitable to think of her aunt like that, especially when she was good-hearted enough to let Thea stay. But her aunt's constant needling ways nicked her soul and drew invisible blood.

The first night had seen Aunt Agatha sigh and shake her head. "I am deeply ashamed of you, Dorothea."

She'd kept her head down and tongue still. Father had expressed a similar sentiment.

The second night: "This is what happens when one marries for money, as your poor mother did."

She'd wanted to argue and say of course Mother hadn't married for money, but she did her best to strive for peace. She had to turn the other cheek, even if she felt like the cheek she was turning was her mother's.

"I cannot understand how an intelligent young lady like you would allow herself to be become enamored of this man."

That was no surprise. Her maiden aunt had been too picky to choose one of her suitors, so Mother had said.

Last night had seen a similar expression of disappointment, and she couldn't wait to hear what tonight's would bring.

She waited as the plates were cleared by the silent maid, silence seeming to be the preferred mode of communication in this place. Then Aunt Agatha eyed her, and Thea internally braced.

"How could you let your heart be beguiled by a married man?"

Shock drove speech to her lips. "Excuse me, Aunt Agatha, but that is incorrect. Mr. Hamill is not married. He would have told me. Someone would have told me."

Her aunt barely blinked at what must be a most unexpected argument, her gaze as beady as ever. "Apparently, someone should have told you, for perhaps we then wouldn't be in this pickle."

Thea's breath hitched, her mind slowing. It couldn't be true, yet her aunt seemed so certain. How could he have spoken with her, looked at her so tenderly, if he was *married*? No, this had to be some mistake. "I don't think we can be talking about the same person."

"Mr. Jonas Hamill, circuit preacher, with family from Lanark, Scotland?"

That was where he'd said his father was from. "Yes, but he can't be married. His wife was not with him."

"I expect not."

"Pardon?"

"Nor his child either."

"His child?"

Wooziness drifted over her, her thoughts unable to settle. Her aunt seemed positive this was true. Why had nobody told her? Why hadn't he? How could a man make her fall in love with him and not reveal such important truths? Nausea lined her stomach, and she was dreadfully afraid she would create a most unladylike mess in her aunt's dining room. How could he have acted as he had when he had a wife and child?

"I. . ." She needed water to lubricate her parched throat. "I don't understand."

Her aunt studied her. Then her shoulders fell, and she rose and exited the room.

Thea sat in her place, unsure what to do. The whole evening felt rather unreal, everything she'd thought she'd known shifting, swirling in a mass of confusion. At least this heavy chair was real. The mahogany table was real. She gripped the edges, the scalloped carving providing an anchor, as her aunt returned and held up a letter. "It's all here in the letter your father sent me."

"Father sent a letter?" Like she was a naughty child? How humiliating.

Her aunt held it out, and Thea grasped it with trembling fingers. No. There had to be a mistake. Had to be.

She slowly unfolded the paper and read her father's strong handwriting, his anger evident in the stabs and slashes of his penmanship as much as his words.

...has made a most unsuitable connection with one Jonas Hamill, who was married and with a child, both of whom were killed in a fire...

She gasped, her heart twisting. How could a man undergo such a thing and still have a heart for the Lord? Oh, the poor man. The poor, poor man. Her heart wrung with pain for him, her eyes filling with tears, which were soon followed by a pulse of anger. How could Father have known this and not told her? Had he told Mother? Who else knew? Oh, this made her feel like such a fool.

Except, "He is not married," she whispered.

"He was."

She met her aunt's gaze. "Yes, but he is not now." There was nothing to be ashamed of in admiring a young man who was free. Perhaps she had been a little unwise in some of her actions, but she had certainly never intended to cause either of them to feel guilty. "His wife and child died in a fire. Doesn't that make you feel so desperately sorry for him?"

"Somehow I doubt your father intended that reaction when he wrote this," her aunt said with a sniff.

Heat throbbed again, and she stabbed at the letter lying on the table. "I know exactly why he wrote this. Father thought this would dampen my feelings for Mr. Hamill, but it has only increased my admiration."

Her aunt shook her head.

Thea had to make her understand. "How can a man continue to talk about the goodness of God and trusting God when he has undergone such a tragedy?"

Her aunt's penetrating stare softened, her gaze lowering to the lace doily that centered the table, topped by matching silver salt and pepper pots.

The steady *tock* of the longcase clock filled the next minute.

Then her aunt sighed. "Perhaps going through tragedy and realizing God has been with him all that time means he can speak with authority on such things."

Thea nodded. She had often heard her aunt speak on religious matters but never in such a heartfelt manner. "Truly he is a man of real faith to believe so."

He hadn't advertised his pain nor dwelled on his grief nor built a memorial to his loss like poor Major Antill had done with his daughter buried on Vault Hill. That suggested he did not wish to be viewed as a grieving widower and would not let the past stop him from embracing God's plans for the future.

At her aunt's continued silence, Thea's gaze shifted to her again. "Aunt Agatha?"

"You. . .you sound like faith is of great importance to you, child."

"It is. And something I desire greatly for my husband to possess."

"You do not care for riches?"

"From my little experience, it seems that wealth might bring a level of material comfort but does not bring happiness or peace."

"Neither does poverty, child."

"But faith in God brings joy and hope." Two things she should probably remember as she sought to trust God with her future.

The silence thickened, then was broken by her aunt's soft exhalation. "Ah, my dear, it does my heart good to hear you say such things. I thought you but a frivolous, vain creature—"

Thea winced.

"—but it appears I have misjudged you. And perhaps I've misjudged your young man too. I know my parents despaired when your mother took up with a man who cared more for appearances than the state of his heart, but it seems you are cut from a different cloth. May I give you a word of hard-won advice?"

Thea nodded, the moment growing weighty with importance. Even the evening birdsong outside had ceased, as if they too waited to hear.

"You will find that if you and he are trusting God, then you can trust Him with all of your future. Both now and in years to come. You may not be with the man you want right now, you may never be with him—"

Her heart protested. *No, no.*

"—but there is great peace in submitting your future to the Lord and trusting Him with all your concerns and letting Him guide your course. It may not be what you want or expect, but if we trust God to lead us, then we can trust that whatever happens is part of His plan for our best. As it says in the book of Romans, 'All things work together for good to them that love God, to them who are the called according to his purpose.'"

Thea's chin dipped, the truth of her aunt's words swirling inside. What if God's best wasn't for her to be with Mr. Hamill? The thought seemed absurd. Yet what if God had another plan? A better plan? Could she still trust Him, even if her heart longed for a different outcome? This promise from the Bible said that was true.

"Whether God intends for you to be with this young man or not, you can trust Him with your future." Her aunt's mouth curved in a rare smile that made her appear ten years younger. "And if it is God's will for you to be with him, then you can trust Him to bring you together at the right time in the future."

The weight on her shoulders slowly lifted as the truth of her aunt's words burned through her confusion. Following God's plans for her life was of the greatest importance, more than the jumble of feelings that had weighed her down in recent weeks. She would take this time apart to renew her focus on God, to let Him truly work in her some more, and trust that He would lead her and Mr. Hamill into all He had for them.

Thea surprised them both by getting up to throw her arms around her aunt, hugging her. "Thank you," she murmured.

"What for, child?"

"For the gift of staying here, for reminding me that God is in control. Not my father, not my circumstances, or my feelings, but God."

Her aunt drew back, studying her with wise eyes as she gently patted Thea's cheek. "It is a lesson we all need to learn sooner or later."

And a lesson she would now be putting into practice every day.

Jonas' remaining weeks in Picton passed in continuing to visit parishioners, caring for the needy, writing sermons, and delivering church services. This included a funeral service for a lonely old-timer who had gone missing during the flood and whose body had been found two weeks or so after the fact. That grim discovery served as an excellent reminder of the fleeting nature of life and that he did not wish to grow old and live alone, forgotten, until circumstances demanded otherwise.

He sang the final hymn, but his thoughts were elsewhere. He had married Mary and had a child, planning to have a future. While his past few years of serving in this interim manner had filled a need, he sensed it was not what God wanted for him anymore. And that was not because of a certain blond who had been exiled to Sydney. It was a certainty that he felt core-deep when he prayed, when he searched the Word of God. Man was not meant to live alone, and while these past three years had been healing, it was now time to make the most of what life he had yet to live.

He looked out at the congregation on this, his last Sunday service before Reverend Carter returned.

"And I'd like to conclude today's service on a personal note, and thank you for your hospitality these past weeks. May God bless you all, now and always." His gaze fell on Mr. Maclean. The man flushed and glanced away. "Now may the peace of God, which passeth all understanding, keep your hearts and minds in the knowledge and love of God, and of His Son, Jesus Christ our Lord, and the blessing of God Almighty, the Father, the Son, and the Holy Spirit be among you and remain with you always."

"Amen."

His lips lifted, his heart tender at the smiles he received in return, and he moved down the freshly recarpeted aisle past the Antills, past the Cowpers, the Cavanaghs, and the Macleans. The odor from the floodwaters had gone with the old carpets being replaced with new. Much as a man's heart needed to be, washed and cleansed, the fibers strong and ready for the future. He felt that way. He was due to return to Sydney this week, and beyond that, he had little idea of what God planned for him. He had some hopes, some secret—or not so secret—wishes, but even those he was content to leave in God's far more capable hands.

He took his spot just outside the door. A breeze held the chill of autumn, and he did not imagine too many of the congregation members would wish to linger today. Still, he did not mind. He had an important call to make.

"God bless you," Mr. Antill said, shaking his hand. "Thank you for what you've done for our little town."

"I'm glad to have had the opportunity."

"I'll be telling Reverend Carter that we'll want you to fill in if ever he's called away again."

"Thank you, sir, but I can't be too sure about my future."

"None of us can be, though, can we?" Mr. Antill clapped him on the shoulder, allowing for the line of handshakes to continue.

The Cowpers, the Cavanaghs—young Mr. Anthony gripped his hand as if trying to crush it—then it was the Macleans. He swallowed. Mr. Maclean had barely acknowledged him since he had torn Jonas' character into shreds following the church cleaning incident.

He held out his hand. "Mr. Maclean."

The railwayman nodded, his grip like steel, his eyes likewise.

No hope for a parting reconciliation there. He smiled at Mrs. Maclean. "Mrs. Maclean."

She offered a timid smile and a "God bless you," which eased his heart some.

"Eliza." He bent a little closer and murmured, "Any visitors today?"

She eyed him seriously. "Do you mean Henry, or do you mean Thea?"

His heart spiked, and the murmurs of those nearby stilled.

"What's this about my daughter?" Mr. Maclean said in a tight voice.

Anything Jonas said now was bound to be misunderstood. He could not talk about Dorothea and would not spill Eliza's secret for the world.

"She's supposed to return home this week," Eliza said. "Father said it would be best to wait until you had gone."

Heat rose up his neck, and he glanced at Mr. Maclean, whose

fiery-hued countenance owned an embarrassment quite similar to what Jonas knew.

The man's scowl, and murmurs of those still waiting in line, drew him to nod, to wish Eliza well, and then to focus on the man behind her.

But amid the words of comfort and congratulations, he was also conscious of the grins from those who were obviously aware of his entanglement and who, now that he was leaving their midst, did not care to conceal their mockery any longer. Perhaps they'd thought that expressing it earlier might result in being targeted in a sermon. He kept his expression as benign as he could, his small talk consisting mostly of generalities about his future. His plans remained uncertain until a few important conversations could be had.

He locked up and moved to where Noble patiently grazed, then hesitated. He had little wish for this interview, especially considering the man's reaction before. But there was no guarantee that Mr. Maclean would be at home this week, and while he gave scant sign of being God-fearing, the man's pride made it a likely bet that he would not risk his reputation on not being at home on the day of rest.

The ride to the Maclean homestead did not take long, and he tethered Noble to the rail as Mr. Maclean exited onto the front porch, a cloth napkin tucked in around his collar. "What are you doing here, Mr. Hamill?"

"I wished to speak to you, sir. But I do not wish to disturb you—"

"Too late for that. I am disturbed. What is it you want?"

"I want to speak to you about your daughter."

Mr. Maclean's eyes narrowed. "You had better not mean Dorothea. She is to have nothing to do with you."

His heart sank, but he bolstered his courage. It wasn't like the man would hit him. At least, it was unlikely he'd do so on a Sunday.

"Well?"

He swallowed then lifted his chin. "Actually, sir, it is about her."

Mr. Maclean muttered something, his hands fisting, the vein in his forehead bulging.

His wife appeared, Eliza by her side. "Ah, Mr. Hamill," Mrs. Maclean said. "Are you joining us for our meal?"

"No, he is not. He is leaving," Mr. Maclean said.

"Oh, please make him stay, Mother," Eliza begged.

"I have no wish to intrude, and I'm terribly sorry to interrupt your meal," Jonas began.

Mr. Maclean snorted. "You knew we would be eating now. You're as bad as those who drop by unannounced when it's time for the evening meal."

"Please, Mr. Hamill, there is more than enough food. And I would like to hear what it is you wish to say to my husband." Mrs. Maclean gave a small smile. "Especially if it's in regard to my daughter."

"She means Thea, not me," Eliza said.

Jonas stifled amusement and nodded.

"Good," Mrs. Maclean said, obviously misinterpreting his nod as a sign he would stay.

"But Margaret—"

"No, Alexander, I suspect this matter is of great import, and we cannot have him leave without matters being resolved." Her smile grew. "Besides, I have already asked Susan to set another place. Come on, let's get you washed up, and then we can eat."

It was only a few minutes later that he was seated at the dining table opposite Eliza, eating beef and roasted potatoes as he tried to ignore the animosity pouring off the man seated at the head of the table.

As soon as his host finished eating, he put his fork and knife to the center of his plate with a clatter, threw his napkin on the plate, and faced Jonas. "So, you've eaten our food, what is it you wish to say?"

Jonas put down his own fork and glanced at Mrs. Maclean. "Thank you for the delicious meal."

"I didn't mean that," his host complained.

Jonas caught a wisp of a smile on Eliza's face, which tugged out his own. Really, Thea's father was like a spoiled child. He smothered his amusement and sat back in his seat. "Again, I wish to apologize for the interruption—"

His host sighed.

"—and reiterate how sorry I am for my role in causing your family to experience strain. I hope you know it was not my intention."

"We have long understood Thea's impetuous nature," her mother said, drawing his gaze. "You cannot blame yourself for her silly infatuation."

Infatuation? No. This was more. "Forgive me, madam, but I beg to disagree. For if your daughter holds me in some regard, then I wish to assure you that I hold her in even more."

Mr. Maclean blew out a loud breath. "I knew you were a fortune hunter."

"I think you mistake the matter, sir." He turned his attention to Mr. Maclean. "It appears your daughter would be the one considered in that light."

"What? You have no fortune."

"I had no fortune," he said slowly. "Until news came of a recent inheritance in Scotland."

"Scotland?" His host frowned. "Where? Who?"

"Alexander," his wife protested gently.

"Thank you, Mrs. Maclean, but I do not mind sharing." He

glanced at Mr. Maclean again. "I believe I once mentioned I was from a small town in Lanarkshire. News has reached me of a house and holding there in Kirkcudbright, on the Solway, that has been left to me by a cousin."

"A house and holding is hardly worth anything."

"On the contrary. The solicitor assures me it is no mean sum." He named a number that caused Mr. Maclean to blink and Eliza's eyes to widen and her mother to smile. "I am as yet uncertain as to what to do with that, whether it would be best to return to Scotland and live there, or whether it would be better to sell it and remain here."

"But why do you think I need to know that?" his host growled.

"Because I hoped this news might make you look more favorably upon me, as I would like to court your daughter."

"You want to court her?"

"I think she is remarkable, bonny in spirit as much as her appearance. I have come to care deeply for her. So that is why I am here, asking for your blessing to pay my addresses to her, with a view to marriage. And while some might consider this a marriage to repair our reputations, I assure you that is not my intention. I love her."

"But she doesn't think of you that way," Mr. Maclean objected.

"Yes, she does," Eliza piped up.

"Eliza," her mother hushed, before stretching a hand toward Jonas. "I, for one, give you my blessing."

"I do too," Eliza said.

Jonas smiled at her, and she grinned back.

"This is not a matter we vote on." Mr. Maclean's frown appeared etched in stone. "I have said no, and that's the end of it."

His hopes sank. He suspected the man's objection stemmed from his stubbornness, something his wife seemed to sense too, as she sighed.

"Alexander, I cannot allow you to continue to make decisions affecting our daughter's happiness simply because of your pride."

"But Margaret—"

"No. My parents were not pleased when you came along and stole my heart, but unlike my sister, who obeyed their decree to break things off with a man they deemed ineligible, I did not. And I have been happy. Which is why I cannot understand why you are so set against poor Mr. Hamill here."

Mr. Maclean sighed. "Very well, then. Here is my objection. How can I trust my daughter to a man whose first wife died?"

"What?" Mrs. Maclean asked.

"You were married?" Eliza's eyes widened.

Jonas nodded and cleared his throat. "I was. And then a fire stole Mary and my son from me. I was away, preaching at a church. And, just like the flood that swept through here, there was no warning. I was told by the neighbors and the poor folk who had witnessed it that there was nothing anyone could do."

"I'm so sorry." Tears shimmered in Mrs. Maclean's eyes, the green color so close to Thea's own.

Jonas blinked back his own emotion then turned to Mr. Maclean. "You can have no idea, *no* idea how much I regretted not being there, of imagining their fear and pain, of feeling guilt at putting my work ahead of my family."

Mr. Maclean's gaze sank.

"What was your son's name?" Eliza asked.

He swallowed the lump in his throat. "Alexander. He was three months old."

"That's Father's name too."

Mrs. Maclean was openly weeping now. Jonas handed her his handkerchief, which she took with broken thanks.

"You've gone and made my wife cry," Mr. Maclean muttered.

"I'm so sorry, Mr. Hamill," Mrs. Maclean murmured brokenly. "I didn't know."

The meal sat heavy on his stomach. "It is not something I ever wanted advertised. It was no secret, and some, like Reverend Carter and Mr. Antill, knew, but I was thankful to start here without the pity and judgment such news often brings."

"I can well understand that. And I'm sure Dorothea would too, if she knew. But I'm sure she didn't."

Mr. Maclean tugged at his collar. "Well, that I cannot say."

"What do you mean?" his wife asked.

He looked at Jonas before casting an uneasy glance at her. "I, ah, may have written a letter to your sister that I enclosed in yours, informing her of the fact."

"Oh no! Agatha is so judgmental, that she is sure to have told Dorothea."

Jonas' hopes dropped some more as regrets twisted within. "I should have told her myself. But I did not see the point, not until I could see a way forward and had secured your blessing." A blessing he did not seem destined to receive. Not now.

"Dorothea is sure to be understanding," Mrs. Maclean said. Pleaded, rather.

"Perhaps." He hoped. He prayed. "But I also know that some might regard the fact that I was married as less than desirable." Like the man sitting at the end of the table.

A patter of rain drew their shared attention to the window. "Looks like another storm is coming in," Eliza observed.

Jonas pushed out his chair. "I should go." His lips twisted wryly. "I have taken so much of your time, and I have no wish to be stranded by another storm."

"But you could stay here," Mrs. Maclean protested.

Stay trapped with a man who openly loathed him? "Thank

you for your hospitality, but I really have much still to do and must leave."

"But Mr. Hamill," Eliza said, "I'll miss you."

His throat tightened again. "And I will you. Please say goodbye to Henry for me."

She nodded, her eyes sad. "And I'll say goodbye to Dorothea too."

His chest panged. He really needed to leave now before he'd have to beg Mrs. Maclean for the return of his handkerchief. "Goodbye, sir, madam."

"But what about Dorothea?" Mrs. Maclean said, following him from the dining room to the door.

He drew on his riding gloves, his heartstrings pulled so tight he could barely breathe. "I hope you will let her know that I care. And if circumstances change, and your husband can find it in his heart to give his blessing, then I hope you might send word through Reverend Carter. Otherwise, I wish you and her a long and blessed life. Good day, madam."

He hurried from the porch to poor Noble and was soon riding through the storm to the rectory. The rain increased its tempo as he galloped through the main street, careless of mud puddles, thankful few observers could see his distress.

For he might be trying to trust God, but the moisture on his face was not just from the rain. His faith felt feeble. How he needed God to intervene.

CHAPTER 8

Thea hugged her aunt. "Thank you for the chance to stay. I admit I did not wish to at first, but I truly feel this has been a good time to learn more about what it means to trust God."

"You will need to remember that when you return. It is one thing to feel strong in faith when one is away from routine, but quite another when facing one's usual challenges and irritations."

Or when one received a letter from her father demanding she return home, as the man she loved had left the district.

She swallowed, refusing to let a single tear fall, and pushed her cheeks into a smile. "Goodbye, Aunt Agatha."

"Goodbye, my dear."

Thea pressed a kiss to her aunt's weathered cheek then stepped into the waiting carriage. This would be the first of several stages on her return to Picton. A final time to reflect on all that she had learned in recent weeks, and to better command her heart.

She nodded to the other passengers—a portly older gentleman, a woman of her aunt's vintage, a young woman wearing widow's weeds—and turned to watch the view as the stagecoach rolled away.

This part of Sydney, near the colony's first train station, held an energy most opposite to what she'd experienced in the quietude of her aunt's house. Tradespeople called, dogs barked, horses whinnied, the busyness distracting. She hoped the other occupants would not insist on constant chatter, as she needed to manage her emotions. Father's letter informing her that Mr. Hamill had already left seemed to be God's answer that he was not to be part of her life. Father had enclosed money for a ticket on the fastest stagecoach, thus allowing Thea this time to think and reflect before facing her family.

Her aunt was right. It was one thing to own faith in good times; it was quite another when things did not seem to be working out. And right now, returning to an unknown future in Picton, with the man she admired goodness knew where, she was feeling older than the woman seated opposite.

"Where is your destination?" the widow asked.

"Picton."

The first stretch of road took them to Ashfield, then across the convict-built Lansdowne Bridge to Campbelltown. They changed horses there for the next part of the journey. The rocking motion of the carriage meant she slept much of that stage as they traversed the road to Narellan, then Camden. They had a short rest at the Plough and Harrow, where the coach and horses changed again, passengers were dispersed, and new ones collected for the last trek over Razorback Mountain to Picton.

Some of her fellow travelers had talked of the recent rains and subsequent floods. Apparently, the water was nearly over the telegraph wires, and she prayed she would get through. But seeing the coachman was eager to get going, to make the most of what daylight hours remained, she joined the others in returning to the coach and watching as they took the road to Cawdor. Lagoons shimmered in the distance, the coach's speed from earlier much slower now as they passed through large boggy-type flats grazed by cows. Then the road lowered, and her heart prickled, as water extended as far as the eye could see.

"I do not like this," a male passenger noted. "The river is too high. I hope this driver knows what he's about."

Thea prayed he did too. They had been fortunate to not get bogged, necessitating hours of delay. A previous passenger, who seemed to revel in depressing stories, had told of a misadventure which had seen his coach delayed by twenty-four hours, when the horses had collapsed after the coach's wheels had gotten stuck in a muddy bog. One horse had needed to be put down after breaking its leg, and all the passengers spent the night shivering, drenched in mud, on the lookout for bushrangers.

She held her breath, praying they would not stall and be forced to wade through water. The horses must be so tired. How much longer until the paddocks returned to green?

A moment later the carriage swerved and dipped, throwing her forward. "Oh, excuse me!"

The man seated opposite gently pushed her back, and she hastily scrambled to her seat, grasping the leather strap. From outside came the sound of cursing, from the man on the roof, the cheapest and most dangerous place to sit.

It wasn't long until they were moving again, and soon they had left the sodden fields behind. The carriage tilted, forcing her to grasp the leather strap more tightly as the coach turned sharply then climbed, ascending the first steep section of the mountain range known as Razorback. This narrow section of road had been built by convicts, cut into the hill with a sheer drop on one side. There was no room for passing, and she prayed the driver would take heed. It was little wonder her father was so keen to see the railway go through. It would take hours off this journey and be much safer too.

She peered out the window, seeing nothing but the tops of trees below. A long valley swept up to distant hills, and when she glanced behind her, the water there seemed like an inland sea. Thank goodness they had gotten through.

This section of road was far bumpier, and she clenched her teeth as they traversed the range. It was not too much longer until Mt. Prudhoe Inn, where they could get out and stretch their legs, and perhaps this nauseous feeling would subside.

The coach veered suddenly, following the sharp bend, and tilted dramatically up on one side then dipped hard on the other. Thea gasped as a yell from up top was followed by a thud and a splintering sound. The coach slowly shuddered to a stop, listing terribly on one side.

"Have we crashed?" she asked.

The man opposite murmured something Thea couldn't quite hear, but judging from his scowl, she was glad she hadn't.

She could hear various yells from outside, but nothing from on top. "I hope the poor man on the roof is not hurt."

"He was likely flung off."

"What?" Oh, she hoped the man was not injured!

Thea opened the door to check on him, but a glance down showed no road. Instead, the valley chasm yawned below her. She screamed and nearly lost her grip when the male traveler jerked her back. She huddled against the other side, her breath coming in short gasps, her skin icy cold. She could have been killed!

"What did you think you were doing?" he snarled.

Shivers rippled up and down her spine. To think, one false move and she could have tumbled to the valley floor! "Thank You, God!"

Through the dimming light she could see the man was pale, his expression as shocked as Thea's must be. "You're all right, miss," he muttered. "Don't get hysterical."

She nodded, working to slow her breathing. She wasn't afraid. God was with her still.

"Now stay here," the man ordered before carefully descending onto the road.

But as soon as his weight shifted, so did the coach, sliding closer to the edge. Her scream joined the yells from the front again.

She had to get out. Now! She stretched to release the door latch, but the coach had tipped, and with a series of thuds, it lurched once more, and she was violently flung back against the leather cushions as belongings toppled past the windows to the valley far below.

"Miss?" The passenger from before stood at the door, holding out his hand, but her fingers couldn't reach his, couldn't reach—

Then time slowed as the coach rolled amid a loud *snap*, *snap*, *snap*, and scream of horses. She caught a glimpse of sky followed by dirt. And then her head smacked the side, and she saw nothing.

Jonas tensed. Something was wrong. He'd had the same sensation on the night of the fire, an eerie sense of foreboding, a feeling he'd since learned not to discount. As he prayed, a sound from the murky twilight outside his window caught his ear. A figure on a horse drew near. He opened the door.

"Mr. Maclean."

Thea's father's mouth opened. "You. . .you are still here."

"As you can see." He should've left by now, but when James Carter had telegraphed to say he would be delayed a day, he'd felt something urge him to stay. Perhaps this was why.

"You don't have Dorothea with you?" Mr. Maclean peered

over Jonas' shoulder.

"Of course not." Jonas stepped out of the way. "You are welcome to look if you don't believe me."

The man pushed past and rushed along the short hall, calling his daughter's name.

A shiver rolled down his spine. "Sir. Sir! Is she missing?"

Mr. Maclean turned, his face wan, his movements shaky. "We expected the coach several hours ago, but there has been no word. I. . .I hoped you might know, but you don't, either."

This was no time to be offended at the man's presumption that Jonas might have somehow met and carried off his daughter. He had to remain calm. "There must have been an accident on the road. I'm sure she will be here soon."

Except the prickle along his spine suggested that was more hope than reality.

"I contacted the coaching office in Sydney on the telegraph down at the station. They said they had heard nothing."

"Then you should not be alarmed. But if it makes you feel better, we could travel the road and search. That way you would have her back sooner."

"You. . .you would help me with this?"

"I love your daughter, sir. Of course I will." Jonas straightened, snapping into decisiveness. "You have driven your carriage here? Have you eaten?"

"I, er, no. I've been too distracted."

"I have some leftover beef and kidney pie, a gift from Miss Larkin. Eat what you wish, and we can take the rest. I'm sure she must be very hungry."

Quickly. He had to think. What else might be required? "A blanket. Ropes, in case the coach has had an accident." He gathered these and a few other supplies then drew on a thick coat. "Come, sir, let's go. There's no time to waste."

The light had almost faded by the time they passed the Razorback Inn, just before Racecourse Creek. Mr. Maclean was silent, his eyes on the road as he slapped the reins, urging his horses to go faster. Jonas held the lamp, shining what light he could so they could traverse the way.

Jonas' heartbeat thudded faster than the horses' hooves. *Lord, protect her. Keep her safe. Give us wisdom. Help us find her soon.* He clutched the side of the gig as Mr. Maclean sped around a corner. *Keep us safe too.*

They passed a dark farmhouse. The silent nature, save for a few dogs, didn't suggest any extra travelers or disturbance, so Jonas encouraged Mr. Maclean to press on. This next part of the terrain was steeper, the slope and pebbles causing the horses to slip as they hurried up the hill.

"We are not far from the Prudhoe inn." Mr. Maclean slapped the reins.

He remembered from his journey over. Perhaps once upon a time the inn had been recommended as a resting place for weary travelers, but with the proliferation of newer accommodations, the only ones who sought to stay there now seemed to be ghosts.

He shivered, tugged his jacket closer, and prayed for poor Thea.

They passed another farmhouse, its stillness also indicative of no drama, so they pressed on. The inn soon passed into view, its exterior just as decrepit as he remembered, like it was the perfect refuge for desperate souls. Or bushrangers. He shuddered and then, as Mr. Maclean steered into the yard, leaped from the vehicle as it slowed.

"Hello? Hello? Is anyone here?"

A man coughed and drew outside, dusting his hands.

"Sir? Has the coach from Sydney pulled in?"

He spat on the ground. "No, and it won't be."

"Why? What have you heard?"

"My daughter is on that coach," Mr. Maclean called.

The man winced.

"What is it? What do you know?" Jonas demanded.

"There was an accident, and I'm afraid the young lady is trapped, and—"

"And what?" Jonas asked, as the man's gaze stole to him then back to her father. *Lord, let her be alive.*

"I have a badly injured man inside. The doctor has been sent for, and I thought it was him when you pulled up."

God forgive him, but Jonas didn't care about the injured man. "And the young lady?"

"I'm sorry, sir, but I fear it is too late for the young lady."

His heart slammed against his ribs. "Where is she?"

"I—I was told she is still in the carriage."

"Which is where? Tell us. Please."

The man gulped. "It's gone off the road and down the cliff."

Jonas stared at him, for a second unable to comprehend. Then Mr. Maclean's exclamation of horror drew his focus. "Enough. Where is the coach?"

"About half a mile that way." The man jerked his thumb to the left. "There is a narrow turn near where the cliffs are, and the horses were spooked, and—"

"There are men there now?"

"Yes, the coachmen, and all the men who were here. They're trying to get to it. I had to wait here for the doctor."

Jonas turned to Mr. Maclean. "Are you able to drive sir, or shall I?"

"What? I—"

"Get in. We need to leave now." That hum of urgency was increasing by the second. "Sir, your daughter needs you. Now."

He snapped his fingers in front of the man's face.

Mr. Maclean startled and came back to himself, and then they drove to where the innkeeper had described. Sure enough, the sounds of frightened horses and shouts of men ahead gave indication to slow at the blind corner. As they came around the bend, they met with a scene of devastation. One horse lay on its side, unmoving. Another limped beside a tree. Two men peered over the side of the road, and it was to these Jonas ran before Maclean's carriage had stopped moving.

"Where is she?"

One man pointed, the dim light from an oil lamp picking out the shattered remains of a coach, its wheel broken in half. It was halfway down the sheer slope, lodged against a tree. "I'm sorry, sir, but there's been no sign she is alive."

"No, she has to be. Has anyone ventured to check?"

"We haven't had the ropes, nor enough strong arms to hoist a man below."

"I have ropes. You can attach them to the horse and lower me."

"But, sir, you might slip."

"I will take that chance. That woman who lies there is to be my wife." She would be, anyway. As soon as Mr. Maclean agreed. Perhaps Jonas' actions tonight might persuade him.

"In that case. . ."

His faith-filled pronouncement seemed to rally the men, and it wasn't long before he had a rope secured around his shoulders and belly, the other end attached to the horse as the men held the rope and braced, calling encouragement.

But he didn't heed their voices, doing his best to listen to the still, small voice of his heavenly Father, as to where to place his hand, his feet, as he was slowly lowered down the side of the mountain, carefully holding an oil lamp. *Lord, protect me. Help us now.*

Inch by inch he descended, taking care not to tip the lamp to extinguish the flame. This venture was already incredibly difficult. To do so in complete darkness would be near impossible.

He grasped a rock as a scratchy bush stabbed at his cheek. He averted his face, coughing, then called, "Miss Maclean? Thea? Can you hear me?"

Silence, save for the creaking of the coach held by wiry branches. His heart sank. No, she couldn't be—he dared not even think the word.

"Anything?" a voice called from above. He thought it might be Mr. Maclean's.

"Not yet," he shouted. "But tell the men to pray. And to be quiet."

He heard this relayed, and the noise above dropped. He continued his descent until he was nearly at the coach, then yelled for the men to stop lowering the rope. He had to be careful now. Any extra weight might be too much for the slender branches holding the carriage, and it could topple farther down, taking its precious cargo with it.

"Lord, help her. Help me." He shone the lamp as near as he dared, peering through the shadows. "Miss Maclean?"

The light revealed a huddled figure curled against the bottom door, blood trickling from her head. "Thea? Oh, thank heaven. Can you hear me? Please, if you can, make a noise."

Nothing.

Lord, please. "Miss Maclean? It's Jonas Hamill. Please, let me know if you can hear me."

He held the light closer. She remained motionless, but perhaps she breathed still.

"Thea? Please, I beg of you, answer me. I need you in my life. I can't lose you. Just answer me, my dearest."

There was a hush. Then a soft groan, and he saw her hand twitch.

Oh, thank You Lord. "Thea, dearest, I'm outside, and I want to help you. But it's dark, and we need to be careful and not move too quickly, so I need you to do exactly what I say."

"She's alive!" he called to the men above. There was a cheer, and then he called for them to carefully lower the rope some more. Somehow, he needed to open the door on this side and extract her without causing the coach to dislodge. It would take a miracle. Good thing he believed in the God who performed miracles.

He carefully placed the oil lamp on the coach's upward side, grasped the door's latch, and turned. It came loose, and he carefully pulled the door open then lowered the lamp farther into the coach's interior. His heart wept at his poor Thea, broken, bloodied, eyes still closed, though he could see the rise and fall of her chest. "Thea, darling, I need you to open your eyes and look at me."

His shoulders ached, his legs threatening to cramp at the unnatural position he was in, his legs behind him as he hung suspended, the rope around his waist. Yet he dared not rest his weight on the coach lest it prove too much for the tree's flimsy branches. "Sweetheart?"

Her dark lashes fluttered, and she shifted slightly before slow blinks preceded her squinting up at him. Her eyes widened, and her mouth opened then closed. She coughed, the action setting the carriage trembling.

"Thea, darling, I need you to hold my hand." He reached down. She remained too far away. He could ask the men to lower him a fraction more, but anything too sudden might send them both tumbling to their deaths. "Thea? I love you. And I'm fairly certain your father will allow us to marry, but you need to hold my hand."

She groaned, louder this time. "Is this a dream?"

Right now it seemed more like a nightmare. "It could be. If you hold my hand. I won't let you go. I will never let you go again."

He stretched, but her fingers were beyond his. "Come on, Thea. I know you can do this. Reach out for me."

She peered up at him, her eyes dark and scared in the shadows. "I can't."

"Yes, you can. If you love me the way I love you, then you can. Come on now. Please try."

She lifted her hand, and he stretched as far as he dared and gripped it, tightening his clasp. "Good." Now came the risky part. He tugged out the other rope secured around his waist, the other end looped and firmly knotted. "I am going to lower this rope to you, and I want you to slip it under your arms."

He lowered it, and she looked at it as if unsure what to do. "Slip it around your shoulders. I know it's hard to do one-handed, but I'm not going to let you go."

She nodded and relaxed her hold on his hand, forcing him to grip harder. "No, don't let go. You can do this. Just ease it around there. . ." His knee nudged the carriage, and it jerked. The oil lamp toppled over, the glass breaking, the flame escaping to lick the painted interior.

Thea screamed, and he knew they had but seconds. He shouted for more rope, and it released so suddenly that he thudded into the coach's side, rocking it. He reached with his other arm, swooped in, and grasped her. The carriage shifted, and she screamed again, clutching him, and he yelled, "Bring us up!"

He used every ounce of strength to haul her from the carriage and hugged her to himself as the flames took hold.

"I'm so scared," she whispered.

"I've got you."

She stared into his eyes then bent her lips upward in the

bravest smile he'd ever seen. "I know."

He smiled back and called to the men up top to pull them up as quickly as they could. "Now hold on tight. We've still got a little climb to make."

"Then we can be married?"

"You heard that?"

"I wasn't sure if you meant it."

"Oh, I meant it. And I meant that I won't let you go. You can trust me, Thea. I love you. And I think I have ever since you smiled at me during that first Sunday service."

She tucked her face into the crook of his neck. "In that case you best get us to the top as fast as possible."

So, along with the brave men above, he hauled them to the top, panting at the exertion, then tumbled onto the road, Thea still in his arms.

Ignoring the cheers and exclamations, ignoring her father, he looked deep into her eyes, lowered his head, and celebrated their rescue with a kiss.

EPILOGUE

They were married by the Reverend Carter four weeks later, Jonas' courage seeing her father bowed into grateful indebtedness and assent. It took that much time for their cuts and bruises to heal, and Jonas was given leave from the ministry to spend time with his new wife.

And now she was married, enjoying a honeymoon in this little town of Berrima, happily ensconced in a cottage for a week or two while they escaped the bustling interest that had surrounded them. She was glad for the chance to be away from her parents, from those neighbors and newspapermen all too eager for her to recall every moment of her misadventure. She did not remember most of it. Only that she'd dreamed of Jonas, and there he'd been, like an answer to a prayer she hadn't prayed. Their mishap on Razorback was being touted as a miraculous rescue, and she felt God's hand in every aspect of their union.

The leaves on the apple tree were now golden, and she was tempted to pluck the last fruit from the tree to bake her husband a pie for his dinner. She'd discovered he was very fond of pies. Her stomach fluttered. And other things.

"There you are," Jonas said.

She turned and smiled, and he stole close, his arms around her always providing a sense of comfort and protection. She tilted her head back, offering her lips. He smiled, bent lower, lower, and kissed her.

Her eyes closed, and she drifted on a cloud of warm sensation. His lips grew more insistent, and she sighed, melting into him in that way she could now that they were married. Her hands stole to his shoulders, his strong broad shoulders that had borne their weight in that awful ascent. She would forever be grateful for this man, this wonderful, courageous, loving man, whose laughter came more readily now.

She drew back, her breath unsteady as she placed her hands on his chest. "Oh, Jonas, I love you."

"And I love you, and always will. From now until eternity."

She tucked her head against his chest, secure in his arms, in his love.

And secure in the knowledge that God, who had seen two hearts that needed each other, could be trusted to work all things for their good. He had done so much already, and they could trust Him with all that lay in their future.

AUTHOR'S NOTE & ACKNOWLEDGMENT

Picton is a small town in New South Wales, Australia, and where I grew up, so the history reflected in this story contains a lot of truth among the fiction. Picton was settled in 1822 by Henry Colden Antill, born in New York, who was the aide-de-camp to Governor Lachlan Macquarie. Major Antill had a large property named Jarvisfield near Picton, and was considered enlightened for his time. He was an earnest Christian, a just magistrate, and a businessman of integrity who upheld equality of opportunity for ex-convicts.

Vault Hill, where members of the Antill family were buried, is one of the most significant landmarks in the town. The flooding produced by Stonequarry Creek is real. In 1863 a significant flood affected the town, including St Mark's Anglican Church. The steep hills continue to affect the town with flooding to this day.

The railway came to Picton in 1863, and while exact dates are uncertain, the building of the telegraph office, Picton's famous stone viaduct, and railway station occurred then, with early photographs attesting to the existence of the steam mill, hotels, and other buildings of note from this period. The blight of wheat rust closed the mill in the late 1860s, and Picton's agricultural focus shifted to dairying and orchards.

The names of all the townsfolk, businesses, and properties mentioned, apart from the Macleans and Jonas Hamill, are real. Sources include the Picton & District Historical Society, *St Mark's Picton* by Kay Weaver and Jan Maloney, *A Brief History of Picton* by Liz Vincent, and *Picton Then and Now*, collated by Joan Brown.

I'd like to acknowledge the wonderful help and support of

my mother, Kay Weaver, whose passion for history ignited mine and ensured many visits to National Trust properties over the years. Her vast treasure trove of books, photographs, and other material truly helped bring the history of Picton alive.

For pictures and to learn more about Picton's history, please visit my website www.carolynmillerauthor.com, where you can also sign up for my newsletter and learn about my other books and upcoming releases.

Carolyn Miller is an inspirational Regency and contemporary romance author who lives in the beautiful Southern Highlands of New South Wales, Australia, with her husband and four children. Together with her husband, she has pastored a church for ten years and worked as a public high school English and Learning and Support teacher.

A longtime lover of romance, especially that of Jane Austen and Georgette Heyer's Regency era, Carolyn holds a BA in English Literature and loves drawing readers into fictional worlds that show the truth of God's grace in our lives.

Carolyn's bestselling historical novels include the award-winning *The Elusive Miss Ellison* and her most recent release, *Dawn's Untrodden Green*.

The Angel and
the Sky Pilot

BY NAOMI MUSCH

This story is dedicated to the one who alone directs my path and sustains me with hope for tomorrow. For Jesus, "the author and finisher of our faith." Hebrews 12:2

CHAPTER 1

Northern Minnesota, 1905

Everett Shepherd hunched in the saddle against the cold and patted his horse's coppery shoulder. "Straight ahead, Buddy. Can't be much farther." He pressed his wool scarf to his face and squinted against the stinging snow crystals pelting down.

Buddy huffed, his head bobbing with his gait.

"I'll give you a rubdown and some oats soon." Everett's stomach rumbled. "Even sounds good to me."

He tucked his chin against another frigid shift of the wind as they rounded a bend in the tote road. A light glimmered faintly up ahead, and soon the outline of the trading post appeared. The scent of woodsmoke trailed past Everett's nose.

Buddy nickered, and his body quivered beneath Everett. "Here we are, boy. See? What did I tell you?" He drew up to the unassuming building with its two front windows twinkling out over a porch. A darkened gable dormer stood above. Everett swung his leg over the horse and found his footing. He flipped the reins over a rail, hoping he'd find welcome at this late hour.

His heels clicked against the step where the wood was beaten with the look of caulked boots having tread up and down a thousand times over the years. Tugging down the scarf so he didn't look like he'd come to rob the place, Everett tapped on the door.

"Yup." A gravelly voice sounded from inside. "Door's open."

He pulled off his wool cap and shook it, then brushed snow from his shoulders and let himself in. "Wasn't sure you were open for business."

"I can be. Isn't barely dark out yet."

Everett stepped toward a tall man with a trim hedge of graying hair around a thinning crown and wearing a well-groomed beard. He stood behind a long, uncluttered counter, polished smooth from years of use. Around the room and behind him were shelves of goods. Among it all, the sweet scent of tobacco wafted along with something savory. Everett's stomach gurgled again, but not noisily, thank goodness.

"Quite a night for traveling," the man said.

"I'm heading out to Camp Twelve."

The proprietor's thick gray brows jumped. "That's a fair piece yet. Six miles."

Everett nodded. "I don't suppose, given the weather, you've got a barn I could shelter in for the night."

He gave Everett a once-over and a slight nod. At the same time, Everett caught the twitch of a curtain behind the man closing off a passage or room. Was someone else here, or did a mouser prowl about?

Everett dipped his chin. "My name's Shepherd, by the way. Everett Shepherd."

"You walk in, or ride?"

"My horse is out front."

"Better bed him up too. Hay and grain will cost you two bits."

Everett opened his coat to reach for his wallet. He spoke again as he paid the man. "I heard about your trading post back in Northome. Seeing the light in your window was a sight for wind-sore eyes."

"I'm the only store and post office near enough for the men in those lumber and rail line camps. Your first time out in this neck of the woods?"

"Been east of here, south, and west before."

The man put Everett's coins in the till. "Name's Adair. You had your evening meal?"

Everett grimaced. "I chewed on a biscuit a few miles back."

"Got some stew that'll warm your belly, if you've a mind to have a bowl. On the house, since it's your first time in these parts."

"That's neighborly, Mr. Adair."

"Just Adair will suit, or some call me Captain." He lifted an unlit lantern from a nail.

"Captain of your own ship right here?" Everett's voice held a smile as he looked around the establishment once more. There were caulk boots and moccasins, food tins and a barrel of potatoes, bolts of cloth and a handful of shelved books. In the front corner near a woodstove sat a checkerboard on a tall log with two shorter logs as stools pulled up beside it. It was a welcoming atmosphere and tidy as a captain's quarters. Everett's glance fell upon a faded captain's hat hanging beside the curtained doorway.

"Used to captain a steamship on the lakes. That was in another life years back. You can use this lantern to take to the barn out back. Get your horse bedded first, then come back in for your supper."

Everett pulled his cap over his ears and nodded as he accepted the lantern and a pair of matchsticks and exited the store.

Snowy gusts blasted him as he unwrapped Buddy's reins from the post. Leading him around the side of the building, he found the small barn tucked beneath a stand of pine. He pulled open the door and led the horse inside, pausing just out of the wind to light the lantern. A glow swept over the space that smelled of fresh hay and horse. A nicker from the back of the barn told him neither Buddy nor he would spend the night alone. He led Buddy to an empty stall beside another housing a tall black horse that flicked his head up and watched the goings-on with interest. In another stall, a cow lowed.

After untacking Buddy, he searched out a bucket and oats and gave him a good rubdown. Then he plumped himself a bed of hay in another dry corner and dropped his bedroll atop it. Everett was used to roughing it. He sang the lines of a hymn. "The Lord's my rock; in Him I hide. A shelter in a time of storm..."

Darkness had fully descended by the time he made it back inside the store.

Adair waved him over. "Hang your coat and get comfortable."

Everett shucked his coat and sat on a stool placed near the end of the counter as a second person swept through the curtained doorway, bowl in hand.

A woman!

And not just any woman, but a young woman. Younger than Everett's thirty years, certainly. She wore a fawn-colored skirt and a pale cotton blouse belted at her small waist. Walnut-dark eyes flashed to him for a second before she set the bowl on the counter and turned away. Everett could only stare at her back and the brown hair plaited and coiled loosely on her head before she flipped the curtain aside and disappeared.

"I...uh..." He thought he'd entered a man's world. He never expected to see a gal this far away from any town.

"Better eat before it gets cold." The captain leaned toward the curtain and hollered, "Bring the whole coffeepot out here." He peered again at Everett. "Looks like you could use more than one cup."

"I'd be obliged."

Everett still hadn't had the chance to assess what might have brought a young woman so far north when the stew's rich aroma made him momentarily push curiosity aside. He bowed his head. *Thank You for the hot supper, Father, and for the hands that made it.* Was it that woman's hands? Likely. *Amen.* He opened his eyes and scooped in a spoonful. It nearly scalded his mouth, but he didn't mind. "Mm-mm." He gave a mouth-closed smile, chewed, and swallowed. "Haven't had anything tasty as this since the church ladies sent me off with a big dinner last week Sunday."

Adair gave him a quizzical glance and took a step back as the woman came through the doorway again carrying a cup and an enamel pot. She set the cup down and filled it without looking at him. He tried not to stare, but he couldn't help taking glimpses of her pretty oval face and dark eyes.

"Thank you, ma'am."

Her gaze flitted briefly at him and away. She bobbed a nod and set the pot down. "Anything else you want?" She directed her question at Adair.

"You can go on with what you were doing." The captain's voice was gentle. Still deep, but void of its gravelly tone.

The girl withdrew behind the curtain again. Everett made short work of the stew, now and then glancing at the doorway where the curtain hung still as a frozen waterfall.

"Kind of late to be starting with the logging season," the captain said as Everett finished.

"I've got another kind of work in mind."

"Oh? You look like a jack to me."

Everett took a long sip of coffee and set down his cup. "Used to be. Like you said, in another life. Nowadays I'm a preacher."

"A preacher!" Was it merely surprise, or was that disgust that coated the older man's response? Adair followed it up with a throaty chuckle. "You don't look like any black-coated preacher

I ever saw. Pretty young for that business too, aren't you?" He raked Everett with a gaze that seemed to assess him more for what he used to be than what he was.

"It's difficult for the older preachers to walk or ride this far up into the woods." The curtain wavered ever so slightly. Everett cleared his throat. "God called me to preach to the fellows up here who can't get out to church or their families much of the year. He didn't seem to take my age into account."

Adair harrumphed. "As if those woods bulls would go to church, even given the chance."

The comment didn't surprise Everett. He understood completely, having been just like those hardened men only a few short years ago. Maybe even worse than most. He offered a grin. "You never can tell. Might be that one or two of them is waiting to hear the good news. They just don't realize it yet."

The older man scratched his chin beneath his beard. Then he crossed his arms and sucked a breath that expanded his broad chest. His cuffed woolen sleeves revealed long johns squeezed tight against forearms as thick as venison roasts. "I guess I don't care much for religion."

"Can't say I'm fond of it either." Everett pushed back the empty bowl. "I know Jesus didn't like it one lick."

"That right?" Captain Adair's tone bespoke tolerant skepticism.

"Yes, sir. The religious leaders of his day preferred rules and tradition, like most religious folk still. Jesus pointed out that they could never keep enough rules to become pure of heart. He came to save the world without man's religion."

The captain grunted and picked up the bowl. "Get enough?"

Everett nodded. The captain clearly had enough preaching, at least for now. Maybe Everett would get to speak to him about Christ again another day.

Everett patted his stomach. "It was delicious. That gal's a fine cook if she's the one who made that stew."

"That young woman is my daughter." The captain skewered him with a look.

"Oh!" The word leaped off Everett's tongue before he could stop it. It hadn't occurred to him to wonder about her role here beyond cook perhaps, but not for a moment did he think she might be this man's daughter. "Pardon me. I didn't mean to sound so surprised." His voice betrayed him again.

There came that look from Adair again, as though he was assessing Everett and deeming him lacking. "Her mother taught her to know her way around a galley."

Everett smoothed his voice. "Well, it was very good, and I thank you both. What do I owe you?" He reached into his coat.

Adair waved a hand. "Put your money away. I told you it was on the house. I don't expect you could have gone another mile in this blow. You can consider it a donation to your *cause*."

Everett pretended not to notice his sarcasm. "My thanks again, Captain Adair. I am fortunate to have met a gentleman of the Northwoods."

"Come back inside before you ride out in the morning. You can join us for breakfast at six. You'll not make it to the camp before the cookee is done cleaning up from the morning."

"You must allow me to pay you for breakfast, at least."

"If you insist, I'll charge you a quarter." The captain lit the lamp and shook out the matchstick.

Everett wrapped his scarf around his neck and picked up the lantern. With a nod, he departed.

The wind had lessened. Now snowflakes fell in thick clumps with only an occasional gentle gust to move them around. Several inches covered his earlier tracks. Belly full and warm, he looked forward to burrowing into the hay for the night.

A shadow moved ahead, catching him by surprise when he recognized the long skirt of a female exiting the barn. She halted when she noticed he'd seen her, and stiffened at his approach.

"I was just seeing to Blackjack. Making sure he's getting on with your horse and settled for the night."

The snow squeaked beneath his boots. "Blackjack is the name of your horse?"

She rocked on her boots with a nod.

"They all right?"

"Just fine." Her gaze flashed toward the barn and back to him. "Does your horse have a name?"

"Just Buddy."

She raised her chin. "Suitable, I suppose."

He couldn't help lifting one side of his mouth in a grin. "We've been companions for nearly six years."

"I heard what you told the captain." She settled her dark eyes on him. They looked even bigger and deeper in the halo of lanternlight. "My mother used to wish for a preacher. We never had one. You come from a church somewhere?"

"I was sent by a group of ordained pastors in Duluth. I've come to preach to the men at the camps up here in the woods. My church will be a cathedral of pine, as it were." He injected a gentle humor in the words and glanced around at the dark canopy, but she frowned.

"I guess I can't imagine that. I wish you were making a real church. One anybody could go to. My mother always wanted that." There was a tone of longing in her voice that uppercut Everett.

"Was your mother a Christian?" A sudden gust and swirl of snow nearly doused his light, but he raised it higher, observing her for an answer.

Her brow pinched again. "I. . .I guess I don't know. I suppose she was. She must have been. I'd better get back inside now, before my—before the captain worries." She spun away.

He wished he could prolong the conversation, but she was right. "You don't want to catch sick."

She paused at the edge of the lantern's glow and flashed him a backward glance. "It would take more than a little November snow to bring me low." With that, she disappeared into the darkness.

Inside the barn, Everett unrolled his bedding on the pallet of clean straw, careful to set the lantern where it wouldn't accidentally totter or catch any stray pieces. He settled, pulled off his boots, and tugged his blanket over himself. "Nice and snug."

He intended to read some scripture, but his thoughts kept drifting to Captain Adair and the daughter who called him Captain instead of Father. He should have asked for her name. Perhaps he'd learn more about both of them in the morning when they shared breakfast.

Or perhaps he should focus his thoughts on the men he'd come here to reach with the gospel. He ought to pray for those he'd meet tomorrow. Yet, as he drifted off to sleep, it was a pair of pretty, dark eyes he visualized, gazing at him with such an expression of heart. *I wish you were making a real church*, was the last thing his memory heard.

CHAPTER 2

A hot fire crackled in the kitchen stove well before dawn, but Angeline Adair took special care not to overboil the coffee. She wrapped her apron around her hand and lifted the bubbling brew off the stove. After setting it on the sideboard, she added a cup of cold water to settle the grounds. Grease hissed in a cast-iron pan on the stove, ready for her to add dollops of flapjack batter. A hearty breakfast would best be served before she plied her father with questions this morning. Ten minutes later, she called him to eat.

He entered the kitchen, rolling up his sleeves and appearing to have washed and combed his thinning hair. Her father had been a handsome man, and maybe for his age he still was. Mama had always thought so. His frame was straight and tall, and while the muscles of his arms and chest weren't as taut as they once were, they could still defy a challenge.

He drew back a chair at the table. "You think that preacher fella's gonna be a no-show?"

She shrugged. "Might be he's foddering his horse."

Her father grunted as he poured himself a cup of steaming black coffee. "Suppose so. Better get him a plate, just in case."

She poured another pair of flapjacks and watched them bubble. "What's that preacher got in mind? He going to build a church somewhere about?" She didn't mention her hopes that he might do more than preach under the pine.

"Why do you care? Don't matter one way or another."

"Mama always wanted a church. I reckon I'm curious. I've not been to a real church service before."

"I think he intends to go up there and scare the devil out of them at that camp." Her father took a slurp of coffee. "I don't believe it can be done. I reckon we'll see him back this way again in a few days, making for civilization, and that'll be the end of it."

She flipped the cakes then turned and leaned against the sideboard. "I hope he sticks it out."

Her father's brows rose as he poured maple syrup over the stack of cakes. "Why is that?"

"I have questions I want to ask him, but I need to think them through first."

"What kind of questions?" He shoved a triple-layer chunk of flapjack into his mouth, regarding her.

"About heaven." She moved the cakes off the griddle to a plate and poured more batter.

"That's what's on your mind? Heaven?"

"I suppose I'd have more to ask about if I heard some preaching. I'm not sure."

He muttered under his breath, and she glanced at him. Then she knew what he was thinking. "Captain," she admonished. "Must every man who comes up our step be someone I'm expected to gauge as a potential wooer?"

"You're past the age most females get a husband, and I know that every man who graces that step notices you." He pointed his empty fork at her. "I don't figure on you picking a preacher man though. Even if he doesn't look like one." He stabbed another forkful of flapjack. "I couldn't help noticing the fine cut of his jib and figured you might have too."

A breath sputtered past her lips. She slid her spatula beneath a flapjack and flipped it deftly. "You insult me, Captain." *The cut of his jib. . .* "Do you think a husband is what I'm after? If you do, you can slow down your thinking. I only want to know about Mama." She didn't bother to add that, beyond that, she didn't know what she wanted. She'd been restless of late, but she didn't think it was for want of a husband. She desired something *more*, if only she could put her finger on it.

The captain was silent for a moment. "No harm in asking, I guess," he conceded.

The outer door opened and thudded shut, and the sound of boots clunked along the puncheon floor. Her father pushed back his chair and rose. He reached for the other plate of flapjacks and the syrup and carried them into the store.

"I'll bring the coffee." Angeline scooped off the last flapjack, adding it to a pile of extras. She moved the pan off the stove and followed her father with the coffeepot.

The preacher carried his hat in his hands. He'd combed back his hair in smooth waves, and he must have found the pump to wash at. "I hope I'm not too early."

"I've already finished." The captain slid the stack of cakes onto the counter. "Angel just pulled these off the griddle."

Their guest gave a nod and removed his coat. "Looks like the storm is over and we're in for a bright day. Still crisp, but the sunshine ought to make traveling comfortable."

Angeline stepped forward and poured the preacher his coffee as he sat down. He gave her a quick glance, and in that moment a warmth exuded from his eyes. She hoped it meant a trustworthiness lived inside him.

"I still think you'll be wasting your breath going up there

to talk God into those lumberjacks." The captain stepped back as the preacher poured a judicious serving of syrup over his breakfast. "But I guess they'll enjoy the entertainment, if nothing else." He cleared his throat. "I didn't introduce you to my girl last night. This is my daughter, Angeline. As you mentioned, she's a good cook, like her mother was. Don't know what I'd do without her."

The preacher smiled at her. "It's a pleasure to meet you, Miss Adair. I don't know if your father told you, my name is Everett Shepherd."

"Preacher." She dipped a short curtsy, wishing she could forget the things her father had said to her in the kitchen. Yes, he had a fine cut to his jib. He was tall and slender, yet nicely proportioned across the shoulders.

Preacher Shepherd grinned. Had she said something amiss? Was she staring? Perhaps she should have been more formal. "I meant, Preacher *Shepherd*."

He took a bite, still smiling with a closed mouth. "Mm."

"My girl has a question or two to ask you."

She startled, coming to attention like one of her father's crew. She'd already told the captain she needed time to form the right words. She shook her head. "Not now. Another time. You have a long ride ahead and lots to think about, certainly."

Preacher Shepherd wiped his mouth on a scrap of cloth napkin. "It's all right. Go ahead with your question."

Angeline's thoughts scampered. How could she corral all her wondering into a single, succinct question? She worked her lips, giving a quick glance to her father, who offered no help. "I was wondering about heaven."

His brow lifted, and she could see that was too broad even before he said, "Heaven?"

She nodded. "I want to know what it's like for the people

there. What they're doing. What they're like now. What it'll be like for the rest of us someday." She pinched her mouth closed. Best to cease now, before she rolled out all her questions like a ball of twine he'd have to unravel.

He puffed out a breath. "Yes, well, those are important questions."

"Her mother passed on some eight winters back," the captain said. "That's what's pushing her to know." He looked at her. "You asked your question. Maybe after the preacher is finished with his breakfast, he can give you an answer that'll hold for the time being."

Preacher Shepherd diced another piece of flapjack. "I'll try."

The captain turned to prying open a crate of tinned meat. Angeline didn't want to ogle while the preacher ate, so she slipped back through the curtain into the kitchen until the captain called her back a few minutes later.

"The preacher's set to head out now."

Their guest's warm brown eyes crinkled. He was handsome, especially when he smiled. *Oh, Captain, why did you have to make me notice?*

"I'm glad you weren't afraid to ask about heaven, Miss Adair. As I said, it's important to search for truthful answers. I'm very sorry about your mother, and I can understand how it is you want to know about her life as it is presently, in the hereafter."

"Is she floating in the clouds all dressed in white? Does she spend the day singing and playing music on a harp? She never played any instrument here on the earth."

He smiled again, but like he understood, and not like he was laughing at her. "I see you've gathered ideas from someplace."

She glanced at her father, who, with his broad back to them, was still busily counting and sorting tins. Mama had talked about heaven with its streets of gold and angel choruses, but

Angeline's notions of bodiless spirits adrift in the clouds came from her father. He'd seemed only to want to assuage her, but she doubted he really knew. Maybe he'd made it all up.

"I don't think your mother or anyone else is floating in the heavens with nothing else to do all the time but sing. And for that matter, in case you're wondering, she hasn't become an angel either."

She blinked at his answer. "You don't believe in heaven?"

"Oh, I certainly do." He pushed a hand through thick brown hair, moving it back from his forehead. "I believe heaven is more real than earth. Earth is the shadow to heaven's reality. And your mother—if she was a believer in Jesus—has much to do to keep her occupied there."

Angeline sucked in her breath. "And there are streets of gold?"

"Scripture describes the future Holy City as having them." He must have noticed how that remark confused her, for he picked up his coffee cup and swirled it as he spoke. "I'll tell you what. I'll look up some verses of scripture about heaven and write them down for you."

She didn't know what had happened to Mama's Bible after her passing, the one she used to read from to Angeline now and then. It had disappeared. Maybe the captain buried it with her. Perhaps he just tossed it away. "I'd like to read them."

Preacher Shepherd sipped his coffee but watched her over the rim like he had something he wanted to ask her too, yet no question came.

She reached for his empty plate. "Thank you for letting me ask about this."

"I only hope that the men at Camp Twelve are as eager to know such things." He rose from the stool and slipped into his coat. "That was a fine breakfast." He worked the buttons closed. "I'll long remember your hospitality."

Her father turned toward them, pushing aside the now-empty crate with his foot. "Glad it filled your belly. Did you sleep well enough out there?"

"Snug as a wintering caterpillar."

Angeline took his plate and wares to the kitchen, brushing through the curtain but listening as her father and the preacher finished their conversation. The captain reminded him to keep left at the fork in the road, or he'd have another day's journey before he reached another camp. Preacher Shepherd chuckled and said he wasn't a stranger to such wilderness ventures. Her curiosity roused further, and more questions brewed in her thoughts. These didn't have anything to do with heaven or about God.

Her father's remark about the cut of the man's jib stirred foremost, and this time she allowed herself to ponder it. She set the plate into the pan of dishwater in the sink, rinsed her fingertips, and dried them on her apron. She slipped back to the curtain to peek out, only to catch a glimpse of the preacher's back as he left the store.

Angeline spun and hurried to the back door. She pulled her heavy woolen coat off a peg and slung it on as fast as she could then hurried outside, careful not to let the door close heavily behind her. With no time to put on her warm boots, she wore her house shoes as she bolted through the snow down the back step, just as Preacher Shepherd appeared around the side of the building. Catching sight of her, he halted his long stride.

"You're right. It is crispy out today." Her words floated out on a foggy breath. She searched for something more to say and turned in the direction of the barn. "Did your horse eat enough? He had a good drink?"

"I fed and watered him first thing. I think he enjoyed the company of Blackjack."

"I'll see to Blackjack now." She followed him into the barn.

"He'll be mad I haven't come to give him his breakfast yet."

"I spared him a few oats. I hope you don't mind." He smiled at her, and it gave her an extra shot of warmth beneath the heavy coat.

"That was good of you. He'd have been jealous otherwise."

The preacher chuckled, and Angeline liked the sound. What kind of voice did he use when he preached? She recalled the way her father described preaching—with fire and brimstone and pounding on the pulpit. Would Preacher Shepherd pick up his Bible and shake it in the air, warning of doom and the eternal agonies of hell? She had a hard time picturing him doing anything like that, even though his voice was deep when he spoke.

She tilted her head with a new thought. "Your family all right with you hightailing it around the country like this?"

"My family is in heaven. Like your mother. My folks, that is." They reached the horses' stalls, and he began saddling up his bay. In what seemed a long-delayed afterthought, he said, "Never had a wife or children."

She grabbed a pitchfork and stabbed at the sweet-smelling hay then delivered it into Blackjack's stall. As he began to nibble, she set the fork aside and reached for a brush. She ran it over his satiny coat. "I didn't mean to be nosy. I only wondered." She brushed all the way down to Blackjack's belly. *Liar. You're nosy as a dog looking for a bone.*

"No harm in it. I believe it's one reason God chose me to call to the north country. I've got no ties to keep me from such a faraway ministry."

She moved around to Blackjack's other side so she could see the preacher over the horse's back. She brushed a long, slow stroke. "Any idea when you might be this way again? I'll be looking forward to reading those Bible verses you're going to write down for me."

He placed the bit into his horse's mouth and slid the bridle over his ears. "That depends on my welcome at camp. I reckon I'll be out again in a week or so for some supply or to visit another camp. I'll not keep you waiting too long."

She eased out of the stall and returned the pitchfork to its place. There was no trace of where he'd bedded last night, except for the lantern hanging on a post. He'd tidied up the area well. She reached for the lantern to take it back with her. Then she followed as he led Buddy outside.

He stepped into the tall stirrup and swung into the saddle, looking for all the world like a man much used to riding.

"Be seeing you sometime then."

He touched his hat in farewell. "Thanks again for the hospitality. Tell the captain that next time I'll insist on paying in full."

She swung the lantern gently. "I'll tell him. Bye now."

Angeline watched him ride off, her head bursting with new questions. Some of them about him being a preacher and how he thought God *called* him. Others about his past, and how he learned to sit a horse. Further still, why he was built more like a lumberjack than a clergyman, at least so far as her father described preachers. A final question rose high in her thoughts. How was a man with so fine a cut to his cloth never married?

She sighed on the cold air and felt the nipping cold tingling her toes. A question like that was better off never brought to the surface and voiced.

CHAPTER 3

Everett whistled hymns as Buddy plodded down the narrow trail. Now and again he had to navigate a section of corduroy road where the logs lay across a stretch of swamp. Everett had driven over more miles of corduroy than he could count. A past life—or nearly so.

On a long straight stretch, a man walked toward him in the sparkle of sunlight, hoofing it quickly through the snow. He drew nearer, until finally Everett reined Buddy to a halt beside him.

"Well now." The fellow set his hands on his hips, his chest rising and falling in ragged breaths. "That's the way to travel. Easier when a horse does the work."

Everett nodded. "That it is." He'd already come three miles or more from the store, likely the only place this fellow could be headed. He hadn't passed any active cuttings. "Sorry I can't give you a ride. I'm headed to Camp Twelve. That where you come from?"

The man reached into his coat pocket and withdrew a chaw of tobacco from a nearly empty bag. He stuffed the pinch into his lower lip. "Yep. Boss isn't hiring though. Crew's full."

"I'm not looking for work, so I reckon I'll talk with him anyway."

The man tipped back his broad-brimmed hat and squinted at Everett.

"I'm a preacher. Name's Everett Shepherd. I suppose I'll be seeing you later if you're from there."

"Huh." He spat juice. "I suppose."

"I didn't catch your name."

"Hankins."

Everett touched his hat. "Nice to meet you, Mr. Hankins. I'd better let you get on your way." He doubted the man was heading to the woods. He was making fast tracks to Adair's, and likely he was hoping to get back before he was greatly missed.

But it wasn't Everett's business. They parted, and Everett moved Buddy on.

Half an hour later, he rode into what looked like a well-established camp. With a quick scan, Everett took in the bunkhouses, the cookshack, the blacksmith shop, another outbuilding that was probably the filer shack, a barn and feed storage, and a smaller shack that must be the boss' administrative office, where smoke puffed out the roof through a tin pipe. He headed straight to that one. Sure enough, a sign with the word OFFICE was tacked to the door. He gave three solid knocks.

"Open."

He withdrew his hat and stepped inside. "Good morning."

A stout man with a thick beard and strong shoulders gave a brief glance up from a desk covered in paperwork. He grunted as he returned his focus to a ledger. "We're full. I hear they need a couple men up at fourteen."

The single room was modest. A small potbellied stove blackened with smoke, a file cabinet, and a tidy, made-up cot filled most of the space. A couple supply shelves stacked with new clothing and sundries seemed to be the extent of the company store. Behind the boss, a thick mackinaw and some extra clothes hung from pegs. "Not looking for a job."

He raised his eyes. "Did you say you *aren't* looking for work?"

"I'm happy to lend a hand anywhere I can, but I came to bring the Word of God."

"Circuit preacher?"

Everett nodded. "I'm not looking for any handouts."

"Little early, aren't you? Sunday is two days away."

"I started out from Duluth a few days back when the weather was clear. When the sky blanketed up, I stopped a night at Northome and then spent last night holed up in the barn behind Captain Adair's store."

"Lucky you made it to shelter."

Everett used to believe in luck, but not anymore. "My horse is strong and able. We're both good workers in a pinch."

The man pushed up from his chair and offered his hand. "John Salverson. You're welcome to bunk up, since that's the case. I don't know how many fellas will turn out for preaching, but you can give it a shot."

"I'll give them something short that won't steal their daylight. I'm sure they have laundry to do and letters to write on their free day."

"You've worked around the camps, I take it."

"Started lumberjacking when I was fifteen. But..." Chagrin stole through him. "I got a little too wild for anybody's good, so God pulled me out a few years back and changed my ways. He set me in a new line of work. Nevertheless, I'm not afraid to heft an axe or pull out a few logs if somebody comes down sick or hurt."

Salverson appraised him. "You figure on sticking around the area all winter?"

"That's my intention. I'm hoping for a base to operate from."

"In that case, you might as well stay here. You might have to split a little firewood or muck the barn, but we've got plenty to eat. Could be a little preaching will do the men some good. Maybe keep some of them out of their gin on Sunday so they're ready to work on Monday morning."

Everett remembered the groggy feeling of too much drink and the vices it lent to. "I'll see what I can do. You said you were full up. Any place I might toss my bedroll? I can take the barn if need be."

"You *are* accommodating. No cause for that. I'm sure we can find you quarters. Might be a little crowded." Mr. Salverson scratched his jaw.

"I'll find a few square feet to fall into." The fellow Everett met on the road flitted through his thoughts. "I didn't pass your cut on the tote road."

"No, you wouldn't have." Salverson thumbed at the back wall. "We're working a stand north of camp about a mile."

"Ah, right." Everett wouldn't divulge having met Hankins on the road—heading east. Hankins was probably supposed to be swinging his axe now, but he was skipping half the day to purchase something likely supplied in Salverson's cabinet, or. . .

The pretty face of Angeline Adair floated past his thoughts.

Or Hankins wanted a glimpse of an angel in a calico skirt.

He shook the image away. He was here to preach to men. Hard men. Men who reveled in their sin and grasped it with a death grip. Men who only God's Spirit could reach, but on whom they must call to be saved.

Upwards of twenty thousand men worked in these woods. Everett had no doubts whatsoever that God had called him to bring them the gospel.

He parted from John Salverson to seek out a bunk in one of the two long bunkhouses. The first, though packed with bunks, hadn't a space left. The second had two. One upper bunk near the entrance, and one lower at the back of the room. The closer upper looked to have a broken board. Scratch that. He moved through the room and tossed his bundle on the open bottom bunk then deftly dropped to the floor and peered beneath, just to be sure there weren't any boards about to drop out as soon as he lay down that night.

Satisfied, he stood and brushed his hands together. He went back outside and put Buddy up in the barn before heading to the cookhouse to introduce himself to the cookee.

A robust man glanced up from his work as Everett approached the kitchen end of the building. A pile of unpeeled potatoes was mounded on his worktable to one side of him, and a heap of red meat to the other. Food enough to feed the army of men that would bustle in at nightfall. Everett cut to the chase. "Good afternoon. I'm Everett Shepherd. Traveling preacher. I'll be staying for a while. I won't ask for anything preferential. Just wanted to say hello."

The man eyeballed him through his short speech then cleaved a large chunk of meat and dropped pieces into a huge pot.

"Need some help around here? I'm not busy."

Another stare.

"I guess that's a no." Everett glanced at the woodbin beside the stove. "Looks like you could use another armload of firewood. Maybe I'll split a little."

The man sauntered to the monstrous cast-iron stove. After a cursory swipe of his hands across his apron, he reached for the oversized enamel coffeepot sitting on the back, pulled a tin cup off a shelf, and poured it nearly to the brim with coffee black as tar and nearly as thick. He held it out to Everett.

"Thanks. Smells good."

Everett took the cup and moved to a bench seat at the end of a long table.

"My boy usually gets the woodbin after supper. He'll be grateful it's done," said the man before going back to whacking meat.

Steam tingled rich aroma up his nostrils as Everett sipped. He never complained about the insipid, caramel-colored stuff the church ladies perked at his sending church, because they happily proclaimed him the nicest preacher boy they ever knew. They wouldn't think he was so good if they'd met the man he used to be.

But that was past. Over and forgiven. Now he lived in the power and grace of the Holy Spirit.

Before long he'd finished the bold brew and hastened to the woodpile. His muscles needed working, and it felt good to swing an axe again. He'd always been called rangy and corded like a leather whip and just as tough to break. Because he was a preacher now didn't mean he should turn soft.

He should have done as much for Adair at his store. Next time he passed through, he'd offer to trade one of Angeline's splendid home-cooked meals for a full woodbox. But would such an overture appear as though he had designs on Miss Adair? If his earlier suspicion about Hankins was right, Captain Adair was probably used to men sniffing around for her favor.

Hankins. Never did give his first name, but soon enough Everett meant to know all the jacks.

It was past dark before the men returned to camp. Hardly a soul took notice of him while they lumbered toward the cookhouse and ate their supper in relative silence. Platter after platter of stewed meat, boiled potatoes, and vegetables appeared, and gallon after gallon of coffee was drunk. Piles of sliced bread disappeared in moments, and it ended with slabs of pie, quartered in tins. Not until the last spoonful was shoveled down and the last belch expelled did the men begin conversing or move from their places.

An animated fellow across the room elicited a few laughs from the man nearest him. Everett ambled over. "Mind if I join you?"

"It's a free country." He was younger, maybe early twenties, with vim customary to the age. Freckles dotted his face beneath a mop of reddish-brown hair.

"That was a tasty meal. Cookee is worth his salt."

The fellow patted his middle. "Yep. Say, you're new here."

"Everett Shepherd." They shook hands. "I'm preacher to the camps. Plan to stay at this one for a while though."

"A preacher!" The guy nearly shouted. "You hear that, Joe? We got us a preacher all the way up here."

A wiry man with scraggly gray whiskers, who must be Joe, sniffed. "I reckon they got to find a man wherever he goes. Can't leave well enough alone."

Everett chuckled. He wasn't offended. "Nice to meet you, Joe. I didn't catch your name," he said to the younger man.

"I'm Fred Barker. Freddy to these guys."

"Nice to meet you too, Fred. Thanks for letting me join you."

"I ain't got no beef. 'Specially with a preacher. Well"—he slapped his leg—"guess I'd better shove off. Say, Joe, walk me out, won't you?" He winked at Joe. Everett probably wasn't meant to see that. Freddy was likely offering Joe an escape.

"Hope to see you both at the Sunday service," Everett said as the two departed. Freddy leaned close to Joe's shoulders, whispering and laughing.

Everett shook his head. A bit of mockery was to be expected. For the next ten minutes, he acquainted himself with one man and another and invited them to the service on Sunday. Only three promised to attend.

Finally, he made his way to the bunkhouse. Dozens of men were inside, most in their sweaty long johns, lounging in one manner or another by the dim light of oil lamps. The room was thick with body heat, woodsmoke, and damp. Stinking socks hung on a line strung across the middle of the room. The odor nearly bowled Everett over, but soon enough he became as used to it as in years past.

He made his way to his bunk, but a fellow jumped up and stopped him from sitting down. "You can't sleep there."

"I didn't think this bed was taken."

"It's got fleas. Bad fleas." He scratched himself.

They all had fleas, no doubt. It came with the territory, but Everett wouldn't argue. "I guess I'll find another place then."

"It's okay. We rustled you up a mattress over here, closer to the fire." He brushed a finger under his nose.

Everett hesitated. Something was up—or maybe he was overthinking things. He gathered up his bedroll, brushing it off just in case. "Lead on."

The mattress lay on the floor to the side of the woodstove. It looked innocent enough. He tossed down his bedroll and bent to undo it when a sudden *whack* stung across his backside. Everett spun around. A few men looked on, grinning from ear to ear or snickering under their breaths. No one was close enough to administer that swat. He determined to ignore the brutal welcome and turned back to his task.

Whack! Harder this time. Everett nearly lost his footing. He spun again. "Who did that?" Anger threatened the edges of his voice, and his torso tightened into bands.

Shrugs.

He glanced them over, one and all. Slowly, deliberately,

he turned around and yanked on the rope holding his bedroll together. There was shuffling behind as if the men were going back to their affairs. He spread the roll open and was about to kneel on it when—*whack!*

This time the blow did topple him. He landed on the mattress and sprang back to his feet in nearly the next instant. He glared at the men, but a slight movement in the rafters above caught his eye. He pretended for the moment not to have noticed the culprit, because they were all complicit. He eyed them, one by one. They stared back. Everett methodically rolled up his shirt-sleeves, exposing hard, muscled forearms. A couple of the older men backed off, while a few his own age took his measure, and one of the younger fellows gaped. Joe—oh, he recognized him—sniffed and shifted into the crowd.

"I don't suppose it was any of you men who accosted me after all." He planted his hands on his hips. "No. I expect it was my new friend Freddy." He purposely used the friendly version of Fred's name. "Wasn't it?" Now he turned his gaze directly upward at the young man.

Freddy lay prone across the beam, eyes bugging out of his freckled face. His mouth opened like a frog's, but he'd no time to spit out a reply before Everett reached up, snatched him by the ankle, and yanked him down in a hard fall. Thankfully for Freddy, Everett knew the mattress would break most of it.

Stunned a little, Freddy got to his feet. His scowl was fierce, but then he looked down at Everett's squared fists. Everett had no plans to hit the boy or anyone else for that matter. But he wasn't opposed to striking a little respectful fear in the man either. And man Freddy was, freckles or no.

"I appreciate the humorous welcome as well as any man, but I know you won't be doing something like that again, will you, Fred?" This time he offered a little mutual respect.

Freddy dusted off his long johns. He turned and bent over to pick up what must have been the instrument of Everett's torture—a long, thin board with a rubber boot sole nailed to it. Everett couldn't resist. He raised his leg and gave one push. Not even a hard one. Just enough boot to send Freddy tumbling onto the mattress once more. Freddy spun onto his back, eyes narrowed.

Everett smiled. "I wouldn't have done that, but I couldn't hear your answer."

Freddy's nostrils flared, but only for a moment. He glanced around the roomful of chuckling men then jumped up. "No, preacher man, I won't be doing that again." He gave a rueful glance at the mattress. "There's your bed." He pushed off through the crowd as the men dispersed, leaving Everett to set up more peaceful quarters.

CHAPTER 4

Angeline climbed out of bed Saturday morning while it was still dark. She longed for the days to lengthen, for the hours of sunlight to peek over the trees while they still slept and to stretch on and linger long into the evening, but that wouldn't happen for months yet. Now was the season of darkness, when shadows finally emerged well past Purty's morning milking hour. Having to rise in the dark usually made her groggy, but not today. She pulled on her layers of woolen socks and underthings and donned her heaviest skirts and sweater. Then she slipped out with a milk pail while the captain still snored. She wanted his coffee fresh and waiting when she told him of her plans for tomorrow, and she hadn't quite worked out the details of her explanation yet. She intended to be on Blackjack heading off to the lumber camp at daylight.

She could say that she was just going on a ride. A good, long, thinking ride. Her father was keen, however, and he'd be on to her, getting out the details, even though riding into the forest wasn't an unusual thing for her to do. Angeline had wandered this country since she was barely old enough to climb over a fallen tree. She'd explored miles of wild territory and knew each river and fishing hole in a ten-mile radius. She found the places where the badgers dug their burrows into hillsides and the meadows where the deer came out to graze. She had done her share of twirling in the tall grass in an afternoon's gloaming, and she had climbed the hills and perched in tall trees to watch the sunsets. Just the same, she'd admired the sunrise from a canoe on various inland lakes.

Now she set down her pail long enough to grab up the shovel leaning against the barn and scrape away the snow so she could pull open the door.

In only minutes, she was lighting the lantern and feeding the critters. Taking up the three-legged stool, she scooted close to Purty. "I know I'm a little early this morning, Purty. I'm sure you don't mind."

The cow chewed, but her big, glassy eye rolled back toward Angeline as though she understood and approved. Angeline rubbed her hands together to make sure her palms were good and warm before she reached for the cow's udders. Soon, the zip of milk sang against the slats of the wooden bucket and quickly turned to the sound of liquid foam.

Angeline hummed softly, a made-up tune. Would they sing in Preacher Shepherd's church service tomorrow? She'd no idea. What was that hymn Mama used to sing? If only she could remember all the words. "I love to tell the story, of unseen things above. Of Jesus and His glory. Of Jesus and His love. Hm…hm…" She didn't think she had the tune right, nor could she recall the other words.

What were those unseen things? Were they golden harps in a glistening, jeweled kingdom? What was heaven really like? Hopefully the preacher hadn't forgotten his promise to tell her those verses about it.

Could Mama hear her or see her? Probably not. Only God

must have that kind of power—unless He allowed her a peek now and then. That was another question she'd ask the preacher about. And was she a ghost, or did she have a body? And what about hell? Who went there? Mama said people most definitely did go there. What made it so? How did God decide? These were the things she must remember to find out.

Oh, so many questions!

Half an hour later, with the milk strained and cooling on the back porch—no need for a tank of cold water in the winter—and with eggs and fresh side pork sizzling in the skillet, Angeline set plates on the table and pulled the boiling coffee off the stove just as her father came into the kitchen, buttoning his shirtsleeves.

"Good morning, Captain."

"Morning, Angel." He moved to the shelving that held his favorite tin cup and filled it. "Kind of at it early this morning, aren't you? All the smells woke me up."

She hefted the skillet with her apron wrapped around her hand and scooped his meal onto his plate. "Couldn't sleep, so I decided to get your breakfast started. Been thinking I'd start early tomorrow too, and then take a little trip west." She forced a nonchalance into her voice as best she could but peeked at him briefly to catch his reaction as she moved around the small table. She dished her own plate and pressed on. "You know, over to that camp where the preacher will be speaking. Figured I might as well hear the man too."

She glanced at him again. He had his cup poised halfway to his mouth, a scowl furrowing his brow. He lowered the cup without sipping. "So, that's what you thought, is it?"

She returned the skillet to the stove. "Yes, that's what I thought."

"What makes you suppose I'm about to let my daughter ride alone into a camp full of rowdy lumberjacks?" His voice was calm, but there was a marked demand to be answered in his tone.

"It's not like I don't ride out alone from time to time. There are men all around these woods."

"Of which you stay clear, I should hope."

"'Course, Captain. 'Course." She pulled out her chair with a little more force than necessary and plopped down. She leaned forward. "But how else am I going to be able to hear the preaching? He doesn't have a proper church and pulpit to preach from like Mama enjoyed when she was my age."

"Your mother wouldn't have missed anything if there hadn't been one."

"How do you know? Mama set a lot of store by preaching and teaching and reading the Bible. You know it, so don't deny it. I think she would have been just as hungry for it as me if she was here."

His eyes flashed, but he lowered them quickly and forked half an egg into his mouth followed by a big hunk of bacon. He chewed, and it wasn't only on the bacon. Angeline could see him gnawing on reasons for her not to go. She wasn't naive. She knew what those reasons were. She also knew her father was loathe to speak of them aloud.

"I'll be careful, Pa." She rarely called him Pa. Though she loved him with all her heart, she'd grown up calling him Captain, and sometimes he jokingly called her his *little sailor*. Both terms were equally endearing, yet while others also called him Captain, *Pa* was reserved for her alone in the whole wide world.

He swallowed and took a draw on his coffee, but his glance came to her over the cup's rim. He slowly set it down. "You can't be careful enough around men like that. They're hellions, and if you rode into that camp unattended, there'd be nothing to stop any of them from getting notions. Some might grab an opportunity if it presented itself."

She knew how it pained him to speak of such things. "I'll take my pistol then." He had given her a pistol a few years back, around the time her womanhood started coming on her. He taught her how to draw a careful aim and shoot straight. He even gave her bullets for practicing with and didn't hold back. It was a little gun, and she couldn't shoot far with it, but he told her it wasn't likely she'd have to. He also said that there weren't many reasons she'd need to carry it, but there were some. A bear might charge her, but only if she bothered it or its cubs. A wolf pack could bring trouble, but she knew where they liked to roam, and she stayed out of their territory. A cougar, now that was one thing in the wild that could raise the hair on your neck, but chances were that if it stalked you, you'd not know it until you were a goner. But if you did know, you might be able to scare it off with a shot or two.

The biggest predator she had to concern herself with, Pa said, was a man with no morals. She might need her gun to scare such a fellow off or to maim him, and even then, they'd have the captain to deal with.

She raised her chin. "All those men know who my father is, and they wouldn't dare bother me knowing you'd put them to the post and horsewhip them."

He took another bite of his eggs, and though it wasn't his manner to speak while he ate, he did this time. "Some of them might not care and think the risk was worth it."

She blushed, knowing just what he meant, but she was firm. "Well, I'm going out there. You might just have to give yourself to praying for my safety until I get back."

"You're just planning to defy me?"

"I'm grown enough to make up my mind. You always say so about other things."

"That right?" He shoved the last morsel into his mouth and

pushed back his chair. He rose and stood so she had to look up at him.

She swallowed slowly, her gaze crawling upward from her plate to his face. "Yessir, Captain. That's right."

He reached for a napkin and wiped his mouth, but his eyes didn't leave her. He crumpled and tossed it back down to the table. "Then I reckon you'd better wake me early tomorrow morning too, so I have time to wash up before we go."

Her mouth gaped a little bit, his words catching her by surprise. "Y–you'll come hear the preacher?"

"That camp is no place for a woman, but if you insist on this strong-willed notion of yours, the least a man can do for his own daughter is accompany her into the den of lions."

She picked up her fork to hide the smile that longed to burst out, but then she decided it didn't matter. She dropped it again and lunged to her feet, throwing her arms around her father. "Oh, thank you, Captain. Thank you. I can hardly wait."

"This won't become a habit."

She sat back down and waited until he nearly reached the door, and then with a twitch in her lips said, "It might."

CHAPTER 5

Everett scratched. Neck, shoulder blades, rib cage, scalp... *Ugh.* He couldn't stop. Never in his life had he been so flea-bitten.

Freddy's eyes had gleamed as he stalked away from his little prank last night. Clearly, whipping the preacher like a bad schoolboy wasn't all the young man had in mind. He'd purposely given Everett the buggiest mattress in the camp.

Everett should have realized. He'd seen this little number done before. Likely, at least a handful of men were in on it, including Joe. He and Freddy had strolled out of the cookhouse shoulder to shoulder last night. Their type liked their pranks. Who better to play them on than a preacher who came to tell them they needed to let Jesus change their hearts? He'd been a ripe candidate.

During breakfast, some men didn't bother hiding their snickers as he twitched. They headed off to the woods straight away after chowing down their plate-sized flapjacks, small log piles of sausages, gloppy oatmeal, runny eggs with crisp edges, and coffee. Meanwhile, Everett dragged out the offensive mattress and gave his bedding a good shaking. Maybe he'd hang it in a tree branch and let the bugs freeze out.

After handling that offensive task, he sat down in the cookhouse to pen a list of Bible verses for Angeline Adair. He pictured her dark eyes and the upturned look on her pretty face when she spoke of wanting to learn.

You're not here for that. You're here to preach the Word.

His old self crept up on him sometimes, taunting him with what he might be missing. Before he met Christ, he'd never let himself pass up time with a woman. It didn't matter who she was, whether she was spoken for, or even if she was married. If Everett wanted her, he took what he wanted as long as the woman was willing.

I'm not that man anymore. He prayed, "I'm not the dead man I used to be. I'm changed, thanks be to You, Father. I submit my flesh to You. May it not overpower me."

A scripture passage whispered through his thoughts, encouraging him. Then the Spirit brought other passages to mind to write down for Angeline and her father, should the captain be willing to read them. Words poured out as he penned her a letter with those scriptures.

Dear Miss Adair, as promised, here are some verses to consider concerning heaven, along with brief explanations we can discuss further in future.

First, let it be settled in your mind that our spirits return immediately to God upon our deaths. There is no sleep for our souls. Some mistake the reference of I Thessalonians 4:13, the state of our physical bodies, with that of our souls. But even our physical bodies will one day be resurrected and made new for eternity, without ailment or sin, for God does not abandon His creation, but rather, by His Son's death on the cross, has made a way to redeem it.

As to immediacy, be assured that the very instant your mother passed, she was ushered lovingly into the presence of her Father.

Everett referenced Luke 23:42-43 and Ecclesiastes 12:7

then went on to explain the soul's conscious state in the Luke 16 story of the rich man and Lazarus.

As to what heaven might be like, one cannot imagine that the God who made the earth would make His own dwelling less glorious. He described it as "paradise," just like Eden.

Everett told her of the future kingdom God would establish with His saints. Scouring the pages of his Bible, jotting references, he considered his own parents enjoying heaven's splendors. One day he would surely see them again, and oh, the stories they would share! One of those stories might even be about tomorrow and his first service preaching to the lumberjacks!

Sunday morning, Everett awoke with just a few new fleabites. With a little ointment smeared on them, he could ignore their irritation long enough to preach his first sermon. He tucked his Bible under his arm and headed toward the bunkhouse door. Halfway across the room, he recognized the fellow he'd met on the road. He nodded a greeting. "Hankins?"

"Hey, Preacher."

"Wondered when we'd bump shoulders. You've been busy the past couple of days."

"That's why God gave us Sunday to rest though, right?" Hankins smirked.

"And as a day of praise and reflection. That's why we call it the Lord's Day. Heading to breakfast?" His question left Hankins without space for rebuttal.

"That I am."

"I'm going that way myself." They stepped outdoors into a clear day, cold as the dickens. Everett's breath came out in a cloud of vapor. "Maybe you'll stay for the service afterward."

"Service! The preaching, you mean?" Hankins sounded surprised that Everett would suggest such a banal way to spend his morning.

Others also trod in the direction of the cookhouse. A couple men stood shaving over a bowl of water that had to be almost as frigid as the air. Still, their suspenders hung around their hips, and they were shirtless in the cold. A few others puffed on pipes around the doorways.

Hankins pulled open the cookshack door and let Everett lead the way. Everett bobbed his head in reply and to clear the low doorjamb. "Just a short sermon. I promise."

Hankins grunted as they got into the mess line. "I dunno. Kind of got my day planned. Pretty well packed full."

Everett held out his plate while the cookee dropped biscuits on it and poured a sludge of sausage gravy over the top. "I'm sure everyone does. That's why I won't make it long. I just want to give you fellas a little bit of encouragement from the Word before you get into a new week."

"I reckon all that kind of talk will just go in one ear and out the other. We've got plenty other things to think on during the week."

"But there's always room for God's voice. Thank you," he said to the cookee.

Hankins brushed past. Everett followed him. Hankins swung his leg over a bench at the far end of the room, and Everett positioned himself on the seat beside the sinewy lumberjack. "I don't recall catching your first name."

"Mick." Hankins squared himself to his plate, fork in hand.

"Mind if I call you Mick, or do you prefer Hankins?"

"Call me whatever you like," he said with finality as he plowed into his meal.

Some men were already finished well before Everett, so he decided to get on with it before they all got up and cleared out. He pushed his plate back and stood.

Mick was already scraping his plate clean. "You gonna eat that?"

"Help yourself."

Without so much as a *don't mind if I do*, Mick pulled Everett's plate close and proceeded to finish off his meal.

Bible in hand, Everett worked his way to the front of the room and cleared his throat. "Excuse me, men. If you've a mind to have a listen while you finish your coffee, I've got a few words to share with you this morning." The men quieted. Only a tinkling of dishware could be heard. Most of them turned his way while others briskly made their escape.

"As you probably know by now, I'm the new pastor around here. God laid a special call on my life to bring you His Word, since you can't get out of the woods to a place of worship on Sunday. It's as simple as that."

Brushing the room with a quick glance and not seeing anything ready to be thrown at him, he continued. "Some of you have asked me why I'd want to do that. Well, there's a fairly simple answer to that too. God changed me. Changed my heart." He held out his hand, palm up. "One day he got hold of it and squeezed." Everett drew out the last word and made a fist in front of him. "He squeezed until I knew there was no getting loose. What's more, I didn't want to." He lowered his arm. "See, I'd been trying to get away from God for a long time, only I didn't know it. Once I figured out it was useless to keep fighting Him, I gave up. I gave in. I gave over."

Some of the men grew more attentive. A few more shuffled out the door.

Everett opened his Bible to a page he'd marked. "We can try to escape God, but there's no escaping hell if we keep running. It says here in Hebrews chapter two, verse three, 'How shall we escape, if we neglect so great salvation?' It's a rhetorical question.

That means the only real answer is, we won't.' "

Three more men hastened toward the door.

He was tempted to let a little hellfire and brimstone fly, but that was his flesh. He reined back. "God says over in Second Peter three, verse nine, that He is longsuffering and not willing that any should perish, but that all should come to repentance. God *wants* to save you. He already let Jesus pay the bill for your sin. But if you spit in His palm instead of accepting it, then it's no good. Won't you—"

The door swung open, letting in a flash of sunlight, but this time someone was coming in instead of going out. "Won't you..."

His jaw sagged on its hinges, and Everett was forced to pull it back up. Even so, his wits scattered.

Angeline Adair—eyes shining, fur-covered boots peeking from her long brown skirt that itself flounced from beneath a heavy woolen coat, cheeks blooming pink from winter air, and a long dark braid draped down over one shoulder from beneath a fur hat—stepped into the room with her gaze already intent on him.

"Won't you join us," Everett quickly amended, his mouth dry and peppery from the sausage gravy. What had he been going to say next? He had no idea.

Her father gave her a nudge and nodded toward a place at the back, but Angeline strode forward, straight to the space at the front table where only one man about her father's age sat. Was his name Willard?

Throughout the room, the men stared wide-eyed at her, grinning like fools. Probably thirty men had stayed to hear him preach. Now a few who'd left after breakfast filtered back inside. No doubt it wasn't to hear the powerful conclusion to his sermon.

The captain loosened his coat and lowered himself beside her.

"It's nice of you both to join us, Miss Adair, Captain Adair." Everett dipped his head. "Welcome."

He faced the room again. One man whittled in the back. Another sucked his coffee down slowly and loudly, grinning after every lengthy slurp.

Everett looked down at his Bible then softly cleared his throat to begin again. "We were just refreshing ourselves with the reminder that God wants no one to perish. He longs for all to accept His gift of salvation, but it's also within each of our power to ignore or outright reject it."

Captain Adair folded his arms snugly across his chest. His burly brows furled. Everett looked away from him in an effort not to let his gaze linger on Miss Adair. The slurper winked.

"Y–yes...so because of that, we all have an obligation to make our salvation sure. To let God squeeze"—he started to make a fist again but thought better of it and lowered his hand—"our hearts. Better yet, to let Him shape them into what He desires them to be."

He no longer remembered where he was going with all this, but the woman seated only three steps away watched him with expectancy. There was at least one soul in this room who wanted to hear the Word. Maybe even more than one.

Give me clarity in my thoughts, Lord. He looked again at the Bible, open in his hand, and then for the next ten minutes, Everett expounded on God's love and craving to have a relationship with man, if man was willing. He described God's gift like a man bringing a present to a woman he was courting—he almost stuttered there but forced himself not to glance at Angeline and instead caught the smirk of Mick—but the gift only mattered if she accepted it. So it was with God's gift of salvation, he explained. If a man saw his sin nature for what it was, so that he might understand his *need* to accept Christ's atonement, he could reach out to God and claim his gift by faith alone. "Just like the thief on the cross beside Jesus," he said as a footnote.

Everett felt breathless when he finished, yet he hadn't preached hard. He offered a final prayer. When he raised his head, he couldn't help a small smile at Angeline. Her father was already shoving to his feet.

Everett hurried forward. "I'm glad you came. I think your presence here might have encouraged a few others to attend too."

The captain's eyes darted to his daughter. "I'm sure you're right about that. Shall we?" He stepped aside for her.

"We don't have to rush out so fast, Captain. Do we?" She gave her father what seemed a teasing smile.

Just then Mick Hankins walked up. "Morning, Captain. Hey, Angel. Surprised to see you here."

Angel? He called her by her father's pet name?

"Good day, Mick. I'm surprised to see you here too." Wryness laced her tone.

"I decided to stick around and see what our preacher man here had to offer."

That was a lie. He hadn't stayed. He'd slid back in after Angeline. Nevertheless, Everett stretched out his hand to the man. "Glad you condescended to sit in, Mick. Every man that comes to hear the gospel encourages another man to do the same."

Mick sniffed. He slid gray eyes at the lady, and Everett could sense him biting back a retort. Instead, Mick smiled at her. "May I walk you out?"

Angeline glanced toward Everett. Her lips pursed in hesitancy.

Everett plunged in. "I'll come along too. I have something to send with you and the captain, if that's all right."

Why did he feel such satisfaction at the look of frustration

Mick was too slow to hide? He whispered to his soul that it was concern for Angeline's spiritual well-being. Even so, his soul whispered back, and none too quietly, that it was merely his own flesh rearing up yet again.

CHAPTER 6

Angel hadn't imagined a sermon to be quite like that. The captain had led her to believe the preacher would shake his fist while his temples throbbed with the shouting he'd do. There might be pacing and gesticulating and a finger pointing at each one of them. They'd be mesmerized with fear.

She'd been mesmerized, certainly. However, Preacher Shepherd's words exuded compassion. He compelled them by God's mercy to repent if they would escape judgment. He'd gestured, but in a manner that described God's longing for human fellowship—as if the host of heaven weren't enough for the Creator. Rather, as though all the saints of the ages stood beside Him, saying, "Come! Join us!" Her mother included.

Angeline could almost hear her mother singing like she used to in the garden.

There'd not been singing during the lumberjack service, and she was mildly disappointed. Her mother had spoken of hymns sung by the congregation in church. There was one Mama always sang while she was outdoors scattering corn to the chickens or pinning laundry on the line or even just walking down the lane with her face tilted to the sunshine. The tune wove through her thoughts. Did the preacher know that song?

She peered at her left where he walked on the other side of her father. Mick strolled on her right, saying something about a visit, but she hardly heard him.

"Preacher Shepherd, don't you ever sing during your services?"

The preacher grinned with some chagrin. "I'm not much of a singer, Miss Adair."

"Oh? The captain is a fine baritone." She eyed her father. "Isn't that so, Captain?"

He grunted. "Just because your mother used to say so doesn't make it true."

"I'll vouch for her word. He carries a wonderful tune." She turned to Mick. "What about you, Mick? Do you sing?"

He winked. "Only when I take a bath."

When was the last time he'd done that? He certainly hadn't bothered recently.

"Hm. Too bad." She turned back to the preacher. "You could use some singing in your service. I bet the men would like a bit of music to liven up their Sunday."

"I'll take your advice into account. Granted, it's the usual order of things." Appreciation twinkled in Preacher Shepherd's dark eyes. "Do you know any hymns?"

"Only one, fully, and some sailing songs the captain taught me."

"And good songs they are," the captain said.

"'Jesus Savior Pilot Me?' Or maybe 'Will Your Anchor Hold?'" The preacher snapped his fingers. "Here's another: 'A Shelter in a Time of Storm.' That's an excellent hymn. Any of those?"

She chuckled. "No, not those kinds of sailing songs, I'm afraid. It seems he's neglected a few." She eyed her father.

"Maybe if you can sing a line or two of the hymn you know, I'll recognize it."

She felt like she might blush but licked her lips and plunged in with the familiar song.

"I sing the mighty power of God
That made the mountains rise,
That spread the flowing seas abroad
And built the lofty skies."

The preacher joined in, and their voices lofted to the skies around the stable.

"You do know it!" She bounced to her toes. "Did you hear him, Captain?"

Her father snickered. "Everyone heard him. It's that tune your mother always sang."

"Yes, that's the one." She smiled at the preacher. "I hope you teach it to the men some Sunday. The captain knows it well, so he will have to join in."

Her father scoffed yet again, but the preacher's smile stretched.

Mick had moved off and begun hitching her horse to their wagon. She caught him eying them over Blackjack's head as he snugged the collar against the horse's shoulders and buckled on the traces.

"Thank you for tending Blackjack, Mick."

"Anytime, Angel." He stepped around Blackjack's head so that he stood close and lowered his voice. "You mind if I poke along with you and the captain a way? I've got nothing important to do that won't wait an hour or two, and I wouldn't mind a good walk."

"I'm afraid we can't linger. The captain doesn't like being away from the store long. It would be better if you had a horse."

He moved over and adjusted the breeching but cast a glance

toward the stable. "I suppose you're right." Besides the teamsters' horses, only a handful of loggers' animals were stalled inside. Most of the workers came by train as far as they could, then traveled on foot. Mick had always walked to the store. She could almost read his thoughts now.

Angeline turned. "How about you, Preacher Shepherd? Would you like to saddle up and ride along for a spell?" *Say yes before Mick asks you for your horse.*

"I wouldn't mind a little fresh air and exercise."

"You're welcome to ride along." Her father stepped to the wagon.

"I'll fetch Buddy." The preacher hastened off, but Mick lingered.

"You're getting pretty well acquainted with the sky pilot, I see."

"The. . .sky pilot? You mean the preacher?"

"That's what the jacks call him in these parts. Going to 'pilot our souls to the skies.'" He rolled his eyes.

But Angel smiled to herself as she took her father's hand. *Sky pilot.* It suited. She stretched her foot to the tall step and climbed effortlessly to the wagon seat. "My mother wished we had a church close by. She'd be glad he's here."

"Having a traveling preacher visiting camp isn't exactly what I'd call having a church."

The captain climbed aboard. "I would agree, but I can see it brings a little light to my Angel's life to hear a Sunday scorching."

She flapped the back of her hand against her father's thick coat. "Come now, Cap, you didn't hear any scorching and neither did I."

"Give him time. He'll soon start to blister the bark off the trees."

"I'm sure you're right about that." Resting an elbow on

Blackjack, Mick knuckled back his hat. "Pretty soon he'll stop being a novelty, and then he'll get to raising the roof." He and her father shared a nod.

Mick sounded jealous that the preacher had gained attention from the men. Maybe he was afraid his friends would give up their drinking and gambling and ruin his fun.

Or. . .was he jealous in another way? Mick wasn't a bad-looking fellow when he cleaned up. He had yellow-brown hair that he combed back with some tonic, and a fair profile. He was limber and strong. He sat a horse well when he had the chance. But there was a sharpness to him that cautioned her, not to mention he was too fond of drink. Whatever gave him the idea he could win her affection was beyond her.

The preacher led Buddy from the stable. Now there was a man who sat well in the saddle, and he hadn't vices, that was certain. She brightened once again. "Ready, Preacher?"

"Sure am. Enjoy your Sunday afternoon, Mick." He tipped his hat as Mick backed away from Blackjack, and the captain raised the reins.

She didn't look back to see whether Mick watched them pull out or if he stalked off.

The wagon creaked along over the frozen ground as the camp fell behind. The preacher drew his horse alongside the wagon.

"I'm not sure I'll ever get used to being called Preacher. If you folks wouldn't mind calling me by my given name of Everett, I'd appreciate it." He caught her gaze, and warmth curled through her body despite the frosty air. She turned her eyes for fear the feeling was creeping out on her cheeks.

The captain assented. "We've been on a first-name basis with most of the men who come to the store. I reckon we can call you Everett."

Should she offer to let him call her Angeline or Angel? Mick took the liberty. All she could sputter was, "Y–yes, I guess that would be all right."

He brightened with a smile that rivaled the sunlight reflecting on the snowy pathway. "Thanks. Makes me feel more at home. After all, you did let me sleep in your barn, and you fed me two fine meals. We're friends, by my estimation." He hitched his shoulders and faced the road, but as she glimpsed him again, he still looked inordinately pleased.

And Angeline felt the same.

"You might as well call me Angeline. Miss Adair—why, no one calls me that."

Her father cast her a sly glance, one she wished she hadn't noticed. He was gathering ideas, for sure.

"I don't believe I've ever met a lady with that name before."

"Her mother named her," the captain said. "She thought God had sent her an angel." The captain's voice changed with a hint of some memory that wrangled it. He took a fast breath. "Angel doesn't always live up to it."

Angeline laughed. "No, that's true. I can rock the captain's boat a bit roughly at times."

Everett gave an understanding nod. "I'm sure we've all given our parents cause to worry now and again. Some of us more than others."

"Not you though."

He shook his head. "Oh, you'd be surprised. I've done plenty for which I'm ashamed."

She scoffed. "I can hardly believe that."

"You mind," the captain said. "A man knows what he is or what he's done. He faces up to it in private if not openly. If Everett says he's done things to be ashamed of, you'd best believe him." He turned a look at their companion. "I've dealt with every manner of man in my life. What manner were you before you took up Bible thump—er—preaching?"

Angeline was a bit surprised that her father would ask so personal a question in her hearing. Maybe he was trying to prove some point. But Everett didn't hesitate for more than a moment.

"That's a fair question. Truth be told, my testimony is important to me, not because I like talking about what a man of degradation I was, but because I like telling how God sees fit to change the worst of the lot."

Angeline slumped. "You make it sound like you were simply terrible."

"I suppose I was like a lot of those fellows at camp. Not bad as you might think, but reckless. I used to make my living in the camps as a teamster. That's how I came to own Buddy. He's done his share of muscle work, I can tell you. It's a piece of cake for him to carry me and a few books around the woods. But back then I caroused too much and cared too little. Spent my money on things that didn't matter and wasted my time in places I oughtn't have." His voice lowered. "Took up gambling and brawling, at the worst of it."

Her father tucked his chin and gave her a shrewd look, which she caught only briefly as Everett went on.

"Found out I was pretty good at a few things I'm not proud of now."

Angeline released a tight breath. No wonder he was built more for lumberjacking than for preaching, and maybe it was a good thing. Some of those woodsmen might toss a spindly preacher out on his ear.

Her father grunted. "Then you *found God*." Maybe Everett didn't catch it, but Angeline noted the bitter edge in his tone.

"Not exactly. Man doesn't go looking for God. I think you'd agree to that."

The captain was silent as he stared at Blackjack's rump

swaying ahead of them.

"No, I didn't find Him. I never even looked for Him. On the contrary. God found me. He wasn't afraid to follow me into the dark and desperate places where I was abiding. He came into the black cave of my life carrying a torch. He picked me up in my worst state of misery and pulled me out into the light of day."

"Sounds like flowery speech if you ask me."

"Captain." This time Angeline really did mean to rebuke her father. She respected him more than any man, but she would not abide his disrespect to the preacher. "It's Everett's story, and if that's the way it was, then that's the way it was. Only a minute ago you told me I ought to believe him if he said so." Determination flashed through her when she spoke his name. "Go ahead, Everett. I want to hear."

He exhaled. "That's about it. I was convicted of my sin. God came by the hand of another preacher. A fellow with a story like my own. He pulled me out of the gutter and got me sobered up." His brow curled when he looked at her. "I was particularly tired of my life just then, but he was a strong man, and I regarded that about him."

He turned his face toward the road ahead. "He began telling me the Word of God. I listened because I figured I owed him. As the Word sank into my heart, however, I saw the darkness of my sin. Pretty soon I was begging God to take it. Turned out I didn't need to beg. He'd been waiting for me to recognize I needed Him, just like He waits for every man and woman. From that day on, things began to change."

He reached into his coat pocket and pulled out a folded-up paper. "That reminds me, here are those verses I wrote down for you about heaven."

She reached for the page and opened it eagerly. Then her heart fell a little. After skimming over the initial remarks, she saw that the full passages weren't written out as she'd expected, but only referenced. "Th–thank you."

"Can you read my handwriting? I admit, my chicken-scratches leave something to be desired."

"Yes, I can read it all right. It's just. . .I don't have a Bible to look them up. I was hoping—"

"That's no trouble. I can read them with you." He offered so quickly that she looked up at him in surprise.

The captain shifted his weight on the bench seat, jiggling her. He likely didn't want to hear talk that reminded him of Mama leaving them, although Angeline figured it would do him the best kind of good.

Everett went on. "Maybe I can ride over again and bring my Bible another day. Would that be all right?" This time he looked askance at her father, who grumbled acquiescence.

"I'll put a venison roast in the oven early on Tuesday if you can come for a midday meal then." She turned to Cap. "Wouldn't you say Tuesday is fine?"

"The girl makes a mouthwatering venison roast," the captain admitted.

"I'd be happy to join you, both of you."

The captain set a hand on his knee. "'Course, I won't be listening to any more talk of heaven—nor hell for that matter. The two of you can yammer about it after we eat."

She chuckled. "All right. Thank you, Everett." His name came easily now.

He smiled, and the twinkle in his eyes pleased her. Men had often noticed her. The lumberjacks, railroad workers, even some of the Indian men that came around. But with Everett her reaction felt different. For the first time ever, Angeline didn't mind.

CHAPTER 7

Everett wiped a gingham-checked napkin across his lips. For the second time he exclaimed how it was the best venison roast he'd had in a year.

Angeline beamed as she cleared their plates. "I'm glad I could appease your appetite."

Everett thought of all the ways she appeased his appetite then reprimanded himself. He was here to teach her, not to court her.

Wasn't he?

He hadn't mentioned to anyone at camp where he was headed today. The men would razz. It was bad enough that he took harassment from the likes of old Joe and Freddy Barker. Willard Skivvens, the older gentleman who sat at the front for the preaching on Sunday, nodding in agreement now and then, warned the troublemakers to leave off. He seemed to have decided to look out for the new preacher.

Everett drew his Bible close and opened it to a passage as Angeline stacked the dirty dishes. Then she drew up the chair nearest him. She pulled the page of verses from her apron pocket and spread it open beside his Bible. "I'm anxious to hear what they say. I fear I'm not only in the wilderness of these

Minnesota woods, which is just fine, but I'm in a wilderness of understanding."

That insight brought him a smile. "We'll just start with this first one then."

"Do people in heaven remember us on earth?"

"People don't stop being who they were on earth. They remember their lives here. They remember the ones they loved, as we will learn when I read to you this section about a rich man and Lazarus."

Angeline pressed her palms to her cheeks. "Please. Read it to me."

For the next two hours Everett and Angeline read and discussed scripture together. Her hunger to know the Word led them down one path and another. It filled and exhausted him, and he loved every second of it.

Eventually the day drew on. "It'll be nightfall soon. We'll read more another time."

Her gaze was alight. Was it so wrong that he found her lovely? Was he stepping beyond God's will for his call by pondering over her in this way? Or maybe. . .just maybe, did God intend something more between them?

"Angeline, may I ask you something personal?" He glanced beyond her shoulder, but the captain hadn't made an appearance in nearly an hour. Not since he'd wandered in for a cup of thick coffee.

The corners of her mouth turned up with interest.

"It seems like most women prefer a life in town. What keeps you in the Northwoods?" He glanced at the doorway once more. "Is it your father? Or. . ." A small sigh escaped. He hurried on, hoping she hadn't noticed. "Is it Mick Hankins?"

Her breath hitched. The smile slipped off her lips. She gave a small shake of her head. "It's not Mick."

His shoulders relaxed.

"Is that what you really wondered? Goodness sakes, Mick isn't the kind of fellow... He isn't the sort of man..." Her chin twitched, and she turned to the sink. "The captain believes I'll get married soon, or at least I should." Her voice was soft, lowered no doubt, so that her father couldn't hear in the other room. "I suppose I shall do so one day, but..."

Everett slowly rose to his feet and quietly pushed his chair beneath the table. "But?"

She turned to face him again. "The captain needs me, even if he doesn't say so. If I married some fellow who comes and goes with the seasons, I might end up far away." Her chin came up.

"But don't you feel alone out here?"

"Alone?" She flipped her braid behind her. "I'm no more alone than you are. If you mean being female, I can handle myself. I can shoot a gun and throw a knife. Uncle Ironstone even taught me how to pitch an axe."

His gaze ran the length of her quick as a flash, and he had to force it not to linger in any one place. "I'm sure you can."

"He's not really my uncle, of course. He's an Indian friend of the captain. When the captain goes to collect merchandise at the train station, he asks Uncle Ironstone to keep an eye on me. He sits on the porch and whittles out spoons or throws his old tomahawk at a stump. If some lumberjack or railroad worker comes to make a purchase when I'm alone, he follows them in and sits by the stove, sharpening that very same tomahawk with a stone he keeps in his pocket. Everybody respects Uncle Ironstone."

Everett could imagine this "uncle" with a keen eye and a sharp blade watching over Angeline.

"You don't go along with your father?"

She shrugged. "Sometimes. But I usually stay to mind the

store." She skimmed her fingertips across a chairback. "I would like to see Duluth sometime. Maybe go to the church you attended."

"I'd like to show it to you."

Her gaze steadied on him. She took a step toward him and laid a touch on his forearm. The gentle pressure of her fingers sent a jolt through him more startling than a shot of rotgut. He pushed away that unfortunate memory and focused on her expression, soft and inviting.

"Maybe someday the captain and I can visit there with you."

With me? For a moment he thought he had said the words aloud as he stared at her pink lips. They begged. . .didn't they?

"Angel? Come on in here when you have a moment." Her father's voice drew Everett out of his enchantment, forcing him to swallow the knot in his throat.

She moved past him, and the clean, violet scent of her hair wafted into his nostrils, stealing his breath. Everett followed her, blinking hard to gather himself.

The captain stood at the counter. Before him lay a heavy black book with *Holy Bible* printed in worn lettering on the cover.

"Mama's Bible!" Angeline gasped. "You found it!"

"It wasn't lost." He sounded sheepish. "I didn't realize how much it meant to you. You might as well take it now."

She ran a hand across it reverently, and her voice quivered. "Everett came all this way to read me the verses." She glanced at him apologetically, but there wasn't the full sound of an apology in her voice.

Everett offered a smile. "It was no trouble. I would have done it anyway."

"Mama's Bible. . ." She picked it up. "Now I can reread all the scriptures we talked about. Oh, Cap." She grasped the Bible to her chest and threw one arm around her father. She pressed her face to his whiskery cheek.

"'Twasn't anything." His voice betrayed him. It *was* something. Adair's eyes had a misty look in them as she released him. "Well," he said loudly. "You'd better get moving, or it'll get dark and your horse will lose his footing on the corduroy."

"Buddy is sure-footed, but you're right. It's a long ride." Everett tugged on his winter coverings. "I'll give a little hay to Blackjack when I go out to the barn."

"Thank you, Everett." Did he imagine it, or did her appreciation extend beyond his offer to hay her horse or read the scriptures? What had happened between them? His thoughts filled with questions he hadn't considered a week ago—or ever.

Most of the men were bedding down by the time he reached camp. The bunkhouse stank as it always did of wet socks and sweat. He tried to remember the sweet smell of Angeline's hair.

It was no good. He couldn't escape the present odors. He dropped down on his bunk.

A balled-up shirt hit him in the chest, and he looked up at a grinning Mick Hankins. "Where you been all day, Preacher? Haven't seen you since breakfast."

Everett yanked off a boot. "Went calling on some folk."

"Folk, huh? Not the railroad camp?"

He shook his head and tugged off the other boot.

"You went to Adair's again today? You were just there on Sunday, if I recall. Getting kind of habit-forming for a man of the cloth, isn't it?"

"I'm not a man of the cloth. I'm just a God-fearing, gospel-preaching servant."

"With eyes for Adair's girl, I think."

Everett's gaze flashed up before he could stop it. What was Mick trying to egg him on for? Just to get at him? Or was he jealous?

"Don't worry yourself, Mick. I'm not courting her. Just helping her grow in her faith."

Mick chuckled. "'Helping her grow in her faith.' Now there's an angle I've never thought of."

Everett didn't like his insinuation. "Angeline is a respectable young lady. We'd do best to remember that."

"Would we?"

Everett was a preacher, but a man just the same. He had to bridle the wayward desires of his flesh just like anyone. But Mick Hankins wouldn't bother bridling himself. Everett knew his type with personal certainty.

He stood in his socks and unbuckled his britches. "Yes. You and I and every man here ought to act with respect toward every woman."

A narrow glint shone in Mick's gaze. "Are you implying that I've been disrespectful toward Angel?"

"I take issue with your suggesting you could pick her up with a line. Sounds more like a desire to use a gal than to know her selflessly."

"Oh, I wanna know her." He said it with the same leering tone that had brought on this discussion.

The urge to punch Mick in the mouth was strong. Everett hadn't anticipated this kind of battle with his past. He unbuttoned his shirt. "Why are you trying to egg me on, Mick?"

"Just wondering what kind of man you are, Preacher. And who you're trying to fool."

"I don't follow." He tossed the shirt aside and undid the top button of his long johns.

Mick snickered. "Sure you do."

Everett sat and yanked off his canvas pants to keep his hands from clenching. Mick was right. Notions regarding Angeline did swirl around in his head. If there was one thing Everett couldn't stand, it was a man who lied to himself, like he was lying now.

"Maybe I am interested in Miss Adair. But I can promise you this: I won't give her lines to hook her into something dishonorable, and I'll be praying long and hard about my actions toward her."

Mick sniffed. "That so? I never yet seen a woman who wanted a man to pray about whether she was worth pursuing. Good luck with it, Preacher. Maybe while your eyes are closed and your head is bowed, I'll go on over and court Angel myself, like I've been doing all along, telling her the things she *wants* to hear and making her *feel* the things she wants to feel."

Heat gathered in Everett's gut. In the old days he'd have swung a leg out and taken Mick down before knocking some sense into him. He stretched out, tucking his itching hands beneath his head. "Why don't we talk about this over coffee tomorrow. I'm tired."

Mick grinned. "Sure. We can have coffee and talk about Angel." He turned to shuffle off then darted one last jab. "But as far as I'm concerned, you're only in the way."

Everett wanted to roll over and not let Mick know he was well under his skin, but he didn't move. Mick was right. Everett was smitten by the girl!

He closed his eyes. *God, forgive my weakness on all counts. I don't want to be angry at Mick. He's no different than I was before you reached down and yanked me out of the gutter. How can I be thinking about a woman now? You've called me into this rough country to preach the gospel, not to court a gal. What kind of life could I even offer her?*

For all he knew, Angeline was no more interested in him than she was in Mick. Did he even dare hope for something more?

Give me wisdom, Father. He finally turned over and, thankfully, peace fell, and he slept.

That simple prayer helped Everett cease wrestling until the men came in from the woods the next evening. They consumed their supper without talking, as usual. But as pie was served and another gallon of coffee set down on the rough table, Everett made his way to Mick's table and swung his leg over the bench opposite him.

"Ready to talk?"

"What about?" Mick mauled his cherry pie. "Angel, you mean?" He spoke too loudly then swallowed and grinned. "I'm just joshing you, Preacher. I knew who you meant. Let me finish this off, and we'll take a walk." He nodded toward his cup. "Can I get you to fetch the pot and refill my cup?"

Everett stood and walked toward the table's end, retrieved the half-full pot, and came back. Mick had a funny look on his face, but when didn't he? Everett filled both their cups.

"Come on." Mick stood with his empty plate and dropped it into a waiting tub as they headed toward the door.

Cold air slapped Everett's face as they stepped out. They wore no coats, only flannel shirts and suspendered pants over their long johns. But the cold air would keep Everett's thoughts clear. Someone in one of the bunkhouses sawed on a fiddle, and the scent of pipe tobacco wafted into the night air.

Mick cleared snow off a log bench and sat down. "Go ahead."

"I want to clear up any misunderstanding." Everett had his speech planned out. He didn't want to have Mick thinking they were in a competition. That would be no way to win him to Christ, nor to help Angeline. "I know how we men talk sometimes. I only want to see Angeline treated well." He sipped his coffee and waited for Mick's response.

Mick took a long slurp. "I ain't offended much. Just a tad jealous, I suppose. I'll tell you square, Preacher, I aim to win that girl. You said you're interested, so you ought to know what you're up against."

"Fair enough." Everett felt Mick's eyes studying him. "Angeline knows her own mind."

"I'll grant you that." Mick gulped down the rest of his coffee. "You done?"

Everett figured he was referring to their conversation, but he finished the quickly cooling coffee and tossed the dredges into the snow. "Now I am."

Mick held out his hand. "Give me your cup. I'll take it back inside. Cookee gets madder than a rabid fox when we take his dishes and don't bring 'em back while his water's hot."

Everett handed him the tin cup. "Thanks for the coffee and talk."

"All's fair in love and war. Isn't that what they say?"

"I don't think you'll find it in scripture."

Mick chuckled. "I suppose not." He went away whistling.

There'd be no beating around the bush between him and Mick from here on. He only hoped there'd never be a reason for them to really lock horns.

His head felt heavy and tired. Probably the result of getting their meeting off his mind.

He stumbled near the door and caught himself on the sill. What in the. . .

Fuzziness crept around the edges of his vision. *Hey.*

His head felt like lead, and he couldn't find the door latch. He spun and leaned against the building, reaching for something to grasp on to, but nothing was in front of him besides the black, cold night.

Voices sounded distant. He stumbled into the snow. Better go to the outhouse. No. Better go to the stable and feed Buddy. No.

Everett swayed, holding his ground. . .almost. With Mick's name tangled on his lips, he tipped headlong into the snow.

CHAPTER 8

"Knockout drops!" Angeline paced across the front porch, her mouth pursed in anger. "The next time I see Mick Hankins, I'll break his jaw myself!" She shook a fist, and her shawl slipped from her shoulder.

Everett pocketed his hands in his red-checked mackinaw. "Mick just wants me to look foolish. I wouldn't want a woman stepping in for me."

She tightened her shawl and peered down the road. He was right, of course. Her tension ebbed, and she felt sheepish at her unladylike outburst.

Mick had brought her a bouquet of princess pine and bird berries yesterday, all tied with a bow of dry grass. It seemed sweet and festive when she set it on the sill of her bedroom window. A fella hadn't ever brought her anything like that before. They came mooning around, but never with a present. What had gotten into Mick to even think of fashioning such a thing?

"It just makes me so mad! Why would he do such a thing?"

"Jealousy makes a man do things he normally wouldn't." His voice lowered.

"Jealousy!" She flashed a look at him, and the glimmer in

his eyes sent a rush through her blood. *Oh.* "You mean. . . You think. . ." Her cheeks heated.

"Does that upset you? That Mick thinks I might be courting you?"

She looked straight at him now, but she could see right off that he wasn't admitting anything. But upset her? Quite the contrary. She only wished it were true. She gave a hesitant shake of her head.

His breath skittered out. "Good. I don't want troubles between Mick and me to worry you. We'll work it out, one way or another."

He sounded so relieved. How much should she tell him? "Mick. . .wants me to have feelings for him. But I never could, especially now." She leaned against a porch post.

"Now?"

Everett's Adam's apple bobbed in his throat, and she wished she hadn't said that last part. As soon as he left, she'd go straight upstairs and toss out that old bundle of twigs Mick brought her. She didn't want or need his presents. She pulled back her shoulders. "After what he did to you," she grumbled. "I don't even know what I did to give him the idea I might like him that way. I don't!"

"Sometimes a kind word is all it takes to pique a man's interest. A gracious smile. A laugh at his jokes. Men are putty to a pretty girl, and their heads can be thick as oak bark." He gazed up the road. "Believe me, we're not very good at recognizing the obvious sometimes."

His words, spoken so soft and gentle, made her feel a little better, but she also felt guilty. She'd probably encouraged Mick to think she liked him more than she did. She never should have taken that nosegay of greenery. Next time she saw him, she'd tell him straight-out she wasn't interested. Straight and to the point, sharp as he might take it.

She peeked another look at Everett. He turned his hat in his hands like his thoughts were brewing. "I did a lot of praying on the way over here. My head feels like lead, but it helped to spend time talking to God."

"Did you ask Him how to handle Mick?"

He rubbed his neck with a nod. "Yep. About other important things too."

Snow started falling lightly, so she dismissed her curiosity over those *important* things. "I've got wash frozen on the line." She stepped down to the ground, and he followed. At the line, she reached for the stiff, frosty laundry. "I'll have to drape it near the stove to soften it up and finish drying."

"I remember my mama doing that."

Her hands moved quickly over the line, removing pins. He joined her and took down a shirt of her father's and some overalls. He laid them in the basket by her feet. She glanced at him over the last piece as she unpinned it—her white cotton nightgown—but he'd averted his eyes. She folded the stiff garment and laid it on the pile then stepped back as he scooped up the basket, and they headed to the back door.

She held it open. "My hands are frozen. Yours must be too. I'll get us some coffee to warm them up."

"You're going to think I come here just for your coffee and cooking."

The thought made her smile. What would it be like to cook regularly for someone besides the captain? "You're welcome to come anytime." They hung their coat and shawl on pegs by the back door, and she moved to the stove to rub her hands above the heat. He came to stand beside her and did the same, and she wondered if he was considering her polite offer of coffee as some kind of overture, the way he warned her a fellow might think of such kindnesses. "Everett. . .do you think you'll stay up here in this neck of the woods, or will you move back to the city someday to be a pastor?"

He left the heat of the stove and stepped behind her. "I only know God called me to reach these men up here. I suspect that'll be the case for a long while. I have no plans to leave the work God's given me unless He clearly calls me elsewhere. I'm His servant."

She turned so that she could see his face. "I don't have plans to leave and go elsewhere either." Her voice filled with confidence. "Why should I? I don't need to chase adventure."

He studied her, and she stared back. It felt as though they were measuring each other, and she liked the way his gaze steadied on her. While it made her heart beat harder, she didn't care now if she blushed. Let him think she was making an overture. Maybe his head wasn't as thick as he let on—or as wooden as Mick's. Finally, she drew a breath and let it shudder out before turning again to reach for an empty cup.

"I hope being a good daughter doesn't keep you from pursuing the dreams God might give you."

"Oh, it won't, and I have plenty of dreams." She filled the cup, her back to him. "Did I tell you that someday I want to explore Lake Superior's shoreline all the way to Canada? I told the captain that once. Told him I didn't care if I went by canoe or on horseback, but one day I was going to do it."

He was smiling when she turned and handed him his coffee.

"Don't you believe me?"

His grin remained. "Somehow, I do. That's a hefty dream, and not at all what I'd have expected. But then, you're not like any woman I've met before."

Her chest swelled at his remark. "'Course," she said airily, "I still want to see Duluth, and maybe someday even St. Paul and

Minneapolis, but I don't think I'd want to stay there."

He squinted against the scalding heat as he took a sip and licked his lips. "You might change your mind."

She turned serious. "I lost my mama when I was eleven. I don't want to run too far off on my father." She hesitated. She needed to make sure he understood that she didn't mean she wanted to live with the captain forever. "Maybe I'll have my own little farm nearby someday."

He lifted his cup halfway to his lips. "When you get a husband, you mean?" He took a sip.

She nodded. "I suppose. No point in moving onto my own place yet. I have the store and Blackjack and even Purty and the chickens to keep me busy. There's plenty here to occupy my time. And now I have my mama's Bible too, so I've got months and months of studying to do."

"How's your study going, by the way?"

"I have questions." She pulled out a chair and sat, and he joined her. "When Jesus went up in the clouds, and the angels appeared and told the disciples that He would come back the same way, what did they mean by that?"

Everett set down his cup. "Just what He said. He'll be coming in the clouds to call us up. We're to keep busy serving Him, but also be watching and waiting for it, just like the people of olden times were to watch and wait for His birth."

"And then what?"

He leaned back with a deep breath. "You don't have any easy questions, do you?"

She laughed. "I don't know. Don't I? Isn't that an easy question?"

"Not according to some folks, but here's the way I see it." He went on to explain how Jesus was coming back in the clouds, just as He went up. Then both the living and those who died loving Him would rise to meet Him in the air. "There are different views on this, but we all agree that when He calls us up, we will get new, imperishable bodies, free of sin and decay."

She thought about his remark. "You told me this before. And you said this includes my mother."

"You and your mother. Yes, she'll rise in newness of life."

"But you said she is in heaven now."

"Her soul is alive in paradise, yes. But one day God is going to call her body from the grave, and it will be new and imperishable, like Adam's and Eve's before they sinned. Christians who are alive when He comes will be changed instantly too."

She was afraid to ask the next question, but there was no way around what she needed to know. "I think I'm understanding all that now, but what about the captain?"

Everett's answer came just as she expected it would. Straightforward yet sympathetic. "We have to pray he'll repent and believe, so he won't be left behind."

"Because if he is left behind. . . ?"

He reached over and placed a hand tenderly on hers. His palm was warm from the coffee cup. "Jesus will one day come fully to the earth again. This time not as the merciful Savior, but as a ruler and judge to the nations and to every soul who rejected Him."

He eyed her for a moment as she listened in silence. "Satan will also be punished for what he did to deceive and destroy all God made."

She was certain Everett was giving her the skimmed-over explanation without all the details, but even that made her stomach clench. She swallowed a painful lump. "The captain just has to believe!"

Everett's hand pressed hers gently. "Let's pray right now." She nodded and turned her palm upward. He clasped her fingers in his and prayed for the captain's salvation to be made sure.

His voice, both tender and strong, resonated with what could only be a deep desire for her father's soul. He cared, truly. Tears came to her eyes, and when she raised her head at his *amen*, his were red with emotion also.

"Thank you, Everett. That means a great deal to me."

He withdrew his hand, and she was sorry to feel it slip away. "You're welcome, Angel. I'll pray for him every day, and I have."

He'd called her Angel. She wouldn't point it out, for she liked it. And she would pray for Everett. Pray for him to receive the answers to his own important questions. She'd begun to feel something solid and steadying in Everett Shepherd. The swirl of awareness that gathered in her middle was delicious and warming to her heart.

He drained back his cup and rose to rinse it in a tub of water sitting in her sink. Her gaze followed him. "You didn't need to do that."

"I know." He gave her a soft smile.

She finished a tepid sip of her own coffee and thought about Mick serving Everett knockout drops in his coffee last night. "You know you'll still have to do something about Mick. He needs to be taught a lesson."

"You've never heard of turning the other cheek?" He sounded disappointed. Was he disappointed in her?

"I'm not saying I want you to get even. I intend to tell him I'm not interested in him, but Mick's the kind of fellow who'll look for someone to blame. He'll call you out, and he'll just think you're soft if you don't do anything."

"Do you think that's the case?"

She looked up. "No!" Heat scurried up her back. "Certainly not. I'm just saying that's what Mick will think."

He stepped forward and braced his hands on the table, his

face a mere foot from hers. "I know what you mean. And you're right." He straightened. "But I have to decide how best to deal with him. I know how a man like Mick thinks. I've been that man. Trouble is, I don't want to be him again." He backed up and propped himself against the dry sink, arms folded and feet crossed at the ankles. "I don't want to respond out of anger or revenge. Just promise me you won't say anything to him about it. To your father either. I need time to think about what I should do and to pray about it, of course."

"Of course," she murmured.

"Pray for me, Angel, won't you? Men need to earn respect from one another. I'd as soon those jacks respected me because of the Word being preached, but I don't think that'll mean much to some of them. They need to see me as one of them first." He rubbed his jaw. "I just have to figure out how to accomplish that."

His request warmed her more than the coffee had. He was getting pretty free with calling her Angel. Did he even realize it? Somehow, she thought maybe he did.

She raised a brow. "You know, if you don't figure it out, I'd still not mind seeing Mick get a whupping, even if I have to dish it out myself." As she spoke, her glance took in the bulge of muscle beneath his sleeves.

Everett chuckled, and with his relief, Angeline laughed, while her insides spun with some unfathomable excitement that she didn't dare think about too long.

CHAPTER 9

Nearly everyone in the camp and the Adairs attended the Christmas service Everett preached. At its end, John Salverson announced a day of festivity to take place after the New Year to shake off the winter doldrums.

The crew hummed about what sorts of competition the festival day might hold. Everett too thought about how he might take part, while he lent a hand in the sawyer's shop a few days later. He cracked his knuckles and chose a file off the workbench. The saws needed sharpening every day, and it was a never-ending job for old Joe, the man tasked with it.

Joe eyed him. "Where'd you learn that anyway?"

"I told you I used to work on the crews before I became a preacher."

"So you did." Joe aimed a wad of tobacco juice into a can and set it aside.

"I can hone a decent edge." Everett grinned.

"Just be careful of them files so you don't lose 'em or break 'em."

"I'll be careful." Everett drew the file along the saw's edge then gave it a half dozen even swipes. He could feel Joe spying for a long moment before turning his attention onto his own work.

"You going to join the festival games?" Everett asked.

"You bet. And if you figure on getting even with me and Freddy for that little shenanigan with the mattress, well, I might not be the biggest or the youngest fella in the outfit, but I can hold my own. Don't you worry 'bout that."

Everett had been in many such competitions before. Sometimes he won, and sometimes he lost. At least there'd be no fighting matches in this one. That was one event he'd be sure to win, but in no way did he want stains from that past marring his work for the Lord here. Those days were long gone, praise be to Jesus!

He chuckled. "No need for getting even. I can take a joke as well as the next man. But. . .I might have a skill or two up my sleeve." Joe glanced over, and Everett winked.

Joe grunted as he settled a saw across the bench. "I suppose so. But I wager I can swing an axe as fast and hard as any of 'em, including you."

"I might take you on." He wouldn't back down from a challenge—not of a friendly kind.

Joe grinned at him, showing stained teeth.

On the festival day, Everett awoke before dawn. Most of the others still snored as he slipped to the side of his bunk onto his knees and prayed. *Heavenly Father, I look at this day as an opportunity from You. I pray that I will acquit myself well and earn the respect of the men. If not, I pray I don't embarrass Your name. Amen.*

Willard Skivvens' voice rumbled low in the darkness. "You praying over there, Preacher?"

"I am at that, Willard."

"Not worried, are ya?"

"Not worried."

"Glad to know you're praying anyway, and I'm not the only one. Mind if I join you for coffee?"

Everett stepped to Willard's bunk and stretched out a hand to help him up. The older man unfolded his body a little slowly and dressed quietly. The others would rouse before long. Already, Everett could smell the sweet, dense aroma of griddle cakes frying over at the cookshack.

Their footsteps squeaked on the hard-packed snow, and the air was so cold it iced their breath.

Everett shuddered. "Might freeze our faces off during the festival."

"Glad we aren't working."

Everett gave Willard a pat on the shoulder as the man swung the door open, and they entered the building lit up by oil lamps set about. Already platters were starting to pile up with bacon, pancakes, coffee, eggs, biscuits, and gravy, all in a swim of smells that made his stomach rumble. He waved at the cookee. "Sure smells good in here!"

"Grab a plate and fill up. They'll all be coming in afore long."

Minutes into his quietly shared breakfast with Willard, the door opened again, and, by twos and threes, men lumbered in.

"Hey, it's the sky pilot, fueling up for the competition," a husky man said.

Everett grinned. "You bet. Don't let my usual manner fool you. Today I'm gonna show you what I've got. I'll let you decide if it's worth anything."

That followed with laughter, a friendly camaraderie.

"I'll lay three dollars on the preacher against all comers in the speed climb. Have you seen his arms?"

"What about his legs?"

"You're on."

"Now hold it. You don't even know if he's gonna enter that race. What do you say, Sky Pilot?"

The banter quieted as Everett set down his cup. He turned

to them as Mick came through the door. Behind him trailed the usual bunch of rabble-rousers that Everett had grown used to causing mischief if not downright trouble. "Get me a pair of caulks, and I'll be happy to race somebody up."

Mick smirked. "I thought preachers didn't bet."

"I'm not wagering, Mick, just competing. What about you?" He eyed Mick meaningfully, and Mick caught on quick.

"Speed climb? I'll take you on. Put me down in a race against the sky pilot. I'll pass the mark and be back to the ground while he's still catching his breath at the halfway."

Guffaws went around the room. Even the cookee grinned as he set another pot of coffee on the table near Everett. "Halfway? Is that the bet?"

"Naw, I'm joshing. Let's just say I'll beat him." Mick held his cup up in a salute.

Everett got to his feet. "I'll see you there, Mick. Just as soon as things get started."

The sun climbed clear of the horizon and streamed through the barren branches as the men gathered in the area set for the competition. A few rough benches had been thrown together for observers, but nearly everyone stood on their feet and crowded around as Mr. Salverson belted out the rules, which were few.

Per their wagering during breakfast, the first game was chopping. The men competed in groups of six, and Everett performed respectably, but at the end of the first hour, neither he nor Joe took the prize for fastest ability to sever a monster log in two.

But he'd warmed up enough to barely notice the icy cold biting his face. The men cuffed up their flannel shirtsleeves and roared with cheer, sweated with effort, or tumbled into the dirty snow with mirth as they raced over logs set on end like pilings. "It ain't the same as running across a creek on a roller," some groused.

Fast and agile, Freddy took that prize. "Put me on the water then. I'll take you all fair and square there too."

"That he would," piped Joe.

At the third event, the tree climbing, money changed hands yet again as Everett took his place along with Mick and a man they called Tug before a grouping of three trees, branchless and straight as arrows. They reached more than seventy feet to the sky. Everett adjusted his caulks and wrapped the end of a strap firmly around his right hand, slung it around the girth of the pole, and wound his left with the other end. He'd use it to propel himself upward. He leaned sideways and winked at a group of onlookers who had bet on him, when a splash of blue caught his eye.

Angel. She and her father were both seated on a bench, awaiting the shot that would send him, Mick, and Tug flying up the trees to reach the marks at sixty feet then hurtle back to earth. The first to have both feet touch the ground would win the ribbon.

In an instant, his drive to simply gain the respect of the men turned into a fuddle of wanting to win Angel's favor. Worse yet, Mick must've seen her too, because he looked past his own tree trunk and clamped dusky eyes on Everett.

He wants to beat me more than ever. Oh, Lord . . . Help me not to think of preening for her now. Help me only think of pleasing You.

But what did that even mean—pleasing God? Was it wrong to want to win, to want to beat out Mick in front of Angel? Was it wrong either way—to try to win or not to try? Should he let Tug have his day? How was God leading?

Then suddenly his uncertainties sorted themselves, and focus was restored. He'd already decided this was his chance to prove himself to Mick Hankins.

"On your mark! Get set!" Salverson fired the shot.

Everett's body responded as every muscle recalled the skill of past years. His arms and legs went into action. He flew up the pole, quickly establishing a rhythm, slinging his strap stride by stride as his caulks found footing. He neither looked to see nor cared how his competition fared on the other poles as he focused all his energy into his own climb. The crowd gave a concerted gasp—not knowing why—he kept on.

At the mark, he began his descent. A quarter of the way down, he turned his hips sideways, holding out his legs and letting his body plummet to the earth with only the pull of the strap to keep him from free-falling completely—a trick he'd learned six or so years ago in just such a race. He hit the ground hard on his feet but instantly straightened in a smothering of cheers and back pounding.

"He did it!"

"Nice going, Preacher!"

"I'm putting my next dollar on the sky pilot."

"He was lucky."

"See that trick he pulled turning his legs? That took nerve."

"He's got nerve aplenty, that's for sure."

"I gotta try that, maybe."

"You're not tired, are you, Preacher?"

"Poor Tug almost lost it there for a second."

The cacophony continued as they parted for him to walk away and make room for the next competitors. At the outskirts of the circle stood Mick, puffing. "I call that cheating."

Everett halted. "Why so, Mick? Because you lost?"

"I didn't hardly. I was only a half a second behind you."

"Half a second is long enough, I reckon."

Angel rushed toward them. "He didn't cheat, Mick. He beat you fair and square."

"He sure did," Willard said, strolling up to them, his ungloved hands in his coat pockets. "I was judge, and I was right there with my eyeballs level to the ground. He had more than half a second on you too, Mick. Beat you by a good ten feet. Maybe twelve." He winked. "Sometimes the better part of wisdom is to just admit defeat."

"Sign us up for another try if you want to, Mick," Everett said with a half smile. "I'll give you all the chance you want."

Mick's eyelid twitched. "I'll do that." He glanced at those around them. "I'd best him in a heartbeat if there was logrolling. That's when you see the makeup of a true jack. That's no place for some namby-pamby preacher who thinks he can match up 'cause he can swing an axe or climb a tree. He probably started doing that as a kid." He gave a nod at Angel. "I hope you can stick around and watch the rest of the competition."

"The captain and I will be here all day. I'll be watching." She smiled, but her eyes were on Everett.

Everyone broke apart at noon for eats and hot coffee. The warmth of the cookshack soaked through half-frozen bodies. Angel removed her hat and gloves and unbuttoned her long coat. Her face bloomed pink from the tip of her nose to her cheekbones, but her eyes glowed warmly. Everett carried her plate to a place at one of the tables. "Are you warming up?"

"My toes sting a little, but they'll be okay. I like a cold snap that wakes up my bones."

Everett sat down beside her.

"That girl was born for the outdoors." The captain set down his own plate. "Just like her mother."

"Mrs. Adair was a country girl at heart?"

"Country as they come. That's why it didn't worry her to move up here with me. She bit off more than I meant to have her chew, but she always did me proud."

"The captain went back to the lakes for only two more years

after he married my mother. I was born during that time. Then he sold his ship and brought us up here to the north country."

The captain swiped his roll in gravy. "That was quite a show you put on up on that pole."

"I always like a good race."

Mick appeared beside Everett, but not with a plate. He dropped a clipboard onto the table next to him. "I signed us up for another race. I hope you won't let me down by backing out."

Everett glanced over, fully expecting to see he'd challenged him to another climb, but when his gaze fell on the name of the event, he set his spoon in his bowl.

"Boom running. You mean that race Freddy already won?"

Mick shook his head. "No, Preacher. Not pilings. I mean a *boom* race."

"The water isn't open." Angel's face looked paler than a moment ago.

"Some fellas are out there chopping it open close to the narrows where the ice isn't so thick."

"It's rushing water underneath."

Mick gave a slow nod and grinned. "That'll make it motivating."

"It can't be two degrees out, if that!" Angel hissed with a hard look.

"Let them be," her father said.

She tucked her chin, but her nostrils flared.

Everett tapped a finger on the clipboard. "I'm not sure it's a good idea. If we go out there and race, somebody else might feel just as foolishly inclined."

Mick's face pinched, and he leaned closer. "You calling me a fool, or are you just chicken?"

Everett regretted his choice of words, but there was no taking them back. Yes, it was foolish. Going out on the river on a snaking band of logs in subfreezing temperatures just to prove a point was downright stupid. But he'd set out to accept Mick's challenges today to avoid a real fight.

He forced himself to nod. "I guess I'll not let you down, Mick. But we're it. Nobody else signs up. This is just a show for the rest. We don't want anybody getting hurt because of us."

Mick snorted. "I don't know how anybody's going to get hurt. It's just running across a few logs and back, end to end. No reason we should get wet if we're able enough. Right?" He cast Angel a cocky grin then strode away whistling.

CHAPTER 10

"Mick's the best boom operator. He can roll logs as well as Freddy." Angel tucked her arm through her father's, sharing warmth as they gathered with the crowd along the riverbank.

"We can be glad he didn't request a birling match," the captain said matter-of-factly. "They ought to both come out all right." He patted her arm. "If the preacher has much sense, he'll let Mick win and get this resentment out of his system."

Resentment indeed.

Mick might strut for her, but his real grievance was that Everett Shepherd was so well respected among the crew. They were drawn to Everett's friendly nature and good words. It would serve Mick right if he did tumble off the boom into that icy water.

She approached the riverside with her father, where workers had chopped and sawn out a section of ice ten feet wide across the narrows. Blocks had been dragged out of the rectangular hole that stretched to the far bank sixty feet or more away. Two booms of logs chained end to end now stretched across the watery abyss. Each log could spin back and forth independently while remaining connected to the next. Black water swirled beneath, arching the lines slightly toward the edge of the hole, but the logs were chained off on land so the current couldn't pull them over too far or allow them to bump against each other.

The two contestants would run as fast as they dared across a boom, round a pole marker that anchored the log chain, and run back while trying to not topple off the shifting contraption.

Angeline pressed close to her father. No doubt he'd seen plenty of stunts in his days. Men racing to the top of masts, diving over sides of ships to attend to issues below the waterline, and any number of other sailing dangers. This was likely little in the way of shenanigans to him, yet he kept a watchful eye on the goings-on.

"You know Mick's doing this for you." The captain's voice rumbled softly. "He means to prove himself to you. Moreover, he's trying to prove that Everett isn't man enough for you."

"Pfft." She sputtered, disbelieving that it went quite so deep as that.

"You don't think so?" The tender tone of his question suggested that there was more behind it. He wanted to know her will on the matter.

Perhaps this was the time to admit her feelings. "Everett is man enough."

Her father held her arm a little tighter. "I see."

That was all there was to it. She suddenly felt lighter. She had chosen Everett Shepherd, and the captain hadn't impugned her choice.

The camp boss explained the rules, but his voice seemed distant as her heart sang out. *I've chosen Everett. I want to be his bride and to stay here in this north country with him for always or for as long as God wants him to stay.* A flood of wanting like she'd never known rushed through her. She pulled in the cold air to refocus on the race.

"Willard will be on the other side, making sure you round the markers there."

Mr. Skivvens gave a wave from the opposite side of the river.

"On your return, I'll make the final call. If there's any question, I'll confer with Mr. Berg and Mr. Sanders, who'll each be clocking a runner, but my final decision—if it's close—will stand. Is this understood?"

Everett stood with his hands clasped calmly in front of him and nodded. "Understood."

Mick rubbed his palms together and gave his shoulders a shake. His nod came slower. "Understood, Boss." His glance went sharp to Everett. "You ready?"

"As I'll ever be."

Mr. Salverson drew out a pistol and pointed it at the sky. The crowd quieted. Clouds of breath hung in the air.

A gunshot popped, and the men sprang forward, leaping half cautiously, half wildly with arms outstretched across the booms that turned and bobbed beneath them so that their feet occasionally plunged to the ankles in the river.

Angeline's belly tightened, and the captain patted her arm. She expelled her breath, murmuring amid the chorus of shouts around her, "Run, Everett."

He wobbled and short-stepped, then leaped to the next length, picking up speed as he gained his stride. Beside him, Mick wobbled and short-stepped too, then sprang forward, his feet gliding like a skiff on a lake, as though he hardly noticed the shifting of the logs.

Everett's steps were light also, like the wind bouncing over whitecaps. How had he ever arrived at such skill?

The animated crowd roared louder, their appetites for the competition growing to a clamor as the racers reached the far bank, dodged around the post their boom was chained to, and leaped onto the logs again. A collective groan went up when Mick floundered, allowing Everett to pass him by two steps, but Mick quickly righted himself and continued, somehow moving faster.

Angeline glanced at the two timekeepers minding the finish on this end, each with thumbs at the buttons of their watches and shoulders hunched to spy the very hairbreadth second their runner's foot touched the shore. Yes, it was going to be close.

Mick made a long leap and passed Everett by a half step, but then the unimaginable happened. Undoubtedly the most experienced river rat on the crew, Mick flicked a glance at Everett, and the log beneath him turned with a jerk as his left foot came down. Mick's right arm flew over his head. He slipped! He landed hard on the log as it plunged forward end down, dipping him to the waist while Everett lunged past.

Everett landed on the last log, which he took in two bounds, and his foot hit the muddy bank. Mick scampered to his feet and finished only seconds behind the preacher.

The lumberjacks roared. Everett's breath panted out as he turned and held out his hand to Mick. Mick looked reluctant to accept it, but he steadied his gaze and took Everett's hand only to give a sharp tug that pulled the preacher off-balance and sent him toppling off the bank and into the water.

A gasp went up, and Angeline's was the loudest. Although Everett managed to land on his feet up to his thighs with a splash, it was uncalled-for conduct that might have erupted into a brawl had it involved anyone else but Everett. Even so, the look on his face wasn't humorous. Several onlookers shouted harsh words that echoed over the woods.

Angeline charged toward Mick and gave him a hard shove. "What's the matter with you, Mick? Are you such a sore loser?"

He sneered. "What's the matter with you, *Miss Adair*? Didn't you come for a show?" He jerked away and stretched down the embankment to extend a hand to Everett. "I guess I shouldn't have done that, but I couldn't resist the temptation. You know how that is, right?"

Everett gave a distrustful glance at Mick's hand then grasped it. Mick pulled him up with a grin. "Just a little fun."

"No harm done."

His smile seemed forced. It would serve Mick right if Everett gave him a good hard shove back into that icy river. Ungracious of her to think so, perhaps, but even so, she had a good mind to do it herself. "You've had your entertainment, Mick. Now why don't you both go dry off before you catch your death."

The two men staggered off toward the bunkhouse as the way parted and dollar bills passed among the wagerers.

"Next contest is axe throwing!" Mr. Salverson announced, and everyone dispersed.

The captain shifted beside her. "You had enough? We ought to head on home if you have. Uncle Ironstone might like to get to his own place before dark."

"I'd like to speak with Everett first, if that's all right with you."

"I expected you would." The softness in his eyes and voice wasn't the same kind of gentleness as when she was a little girl, or even like when they spoke of her mother. It bore the realization that she was a grown woman, with her own mind, her own will, and her own new love. "I'll go ready the wagon."

"I won't keep you long. I promise."

They left the riverside, and Angeline trudged through the rutty snow, coming to a halt not too near the bunkhouse but spying the doorway. The cold bit her fingers and toes as minutes passed. Finally, Mick stepped out. He caught her eyes on him immediately then strode away. *Mick. . .ignoring her!* She took a deep breath and let it out in a trail of fog. More minutes passed. Would Everett come?

At last, the door opened again, and he came out in dry clothes and donning his thick mackinaw. She took a step, and he came toward her. "That turned into more of a show than I bargained for. I didn't expect to win, but I didn't expect to go swimming either."

She expelled a loud puff of breath. "That was all Mick's doing."

"He doesn't give up a grudge easily."

"He should learn when it's time."

He held out his elbow, and she slipped her hand through. "He doesn't like me being here."

She lifted her chin, feeling bold. "I suppose that's true. He's jealous because I like you more than I like him."

His arm tightened. "Let's get you inside where it's warm." He led her toward the cookshack and opened the door for her. A full coffeepot waited on the counter. Everett poured them each a cup, and they took seats across from one another.

She held her cup between her palms to warm them while Everett set his on the table, but neither of them drank.

She chose her words carefully. "Please don't mind what I said."

Everett stared at his cup. After what seemed a long wait, he finally looked at her. "Are you certain you want Mick to let things go?"

She stared back with the most heartfelt gaze she hoped to muster and nodded. "I told you. I'm very sure."

He studied her in a way not too different from how the captain had a short while ago. "Then I might as well tell you, we're in for a tussle. I need to settle things between us once and for all."

"I'm loving you, Everett. Does that settle things?"

The air gushed out of him. He reached across the table then

drew back before he touched her hand. "I meant *Mick and I* are in for a tussle. I didn't mean Mick and *us*."

"But if I'm the cause of the trouble—"

"Angel…you're a one-of-a-kind woman, and I admit you have a lot to do with it, but this is my fight." He parked his elbows on the table and glanced away at a pair of men conversing and laughing across the room. "Mick isn't going to stop pecking away unless I put him in his place. It's not the way I want it, but I see no way around it."

Her breath hitched. "Meaning?"

"It's going to be a fight. He's agreed to my terms."

"Terms?" Her voice took on an edge, and she repeated the question softly as the door opened and four more men came inside. "What kind of terms?"

"No audience except two men to keep it square. If Mick wins…" He shrugged. "Bragging rights. He can rub it in as much as he wants. If I win, he comes to hear the preaching for the rest of the season, and he doesn't make a peep to cause distraction."

"And you're sure you'll win?"

He let out a little gust of sound. He'd never told her about his past entirely. "Reasonably." He picked up his coffee then and took a long swallow. "Mm. That's good."

"If you're reasonably sure, then I'm sure."

Lowering his cup again he reached across the table, and this time he took her hand in his and caressed it. The calluses on his palm felt warm and soothing across her skin, and something more meaningful in his touch made her heart swell.

"About what you said a minute ago. I care deeply for you too. I want what God has planned, and I've come to discover that everything I *thought* He wanted for me has turned on end. I'm not sure what tomorrow holds. I don't know if this camp is going to ride me out on a rail after I meet up against Mick.

But this part is certain. I never expected to find a woman out here in the woods who could change everything I ever thought about marrying one day. I'll tell you now, Angel, I feel things that are new to me. And I welcome them."

Heat raced up her neck and over her face and singed the roots of her hair. A blush must have shown, because his wonderful smile seemed to hint at his heart.

The door opened again, and the captain stepped in. Everett let go of her hand.

Angeline rose. "I'm ready now, Captain."

"Just rest there and finish your coffee. I'm going to have a cup before we go. You ran a good race, Everett."

"Thank you, sir. The exercise felt good, though I didn't like the getting wet part. I've no desire to leave preaching and become a birler anytime soon."

The captain filled a cup. "Can't say as I blame you. I've experienced my share of cold and wet in my day."

"You stick to storekeeping and I'll stick to gospel preaching. Sound good?"

With a nod of agreement, the captain sat down beside Angeline. "Those days of trying to stay warm and dry while the lake battered against my hull are over. My rudder has shifted me in a new direction. Not unlike yours has." He took up his cup. "It's calm seas for me now."

Angel smiled at Everett, but now the look in his eyes said that he believed his rudder had somehow broken loose. And at the end of the day, no matter how he came to the decision to fight Mick, she was the one battering his hull.

CHAPTER 11

A week passed, giving him too much time to think—or over-think. There just seemed no other way for him to get out from under Mick's badgering. Everett hoped God still had his back.

Mick would do his best. He was strong, agile, and probably had his own experience brawling after too much drink. But Everett was trained. He might have stumbled into the ring to begin with, but once he had an agent, he'd been taught how to hold out and land a punch on his own terms and timing. The boom race had proved he was still light on his feet.

He would win, and Mick would tuck tail. But when all was said and done, would Everett be able to live with the results? So much for turning the other cheek.

My head's all muddied with pride and my feelings toward Angel. Give me wisdom, God. Stop this nonsense if I'm going all wrong.

A January warmup had busted the cold snap. Twenty degrees and climbing, it would be good weather for their meeting in the woods. Only Willard Skivvens would attend as Everett's choice and old Joe as Mick's, but Everett insisted they inform the boss of their actions. Mr. Salverson agreed to let them fall out to their own demise. He'd leave the witnessing of it to Willard and Joe, and they could report to him if anyone needed more than casual bandaging when they were through.

There'd be no rounds. Just a knock-down-and-drag-out of the type Everett never expected to partake in again. How wrong he'd been.

January darkness fell early. Neither man took comfort in a warm meal before the fight. Everett and Willard walked together down the trail toward a chosen clearing. Mick and Joe were already there. They'd put up several torches for light and inspected the area for any branches or rocks that could cause injury.

"Let's keep it inside this area, fellas," Joe said.

Everett nodded.

Mick sneered and pulled off his coat. "Time to get on with it. I've got a plate of supper waiting on the back of the cookee's stove."

Everett handed his mackinaw and flannel shirt to Willard and pushed up his long john sleeves. The old anticipation coursed through his blood, but with it, a fair dose of regret.

"You certain you want to do this? We've got nothing to prove, Mick, either of us. The fellas like you, and they like me. We can quit while we're both ahead."

"You've forgotten one thing, Preacher. *I* don't like you." Mick took three slow strides closer. "And I just want to wipe your smug face with my fist."

"I'm sorry you feel that way. I assure you, I'm not feeling smug. I've got no axe to grind against you, Mick."

"What about Angel? You saying she isn't worth fighting for?"

"Is that what it comes down to then? If you beat me, you think Angel will see what a better man you are?" Everett's blood heated.

"I don't have any such illusion that she'll see it that way.

But"—he gave a sharp nod—"yeah. It does come down to satisfaction. Way I figure it, you owe me something for stealing her."

Everett squared himself. "I can see there's only one way to bring you to your senses."

Mick thumbed his nose. "As if."

They strode off to the sides of the snowy arena. Joe spoke in fast, low tones to Mick. Willard gave Everett a pat on the shoulder and said simply, "I'll be praying. You just finish it up quick, so nobody gets hurt bad."

Everett let those words wind through him, wondering at Willard's calm, but he'd spent a lot of years with the restless jacks out here in the woods.

"Anytime you and your *coach* are ready," Willard hollered to Mick.

Mick came into the arena, fists up, and Everett moved in. For a few seconds, they measured and moved in a circle, then Mick drove in with the first strike.

Everett knocked the blow aside and sidestepped as Mick came back again. Three times Mick tried. Three times Everett skirted, ducked, or dispatched the blow. Then it was his turn.

He came in fast with two quick strikes, one to the chest and one to the chin. Mick's head snapped back. Fire lit his eyes in the glow of the torchlight. He swung back hard, but Everett caught Mick's arm with a left block and struck him to the side of the head with his right.

Mick staggered, and Everett landed several more punches, dropping Mick to his knees. He reeled there for a moment, and Everett backed off, waiting to see if he'd get to his feet.

He did, wobbling. The man had grit. Everett would give him that. Mick came again, slower this time. Everett let him lunge, and when Mick's fist glanced off Everett's shoulder, he fell against Everett in a bear hug. Everett wrestled him off and they fell apart, but not before one jarring punch connected hard to Everett's ribs.

Everett let his breath out with a painful gust. He was fired up now. Ready to end this. He went at Mick, unrelenting, knuckles splitting.

It felt like raining fury, but in reality only four hard and heavy blows sent Mick spiraling face down to the earth. This time he didn't get up.

After Everett counted his breaths silently to himself, he staggered to the edge of the darkness. Joe went in and turned Mick over. "You gonna wake up?"

A murmur told him that Mick was coming to.

"That's that," Willard said. "Come on. I'll get you a bucket of water so you can wash up."

"You don't seem surprised," Everett said without enthusiasm. He had garnered the expected outcome, but he couldn't feel pleased about it the way he might have a few years back. Hopefully, he'd beaten sense into Mick, but he hadn't pounded any spiritual good into the man—and his own spirit felt wounded.

Willard plucked up a torch. "I ain't."

They made their way back to the camp pump house where Willard filled a pail with cold water. Everett rinsed blood off his hands. He bent to splash icy water over his face.

"Isn't the first time I've watched you fight."

Everett's head shot up. "What's that?"

"Seen you down in Duluth a few summers back." Willard chuckled. "That was a real fight. Not like this goofing around you got from Mick."

Everett toweled his face, his mood sinking further. "You saw me in the ring?"

"Mm-hm."

He drew the towel away. "So you probably think I'm more cut out for prizefighting than for preaching."

"I didn't say that. I doubt there was any way around it."

"I fear I'll lose the men's respect."

"Or gain some. Don't you worry about the fellas. God sent the man He wanted here to them, and He cares about their souls better than you or I. Mick's too. You did what you had to do, I figure." He let out a chortle. "You gave Mick a whupping, sure thing. Come on." He laid a hand on Everett's shoulder. Let's get you some supper. I set aside a plate too."

"Don't know if I can eat."

"I'm thinking you'll change your mind when it's sitting in front of you."

The next morning, Everett roused along with the others. He didn't look at Mick. One glimpse last night told him that Mick was going to be sporting the colorful rewards of their fight for some time. Guilt punched his gut. He wouldn't be able to rest again until he got into the ring with the Lord and took whatever discipline he had coming.

He heard his moniker whispered none-too-softly as he tied his boots. "Sky Pilot. . ." Mick's name drifted past his hearing, and a sleepy voice chuckled. Men eyed him as they headed out of the bunkhouse. Some even dared quick glances at his knuckles before he stretched his fingers into his coat and gloves. Were they comparing the condition of his hands to the marks on Mick's jaw that would be swollen and purple this morning?

Before anyone could waylay him, Everett tugged down the brim of his hat and made his way to the barn to saddle up.

He hadn't slept well. He'd tangled up his blanket with his tossing yet couldn't bring himself to pray. He'd felt the urge to give in and simply head to the next town and buy himself a bottle. It was an old but all-too-familiar temptation, one that seemed to come back from a two-year trip away. But he hushed its whisper while he cinched the saddle tight and took hold of Buddy's reins.

"Let's go." He led the horse out and swung himself into the seat. With a nudge, he turned Buddy up the corduroy road.

He had packed his Bible as his plan slowly evolved. He would head to Northome to stay for a night or two. He'd do battle, praying and reading until he understood what God wanted him to do. If nothing came out clear, well. . .

Brush hung like shining white curtains alongside the dark trail. He couldn't see very far, just like looking into his future, but he'd stand in that ring until God showed him if He still wanted Everett for His work. If it took a day or week, that's what he'd do.

Dawn cast a bright shine behind silvery clouds by the time he made it to the crossroads an hour later. Adair's store stood straight ahead. Smoke curled from the chimney, beckoning him. "Not today, Buddy. We'll go another mile or two and then stop for a rest."

He slowed and watched the house and store, his heart divided in two. The horse came almost to a stop and nickered, sensing a warm stall and oats nearby.

Crystals sparkled on the branches all around him, and the roadway glistened. Then the door cracked open, and Buddy's head jerked with a snort.

Adair. The captain's hatless head came up. "Well, hello there. You're out mighty early. Stopping in, or heading to the next camp?"

Everett didn't move, though he felt like he'd been slugged and was stumbling. Could the man see his uncertainties? "Heading to Northome, but I wouldn't pass by without stopping to say hello."

"Angel's getting breakfast on. You're just in time."

His stomach rumbled, and he was glad that the captain was too far away to hear it and note his misery. "You win, Buddy. Let's get you those oats."

A minute later he dismounted and hitched Buddy to the rail. Everett followed the captain inside where his nostrils were assailed by the smell of frying sausage and boiled coffee. "Glad I skipped out of camp early this morning." He put on a smile.

"Come on back to the kitchen. Uncle Ironstone is with us this morning."

Everett had never met the Indian. Now he spied him in the front corner of the store by the woodstove, whittling on a block of wood. "Good morning."

The Indian nodded. His age was difficult to determine. He looked neither old nor young. His face was weathered and sage, but there was still an uprightness in his bearing that showed strength.

"Uncle, this is Everett Shepherd."

"The sky pilot." Uncle Ironstone's eyes creased with a twinkle. "Angel told me what they call you."

"That's right. I'm not used to it yet."

"And I am not really anyone's uncle. I do not even have a brother or a sister. My wife, when she was young, had two children, but they did not live, and now she has gone on too." He spoke matter-of-factly, but with a smile and creases at the edges of his eyes. "I will see them another time, and I am happy for it."

Would he? A pang of another kind went through Everett. Did Uncle Ironstone know about Jesus?

Everett glanced at the captain. Best to get it off his chest or he wouldn't be able to swallow a bite. "Before we go in to breakfast, I feel I need to apologize."

The captain frowned. "Apologize? What for?"

"I suppose you'll be hearing about my fight with Mick last night."

"A fight between you and Mick?" The captain tilted his head, and he gave a swipe at some imaginary dust on his countertop. Somehow, Everett had managed to surprise him. His expression turned bemused.

"I'm sure the news has spread." Knowing he'd be the center of talk didn't help his growing self-contempt. "I don't like that our quarrel went so far. At the time I figured—"

The captain held up a hand. "Hold up. Mick's needed someone to take him to task, and he wouldn't have quit bedeviling you until he'd run you off a laughingstock, if he could manage it." He scanned Everett. "You don't look any worse off. If you gave him a flogging, you were in your rights to do it."

"I don't feel like I was in my rights."

"Maybe you ought not allow yourself to be cast adrift on your feelings. If you were men on my ship, I'd have given you the ring myself so you could get it over with. But you're steering your own boat, and you're man enough to handle whatever comes against you, or so my Angel believes."

Angel had told her father *that*? "Sometimes our feelings are convictions, sent by the Holy Spirit."

"And other times they are nothing more than human guilt about handling difficult situations without a perfect solution. Take my word for it—as someone who once commanded a ship's crew, which in many ways was easier than governing a single daughter—occasionally life forces difficult choices, and you make them despite the probable fallout. You must set your course and hold fast."

The captain's steely gaze fixed as though he stood forecastle. "Whatever happened between you probably did Mick better good than he's willing to admit just yet. And I'd bet my bottom dollar those lumbermen are setting you on a pedestal. 'Now that's a preacher.' That's what they're saying." He thumped his fist on the counter as if the matter was settled. "Let's eat."

Everett removed his hat and coat and followed the captain to the kitchen ahead of Uncle Ironstone. Despite his fog of self-incrimination, it hadn't escaped his notice the way some of the men looked at him as he hurried to get away this morning. Pulling off their caps and nodding. Was it Freddy who patted him on the back and offered congratulations as he ducked out the door?

But what would Angel think? That was another question. She'd declared she'd like to take Mick down a few notches herself, and her father might say that she alleged him man enough, but for what? Was he Christlike enough to control himself against critics and mockers? That's what mattered.

"I brought another guest for breakfast," her father announced, coming through the doorway.

Angel's eyes lit up when she saw him. That was a welcome sign, for the moment. "Everett! You've come, and you've met Uncle Ironstone."

As Uncle Ironstone took a seat, she slid a stack of pancakes and sausage in front of him, along with the jug of maple syrup. "I promised him the first ones."

"Mm. Best flapjacks in the north," he said, drowning them in syrup.

She winked. "He says that because he made the syrup."

"Either way," he said.

"Take a seat. Yours and the captain's will be ready in a minute." She turned back to the stove, and Everett couldn't help but admire the lightness of her movements and brightness with which she filled the room. Who wouldn't fall in love with her? Surely, he and Mick weren't the only ones.

"Angel, before I sit down, I need to tell you that Mick and I had our tussle."

She watched the batter bubble on the skillet. When she finally slid her spatula under a flapjack, she answered as adroitly as she flipped the cake. "Mick deserved whatever you gave him. He should have let things go when he had the chance."

"I wish I was so sure."

Her smooth brow marred with a frown. "I hope you didn't get hurt."

"I'm all right," he said gruffly.

"Sit down, son," the captain urged.

Everett obeyed. Uncle Ironstone ate quietly, and the captain rested his elbows on the table as he awaited his meal. Angeline slid a plate in front of her father.

Now was the time to tell her those parts of his past he'd only skimmed over before. Like the captain said, he had to stick to his course despite the fallout, even if it made her change her mind about him. "I'm not feeling much like a man of God right now."

"I hope you aren't sorry for waking Mick up."

"I might be. Truth is, it's causing me to wrestle with some things. Besides. . .there's more to my story you need to know."

The captain's mouth worked extra slowly around his bite of sausage. Uncle Ironstone's glances sharpened, even while his progress with his meal didn't wane.

"You'll remember how I told you I was a carouser and brawler before I met Christ, but that was just the small of it. Fighting got me plenty of notice. I quit lumberjacking and got paid to fight in the ring."

Her gaze didn't leave his face, and he had to force himself to return it.

"I had an agent and proper training. Made a name for myself in fights as far away as Minneapolis. Money came easy, and went out in ways I hope you could never imagine."

"That's why you knew you could beat him."

"I said those days were over, but now I feel like I've stepped backward. I'm not proud that I cut my knuckles on Mick Hankins." He glanced at the marks on his hands and nearly spat the final words. "Not proud one bit."

Angel's eyes were wide, but she set the edge of her spatula on the table with emphasis. "There are a lot of things I don't know about God yet, but I believe He allowed you to have those awful experiences in your past just so that you'd be the right man to preach to men like Mick—or to put him in his place."

"I'm supposed to be changed."

"You *are* changed. You didn't fight Mick for money or pride or—or vengeance. You were more than willing to turn the other cheek! You understand those men like my father understands a sailor. Why. . .those other jacks, they'll all respect you for doing what you had to." Her voice softened. "I respect you." She glanced at her father with a jerk of her head. "The captain respects you."

Captain Adair straightened, his fork paused halfway to his mouth. "I. . . Yes, I suppose that's true enough."

"You don't have to agree with her, Captain." Despite saying so, Everett's mood lifted a little.

She snatched her spatula back and turned to the stove where the butter had burned in her pan. "Eat some sausage and drink your coffee while I start over."

Ironstone belched. "Interesting talk. I go smoke now." He stood and sauntered off.

"I'll join you." The captain got up, taking his half-eaten breakfast and coffee with him into the store.

Everett gnawed on a bite of sausage as the hiss of batter hit the hot pan on the stove. A few moments later, Angeline draped a flapjack over the edges of his plate. Before she could move away, he reached up and stopped her with a touch to her wrist. "I know you don't want to hear an apology right now, but I'm sorry you have to see me out of sorts like this."

"I expect that people who care about one another see all the sides of each other eventually." A blush rose up her cheek, and Everett couldn't help a caress to her wrist before he released her.

"I thought I had God's will figured out before I came up here. I came to do the teaching. Turns out God brought me here to teach *me* a thing or two." He dolloped butter and syrup onto his pancake, folded it in two with his fork, and cut into it.

"But He *did* bring you here," she said with tender certainty.

He thought on that awhile. He'd known difficulties would arise when he said yes to God's call, and running off to Northome wouldn't solve anything. "I suppose you're right. Come Sunday morning, I'll get up and preach, and I'll see if Mick shows up."

"I reckon Mick will keep his word."

"We'll see."

She set another flapjack over the first one, this one not quite so large. "Eat up. You don't want to face your business on an empty stomach."

He thanked her with a smile and a look that lingered. She was a good woman. The right woman. Maybe finding God's will wasn't as difficult as he was making it out to be.

CHAPTER 12

Angeline gave Blackjack a long, easy brushstroke. "You should have seen the way he looked at me, Jack. His expression—it was kind of wanting but unsure. Then he smiled so sweet. I think it was the wanting that won." She let out a long, even sigh, and the horse's ears twitched. "Lord knows, I'm wanting him." She gentled the brush over Blackjack's withers, and the horse gave a little toss of his head then returned to munching hay. Angeline chuckled. "You know I'll always love you. And if I marry the preacher, you'll have Buddy. The two of you probably understand each other better than you understand me anyway." She took another deep breath. "I haven't ever met a soul who understands me the way I think Everett does. Given a lifetime together, we'd be like a left hand is to a right."

She set the brush aside. "That's enough breakfast. I've got to get you hitched up. We don't want to be late for the preaching."

Her father entered the barn, humming.

"You sound like you're in a good mood for churchin'." She backed Blackjack out of his stall.

"I'm curious to see how Everett fares after the big scuffle."

"He'll do just fine. I'm sure of it." She gave her father a look.

"Fact is, I'm sure of Everett Shepard all the way around, if you understand my meaning."

"I saw it coming."

"And you don't mind?"

"'Course I mind." He took the traces from a nail on the wall and hauled them out the door with Angeline leading Blackjack behind him. "You're my daughter. I don't figure there's a man in the world worthy of you. But if you're dead set on finding one anyway, I wouldn't say no to the preacher."

"I thought you wanted me to marry. You've mentioned it often enough."

"I wasn't hinting. I was trying to ready my own mind."

She scowled. "Could have fooled me."

She caught the scent of tobacco smoke and turned to see Uncle Ironstone on the back doorstep, puffing on his pipe. "Will you come along to hear the preacher, Uncle?" she hollered.

"Today I promised to stay at the store. Another time the captain can stay, and I will go."

She gave him a wide smile. "I like that idea!"

Her father lifted a brow. "You think you'll get that old Indian converted?"

"I don't think *I'll* get anybody converted. But there's no knowing what God will do. Wouldn't you say?"

"I say you sound like your mother."

His remark was enough to warm her all the way to camp, even though the day was frigid and the ride felt longer than ever. She could hardly wait to see Everett and hear him preach again. Could hardly wait to slip her arm through his. . .

They arrived just in time. Was that singing coming from the cookshack? The deep, occasionally discordant blend of male voices pulled at her to hurry.

She adjusted her coat and smoothed her woolen skirts while

the captain unhooked Blackjack from his traces and turned him over to the camp hostler. He offered her his arm. "I haven't been to this camp so much in five years as I've been the past two months."

She winked. "Thank you for not complaining."

Angeline stepped into the shack where it appeared nearly half the camp was in attendance. Two fellows near the door offered their seats as Everett led an opening prayer.

He raised his head and proceeded to read to them from the book of James, chapter one. After reading about the testing of a person's faith, he concluded with the verse, "Wherefore, my beloved brethren, let every man be swift to hear, slow to speak, slow to wrath: For the wrath of man worketh not the righteousness of God."

He surveyed the room. "I confess to you that I am not a pillar of strength in this area. My fuse can be short. Like most people, I am prone to *reaction*."

Angeline followed the line of Everett's vision to the back of the room. Mick Hankins sat at the furthest table. He pushed a hand through his lank hair and slowly rose to square himself to Everett. Angeline's heart lurched. Would he further embarrass the preacher—and break their agreement—by spouting off some nonsense during Everett's sermon?

She clutched the edge of her father's coat, as much to keep herself from lurching to her feet to stop him as anything.

Mick cleared his throat. Everyone turned. The purple in Mick's jaw was stark, and his left eye remained a bit swollen with a big cut scabbed over across the bone beneath it. "Well, Preacher. . . I don't suppose you'd be much of a man if you didn't use the abilities the good Lord gave you. If you're talking about reacting to me hectoring you, and if you're saying to these men here that you were wrong for giving me this shiner. . ." He chuckled. "Well, you'd be making a mistake to do that. It was a fair fight." There was nodding and murmuring, and Mick spoke up a little louder. "They don't blame you any. They all seem to think I had it coming. Like I said, it was a fair fight."

Angeline's fingers unclenched. What was this? Mick confessing his foolishness in front of them all?

"I plan to hold up my end of the bargain without complaining." He looked across the gathering and at Everett again. "I'll be coming to hear what you have to say on Sunday mornings without pestering. I owe you that."

Was God perhaps getting Mick's attention? As he sat back down, Angeline silently prayed that was the case. She looked at Everett, who continued to stare at Mick.

"Amen," came a voice sounding like Willard Skivvens' from near the front. Around the room, other men nodded, a few adding halting *Amen*s.

Behind her, someone said, "That's a preacher who can swing a fist as well as he can wave a Bible. A man's man."

Everett rubbed his chin then held up his hands to quiet the growing consensus around the room. "I've a bit of a story to tell you." Was that a light coming back into his eyes? "I haven't always wanted to follow Christ. In fact, you may have heard a few rumors about me. If you did, it doesn't matter what they are. They're probably true. Yes, I was a brawler, a carouser, and many worse things besides. But when the Lord captured me, He gave me a better way to live.

"There's a hymn that was written just a few years ago. Don't worry." Smile lines returned to the corners of his eyes and mouth. "I won't torture you by singing it. But I memorized the words sometime back, because it seemed to be written about my life. This is what they say.

"'Years I spent in vanity and pride,
Caring not my Lord was crucified,
Knowing not it was for *me* He died
On Calvary.'"

Everett raised a finger heavenward.

"'Mercy there was great, and grace was *free*;
Pardon there was multiplied to me;
There my burdened soul found *liberty*,
    At Calvary.'"

His features smoothed and his voice softened:

"'By God's Word at last my sin I learned;
Then I trembled at the law I'd spurned,
Till my guilty soul imploring turned
To Calvary.'"

A bright sheen filled Everett's eyes.

"'Now I've giv'n to Jesus everything,
Now I *gladly* own Him as my King,
Now my raptured soul can only sing
Of Calvary.'"

Everett raised both arms, as he cried out:

"'Oh, the love that drew salvation's plan!
Oh, the grace that brought it down to man!
Oh, the mighty gulf that God did span
At Calvary!'"

Angeline joined in a chorus of *Amen*s. She turned a joyous smile toward her father, stunned to see moisture in his eyes also. She pulled her glance away but leaned against him and reached for his hand. Her heart nearly exploded from her chest when he squeezed hers back.

Everett thanked them for their understanding about the fight, but he pressed them again to come to God for salvation and to let Him take away the soul-sicknesses that waged war against them.

After a final prayer, men cleared out of the cookshack, many of them greeting Angeline and her father kindly as they passed by. Then Mick approached.

"Good morning, Captain. Miss Adair." Gone was the snideness he'd used the last time he spoke her name.

"Good morning, Mr. Hankins," her father replied with a measuring look.

Angeline greeted him. "That was a fine speech you gave. I hope you meant it."

"You never could pin me for being a liar. No, I meant it all right. I'll keep my word." He gave an emphatic nod. "And the preaching wasn't too bad. I might even learn something."

"I hope you do."

"I'll take that to heart." He looked about as if to say something else but drew his lips into a smile instead. "You folks have a good day now." He left them, and Angeline could hardly believe Mick didn't press her for attention any further. Had his fight with Everett even accomplished that? Or was it Everett's message?

She raised her eyes to look at the man who stood in front of the room, tucking his Bible beneath his arm as the last man walked off. He caught her gaze. She pushed back her shoulders as he approached her, his expression inscrutable. Uncertainty still? Weariness?

He shook her father's hand. "I'm not sure I wanted you to hear that again, but it's best you know all about me."

Angeline raised her chin. "There are things you ought to know about me too. For instance, I'm terribly headstrong, isn't that so, Captain? I can throw a real tantrum if I put my mind to it."

"Don't make her show you," her father said. "I'm going to go find John Salverson, if you two don't mind. I'm sure there's more you'd like to talk about before we drive back."

"Yessir."

"Thank you, Captain." Angeline whispered. She stretched to kiss his cheek. He sniffed and turned away.

As the door closed behind him, Everett set his Bible on the nearest table and gently took her hands. "I feel like the air has been cleared. I can breathe easy again." He rubbed her fingers. "I never saw any of this coming when I mounted up and came to the Northwoods to preach. My saddlebags were packed with high ideals. Seems that, even for a preacher, God only reveals His will along the path one little bit of torchlight at a time. With one step, and then another, He says, 'This is the way, walk ye in it.'" He gave a rueful chuckle. "I sure never pictured myself in the ring again, albeit a ring of moonlight. I thought I had His way for me figured out. I'd not kept to the Word where it says, 'ye *ought* to say, If the Lord will, we shall live, and do this, or that. But now ye rejoice in your boastings. . .' My own pride, I suppose." His brown eyes searched hers. "But He is merciful. I think He's giving me a bit more light for my way."

"Is He?"

He tucked her hands against his chest. His heartbeat pulsed against her knuckles. What if one of the jacks came in? As it was, she was sure that the cookee could see them while he worked quietly in the back of the kitchen. Everett didn't seem to care. He studied her then kissed her brow, and a riotous warm flood washed through her.

"I've been in that ring wrestling with God, asking Him if He was sure I was the right man for the work. . .and for you."

She barely breathed. "And. . .what did He say?"

"He told me to ask you what you thought and to stop measuring His love by what I know I don't deserve." He brushed a strand of her hair from the very place his lips had briefly touched.

A shiver raced over her skin. "You are the right man for this country and for me, Everett Shepherd."

"Then you'll have me, Angel? As your husband?"

Her heart lunged, and she squeezed his fingertips. "Everett."

"Of course, I know I'll have to ask the captain's permission, and he'll—"

"He'll say yes," she blurted. Heat flooded her face. "He knows my mind on the matter."

"Does he?" He grinned.

She bent her head against his chest. "Oh, you're teasing me."

One arm came around her, and with his other hand he raised her chin. "I wouldn't tease about how I feel. I've never met a woman like you, Angel. I'm sorry for my past, because all this time God knew I would love you."

She felt almost dizzy with joy. "You're a warm, strong, courageous man, Everett Shepherd, and I'm going to claim you."

"Forever?"

She nodded.

"Then we have a bit of unfinished business to take care of."

She couldn't imagine what that could be, but her pulse quickened to the answer as he bent his head to hers, and Everett did the claiming.

Angel never imagined a real kiss, nor especially that a *preacher* might kiss like this. His lips softened over hers, and their caress stole her breath. She didn't mind. He tightened his embrace, and for a moment longer, she didn't care if she ever breathed again. Then he shifted, and she inhaled, and the kiss intensified.

Oh heavens! Her legs wobbled, and if not for his arms around her, she would collapse.

Then his breath fanned her cheek. "Angel. . .my angel."

Angeline hadn't known what she wanted in life. Now she did. She wanted to share Everett's faith and his heart. And she wanted to share his words. "I love you so."

His gaze, soft yet hungry, swallowed her whole, and he kissed her again.

The cookhouse door opened, and an icy breeze gusted across the floor. There was a whistle and a whoop, and whoever did it went right back out again, but his voice carried. It had to be that young Freddy Barker.

"Hey! Looks like there's to be a wedding, and we'll be having a shivaree for the preacher any day now. He's kissin' on Miss Angeline like there ain't no tomorrow!"

Everett groaned even as a half smile bent his lips. "There goes my chance to ask your father properly for your hand before the word went out."

"I don't think it would've come as a surprise in any case."

"You're sure about that?"

She chuckled. "Quite sure. The captain doesn't run the tight ship he once did no matter how he might bluster and blow. However, should another fellow come strolling in through those doors, I'd hate for him to spread any doubt about how resolved I am to marry the preacher. I think you ought to kiss me one more time."

"Has the captain grown lenient because of his strong-willed daughter, I wonder? There's a good way to handle that kind of mutiny."

"It might be the reason. And speaking of my mutinous nature—"

Before she could finish, his eyes darkened again, and another kiss made her forget what she'd been going to say. There would be other times for talking and laughing and asking questions, and even for reading and praying together. There was no hurry to speak of everything now, because she would have Everett Shepherd, her own sky pilot, helping her find her way, for always.

HISTORICAL NOTE

Christ to the Lumberjacks

I first read about God sending the gospel to the thousands of men working in the lumber camps of Minnesota's great Northwoods in a fabulous biography by Harry Rimmer LL.D. titled *Last of the Giants – How Christ Came to the Lumberjacks*. He told how God placed the call on the first "sky pilot," Frank Higgins, who later passed the mantle to John Whitman Sornberger, and it eventually rested on Elwyn "Al" Channer. The unique stories of these spiritual giants read like the most adventure-some fiction, since these preachers came from colorful back-grounds before they met Christ. Yet their hearts were changed, and God chose them to carry salvation to the lumberjacks whose way of living they knew so well.

In my novella, *The Angel and the Sky Pilot*, Everett Shepherd's character is a compilation of men such as these. In one scene, Everett tells how a preacher pulled him from a gutter in Duluth, led him to faith in Christ, and trained him for the ministry. Although I don't name him, in my imagination that preacher was Frank Higgins, and Everett's background as both lumberjack and prizefighter was loosely based on the testimony of John Sornberger. Pastor Sornberger had personal experience with knockout drops prior to his salvation. Their use was common in the barrooms where men spent their hard-earned money with abandon. They might enjoy a wild night on the town only to wake up in an alley the next morning with their pockets turned inside out.

The lumberjacks created their own entertainment in the

camps. The pranks played on Everett by Freddy and old Joe were just the sort of thing men might do, as well as giving a newcomer the filthiest mattress nested with bedbugs.

As to the characters of Angeline Adair and her retired ship-captain father, since shipping and trading on Lake Superior have always played such vital historical roles for our country, and northern Minnesotans in particular, it seemed circumspect to bring those enterprises to light in my narrative. The fact that Angeline is the only female in the story plays on the significance that northern Minnesota was still a vast backcountry in 1905.

However, the landscape quickly changed with the influx of newcomers by railroad and steamship. New wilderness riches were soon discovered. The north country has ever since been characterized by giant tracts of woodland, resilient people, and exciting history, and Duluth remains an ever-changing, ever-growing city. I hope you enjoyed reading about this great American panorama.

Naomi Musch is an award-winning author who writes from a deer farm in the pristine Wisconsin Northwoods, where she and husband, Jeff, enjoy time spent with the families of their five children. When not in the physical act of writing or spending time loving on her passel of grandchildren, she can be found plotting stories as she roams around the farm, snacks out of the garden, and relaxes in her vintage camper. She also finds inspiration getting away to the water with her kayak. Naomi is a member of the American Christian Fiction Writers and Faith, Hope, & Love Christian Writers. She loves engaging with others and can be found all around social media or at her site naomimusch.com.

Mail-Order Minister

BY KARI TRUMBO

CHAPTER 1

Bakers Nook, SD, 1889

A bright orange feather in Belta's new hat distracted Olive Torey only a moment. In that second of distraction, her friend was able to ask the question Olive had been staving off for the last twenty minutes. Drat her persistence.

"And what was it you were saying about your parents and the mail-order minister? Ghastly business. A minister should have to prove himself before being given such a position." Belta waved her hand, sending the large feather bobbing.

"I don't see what's so ghastly about it. The church split, and now we need a minister. That's all there is to tell." She bit her lip and said a prayer her heavenly Father wouldn't hold the falsehood against her. Belta was the worst kind of gossip, and Mama would be so disappointed in her for sharing too much.

"My parents were laughing and laughing last night over what they heard. They said your parents had sent off letters only to eligible men." She gave a dramatic pause and covered the lower half of her face with her fan. "I wonder why that would be?" She fluttered her lashes and whipped the fan away to show off a pretty pout. "*Our* elders specifically looked for a married man.

One who would be stable and stay with our church. Not one who would move along the moment he gets a mind to marry."

That was just the trouble. Olive wasn't supposed to know the particulars, because she shouldn't have been listening at her parents' door while they discussed their options for a suitable pastor. They'd looked over the applicants and realized the ones they liked were also men whom they would gladly choose as a husband for their only daughter. Coincidence? Olive wasn't so sure but wasn't going to malign them in any case.

She wasn't going to be easily swayed to their plot, but they didn't know that. Just a year ago now, they had enrolled her in the Spearfish Normal School for teachers without telling her. She'd begged them to reconsider, and they'd finally allowed her to stay with them. Teaching was not what she wanted to do with her life, and her parents' actions had set the framework for her to fear they would continue trying to control her future.

"I know of no such thing. I think my parents hoped to find someone young, with new ideas, to draw people back to our congregation. The families remaining at our church are mostly young. My parents are the only elders." The excuse, though a bit illogical, sounded good enough to her own ears. Hopefully, it would pass Belta's inspection.

"I heard they were trying to find a match for their *almost spinster* daughter." Belta raised her chin a notch and stared at Olive.

Olive laughed and glanced around her loud friend, farther down the boardwalk, to see if anyone else might hear their conversation. "Well, if I am, then so are you. We're the same age, and you're unmarried, same as me."

Belta sniffed. "Not for long. Anthony will ask for my hand. I'm sure of it." Her glance dodged everywhere but at Olive's eyes. "Is that the stage?" She bobbed her head toward the end of the street, sending the poor feather in a frantic wave, barely missing Olive's eye.

The noise of six horses and a cloud of dust that rose above the puny buildings of Baker's Nook announced the coming of the stage. Against the backdrop of the Black Hills, the sight was impressive. Olive's stomach flipped at the idea of who was on that stage. The new minister. The man her parents hoped she'd marry.

She gave herself a mental shake and sat up straighter. She was a woman of the new state of South Dakota, a pioneer in so many ways. Strong. Resourceful. She didn't need a husband. But, *honour thy father and thy mother. . .* She had to respect her parents, which meant respect for the man they'd chosen to lead their now-tiny flock.

The stagecoach driver tugged on a handful of thick lines until the horses slowed to a stop in front of the stagecoach building. Olive had purposely chosen a seat outside the barbershop, two storefronts down from the station, so she could get a good look at everyone getting off without appearing overly curious.

One man climbed down the straight stairs and landed in the dusty road. Black boots led to black trousers and a vest that fit nicely over an ecru linen shirt. He smiled up at the driver and thanked him before catching a bag the driver tossed off the top. Apparently, he was a man of few belongings, or he didn't plan to stay.

He glanced up and down the street with that same warm smile. Did he like what he saw? She hoped so. His mission would be difficult if he wasn't used to living so far removed from a larger city. For a drawn-out moment, his gaze caught above the buildings, and she followed where he stared. She took in the pretty morning haze that clung to the mountain spruce trees. The frondescence itself had offered a welcome.

Belta gasped. "Will you look at him? Is he the preacher your parents requested?" Her gaze finally hit Olive square in the face, and she whipped her fan so fast the feather laid straight back. "You'd be an absolute fool not to let that man marry you."

"Then a fool I'll be. You don't even know him. He could be horrid. He might have food in his teeth or smell." She gestured toward the man with the preacher's collar and groaned inwardly as the motion caught his attention. He nodded at her and turned his steps their way.

"You'd best keep your mouth shut." Olive wasn't at all sure what her parents had put in the letters to this preacher, Mr. Handsome, whose name she couldn't recall.

"Good morning, ladies." He gave a quick nod to each of them. "I'm Reverend Finch Presly, and I'm looking for the home of Mr. and Mrs. Torey. Would either of you happen to know where they live?"

Belta snorted in a most unladylike way. "I should say so. This is Olive Torey, their daughter."

His focus swung from Belta to Olive, and her face heated by degrees. If his sermons were anywhere near as attractive as his face, the town would beg to keep him and he might even bring the two churches back together.

"Good morning. I can take you to see them." She stood, and her knees wobbled under the weight of all her questions. Would he ask about her parents along the way?

"Be good now!" Belta laughed as she dashed off in the other direction.

Olive flinched. The entire town, all six hundred and two of them, would know about her situation within the hour.

Reverend Presly ambled along on her left, clutching his full bag and matching her shorter stride. "Is it far?"

She shook her head then thought better of the action as she

made certain her curls were still under control. "If you have no need of your bag straightaway, I can take you to the parsonage first. It's ready for you. I helped Mama freshen it up yesterday."

"If it's closer, I'd thank you." He laughed, adjusting his hold on his bag. Only then did she note the strap of his haversack was broken, so he couldn't carry it easily.

"It is. Down this street. Not even a block." She turned and headed toward the church at the edge of town. Two steeples now dominated the landscape instead of one.

"I didn't realize Baker's Nook was large enough for two churches." He nodded down the street. "Your parents didn't make any mention of it."

She bit her lip, unsure how to tell him of the divide that made finding two new pastors necessary. "That is the reason you're here." Well, there were two of them, if she counted the reason she wasn't supposed to know about. "Our church recently split after some differences over elders."

"And the other congregants have a minister?" He stared down the street as he spoke, the first hint of doubt seeping into his strong voice.

"I've heard they've contacted an older man who has a wife and grown children. He too is on his way."

They arrived at the small parsonage, and Olive pushed the door open. She let Reverend Presly walk inside and waited for him on the front stoop. She knew the house as well as if she'd grown up there, since the former pastor had been close friends with her parents.

On the inside to the left was a welcoming sitting room with two rocking chairs and a horsehair sofa. The fireplace was sturdy yet held an attraction as well. The kitchen was to the right with a small but efficient dining room behind it that led right back into the sitting room to form a circle. Stairs in the sitting room led up to the small half story with two bedrooms.

Reverend Presly poked his head out the front door with a grin on his face. "It's quite spacious for just me. Will I be sharing with the other pastor?"

She'd never asked her parents such a question, but with the divide of the church, so was a divide among friends. "I doubt that, but my parents will be able to answer all of your questions. I'm not privy to such things. They are the only remaining elders of our church."

He offered his arm. "Lead the way." After they'd gone only a few steps, he continued, "We'll have to look into more elders. I hate to force change so soon, but a church needs more than a pastor and one couple to lead it. I hope your parents can recommend others in the congregation who have stayed."

He couldn't possibly know their plans for him if he asked that question. Marrying their daughter would certainly be a change. If he didn't know, she wasn't going to be the one to tell him. "Yes, they would be happy to help you find others to take on leadership. Other changes... You'll have to ask them."

He patted her hand as he waited for her to direct them which way to go. She nodded in the direction of First Street, and he continued walking, his presence drawing people out from businesses to stare. "All change comes at a price." His low voice seemed only for her, making her heart stutter strangely.

Within a few minutes, they turned down the street where Olive lived. She had always been secretly proud of her family's home. It sat on the edge of town on a soft slope, so the front yard seemed to spill down into the street with flowers and two neat rows of low-growing hedges that led to the front door. Father had ordered special paint to make their grand house stand out, though she would never say it was ostentatious. It was home and always had been.

"We're here." She strode forward a few steps then stopped, realizing she'd left Reverend Presly behind. "Is something the matter?"

His mouth hung slightly agape as his gaze rose up higher and higher until he shielded his eyes with his hand. "All this will take some getting used to." He squared his shoulders and headed for the door.

Finch refused to be cowed by the situation. The town was little more than a smattering of short buildings all butted up next to one another in a tidy row, nestled in the crook of a few mountains. The street was dusty from a midsummer dry spell, and the noise of horses, wagons, and traces seemed to come at him from all sides. Yet his main concern was the house he was about to enter.

His new life was hundreds of miles from the old. What he'd always known was nothing like this. He needed to be a strong, decisive leader now, not the man he had been. Kansas had once been home, the flat part, where a man could see for miles in all directions. These hills gave him the feeling of being boxed in, and the Torey house only added to his concern.

A house was a house, and this one was many days' ride by stage away from the other that looked very similar. The house in which his former intended, Felicia, used to live with her parents. The one he'd left behind when she'd married someone else. He cleared his throat as Mr. and Mrs. Torey appeared at the front door.

Both graciously welcomed him, and he noted characteristics about each of them that were similar to Miss Torey. Mrs. Torey had golden hair woven on the back of her head in a becoming style. Miss Torey's dark blue eyes came from Mr. Torey, as did the crescent dimple on her right cheek when she smiled, though it was more attractive on her.

"Good morning." He took the time to give both a firm handshake then followed them. Mrs. Torey indicated a place at the table for him.

"I've just served up a small breakfast, knowing you'd be arriving on the stage and you'd be famished."

Mrs. Torey's idea of a small breakfast filled the entire table. There were thick slices of toasted bread with honeyed butter. Flapjacks sat in a perfect stack at the center with three kinds of jelly nearby. The scent of fried bacon set his mouth to watering.

"My, what a gracious offering. Shall we?" He brought Miss Torey forward and gently laid a hand on her back to guide her to a chair.

The moment he touched her he pulled away, feeling a tension that made him somewhat nervous. She looked at him, a question lifting her pretty brows. Had she felt the same when she'd touched his arm earlier?

"Yes, yes, sit. Let's eat together, and I can answer any questions you might have." Mr. Torey broke the unease in Finch's belly. Asking questions about his new position was safe, whereas thinking about what had just happened was not. He forced a smile, pulled out the chair next to him for Miss Torey, then seated himself.

He waited for Mrs. Torey to pass the bacon and to ask him the first questions families always asked. They usually wanted to know why he wanted to come. How long and where had he studied? He was used to their inquiries, though no congregation so far had decided to keep him on as their pastor. They'd all thought him too young for the job.

He took two slices of bacon and handed the plate to Miss Torey. Her fingers brushed his, and she jerked back slightly, almost dropping the plate. He caught it quickly and laughed, hoping to set her at ease.

"I'm so sorry. It was—" She paused, staring at him as if for help.

"Slippery," he said, almost unable to find his voice. Where had the Lord placed him? Finch had begged and pleaded to be assigned anywhere he could be of service—except somewhere with women who would remind him of why he'd left Kansas.

"So, Reverend Presly, tell us about Kansas." Mr. Torey piled a stack of flapjacks on his plate then passed them to his wife.

Praise God, a subject he could talk about in his sleep. "The part I come from is full of wide-open spaces. Not a hill within miles." He took a sip of coffee, letting the rich flavor linger over his tongue. "These hills just drive your thoughts to the sky, to the heavens. 'The heavens declare the glory of God; and the firmament sheweth his handywork.'" He took a deep breath, taking in the scents and all the wonder around him and letting the familiarity of the Word calm his disquiet.

"I hope you don't get homesick. These hills are vastly different from the prairies." Mrs. Torey wove her fingers within her husband's in a sweet gesture.

"We should know. We made our home in Nebraska when we first married, then came north and started a family," Mr. Torey explained.

He glanced over at Olive just as her cheeks darkened in a pretty blush. He nodded her way. "Thank you for meeting me at the stagecoach station, Miss Torey. You made my arrival much easier."

Mrs. Torey smiled. "That's wonderful. You may call our daughter Olive, and she can assist you in whatever you need. She is so helpful. The town can be a little prickly with newcomers at first, but we warm up quickly. She can introduce you to everyone."

Was he being dismissed by the two people who were supposed

to be his right hand in the church? "What do you see as your role in the congregation?" He abandoned the food and got right to what was on his heart.

Charming as their daughter might be, he had no desire to spend any more time with her than was necessary. The heart was a fickle thing. Better that he focus on his soul and his mind. Two things he had some say over.

"It's our responsibility to ensure you're preaching from the Word as you lead our small congregation. We are also there to help whenever you plan anything outside of your Sunday duties. The last pastor held a Bible study for those of us who lived in town and wanted to join him. The parsonage was too small, so we held those here." Mrs. Torey smiled with a touch of pride reflecting in her eyes.

"And is that something you'd like to continue?" He'd never done anything of the sort beyond the small study he and some friends had put together in seminary.

"Dear, let the man get settled in before we start adding to his duties." Mr. Torey patted his wife's hand. "If we want him to stay, he has to get to know people, and they have to like him too."

Mrs. Torey's face fairly beamed. "You're right, of course. How silly of me. I'm just so excited to finally have a preacher again."

He glanced around the table, letting the welcome of this family seep into him. He wouldn't be shaking the dust off his boots so quickly in Baker's Nook. Maybe he'd finally found a place the Lord would ask him to stay.

CHAPTER 2

Loud thumping downstairs alerted Olive to the fact that she'd taken too long to dress. "I'll be right down!" she called to the closed door as she shoved a pin deep into her curls.

Why was she taking so long this morning? Dressing wasn't usually an affair that took more than fifteen to twenty minutes. Belta was the one who cared about fashion. Olive stood and brushed her skirts, taking an extra moment to look in the mirror. Fine. She was just fine.

Mama bustled about the kitchen as Olive entered, handing her two flapjacks as she rushed by. "You look lovely, dear, but you need to be on your way. You don't want to keep the reverend waiting." Olive felt a pang of guilt as she watched Mama wipe down the breakfast table.

"Surely he'd wait a few minutes while I help you. I'm sorry I took so long to get myself ready."

Mama waved her away. "Making breakfast for three people is not that hard, and I don't complain. Don't worry on it for one moment."

With Mama practically shoving her out the door, Olive slid on her small wristlet then rolled her flapjacks into a tube so she could eat them quickly before anyone saw her. The street was full of people already, which was good, since the entire reason she was going to see Reverend Presly was to introduce him about town.

That very reverend was out on his porch, sweeping the morning dust away. He looked fresh, well rested, and broader across the shoulders today than he had yesterday. Olive closed her eyes and steadied her wayward thoughts. Continuing to think of the preacher as handsome would only serve her parents' purpose.

She squared her shoulders and headed for the front porch. Reverend Presly sang a hymn, with great enthusiasm but slightly off-key. If she could see a flaw in him she couldn't be infatuated with him, could she? Didn't love make a person see someone as perfect? Liking him as an acquaintance was natural, as they were quite close in age. At least, he appeared to be. So that had to be why she was letting him take residence in her mind so.

"Good morning, Reverend." She stopped at the base of the two steps leading up to his narrow porch, giving him a moment to prop his broom by the door.

"A fine morning it is." He turned and gave her one of his smiles the way he had the day before, the one that set her knees quivering.

Olive reached for the stability of the railing and gave what she hoped was a sure smile in return. "Are you ready to meet the town?"

Reverend Presly ran his hands down the front of his black vest, touched his collar, and then grabbed his hat off a nearby chair and set it atop his head. "I am. Where should we start?"

Even though the church was mostly empty, she wanted to show him the reason he was here. "How about the church? Alma will be there now, counting last Sunday's offering before she takes it to the bank."

"Someone who isn't an elder counts the offering?" He fell

into step alongside her, his words merely questioning, not condemning.

"She's the banker's daughter and offered to do the task. My parents count it first, but she verifies the amount and has always been honest. She's two years older than I am and married to one of the Whisk brothers." Who married her for a connection to her father. Mark Whisk had struck gold in one of the mines, and he wanted a safe place to keep his money. Alma's hand ensured the bank took special care of his account. Olive hoped he took special care of Alma too, but Mark had never attended church, so she didn't know.

Reverend Presly opened the right side of the double front doors and held it for her. She entered the dark narthex and waited for him to close the door. Just being in the church gave her a feeling of peace and rest. The church was like a second home to her.

"Alma? Are you here?" she called quietly. Her voice echoed off the vaulted ceiling.

"Olive? Is that you?" Alma peered from behind the door to Reverend Presly's new office. "Oh!" She stepped out and whipped off her apron. "I was just doing some tidying in here in preparation for the new preacher. You caught me." She laughed as she tucked a strand of dark hair back into her bun and stepped forward. "You must be he. I'm happy to meet you." She gave a slight head bob, like a curtsy.

He gave her a gentle smile that seemed different from the ones he'd been bestowing on Olive. "Alma Whisk, this is Reverend Finch Presly."

Alma stepped aside and gestured to his new office. "I'm sure this is what you would like to see." She headed back to the door and held it open. "It's not much, but it's quiet in there."

Reverend Presly stepped forward and then into the small

space. That too Olive knew well. There had been so many meetings in the office over the direction of the church between the former three families of elders and the pastor. Everyone had been stuffed in there like quilts in a trunk. When she'd been very young, she'd played on the floor as her parents talked to the pastor.

Reverend Presly ran a finger across the desk and left a dark line in the dust. "There hasn't been a preacher here in quite some time."

"No, sir." Alma ducked her head. "It's been quite a few months. Most of the congregants are young, many newly married or with small children. A good number of them live outside of town, so helping with the church is difficult. I would gladly come in and tidy, if someone is needed." Though she hesitated in the delivery of her offer.

Olive had heard all the reasons the church had been left without upkeep before, and they were valid. Everyone was busy. "I can help." The words escaped her tongue before she could think them through.

"Oh, bless you." Alma sighed in relief, and Reverend Presly grinned. "Then I won't have to do all the work alone."

What had she just agreed to?

Finch kept pace at Olive's shoulder, reminding himself that he had to think of her as Miss Torey, not Olive, when she stopped abruptly. He barely caught himself before barreling into her. After meeting a handful of the nicest, most genuine people, the one in front of them didn't seem to fit the mold.

Olive's voice trembled only for the first syllable of the woman's name before she got her fears under control. He silently cheered for her. Facing people who obviously weren't pleased to be faced was one of the most difficult parts of his job.

"Bethanne Gould." Olive squared her shoulders. "This is our new pastor, Reverend Finch Presly."

Miss Gould tipped her head slightly, her pert nose pointing in the air. "Not our minister. He's coming by the end of this week."

Olive took a deep breath, and he could feel the tension running through her though he wasn't touching her in the slightest. "Yes, I know, but Baker's Nook is a small community. I thought you might like to meet the newest member."

He stepped forward to take the pressure off her. "Good afternoon, Miss Gould." He'd had to remember what time it was after they'd stopped for a pleasant luncheon at the bakery. "I'm pleased to meet you."

Miss Gould whipped her hands behind her back and took a step away. "Don't you dare make it appear to anyone as though I might go back to your church. I'm proud to attend services where I want. Where I'm welcome." Miss Gould gave them a wide berth as she stomped around them.

Olive spoke to her as she passed them by. "We were friends. . . Why are you doing this? Reverend Presly has done nothing to you. *I've* done nothing." Her voice didn't quiver in the slightest, but he heard the pain there and wanted to lay a reassuring hand on her back. He was so proud of her for saying what was on her heart.

Who could harm this woman who gave of herself everywhere they'd been? There wasn't a person she'd avoided, even with the obvious discomfort. She hadn't had to defend his presence until now, and he wouldn't let her be the only one to have strength.

He touched her elbow gently then pulled his hand away as that same fission of energy popped through him. He raised his voice to be heard. "It was nice to meet you, Miss Gould. I won't try to pull you away from a church that gives you a sense of community and teaches the Word of God. Good day." His words halted the young woman, and she turned, her mouth gaping as he directed Olive away. Had she expected him to call for fire and brimstone to rain down on her?

Olive trembled slightly at his side and kept looking away from him. Finally, she swiped at her eyes with the back of her hand. He stopped her swift progress with a slight clearing of his throat.

"May we take a brief break in the churchyard? There's a lovely tree there, and it seems the perfect place to rest and give you a moment." He hated to point out the delicate notions of women. Some preferred for no one to know when they cried, while others used their emotions to twist people into doing what they wanted. He doubted Olive was the latter, but kindness was never wasted.

She nodded and did an about-face so perfect, military men would probably vow she'd been a soldier. She marched two blocks without a word then sank down in the soft needles beneath the lone tree in the front yard. Her eyes were slightly red, and her spine seemed to have lost most of its starch.

"Want to tell me about what happened?"

She sniffled, and he dug a handkerchief from his pocket. He'd learned early on in his ministry to keep more than one neatly pressed square available in his pocket. Settling down next to her, he waited for her to calm down enough to speak. He couldn't offer comfort other than a listening ear. He'd easily offered brotherly compassion to some women when he'd copastored with his minister back home, but he'd known them his entire life. Olive was a mild temptation for him. He prayed for the right words to say and the right heart to deal with her pain.

She dabbed delicately at her nose then looked away. "About

a year ago, our pastor started preaching fire from the pulpit, and some of his words caused dissension among the members. Two of our elders were unhappy enough to leave, and they took much of the congregation with them." She tucked her chin, hiding her face.

"I don't understand how his preaching could lead to such a rift." Finch crossed his legs and made sure he was giving her enough space so anyone who witnessed them would know this was not a romantic outing. He had to maintain a respectable reputation.

"When our preacher realized that he was the reason for the divide, he left."

"Which is why your parents are the only elders."

She sighed and wiped her eyes. "Yes, most of the young families stayed while the older members of the town left our church. My parents moved to Baker's Nook twenty-five years ago, which was well after most families established themselves in this mining town. We are still sometimes seen as outsiders."

He was saddened that someone who had lived her entire life here could still feel like an outcast. "I'm sorry. I understand how you feel. Thank you for defending my reason for being here to Miss Gould, but I think my service to the community should do that. Let the Lord do that. If they are convicted to come hear me preach, then they might see that it's safe to visit old friends again."

She slowly shook her head. "If trying were an option, it would've worked by now. The only person I've managed to continue a relationship with is my friend Belta, and I suspect she stays by my side because she likes to hear what's going on with our church."

He tried to recall where he'd heard that name. With all those he'd met, the people of Baker's Nook were starting to become mixed in his mind. "Was she the one sitting with you when I came off the stage?" He stuck one finger straight up along the side of his head like a feather. "With the hat?"

Olive grinned, then laughed. "Yes, she's known for her hats and her wagging tongue." Her cheeks and nose turned pink. "Oh, I shouldn't say such things. It makes me as terrible of a gossip as she can be."

He wanted her to feel comfortable enough with him to speak her mind and to laugh more. "Have we had enough walking about town for one day? I'm afraid if we meet many more people, I won't remember a one of them."

She slowly nodded. "I think I have. Would you like some tea and scones? Mama makes some every afternoon."

He couldn't miss the urgency in her voice, a need to be home. While her house offered him no comfort, since it was so much like the home of the woman who left him behind, he couldn't deny Olive when she was obviously distraught. "That sounds nice."

He pushed to his feet and offered her a hand getting off the ground. Though it was the gentlemanly thing to do, he fought the urge to keep his excitement at her touch under control. Why did his heart race when he was near her? What was this strange sensation to protect her when she was obviously a capable woman? Clearly, he needed a little distance.

She walked alongside him, tucking his handkerchief in her sleeve. She'd wash it and return it to him, but the notion of her keeping something of his was making his mind whirl. Once they arrived at Olive's home, he held the door for her.

She immediately removed her hat, revealing her blond curls tucked neatly at her nape. After she hung up her hat, she waited for his. He'd completely forgotten what was on his head and fumbled it for a moment as he took it off, making her smile.

"Olive? Is that you?" Mrs. Torey's cheery voice came from the back of the house.

"Yes, Mama. Reverend Presly is with me." He found himself wishing she was comfortable enough with him to call him Finch, as she had when she'd introduced him all morning.

"Oh, Reverend, come inside. Olive? What's the matter?" Mrs. Torey wrapped Olive in a swift embrace.

"We came upon one person who wasn't nearly as friendly as the others. Your blacksmith, banker, and hotelier are all wonderful people," he offered.

Mama held Olive's shoulders and gave her a little shake. "Don't you let anyone look down on you. They've got no call to."

With that, she turned on her heel, and Finch held in a laugh. Now he knew where Olive had learned to have such backbone. In the kitchen, Mrs. Torey had set out a tea service and a plate of scones that looked appetizing. Though they'd eaten just a few hours before, his stomach grumbled at the sight.

Olive pulled out the chair she'd sat in the morning before, and he rushed to seat her then took the spot next to hers. He wasn't about to let Olive bring up Miss Gould again, not when he'd just tried to get her to forget what had hurt her.

"We've decided to mix our meeting the townspeople with working on the church." Finch took the pot and poured tea for Olive, her mother, and then himself.

"Thank you, Reverend." Mrs. Torey smiled at him and then Olive as she took a scone and set it on her plate. "Meeting the first few people went well?"

"Most of them, yes. We started with Alma at the church then went to as many of our congregants as we could here in town." Olive added a drizzle of honey from the pot on the tea tray.

Mrs. Torey nodded. "I'm hopeful many of them will return now that we have a real preacher and not just your father. He did his best, but the calling was never on him." She took a sip of her tea.

Everyone they'd met from the church had been in their twenties or very early thirties. While he could make young people elders, generally he liked older couples to assist him in leading the church, since they had time and experience to guide them. This wouldn't be an easy assignment, but if it was where the Lord wanted him, then his efforts would be fruitful.

Olive delicately held her teacup. "Yes, I think tomorrow will be a day of focusing on dust and repairs at the church rather than rebuilding dusty relationships."

That also meant he'd have a day alone with Olive in the small, out-of-the-way church that no one used except Alma. Maybe he'd have to pray some of his new congregation would stop by as they worked, or he might have trouble concentrating on the task of cleaning. Focusing on the lovely lady with him would cause quite the dustup in the community indeed.

CHAPTER 3

Finch pulled a squeaky wagon behind him, borrowed from the mercantile, carrying a load of white paint for the walls. Shoved in along the back sat a small can of black paint for the trim. One wheel wobbled in protest, and he whispered a prayer that the dilapidated cart would hold up until it had served its current purpose. Olive had told him there was a limited budget for repairs after paying for his train ticket, which meant the paint could not be replaced if it spilled.

He waved to the baker, Mr. Stansteader, whom he'd gotten to know well over the past few days, since Finch wasn't a cook. Mr. Stansteader made cakes, pies, and bread but also sandwiches. Relying on the kindness of the Torey family any more than was expressly necessary was out of the question. He was already spending more time with their daughter than he should. Additional meals had to be taken alone or he risked a deeper friendship than he could allow.

"Hello, Mrs. White!" Olive's cheery voice carried across the grassy lawns that spanned between him and where she walked toward him. He could practically see her without looking. She would be wearing her blue dress today, the sturdy work dress that she wore interchangeably with a green one when helping him. He'd found her steady routine in things even as trivial as her clothing to be comforting to him. He never had to worry that she would be ostentatious, nor would he have to go out of his way to maintain propriety. She was forever one step ahead of him and completely above reproach.

He slowed his pace, allowing her to catch up, secretly happy when he heard her footfalls quicken to reach him. "Good morning, Reverend."

Her exuberance lifted his mood and made him happier about the prospect of working. Painting was one of his least favorite tasks, but her pleasant mien and cheerful countenance would make the day pass quickly. "It is a fine morning." He grinned but stuttered to a stop as suddenly one of the wagon wheels buckled and refused to turn.

"Oh!" Olive stopped next to the cart. "At least the buckets of paint only slid, they didn't spill." She looked expectantly at him, and he felt something he hadn't experienced in a long time. Confidence. She believed he could and would take care of the situation.

He smiled at her. "Let me carry the drum of paint to the church. I think I can manage without the cart, though the can is heavy. I'll come back for the black paint."

She nodded her agreement to the plan as if she trusted he could move the entire earth if he wanted to. "I'll wait here with the wagon."

He held his breath. *Lord, this isn't pride asking, but please let me be able to lift this. Not only so Olive doesn't have to assist me but so that I don't look the fool.* He had to be honest with himself. God knew his heart and his intent, so hiding his true feelings would be a falsehood.

He checked the rim of the barrel for any wet paint where

they'd sealed the lid. Finding none, he wrapped his arms around the container and lifted with his knees, trying not to grunt like he had no manners at all. He'd only gone a few steps when the strain nearly forced him into giving up on manners completely.

"Reverend, you need some help there?" Adolf, the blacksmith, jogged toward him, waving a hand for him to stop. "Your face is red as a beet. Let me get that for you. To the church?" He didn't wait for a reply, which was good because Finch couldn't have said a word if he tried.

Turning back to Olive, he saw her friend Belta approaching at a jog, her hat a grandiose banner announcing her arrival. He wanted to groan but held it in. Belta was a friend of Olive's, though she didn't treat Olive all that well. At least, not from what Olive had confided to him as she had introduced him around town last week.

"Olive." Belta stomped to a stop. "What do you think you're doing?"

Olive's cheeks colored slightly. "I'm going to the church to help paint. We'd like it to be ready for this Sunday's service."

"It's unseemly." Her brows rose as she noticed his approach, and then she pounced on him. "What are your intentions, Reverend?"

Don't cross your arms. She's just looking out for her friend. State the plan kindly with firmness. "I intend to accept any assistance offered to me to get the church building ready. Would you like to help?" Her hat had some type of accessory that looked a little like a paintbrush, reminding him they'd only purchased two. Thankfully, she was already shaking her head.

"I would never. . ." She gripped Olive's shoulders, almost pushing her into the cart. Finch grabbed the smaller can of paint and moved the wagon before Olive could stumble over it and hurt herself.

"Olive, think about your reputation and his. You can't spend days upon days with the preacher alone in the church." Belta scowled at him like he was a reprobate.

"The door has remained open the entire time. In fact, the only time we've been behind closed doors was when we were in my house with my parents," Olive protested.

Belta sniffed in indignation. "That may be, but if you're working in his office, no one can see from out here if the door is open or closed."

Olive gasped and turned as red as Adolf had said Finch was a few minutes before.

"I can assure you all doors have been left open in the church, and the windows," Finch said firmly. "We've been dusting, sweeping, and repairing the pews. Tomorrow, we're going to bring them outside to stain them and the floors, but only if we can get the inside painted today."

"Need help with that can too, Reverend?" the muscled blacksmith asked as Belta eyed him and stepped back two paces.

"That would be just fine, thank you, Adolf." He handed Adolf the paint can and hoped he could convince Belta to move along as quickly.

"Miss Collins, Anthony will be waiting for you in his office," Adolf said. He nodded at her with narrowed eyes.

Belta huffed and stomped off the same way she'd come. Finch immediately felt more comfortable until he saw Olive's pinched face. Had she taken what Belta said to heart?

Olive took a deep breath as Belta walked away. The last thing she needed was the only person her age who still spent time with her telling the entire town that she was having some make-believe tryst in the church with the new reverend. People might not truly believe Olive would do that, but they'd spread the news merely to hurt her family. The majority of her parents' friends had moved to the other church and were angry that Olive and her parents hadn't chosen to go as well.

"Are you all right? I'm sorry I didn't save you from Miss Collins' unkind words." Reverend Presly ducked his head.

Olive would have none of that. She wanted him standing in front of his new flock with authority and conviction. "She did me no real harm." She knew that tongues might wag over the amount of time she'd spent with the preacher. But he was truly becoming a friend, even in only a few weeks.

When she'd introduced him that first Saturday, they'd invited everyone to Olive's home for the first Sunday service. He'd given a rousing and impressive sermon. They'd talked at lunch when everyone had left, giving her more time to feel comfortable about her offer to help him. After the first day, they'd fallen into a routine that was comfortable and exciting all at once. She enjoyed talking and working with him. He was strong and capable with a quick mind and a handsome smile.

Knowing her parents wanted to marry her off to this man was keeping her heart where it needed to stay though. She couldn't let them dictate her life. He could be her friend and nothing more. And she wasn't going to let Belta's pesky rumors do what she was trying to prevent. There wouldn't be a wedding simply because people wanted to gossip.

She fell into step at Finch's side as they headed for the church. Though she couldn't call him by his first name, he was Finch in her thoughts. "Which room would you like to paint first? Nothing has been done to the inside for years, and before we got to it, it hadn't been cleaned for three months."

The cobwebs and dust they'd removed spoke to that. While the church could be cleaned and then used as it was, Finch had maintained that a transition to a new pastor was the best time to make needed repairs, and Olive agreed. Even if she was the only one offering to help.

He released a long breath. "The sanctuary first. That's the room that will get used the most. If there isn't enough paint for my office, I'll make do with the walls as they are. It's much nicer in there after you scrubbed it down yesterday."

His notice and praise warmed her from her chest outward until the embarrassment from the meeting with Belta slipped away. "Thank you. I'm glad you like it." Helping Finch had given her something to do besides worry over the friends she'd lost to the separation. When she was here working, she had purpose and focus and. . .a friend. The conversation and company were pleasant, especially when Finch rolled up his sleeves and moved the pews to sweep. The man had lifted more than books in his life.

He opened the door for her and propped it wide with the same rock they'd used the days before. Then he started opening windows. Without a breath of air moving, the building was stifling.

"There. These are not the best conditions to paint. A rare sweltering day." He glanced out the window toward the town, drew his handkerchief from his pocket, and swiped his brow.

"If you think today is not good to start, we can wait." She'd helped her mother paint the outside of their house, and that had been an undertaking, especially going up and down ladders in a skirt.

"I think we'll manage. I do need to go thank your parents for the paint sometime."

He'd been absent from supper almost since his arrival, much to Mama's consternation. Olive knew she wasn't supposed to know why her mother was so frustrated by Finch's avoidance of their house. She'd speculated that perhaps he'd been able to read her parents' intentions from the start and was making his objections known by keeping his distance.

Olive's cheeks burned. What if he thought she had something to do with their scheme? "I know you'd like to tell them yourself, but if you're too busy, I can share your appreciation." She tied the strings of her apron, ready to get to work.

Outside, a group of boys had gathered for a game of midsummer baseball. The planting was in, and calving season had mostly passed, meaning the boys had a few weeks where, once they finished their chores at home, they could just be boys. Olive longed to sit outside under a parasol and cheer for them.

Finch arrived at her side, his tall presence oddly both comforting and unsettling as her heart first sighed then raced. She'd never felt these odd, tremulous emotions for anyone else. Why this man? Certainly, he was of good character and handsome. Those were fine things. But she wasn't about to let her parents choose a husband for her when she had no desire to marry yet.

"Looks like they're having fun. Have you ever played?" Finch grinned, giving him a sweetly boyish appearance.

"Me?" She shook her head. "Never. I used to watch from the front steps of the school while I ate my lunch. I always marveled at how quickly the boys could eat so they would have a few minutes to play. Then Mama told me that at home those boys have to eat their lunches while they work. My own stomach would protest."

Finch nodded, and his lips flattened. "I remember Ma handing me a sandwich while I was pitching hay. It's hard work. Sweaty work. I peeled off my glove, prayed there wouldn't be straw on my fingers, and didn't look at what I was eating, because I didn't have time. The first few times you do it, you get a gut ache. After that. . ." Finch shrugged. "You get used to doing what's required of you, and skipping a meal is a bad idea when you have to work so hard."

"You were a farmer?" She'd had no idea, though because he came from Kansas, the idea made sense. Kansas was a farming state.

"My father was, yes. When I told him I had to pay to get an education further than eighth grade, he wasn't pleased. He told me that if preaching was what I was supposed to do, then God would provide the money, because he certainly didn't have it. I was offended at first that he would be unwilling to support my decision, but now I don't hold his words against him."

"Why would your father have to help you?" She was confused. Her friends had worked and paid for their own educations, the few who went on.

"My father had saved for me, or so he said, enough money to build a house on his land. I hoped to use that for my education when the time came, but he wouldn't allow it."

She wanted to reach out and touch his shoulder, to assure him he'd done the right thing by answering his call. His preaching was beautiful and from the heart. God wanted him to preach, that was certain. But how would she feel if she'd disappointed her parents? "Are you the only son?"

He choked on a laugh. "I'm the only child born to that generation, either for my father or my uncle."

"Oh." What else could she say? Was it possible his family understood now, or were they still disappointed in him? "Is your father now happy for your choice?"

Finch headed for the open doorway as the first crack of the baseball made her flinch. "He's not. After I was unable to secure a wife, it was better for me to leave home than to see the disappointment of both my uncle and my father, since they'd hoped I would continue the family line. I know I'm doing what I'm supposed to. But that doesn't make the choice easier." He indicated the can of white paint. "I think we have enough here for the inside and the outside. Mr. . ." His face went blank.

"Mr. Clark?" She filled in the name of the mercantile owner.

Finch grinned, and she couldn't help but smile back. "Yes, that's right. Mr. Clark at the mercantile assured me that both of these paints could be used inside or outside as long as we had the windows and doors open."

That was a requirement anyway. She dug in her apron pocket for the paint can key her father had loaned her and handed it to Finch. "Here you are, Reverend."

He took it from her, his fingers brushing pleasantly over the palm of her hand. Goodness, she needed to pull herself together. She shouldn't long for his touch. *Lord, help me control my wayward feelings.* "Perhaps I should wash these windows first?" If she had to work right next to him, she might feel this strange giddy feeling all day.

He tilted his head and stopped, obviously thinking. "I think it would be better to wash the windows after the room is finished, in case we drip."

Father had given her a tool for that too. A dull knife lay in her other apron pocket just for that reason. If her father had said the same thing, she might have tried to convince him otherwise, as it was in her nature to give her opinion, being the only child. Father had always humored her and even encouraged her to voice her concerns. However, Finch's simple statement had her swallowing her objections.

Surely he couldn't know what her parents had plotted if he wanted to work alongside her for the next few hours. Possibly many hours. Gracious, she hoped she could paint in a straight line.

CHAPTER 4

Finch tried not to worry about the paint spatter adorning Olive's apron, but thankfully the mess had missed her dress. He'd tried all morning to avoid coddling her with requests to take a break when she clearly could do more than he wanted her to. He had to remind himself often that she'd volunteered to help him. She knew the work that needed to be done because she'd seen the church when it was still in fine condition, with a pastor who took great care of it.

Olive wiped her brow with her sleeve and heaved a satisfied sigh. "That was a lot of work, but if you step back and look at the progress, the building looks new." She grinned. "Thank you for letting me help, Reverend."

Though he'd thought of her as Olive for days now, he still couldn't bring himself to tell her he would prefer to be called Finch. How could he even ask that of her? He was supposed to be her pastor, her spiritual leader, so why did he feel like God had meant for her to be more to him? Because of his recent failure to choose a bride wisely, he'd begged God to leave a relationship out of any assignment, yet he couldn't deny he was drawn to her.

"Letting you? I don't think that's how this happened. I think you took the initiative, and the work you started was blessed." He meant his words, and he wished he could give her more praise. Who else would have helped him? The members of his young flock were hard workers, people who needed to make use of every minute of every day to make their lives the best they could be. He'd known this would be a difficult assignment, but Olive seemed to have been selected to make his time easier. For that, he was thankful.

"Goodness, I didn't realize how late the hour is. Mother will wonder where I am. I should've been back to help her with supper an hour ago." Olive untied her apron and yanked it over her head.

He glanced around, only now noticing the waning light. The fresh white paint in the large room made the area brighter, less dingy than before. He'd lost track of the time. "I should walk you home." He wiped his hands on a rag. "When I return, I'll come by here and close the windows in case of rain. The walls will have some time to dry then."

Olive's glance darted around for a moment, and she pressed her skirts with her hands. "You don't have to walk with me. I'm sure no one would hold it against you if you didn't act the gentleman this once." She smiled, but it held a touch of nervousness that bothered him. Why didn't she want him to walk her home? They'd had a lovely day, chatting and working.

"I insist." He followed her to the door and locked it behind them. The sky had turned a lazy dark blue that seemed in no great hurry to go dark. Even the sky was different in the mountains from the prairie. It should have appeared smaller, since he felt boxed in by the surrounding hilltops. Yet, when he cared to gaze up, he was struck again by its vastness.

Olive silently walked next to him, her stride short despite

her assertion that she needed to hurry. "Is something the matter? Have I done something to bother you?" he asked. She was his only dear acquaintance so far in Baker's Nook, and he didn't want her upset with him. Better to ask forgiveness if he should than let her remain in a pique with him.

"Not at all. I've simply noticed that you've made other supper plans since the first few days after your arrival. I assumed there was a good reason. I didn't want to force you to go where you didn't wish to."

Her words, quiet and steady, took away his ability to reply. He had fully intended to evade her parent's home, but their friendship would suffer if he told her the truth—that he had to avoid the comfort of her home or risk encouraging the growing feelings inside him.

"I didn't mean to hurt you with my avoidance." He took a deep breath and decided it was better to avoid the question, so he didn't hurt her. "I hope to join you again soon."

Olive's eyes met his. "To be honest, I'm worried about walking home with you. Belta's allegation this morning, that your reputation could be marred because of me, greatly concerns me. I would never try to injure you in such a way. I'm worried that if someone sees you walking me home, they might assume things that aren't true."

It was obvious that she meant she did not want people thinking there was a romantic link between them. Perhaps she had a beau already, or perhaps she simply didn't see him in that light. Good. Now he knew his burgeoning infatuation with this woman was one-sided and he needn't worry about visiting her home. She would never return his favor.

"Life is difficult when you're worried what people will think. If you would like for me to stay behind, I will, but I would rather make sure you arrive safely at home. I can't very well ask for righteousness from others if I'm not willing to do what is right." Though he didn't feel particularly righteous with the way his heart raced as he looked down into her beautiful face.

She smiled up at him. "Of course, you're right. I shouldn't let gossip bother me. Living in such a small community where wagging tongues are often the only entertainment makes taking the narrow path harder."

"This is true." Which was why he hadn't offered his elbow to guide her, though he wanted to.

As they walked up the footpath to her front steps, the scent of flowers washed over him. Then, a moment later, his mouth watered at the aroma of roast beef. His stomach protested his plan to immediately leave, go home, and eat the sandwich he'd purchased earlier.

"You should come inside. You've worked hard all day, and my parents would love to see you again. You can also thank my father in person as you wanted to earlier for the paint." Olive held the door open for him, offering him the chance to accept her request.

"I. . ." He opened his mouth to refuse, but Olive was distracting. He needed to remember his purpose for coming to Baker's Nook. It wasn't for love. Well, it was, but not for loving one woman. He needed to love his whole flock equally. "I shouldn't," he managed.

She tilted her head and questioned him with her dark eyes. "My parents are the only elders left in the church. Let them feed you after you've worked so hard today."

He wanted to run, but her soft smile stole his refusal from his lips. At least he was the only one of them that felt a pull. He had to be strong enough to win this battle with his own heart.

Questions swirled in Olive's head. She'd tried to keep her thoughts straight all day, but talking to Finch was such a pleasure. He never made comments that had her questioning if she understood some hidden meaning behind a turn of phrase. He didn't look down on her, nor did he look at her in any way that made her uncomfortable.

That was, acutely, the issue. She was far too comfortable talking to him and looking at him. He was intelligent, supportive, kind, honorable, and handsome. She couldn't have chosen a better husband for herself if she were looking for one. But it was her parents who'd chosen him, and that was unacceptable. She couldn't let them run her life. She was an independent woman who knew her own mind.

She strode through the house, tossing her hat on a sideboard as she made her way to the kitchen with Finch a few steps behind her. "Mama?" she called when she reached the kitchen and found no one there. Had they already eaten and retired to the library?

"In here!" Father called from the study.

She backtracked out of the kitchen, taking Finch's bemused expression in and hoping he didn't bolt with the change in plans. Down the hall to the right of the kitchen was a room Father called his study but Mama playfully called the library. She said that a library was welcoming, whereas a study blocked people out. She'd said if she was welcome in there, it wasn't a study.

The sliding pocket doors had been left ajar about an inch, and Olive slid one to the side to reveal walls of books with sturdy desks placed in two of the corners. Two couches sat facing one another in front of a massive fireplace, its masonry ascending to the ceiling. Finch gasped quietly behind her.

Father looked up and beamed. "Reverend! I'm glad you could join us. You've been so busy the last week or so, we haven't wanted to pressure your attendance, but you are welcome to eat here any time. It is, in fact, part of your pay. I thought that was clear in our offer letter, but I'll repeat it in case you've forgotten."

"Oh." Finch appeared at Olive's side, and she couldn't miss the slight reddening of his neck.

She came to his defense. "Perhaps, having so many people surround him all day long, he would enjoy a little solitude in the evening. I could take a plate to him, so we don't short his payment and he doesn't have to come if he doesn't wish to." Of course, that would mean she would have to walk over there every evening. She wanted to see him, certainly, but a schedule like that meant permanent meetings would be set before them. At least until Finch married someone.

"I couldn't ask you to do that." Finch flushed even deeper red. "I'll continue to do as I have been."

"Nonsense," Father intervened. "If Olive offered to do the task, she means to. She's a woman with her own mind."

Olive almost laughed that her father chose that moment to discover her independence, or at least to say as much out loud. In any case, she wanted to make sure Finch ate well. If that meant carting a plate through town, she would. "I really don't mind, Finch."

Everyone in the room gasped at her gaffe, including Olive. She'd told herself time and again that calling Finch by his given name could only happen in her head or in introduction to others. Saying it out loud would get her in trouble. At least she'd done so only within the walls of her own home.

"I'm sorry." She felt her cheeks grow hot. "I didn't mean to be so forward. I've been introducing you using your name for over two weeks, and I'm quite tired after all our work today."

She hoped the excuse sounded more plausible to the others than it did to her.

Finch gave a soft snort of laughter. "All is forgiven and forgotten. We've worked so hard, it's no wonder you slipped up."

She searched his eyes, sensing that he wasn't truly bothered even if she was forgiven. Was he sad that she'd apologized?

"Well, let's get both of you fed. You must be starving after such a long day." Mama pushed herself out of her chair. "Father and I have already eaten, but the roast is still in the warmer. It may be a little tough, but the carrots will be tender."

Since they lived in the middle of ranch country, the main meats sold at the butcher were beef and mutton, from animals raised locally. Her parents also purchased chickens from nearby farms, especially from families that needed a little financial help. They were always trying to assist those in need.

Mama strode to the kitchen and retrieved a towel then opened the oven's warming drawer. She pulled out a pan and took the lid off, releasing a waft of steam. The scent had been subdued in the kitchen until that moment, and Olive's mouth watered. Her stomach made an unladylike noise. Maybe she was hungrier than she thought.

"Olive, why don't you set a few plates on the tea table so you two can eat in here. Father and I are just down the hall."

Mother headed out quickly, only leaving the door open an inch. For the first time since meeting him, Olive felt awkward around Finch. She'd called him by his name instead of the title he'd earned, which changed something she couldn't explain between them.

"Shall we?" Finch headed to the washbasin to scrub his hands. Then he brought the roast to the small table and started cutting portions.

That left her to gather the plates and silverware. *Pull*

yourself together, Olive. Obviously, her mistake hadn't bothered him. That thought almost made her nervousness worse. Why wouldn't he care?

How would she feel if he mistakenly used her name? She imagined him calling her Olive, and her heart raced. Only those she knew very well used her given name. They were her closest friends and family, but Finch was different. He was young and unmarried, and no other man like him did so.

Olive took her turn at the basin then brought the plates to the table. She arranged them on either side then laid forks and knives beside the plates. She filled both glasses with lemonade. The cool drink would be refreshing after all the work they'd done that day.

After they'd seated themselves, Finch bowed his head and folded his hands. Olive followed his lead and waited expectantly as he prayed over the meal and thanked God for his new flock. She resisted the urge to feel pride in helping him. She wouldn't make any difference in the attendance. Whether the paint was fresh or the pews oiled, his message was ultimately what would keep people coming to the church because he truly loved the Lord.

"Are you nervous for Sunday?" She wanted to be a good hostess and talk about something he would be interested in.

He chuckled. "I shouldn't be. Fear can be sin. But if I'm honest, I am. I have doubts in my ability. I need to remember that Sunday isn't about me. As long as I say the words I'm supposed to in the position the Lord has put me, then I've done what He intended of me. I can't make a single person listen or believe what I say, but the Holy Spirit can. 'But this I say, He which soweth sparingly shall reap also sparingly; and he which soweth bountifully shall reap also bountifully.'"

She nodded. "My father used to say something similar when

he would get nervous about delivering a message on Sunday morning. God always gave him the words to say." Though her father didn't deliver his messages in a particularly powerful or captivating way like some of the traveling preachers did.

Finch cut a piece of meat and stuck his fork into it then paused. "Being a preacher can be a very lonely profession. Rarely do we find friends who aren't afraid we'll judge them too harshly or who don't want us to fix every problem. I've appreciated your companionship. You've helped me greatly since I arrived. I wouldn't be nearly as close to finishing the church if not for you. Thank you."

His gaze bore into hers, and he opened his mouth, ready to say more. She was sure he was about to bring up what she'd called him, and she'd already determined to leave her mistake in the past. She quickly laid her hand on the table just a few inches from him.

"Thank you for accepting my help. I don't know what I'll do with my days once the church is finished." She laughed, immediately realized she was too loud, and softened her voice.

"What did you do before I came?" Finch started eating again.

Olive sighed, letting her worry release. Bringing up her growing infatuation with the preacher would serve no good purpose. She couldn't fall for this man. Marrying the man her parents had chosen for her would send them a sign that they could manipulate her life anytime they chose. They may have had good intentions, but she wouldn't give them the satisfaction of believing they were right.

"I helped my father prepare for his sermons by listening. I've also been helping Alma at the church as much as possible." She had spent some time with Belta almost daily, but she needn't say that. "I also enjoy reading."

A comfortable silence rose between them while they finished

eating. Finch wiped his mouth. "Before I came here, I traveled to various churches, filling in for a few Sundays at a time, always hoping the church would choose me as their pastor. I can't tell you how shocked I was to be offered a job without preaching here first."

Olive choked slightly on a large piece of carrot. Her parents would never tell him they hired him exclusively because of his age and mainly because it was so close to hers. She sipped her lemonade to clear her throat. Finch looked alarmed for a moment then relaxed when she finished her drink.

When she could speak again, she explained what she could. "My parents wanted a young pastor because so many members of the church are young. Our former pastor was beginning to have opinions about marriage, which caused part of the divide. He said that anyone under twenty-one was far too young to make such a decision. I'm not a preacher, but I don't think there's anything in the Word saying one should avoid marriage before the age of twenty-one."

Finch set his fork down. "While I think it's important that preachers have opinions, I think individual beliefs need to stay out of the pulpit unless they are directly supported by the Word of God."

Olive had been afraid to bring up the reason the church needed Finch. He could have easily sided with the former pastor in this case. If that happened, they would have to start hunting to replace him all over again.

"That relieves me. My parents thought the same. They supported Reverend Percival until they simply couldn't anymore. Unfortunately, many people in the church took his departure as a reason to permanently split what was already broken."

"Institutions like marriage are an interesting thing." Finch took a slice of bread off the bread tray and used it to mop up the last remnants of food from his plate. He obviously enjoyed Mama's cooking. Olive couldn't blame him. She'd been trying for years to learn Mama's secrets. Even if she didn't plan to marry just yet, she still needed those skills.

"That is true. Marriage should be a matter of heart and mind." She sighed, feeling better because he was in agreement with her.

"I wish I could tell you that separations like this are abnormal, but they're not. Oddly, it seems to be mainly in churches, but many groups seem to want to separate into their own divisions. Perhaps there is some comfort in worshiping with those who are like yourself. I don't know the answer. I hope the other church finds a pastor soon."

"He should have been here last week." Olive had heard the news from Belta, though, so she couldn't be sure of the veracity of her claim. Belta was the only person from the other church who still spoke to her with anything beyond courtesy, so that was where she had to get her knowledge.

"I look forward to meeting him. If he's amenable, we could try to create a connection between the two churches. There must be friendships that were hurt by the split."

Olive closed her eyes, recalling all the wisdom she'd gained from the older families. Her parents literally had no one to speak to now. If the chasm between them could be bridged, Baker's Nook would be a wonderful place to live once again.

"Without knowing all the reasons why the church split—and I'm sure there are more—it will be difficult to gain that agreement."

Finch reached out and touched her hand, shocking her momentarily. Her first instinct was to pull away, to immediately stop all the fluttery feelings that his touch brought on, but she didn't move. She let him gently pat her hand and give her comfort.

"I know it won't be simple, and it may not be soon, but I

will work to see it happen." He stood and took his plate to the soaking pan. Mother had left the dishes for Olive, since she'd had to cook without Olive most of the week.

"Thank you. I hope you can. You've already been a blessing to the community, and healing the wounds, whatever they are, would mean the world to a lot of people."

He pushed in his chair and wiped his hands on the cloth napkin before tossing it into the linen hamper near the stove. "Would it mean the world to you?" he asked, his eyes searching hers.

She swallowed hard, knowing Finch was asking for personal reasons. She couldn't let her heart fall for him. Nor could she let herself enjoy the fact that he wanted to do something so amazing for her. He shouldn't. He should want to do these things for everyone. But, if having her stamp of approval made him happy to do what was best for the community, then she wouldn't hold back the truth.

"Yes. Yes it would."

The side of his mouth lifted, and her belly did a little flip as his eyes lightened. "Then consider it done."

CHAPTER 5

The streets seemed overly full of curious faces as Olive made her way to the bakery for breakfast. Mama hadn't been feeling well that morning, so Olive had convinced her to head back to bed. The bakery would make for a nice change, and she could surprise Finch with one of Mr. Stansteader's amazing breakfast rolls.

She pulled open the front door, and four faces stared at her as she made her way to the glass front countertop. The store smelled of baked sweetness, like the scent was a permanent part of the spotless fixtures all around. The three people who'd appeared to be waiting in line backed away, and a subtle whispering tickled her ears as she stopped to look at the selection.

"Olive," the baker said in such a stern voice that she took a step back.

"Good morning, Mr. Stansteader. I'll have two of those." She pointed to a tiny loaf of sweet bread. While that may be more than either of them needed, what was left over would make a good treat for after lunch.

"I don't think that's a good idea." He didn't move to open the case, instead taking a step back and crossing his arms over his chest with a glare that was clearly meant to scare her off.

"What?" Olive didn't know what he meant. She'd never been turned down at the bakery before.

"You heard what I said. What you and your family are doing to that new preacher is, frankly, ugly. I can't believe you'd agree to it. I thought you were a sweet girl, but I can see I was wrong." He braced his hands against the lower counter where the large till sat and scowled at her.

"I haven't done anything. I've been helping him fix the church." How had anyone found out about Mama and Father's plan to marry her off? Even if she didn't agree with her parents' scheme, she wasn't going to let someone tarnish their name over something that was only supposed to be known behind the closed doors of her home. "My parents are the elders of our church, so offering to help the new preacher is our duty." She raised her chin but felt the unease of defending something that was untrue settle over her.

"Belta was in here yesterday afternoon and told many of us exactly what was going on with your parents and that preacher. You must be in on it because you've been with him every day since he arrived. I've never seen such a pursuit of power in all my life," Mr. Stansteader continued.

"Power? I don't understand what you mean." She hated to make him repeat whatever lie he'd heard, but how could she fight what was said if she didn't understand it?

"Your parents want to stay on as elders, and they will stop at nothing to keep that position of power over the new preacher. Since they are now the only elders, they can control everything he does. They can even convince him to marry their only daughter, securing their spot as his most influential parishioners." He glared down at her. "I don't even go to that church anymore, and I think it's wrong."

"He's going to add more elders." He hadn't chosen them

yet, but that was his plan. Her chest ached because no matter what she said, they wouldn't believe her. "You've known them for over twenty years. They have no reason to try to influence him. Reverend Presly has already told us he's going to choose additional elders, and my parents are happy to have more assistance and support."

Mr. Stansteader pointed at her with an accusing finger. "Your father was the one who took over the pulpit when Reverend Percival left. He *gladly* took that over because he likes the power. I doubt he's willing to step down so easily."

The other three people hadn't moved, and Olive could feel their eyes on her back, heard the murmurs of agreement as they waited for her response. What Mr. Stansteader said made no sense, but rumors rarely held up to scrutiny. Why did people love to watch confrontation so much? "We all used to be friends. What happened? Why are we arguing so?" Olive wasn't the slightest bit hungry anymore but couldn't leave either. "My parents would step down right now if there were others to come forward and do the work."

"So naive," said someone behind her.

Mr. Stansteader shook his head. "I'm not helping you trick that man, luring him into something when he has no choice in the matter. Shame on you. Go back home where you belong." He pointed to the door.

Olive dashed from the store and still felt judgment on her as she walked as fast as her feet would carry her. Eyes burning, she could hardly see where to go. Father and Mama couldn't have planned anything so evil as what Mr. Stansteader—and by extension, Belta—had accused them of doing. They'd wanted rest, not power. They'd wanted to hand the church off to someone they could trust.

But she couldn't deny the fact that they wanted the new

preacher as a son-in-law. She thought back to the nights when her parents had been praying over the various applications they'd received after they'd put out word that the church needed a new pastor. They'd admitted to each other, though not to her, that they were looking for a man who would be perfect for their daughter, *not* perfect for their flock. They'd said the two were one and the same, but were they?

Olive slowed her steps and headed for the edge of town where a small river flowed, providing water to the water stop depot down the street. There were few places to go in Baker's Nook where she wouldn't be seen, and the church was one of them. Except now Finch would be there, and he would wonder what was wrong. Especially since she was late to meet him.

Explaining what had happened to her would involve telling Finch the truth about her growing regard for him and her parents' reasoning for inviting him. She recalled how he'd said he'd preached at many churches over the last few months and none had offered him a job. Without Baker's Nook, he wouldn't have employment again. If he assumed he'd been hired for a purpose other than to teach the Word, he might leave.

She couldn't do that to him, but he was bound to hear the rumors soon. When he did, he'd put an end to their friendship. He would have to for his own reputation, which had to be spotless. A preacher couldn't afford to have a mark like that on his character, nor could he look weak, relying on his elders to make decisions for him.

She headed for the cover of the evergreen trees alongside the small river and sat on a large granite boulder near the edge. The sound of the water rushing over the rocks and fallen branches created a soft noise that was pleasant, but not enough to distract her from her thoughts.

Someone called her name from a few yards behind her.

"Olive? Are you all right? I saw you dash by my window, and I was worried about you."

She turned as Alma approached. She often sat by her sitting room window on days when her husband was at the mine.

Olive swiped the tears from under her eyes and tried to smile over her shoulder at Alma. "I'm fine. Quite fine. Just wanted to enjoy a minute by the river and couldn't wait to get here." She bit her lip at the sound of her trembling voice.

"Truly?" Alma had come closer, the rustle of her skirts over the twigs and dead grass like a warning. "You didn't seem happy when you ran by. I could be wrong, of course."

Olive had already come far too close to deceit that day and wouldn't cross the line into a full untruth. "I just needed a few minutes. I was accused of something in town because of wagging tongues with nothing better to do."

"You mean what Belta is telling everyone?" Alma sat on a boulder nearby. "I'll admit, at first I wondered how much truth was behind what she said. People want to believe things that sound sensational. At the same time, you have been spending every day with the pastor, and I've seen you walk past my window at his side nearly every evening. I can see why your parents want some assurance that you'll be taken care of. I know that was a strong motivation for my parents' agreement to my marriage."

"You didn't marry for love, did you?" Since Alma had brought up the topic, the offer to change the subject was like a blessing.

"I didn't, but Mark treats me well. I hope to someday get him in church. He feels that his soul is as dirty as his hands from working in the mines. I've told him that forgiveness from the Almighty is stronger than any stain, but he's not ready to understand that yet."

"I pray he sees the truth." Olive took Finch's clean handkerchief that she'd washed and pressed in preparation to return it to him from her pocket and dabbed her eyes.

"Have you considered that I might be able to use your situation to share the forgiving power of God with my husband? Belta has made a terrible mess. If you and Reverend Presly can forgive her, perhaps my husband will see the truth. And don't worry. The Lord will not let a false rumor tarnish a preacher of His Word."

Unless that rumor held a grain of truth. The Lord might not let Finch's name be tarnished by what had been said, but her parents wouldn't be free of guilt if they'd lied about the intent to hire him. Her thoughts turned to Ananias and Sapphira in the Book of Acts. They had done the right thing by giving a portion of their profits to the church but fell dead at Peter's feet because they'd lied when they told him they hadn't held anything back. The ministry wasn't affected, but the liars were.

"I know you're right and He does work all things for His glory. I just feel so beside myself. What if Reverend Presly decides to end our friendship because of the rumors or removes my parents as elders because people believe they were seeking power?"

"I know you can't see the answer, but I promise it's there," Alma said.

"I'm going to have to talk to them." Olive hung her head. "Belta took things that I said and twisted them. I'm the one who must fix this." And that meant telling her parents and Finch what had been said. The three of them would have to pray and make a decision on how to act going forward. She would have no other say in the matter.

She wanted Finch to remain their pastor, but knowing that her time as his confidant and even friend would be ending left her heart aching. Since the church split, she hadn't felt so close to anyone. Losing Finch was like losing her friends all over again.

"Yes, I think that's a good idea. Your parents don't listen to gossip, and I doubt anyone would be willing to accuse them to their faces. They confront you because you're a softer, sweeter soul. You're less likely to push back against the lie. Talking to them will get all this mess out in the open, so that those it really affects can handle it. Let this worry fall off your shoulders. It's not yours to bear."

Alma came and sat next to her, wrapping her arm around Olive. They'd never been great friends, but perhaps Alma was looking for someone just as much as Olive was. "Thank you for coming after me. I wasn't sure what I wanted when I was looking for a quiet place to think, but you said just the right things."

Alma laughed. "I'm thoroughly out of practice. My own friends all moved away once they married. Since Mark doesn't attend church with me, people often assume there's something wrong with him or us, making friendships difficult. I'll pray that you have the right words to talk to your parents. I don't know how Belta came to the conclusions she did, do you?"

That was another side of the situation that made talking to her parents even harder. She'd never come right out and confirmed Belta's accusations about her parents' plan, but that didn't seem to matter. Was she completely innocent, or had she, by her inaction and lack of defense, been the one to start this awful rumor?

Olive thought back over her words and actions since Finch's arrival. Though she'd felt many things she wasn't going to share with anyone, her actions were above reproach. "I'm not sure I can answer that. At least, not completely. For some reason, she was convinced my parents were planning to have me marry the preacher."

"Are you certain they weren't? I love your parents, and I don't think there was a hint of malice involved, but faithful parents would want nothing more than for their daughter to have an upright man to lead her through life. They know they won't always be here for you. . ." Alma's voice faded away.

"Do your parents worry about you?" Olive reached for Alma's hand, feeling a bond with her like she never had before.

"They do. Mark is a good man, but he's not a Christian. We're all praying for his soul. I only worry that once my father is gone or retires from the bank, Mark will grow cold. I know he married me because of my father. He didn't keep that fact secret. But I pray he cares for me enough now that even if my father had nothing to do with Mark's bank account, he wouldn't leave me."

Alma's voice had quieted to almost nothing. Olive squeezed her hand. "You know him best, and you know you are a child of God. He will protect you." But even so, God didn't promise that people wouldn't have hardship.

"I know. I wish my future was more secure. Being the daughter of a banker, I learned from a young age that security is best." She laughed. "I'm still not sure why my parents agreed to the marriage."

"Perhaps they saw something in him, a glimmer of hope to come." Talking through Alma's problems made her own seem less severe. Just like Alma, the Lord would be with her too. She just had to believe that He would.

"I dearly hope so." Alma stood, still holding Olive's hand and tugging her to her feet. She pulled Olive into a surprise embrace. "Thank you for letting me speak my heart. I haven't shared those thoughts with anyone."

Olive gave her a final squeeze then freed her new friend. "Thank you for sitting by your window and caring enough to come check on me. I'd better go do the work I dread." Mama and Father wouldn't take her questioning well.

"I'll pray they have calm spirits and minds." Alma waved as she headed back to her home.

Olive took a deep breath and glanced out over the babbling river one last time. Her problem was just the same as it had been when she'd come here, but now she was fortified to do the work she had to do.

"A friend will stick closer than a brother. . . Well, I don't have a brother or a sister, so a friend it must be." Olive laughed because the closest friend she'd had to that point was Belta, who hadn't acted as one.

She made her way back into town, ignoring the looks on the faces of everyone she met. She ducked her head and watched her feet as she headed for home. No one could accuse her if she couldn't see the accusation in their eyes.

The path ahead was so familiar she could find it in her sleep. She trudged between the hedge of flowers up the walk. The scent wrapped around her, familiar and steady, the aroma of summer and home. She bent, plucked a new bloom, and tucked it into her hair. Just as the flower would be with her, the Lord would be with her and give her the words to say. Truth was right and good.

She took a deep breath, taking in the scent of the flowers and the calm outside her front door. Inside would be turmoil once she opened her mouth. She'd never caused her parents strife before, but what they'd done had to come into the light.

Pushing open the front door, she listened. The house seemed more still than usual. Father wasn't sitting in his reading chair. The room was dark with the curtains drawn shut. "Mama?"

This was abnormal for her family. They had a routine, and she knew where they were at all points of the day. "Father?"

She took a few more steps into the house and heard a faint

sound that tore her resolve from her and stomped it on the floor. Mama's soft crying from the library rent her heart. "I'm coming!"

CHAPTER 6

Olive rushed to the study and pressed her ear to the door. Mama never sat in the study during the day, only in the evening when she shared a cup of tea with Father as he read his newspaper. Why were they in there, and what had happened? Had someone told them about the rumors?

She knocked softly. Obviously, they'd wanted privacy if they were behind closed doors. "Mama, Father, is something wrong?"

Heavy footfalls told her Father neared the door. She took a step back and waited. He slid the door open, his face a stony mask. "Olive, come in. We've got something very important to talk about."

Would they tell her the truth about why they'd hired Finch? But why would that make Mama cry? Even now, she dabbed at her eyes from her chair across the room. Only Father's gentle hold on Olive's elbow kept her from rushing over and kneeling at Mama's feet. She hated to see Mama distraught.

"What's the matter?" Her voice sounded frantic to her ears.

"Mr. Dogwood came to speak to us just a half hour ago."

"From the new church?" Olive asked, surprised that one of their old friends had reached out to speak when the silence had been almost palpable for a year.

"Yes, but not with news of welcome, or even goodwill." Father sat in his large leather chair and leaned forward to take Mama's hand. "He came over here to tell us that their pastor turned down the assignment before he arrived in Baker's Nook. He found another position in Colorado and didn't want to come this far north."

"Oh." Olive wasn't sure what else to say. Belta had been so sure their pastor would arrive on time and be better than Finch, since the man they'd chosen was well on in years.

"It's worse than that," Mama said through her tears. "So much worse."

"Now is not the time," Father chastised.

Mama looked up at him. "If not now, when? She's got to know. We did all the work, and it will be for nothing. Just like applying to the Normal school."

Olive stiffened her spine, willing her knees not to buckle. What was Mama talking about? There had to be more to the story than she knew. "Mama? What do you mean?"

Father sighed. "Olive, sit down like the adult you are so we can talk this through."

She'd never been asked to sit with them in the room where they sought privacy. She'd known even as a child that the study was not for her. She went to the wall and moved one of the ladder-back chairs close to theirs then settled into it.

"Olive, your mother and I prayed fervently for someone to lead our church. A man who could bring knowledge and leadership. But not only that." He glanced at Mama then squeezed her hand. "We prayed that he would also be a fine match for our daughter. How could we not when no one else in town had caught her eye?"

Olive held up her hand. "This isn't about me. What has made Mama so distraught?"

Father softened his voice as if she were a small child. "Dear, when the other pastor sent a telegram that he would not be coming, the elders of the new church convened. They agreed that the man we chose was a good man. They've seen him welcome everyone, not just those he was hired to lead. They decided he would be good for their church, but he must marry one of their members. They will offer Belta if he can't choose. Since you've had no interest in anyone else but seemed to be getting along well with Reverend Presly, we'd hoped our plan would work without any further intervention. However, if he marries someone else, that can't happen."

Olive's hands went cold, and her head spun. "Marry Belta?" Hearing he may marry someone else made her sick to her stomach. How could he choose to marry someone just to preach at their church?

A conversation they'd had a few days prior came immediately to mind, and she knew what his answer would be. He would do anything the Lord led him to do if it would bring lost souls to Christ. Including marriage. She fought the urge to cry just like Mama.

"Does he know?" she asked, holding her emotions behind her own firm wall.

"Not yet. I asked them not to speak to him until we'd had a chance to think and pray about this. I don't mind sharing a preacher with them, but I'm opposed to them requiring he marry one of them to do so."

Her parents had never required Finch to marry Olive in order to pastor their church, but they had hoped for it. Hopes and ultimatums weren't the same, but the intent was similar. "Belta will not agree. She's in love with Anthony."

"Her parents were part of the meeting. They agree that Belta is the best choice, since Reverend Presly might convince her to stop her wagging tongue."

"Or she could ruin his reputation." Olive couldn't stop her heart now as tears burned her eyes. Finch's situation was so much worse than her own fears of confronting her parents. "I shouldn't be so spiteful, but she will never stop gossiping. His reputation will be destroyed within a fortnight. He's come all this way, and this decision will be disastrous."

Finch seemed to slip further from her the longer she spoke with her parents. There was nothing she could do short of marrying him herself to stop this tragedy from occurring.

In the span of an hour, she'd gone from hope for a good day with Finch, working on the church and getting it finished for Sunday, to seeing that her parents' choice for her might not have been so far flung. No one had ever made her feel so at peace yet so wonderfully fluttery at the same time. Finch was all at once steady and exciting.

Now he would be completely out of reach. If she had been as convinced as her parents were from the start that she should try to win his hand, this predicament might have been avoided. She might have given him a hint to what she was feeling. Belta's interference wove its way through her thoughts, and she realized why they'd chosen her to wed Finch.

The townspeople who were now members of the new church were still hurt Mama and Father had chosen to stay with the old church. They'd considered Mama and Father's desire to shepherd the small flock until a new pastor could be found an insult.

"They're offering Belta not as a way to control her, but to get back at you," she told them. "There's a rumor going around Baker's Nook, started by Belta, that you hired Reverend Presly specifically to marry me so you could stay on as elders. A match made between us would mean your place was secure." She could feel the right words coming to her, just as promised. She felt to her very core they were true.

"We never considered that, Olive," Father said. "We hoped you both would become close, even prayed for it, but our hopes were for you, not us. We wanted you to find a man who would appreciate your independent spirit and the hard work of your hands. We prayed you would find a new way to direct your energy into the church. We're glad he's only been here a few weeks, hopefully too soon for you to make a connection with him."

If only that were true. She'd spent every day with him, from morning until evening, working with him, eating along-side him, and talking with him. She now knew Finch better than almost anyone else in Baker's Nook. Much better than any other man in town. "That is a blessing." She squeaked the words past her tight throat.

She prayed she would not fall into tears the moment she saw him and that her parents didn't see her true feelings in her actions.

A knock on the front door reminded Finch he was supposed to be at the church already, working with Olive. He glanced at his pocket watch, and worry settled over him. That knock had been too firm to be Olive, yet she was to have come to his door over an hour before.

He stood and headed for the front, stopping at the window to see who it was. Mr. Dogwood and Mr. Collins, Belta's father, stood outside. He quickly put on his collar and adjusted it then opened the door for them. "Good morning, please come inside." He held the door wide, unsure why they would be visiting but hoping his prayers for a unified church had been answered.

"Reverend Presly," Mr. Collins said, "I wish we could say

we've stopped by for a friendly chat over coffee, but that is not the case. I hope you have felt welcome in Baker's Nook."

Finch glanced around the room and realized he had nothing to offer them. He hadn't even made coffee that morning, since Olive always brewed a pot at the church when they met to work. He wanted to get the meeting with these men over quickly so he could check on her. He'd been so focused on his study of Acts that he'd lost track of time.

"I would like to get right to the point of our visit, Reverend." Mr. Dogwood sat in one of the chairs in the sitting room like he was very comfortable being there, and Mr. Collins followed suit.

"Please." Finch sat across from them, hoping the reason behind their strange arrival would lead to good.

"We received an urgent telegram yesterday that our preacher has declined our offer of a job. We have been looking for many months. Despite the warmth right now, the cold is coming. Soon, trains will struggle to get to Baker's Nook, and the stage will only come when the snow doesn't block the way."

Finch calmed his suddenly racing heart. The mountains already felt like walls around him, and now he would be trapped by snow. "Do you have anyone else who might come? This could be God's way of telling you someone else should be leading you."

Mr. Dogwood shook his head. "No. There is no one else. I don't wish to steal you away from the other church, but we're in need as much as they are. We're willing to hire you to preach for us as well, but there would be one stipulation, which I don't think is that terrible. We need some assurance you will stay."

"I'm here, aren't I? I have no plans to leave. I'm enjoying Baker's Nook and all its people, not just those I've been hired to lead." He was growing quite fond of one member of the town especially.

"What you're saying is all well and good, but we know after the last preacher left and after this one never arrived that a man of the cloth doesn't always keep his word. Even a signed document saying you will stay is not enough."

If there was no trust, could he lead anyone? Would they always compare him to those who came before? "What can I do to convince you I won't leave? There's nothing pulling me from Baker's Nook."

Mr. Collins looked him in the eye, and the room grew silent. "You can accept my daughter's hand. You understand, it's part of our new bylaws that our preacher be married. If you're married to one of our members, you'll stay. You can still lead the other church if you choose."

There were at least two flaws in Mr. Collins' plan, the main one being that Finch could simply marry Belta and still leave if he had a mind to. The second, and one that Mr. Collins couldn't possibly know, was the fact that his heart was already becoming entangled with Olive's. She, however, didn't seem to be aware of it or even desire it.

"I'll need to think this through and pray about it. I can't just give you an answer on the spur of the moment." Hopefully the decision would become clear once he had time to mull it over.

"We would expect no less." Mr. Collins stood and held out his hand to shake.

Finch hesitated only for a moment, feeling like the handshake was a trap, then thought better of it. These men weren't going to hold him against his will and walk him down the aisle. Belta had a mind of her own, and she wouldn't unwillingly agree to a union. They couldn't have spoken to her yet, or the whole town would know.

"We'll stop by to see you in a few days. I'm sure you understand we can't wait long due to the reasons we already mentioned."

Mr. Dogwood headed for the door.

Right, those reasons he'd forgotten about in the shock of hearing their expectations. He'd be trapped in Baker's Nook until spring like he'd never been walled in before. There wouldn't be a way out of a marriage either.

He shut the door behind them and prayed he'd been hospitable. *Lord, how do I answer this call? Surely you don't want one of your churches to be without a leader, but. . .marry Belta?* God had called Jonah to do something he didn't want to do, and everything had turned out fine. They would've been even better if he'd followed God's direction from the start. Now Finch just needed to decide if Belta was his Nineveh, or if the leaders of the new church were inadvertently trying to lead him astray.

CHAPTER 7

Helping Mama at the stove for supper usually quieted Olive's racing thoughts, but not today. Mama hadn't said anything, but she had to have noticed Olive's distraction. She'd already added milk instead of cream to the mashed potatoes. Mama had assured her they would still turn out fine, but now she was even more preoccupied. What would Finch think of her cooking skills?

"Dear, go get ready. Our guest will be here any minute." Mama laid a gentle hand on Olive's shoulder.

Olive tucked a strand of unruly hair behind her ear. She wanted to argue that how she looked didn't matter now. Finch would marry Belta. She knew he wanted to unite the two congregations any way he could, and this would be the best way to bring that to fruition. If only she could go back to the beginning of their acquaintance and let him know he was turning her head.

"Thank you, Mama." Her chin trembled against her will.

Mama gave her an understanding look. "Whatever is wrong will turn out in the end. You'll see." Mama patted Olive's back then turned her attention to the stove.

At least one of them could still manage to cook in a crisis.

Olive headed for the stairs, willing herself to be stronger. Look at Mama, doing all the work. She'd had her tears, freshened her face, and done the work. Since they'd invited Finch earlier and he'd decided to join them, there was no choice but to make supper, though no one felt like eating.

The mirror wasn't kind as Olive stood in front of it. She turned right and left, but her face and eyes were still puffy. Her dress was still the same blue dress she'd worn every two days since Finch's arrival. Putting on a new one wouldn't help the situation, but it might make her look fresher, less distraught.

She quickly stripped out of her sturdy cotton and into one that would usually be used for a party. The evenings were getting a slight chill, and a wrap would complete the look. Finch wouldn't notice her anyway. He hadn't given her any show of affection since he'd made the promise to unite the churches, and that seemed long ago now.

Her thoughts wandered to the time they'd spent together, and she couldn't recall any other moment he'd said or done anything that hinted at his feelings. He seemed more brotherly to her than anything, which was terribly sad. Of all the men she could lose her heart to, God had chosen the one who would never look on her as anything but a friend.

Olive opened a small cedar box on her writing desk. It was full of mementos from her childhood. There was a ring from her grandmother, a note from her father, and a testimonial from a teacher who had left South Dakota to teach at a school in Montana.

Perhaps moving, like that teacher, would be her best option, no matter that she loved South Dakota and everyone she knew well was here. Montana might offer an escape from watching Finch and Belta get married and have children. She would miss everyone, but the alternative was painful.

She heard Finch arrive downstairs. Her father's booming voice welcomed him as if they didn't know the situation and what was soon to happen. Would they talk about it over supper? Would he be excited? She swallowed hard. If she cared about him—not an infatuation, but true care—then she should be happy for him to be able to do the work he was called to. Finch wouldn't resort to marriage without praying first, which meant the decision was God's will.

She took a fortifying breath and headed down the stairs. Finch stood in the sitting room, talking with her father. He turned as she came down, and his mouth fell open slightly. He stopped talking until she'd fully descended, seemingly forgetting that her father was right there.

"Miss Torey. Good evening." He gave her a half smile.

She wished to hear him call her Olive, just once, but that wasn't meant to be. They would have to stop working together if he was promised to Belta.

"Good evening." She tried to sound friendly instead of stiff. Pretending that nothing was wrong was one of the most difficult things she'd ever done.

He turned back to Father. "Thank you for the invitation. I was in no frame of mind to make my own supper tonight."

Mama entered the room, her hands folded in front of her. She'd already removed her apron, and her hair was in perfect order. She certainly didn't appear like she'd been fretting over a stove for the past hour.

"Mrs. Torey, good to see you." Finch gave Mama a smile.

"Shall we sit for a few minutes and let supper cool?" Mama gave a weak smile as she headed for her usual chair.

Father followed suit, leaving only the sofa for Olive and Finch. She gingerly sat down, leaving plenty of space between them. Finch looked slightly confused and perhaps uncomfortable, clearly searching for a reason for their odd behavior. All the other times when he'd come for supper, they'd sat right down to the meal.

"Reverend, we feel we need to confess something to you," Father said. He took a deep breath and looked over at Mama.

"You don't need to confess to me, sir. Anything you've done can be brought straight to Jesus." Finch held up his hands.

"Not when the offense is against you," Father said.

Olive couldn't hold in a gasp. What was going on? Were they going to tell him why they'd hired him? He might leave the church completely.

"Father?" Olive's voice quavered. Could the situation get any worse? *Lord, please, do something to stop this!*

Father let out a long breath. "I'm sure you've wondered why we would hire you without ever hearing you preach. From what you said when you arrived, you know that's not usually the case."

"That's true," Finch said slowly.

Olive clasped her hands together to keep from reaching out to him. The poor man looked like he was worried he might be sent off.

"You were hired for two reasons. One was pure faith, the other, pure hope. However, there is no hope outside of God, so we felt we were justified." He glanced at Mama again then continued. "We were pleased with what you said in your letters, enough that we knew you would make a good minister. But our hope was that you would also make a good husband for Olive."

Finch jumped to his feet, and Olive felt all the warmth drain from her body. He didn't look angry, but he also didn't look happy. The man had never so much as raised his voice except during one of the sermons he'd delivered, and that was out of joy, not anger.

Finch glanced down at her. "I don't know what to say."

Finch ran his hands through his hair, unsure of how to deal with the situation. How could God have done this? He'd begged for a placement where he could care for the entire church, not a woman. Yet he was far too close to Olive as it was, and her parents had obviously pushed them together for that purpose.

He thought about that very first day Olive met him when he arrived on the stage. He'd thought her presence was providence, but now it seemed more likely to be her family meddling. Then, not an hour later, they'd given her the job of introducing him around town. They'd orchestrated every meeting, making sure Olive would spend time with him, and he hadn't suspected a thing. Mainly because he hadn't minded in the slightest.

"I need to be clear with you that I came to Baker's Nook with the intent to remain a bachelor. I want nothing to do with love. I have no desire to find a wife."

He wasn't sure if he should mention the offer he'd received from Mr. Collins, but now seemed like the time he should. He strode to the hearth, giving himself a moment to compose his thoughts. If the Toreys could confess, then so could he.

"The truth is, I've been offered a position by the other church. They don't mind sharing my services with your church, but they do require I marry one of their parishioners." And in light of the situation, perhaps that was God's way of telling him he should take it. He wasn't good at this love thing or choosing a bride. Felicia had made that very clear when she left him at the altar. The only way he could stay in Baker's Nook without having his heart involved was to marry Belta.

"Mr. Collins and Mr. Dogwood came to me today and offered me their pulpit in addition to yours if I would marry Mr. Collins' daughter."

"In light of our hopes, I know I have no right to say this, but I feel that is an unfair request. Marriage is to last a lifetime. What if you aren't suited to Belta?" Mrs. Torey said.

"Suited or not, I feel like this would be a good opportunity to bring the two churches back together. At the very least, we could rebuild the friendships torn apart by the split. Perhaps I came here for such a time as this." Though saying the words aloud didn't give him any reassurance.

If Belta's father shared with her this evening what he'd offered Finch, she would tell everyone by tomorrow. Would he have any choice left in the matter?

As friendly and willing to help him as Olive had been, he couldn't be certain she wasn't in on her parents' scheme. He couldn't abide the thought that she was as interested in him as he was in her. It was one thing to believe his regard was one-sided. If she had the same feelings for him, he might be tempted to give in and explore what he felt.

Finch closed his eyes and prayed for wisdom and the right path. "I think it's time we eat before the food is cold and before we say anything that will hurt each other unnecessarily. I forgive your planning, and I intend to stay on as the pastor of your church if you still want me to do the job."

Mr. Torey stood and held out his hand, and Finch shook it. "We'd be pleased to have you as our pastor. I'm glad you've decided to stay, even if you lead both churches. I hope they will reconsider the requirement."

Finch followed Mr. Torey to the table then held Olive's chair as she sat a moment later. Her hair had a lovely scent, like that of rose petals. He shouldn't compare Belta to her. That wasn't a fair comparison. Olive was sweet and quiet, unassuming, witty, and delicate. Belta was loud and brash, and she desired to be noticed. Everything from her brightly colored clothes and hats to the words that left her mouth proved that. The two were complete opposites. If he'd had to choose between the two based on his feelings, there would be no question. But he'd made a disastrous decision before, based on those same feelings.

What do You want me to do, Lord?

He listened, but the Lord gave no reply. They ate supper in relative silence. This time, as the plates were passed, he was careful not to touch Olive, because he enjoyed the contact far too much. He must not do that anymore. If he did this thing and Belta agreed, he'd be promised to her, and she would be promised to him.

He'd barely finished his meal when Olive excused herself, complaining of a headache, and headed upstairs. He watched her leave until she disappeared around a corner. Odd that it felt like he would never see her again, not in the same way.

He offered to help Mrs. Torey clear the table, but she wouldn't hear of it. She shooed him and Mr. Torey from the dining room with a quick wave. Mr. Torey closed the pocket doors of the study behind them and then offered Finch a seat.

"We've only known each other a month," he said, "but I feel like I know you. I feel like I can speak plainly with you, and I hope you feel you can do the same with me. The last pastor had that relationship with us, and he found it to be refreshing. Everyone needs a place where they can say what they mean."

Finch sat down as Mr. Torey lit a small fire in the grate. He wasn't sure why, as it wasn't overly chilly in the house. Mr. Torey looked over his shoulder and smiled then pointed upward. "My daughter's room is right up there. She's upset. When she gets upset, she gets cold. I'm making sure she's warm enough in her room, even if it means I'm uncomfortable down here. That's what love does."

Finch wasn't sure what Mr. Torey expected him to say. He

wasn't going to complain when the man was obviously caring for his only daughter. As a preacher, he would be expected to start a family as soon as he and Belta were able. He tried to picture what life would be like, but the only image that would come to mind was that of Olive.

"I'm sorry she's hurting. I hope her pain is relieved soon."

Mr. Torey stuck the poker into the small logs, pushing them back near the brick of the fireplace. "She will heal. In time."

Wouldn't a headache go away fairly quickly, if that was what was truly the matter? Though with Olive's silence throughout supper, he had to wonder if her true pain had stemmed from the conversation prior to eating. He hated the idea that something he'd done could be hurting her, but he wasn't qualified to care for a woman. Now he'd have to rely on God to change his heart.

"I should go back to the parsonage. I've got many things to talk to God about tonight."

Mr. Torey put the poker back in its holder and straightened. "It sounded earlier like you had already come to your decision. I'm glad to hear you still need to pray about it. I'll pray for clarity myself."

"Thank you." Though he wondered if Mr. Torey's prayer would be for clarity or for his daughter. "And thank you for telling me the truth. I may not be able to marry your daughter, but I will lead this church to the best of my ability. I'll pray that the Lord blesses me with the right words to say every week."

Finch headed for the door, the heat from the fireplace already leaving him sleepy. As he passed the staircase on the way out, his eyes wandered to the spot on the stairs where he'd seen Olive earlier. She'd looked so lovely in the cream-colored dress. Her eyes had been the deepest blue, and her hair was the color of fine wheat. His heart had betrayed him in that moment, and he'd wanted to tell her exactly how he felt.

Thankfully, he'd held his tongue. If he hadn't, the rest of the evening would've been even harder. He'd have had to explain his failure back home and why he couldn't marry a woman based on his feelings. He couldn't be trusted to choose the right woman. He'd been wrong about Felicia, and she'd left him for someone else. He couldn't go down that path again.

CHAPTER 8

Morning coffee wasn't the same knowing Olive wasn't coming to the church to share it with him. Finch stood next to the small stove in his office and stared at the carafe he'd set to percolate an hour before and had promptly forgotten about. There were too many things to mull over, and he hadn't had enough coffee to remember that he needed more.

He wandered over to replenish his drink when he heard the sanctuary door open. Setting down his ceramic mug, he went to see who'd come in. Today of all days he wasn't sure he was happy about anyone coming by.

Belta stood at the door. Her ostentatious hat had a giant red bird perched on the brim, a decidedly worried look frozen upon its face. Belta, to his amazement, looked positively distraught.

"Miss Collins? Is there something I can do for you?"

She nodded, her chin quivering. "Forgive me."

There were many things she could be asking forgiveness for. He only knew of one thing she'd directly done to him, and if they were to be married, that thing would be forgotten by the town soon enough. "Forgive you?"

"Because of what I did, Father is using you to prove a point.

Do not misunderstand me, he firmly believes you'll be a fine pastor. But he also believes that my tongue has gone too far and that I need someone else to guide me. He feels he and Mother have failed. I've never been good at keeping secrets, like my parents. When they talk about people behind closed doors, I can't help but listen in. I've done so since I was very young."

"And now you regret honing such a. . .talent?" He wasn't sure how else to say what needed to be said without driving her away.

"Talent is a very kind way to put it. Let us be honest with one another. I sneak around and eavesdrop." She came fully into the sanctuary and sat in the nearest pew. "I don't want you to think I'm unhappy with my father's decision."

He chuckled because even though Belta never hid her feelings, today they were even more obvious than usual. "But you are unhappy."

"I am. I wish I'd never said a word. I'm so sorry about the pain I caused you, Olive, and her parents. My parents were just speculating about what was going on. Nothing more, but I didn't know that. I thought they knew some secret information. I thought they'd been meeting with Olive's parents on the sly, because they were such good friends before the split. How was I to know that they were just being spiteful and making up stories?"

"That's still no excuse for you spreading those lies." He felt a pang of his own regret. He'd thought less of Belta because of her actions, never assuming that the behavior had been learned at home.

Belta hung her head, but her hat stayed firmly attached to her hair, making it all the more difficult for him to take her seriously. The bird gave him a condemning stare as he took a deep breath.

"If you're looking for forgiveness, you have it." Holding on to a grudge wasn't going to make their lives any easier, and he truly felt sorry for her now.

"I'm in love with someone else," she wailed. "Father knows, but he doesn't care. They are both good men but don't see eye to eye because Anthony attends Olive's church. Most of the people my age do, so I've been seeing him in secret."

Finch sat in the pew in front of her and turned so he could look her in the eyes. "Secrets rarely come to any good."

"I know." Her chin trembled. "I know I must do what my father tells me to, but I don't want to. Anthony doesn't know yet, but it won't be long until he hears. When he does, he'll be furious. He warned me that if I didn't behave, Father would take measures I would regret. Anthony was right, but I never thought my father would force me to marry someone against my will." She drew a dainty kerchief from her wristlet, and he was reminded that Olive still had one of his. He hoped now that she kept it.

"The only way out of this would be for me to refuse the position, but who will lead your church if I do so? And will my refusal ruin the rapport I've built with a few members of your church? I must think of these things. If this offer was given because I was meant to take it, then I have to consider what I should do."

"I understand." She dipped her chin again. "I hoped that if I came here to tell you that I will do what my father asks but that I'm opposed to doing it, you might find a way to do what is needed without a wedding."

"That would involve convincing your father you've learned your lesson, I would say. To do that, you might want to attempt to reverse the rumor you started and perhaps apologize to the one it hurt the most." Though he wasn't going to tell her that her assumptions had come dangerously close to the truth. Olive's parents had, in fact, hired him in the hopes of his wooing their independent daughter. A beautiful scheme that had worked, despite very little prodding from them outside of the first day.

"Apologize to Olive." She paused with her lips slightly open in a grimace. "I know you're right. I love her, but she can be such a mouse. I'm sure I take advantage of that with all my ranting. She puts up with me better than most." Belta stood and wiped her hands over her hips twice, as if to shake off what she had to do. "Please think of a way to get us out of this mess."

He'd been awake all night fitfully trying to think of a way around what it looked like he had to do. Just as Jonah had wanted to do anything but face Nineveh. Why was this bothering him so much when it was the answer to his prayer? He'd asked the Lord for a church where he would never have to worry about choosing a spouse himself. If he was married to a woman he didn't love, then he could work for the remainder of his days with a partner who never distracted him, never came before the Lord, and never walked away from him the way Felicia had.

Now that he'd gotten what he'd asked for, he realized the drawback to his request. Marrying someone who didn't love him, and whom he didn't love, meant he would have someone at his side who had no wish to be there. Belta couldn't support him to the fullest, because she was in love with another man. The life of a preacher wasn't an easy one, and Belta was accustomed to ease. He groaned. Was he just making excuses and listening to his own mind instead of the leading of the Holy Spirit?

"I'll keep thinking, but I have to do what I'm led to do."

Belta gave a quick nod, hiding a sob, and headed for the door. "I'm off to talk to Olive and a few others. Good day, Reverend. Thank you for forgiving me."

He watched the door close and took a deep breath. The

Lord never asked for easy things. If He did, everyone would follow. He'd asked Hosea to marry a prostitute to show Israel how they were acting. The Lord wasn't above using marriage to show people that they needed to change. Hosea had loved his wife, trying to woo her back home time and again.

Why wasn't the answer clear in this case? He didn't feel a tug in his spirit as he usually did when making a decision. When he'd been looking for a church, the letter from Olive's parents had arrived, and he'd known without question that he was needed here. But this decision wasn't coming nearly so easily. "I'm praying for you, Miss Collins." He wondered if he'd be praying for her for a lifetime.

Olive sat in the sitting room of her parents' home, alone. Before Finch, she would have gone out looking for Belta to sit and chat in the sun. Now, she couldn't seek out either one. Belta would either know the plan her father had made for her by now or would soon learn. Finch knew, which meant she had to have a very good reason for seeking out his counsel. No more could she turn to him as a friend.

Since she'd had so few she could count as true friends, the loss felt all the stronger. Worry always made her chilled to the bone. She curled her feet under her, despite the warmth in the room, and hugged her book to her chest.

Mama entered the room, came over, and patted her knee. "Things will work out. You'll see."

Olive cringed inwardly at the idea that her parents had to know that they'd chosen a man for her and she'd fallen for him. The only thing left to do was say what they clearly knew aloud.

"I'm not so sure my plan is God's will. If it's not, then it won't work out for me. I'm not yet ready to say, 'All glory to God,' because my heart hurts. I care for him more than I thought I could." She hated that she sounded fretful, like someone who complained perpetually.

"It's all right to be unhappy. It's not good to stay there though. I wish your father and I hadn't planted the seeds of hope. We tried not to. We kept our speaking to quiet moments we thought were secret, but I suspect you knew our plan." She brushed back her hair, which had been fixed in a neat bun a few hours before. "I feel like I need to repent for my part in this."

"I thought what you did was wrong, though I now believe your heart was in the right place." Olive held the book tighter, firmly believing her words. She'd known the truth from the start and had fallen anyway. "I could have easily avoided him if I'd chosen to." The trouble was, her heart didn't want to be away from him. From the moment he'd descended the stairs of the stage, she'd wanted to be with him.

Someone knocked on the front door, and Mama rushed to answer it. Flowing lace curtains prevented Olive from seeing who was outside, but she heard Belta's voice, though she didn't sound as brash and loud as usual.

"Good morning, Mrs. Torey. May I come inside? I'd like to speak to Olive, if she's available."

Her first instinct was to run and hide. After thinking the problem through all night, she'd realized that not only had Belta spread the lie about Olive and Finch and her parents, now she'd marry Finch, which would make people wag their tongues all the more. Why would Finch step around town with Olive and then marry Belta? People would call his character into question. All because Belta had spread vicious lies.

"Olive is still in her housedress this morning and isn't taking callers. I can give her a note if you wish."

Belta sighed. "I don't mind, if she's willing to see me. I owe her a deep apology, and I'd prefer to do so with my own words, not on paper."

Mama was obviously struggling to come up with something she could say to prevent Belta from entering their home. "Well, she—"

"I owe you and your husband an apology as well," Belta interrupted. "I said things that weren't true. I heard my parents talking and thought what I repeated was fact. I shouldn't have said anything to anyone, but I did. For that, I'm very sorry. I know my words caused you pain and discomfort."

This wasn't like anything Belta had ever said before. Was Finch already changing her? Olive stood and approached the door. "I'll speak to her. Thank you, Mama."

Mama gave her a nod. "I'll pass along what you said to my husband. Thank you, Belta." She headed for the back of the house where Father was probably sitting at the table with his morning coffee.

Belta stood in the doorway and stared at Olive. "I assumed your mother wasn't telling the truth about the housedress."

Olive had never known her mother to tell an untruth. "I am, but obviously I'm here. Why don't you come in and have a seat?" She motioned her inside.

Belta entered, and Olive shut the door. "What can I do for you?" The friendship they'd shared since they were children had disappeared. She felt no desire to speak to Belta or give her forgiveness. She asked the Lord to soften her heart.

Belta went into the sitting room and sat in a chair near the sofa where Olive had been. Olive took her seat once again, placing her book on the table next to it.

"Olive, I know I hurt you. I'm so sorry. I heard what my

parents said, and I couldn't keep it to myself."

"So because it was gossip, you told everyone." Olive swallowed back a sob.

"I did. And now I'll pay for my words. I'm sure you've heard about my father's offer to Reverend Presly. I can't even imagine marrying him. I don't want to. I'm so sorry for what I've done. I didn't intend to take the man you care for."

"I don't know what to say. I'm hurt. Your words hurt me. You're supposed to be my friend. We promised to stand by each other, even after the separation, but you've changed. We used to chat and enjoy each other's company, but then you started talking about me and the people in my church. I'm not the only one who needs to hear your regrets."

"I have quite a few. Father is angry because the words that he spoke with Mother in private were spread through the town. Perhaps no one knows that they were his words, but he knows." Belta hung her head. "You have been my friend for many years, and I broke your trust. Will you forgive me? I have gone to the people I originally went to, and told them the truth. No one wants to hear a story that isn't sensational. No one wants to hear that there was really nothing to talk about. One of them even asked me why you were with the preacher all the time if there was nothing to what I'd said. I couldn't answer that. If I had, I would've broken another trust with you. I would've had to tell them that you do carry a torch for him."

Heat burned up Olive's chest to her cheeks. She drew her wrapper around her waist tightly. "I think 'carrying a torch' is perhaps a little strong." Olive couldn't look her in the eye.

"Is it? I've seen you around him, and I know you well enough to know what I'm talking about. And trust me when I tell you I understand what you're feeling. I'm in love with Anthony, and this marriage will mean I will never see him again. My father has forbidden me from even talking to him. I spoke to the reverend this morning, and he's talking about going through with this." Belta shot to her feet and strode to the other side of the room. "I'm at a loss, Olive. You've always been the wiser one, the one with the ideas that make sense. Please, tell me what to do."

Olive swallowed her pride and went to her friend. She wrapped her arms around her and laid her head on Belta's shoulder as they both looked out the window. In that moment, she knew that Belta wasn't the only one who needed to hear from her. "I can't tell you what to do, my friend," she said. "But I know what I must do."

CHAPTER 9

The sanctuary seemed like the best place to be when Finch's mind wouldn't quiet down so he could think properly. *You must die to self.* He bowed his head, trying to have faith, trying to accept what was expected of him. But no matter how he tried, his flesh rebelled against the idea.

Was there a way to make sure the other church had a preacher if he didn't take the position? Was he refusing God's plan if he didn't take it? He'd thought the Lord had sent him for Olive's church, but what if he'd actually been sent there to help Belta's? He didn't know what course to take, because nothing stood out clearly as the right path.

He bent his head and scrubbed his eyes. He knew how to pray, to stop and listen for an answer. The move away from his family and friends hadn't been so worrisome as this. His decision could leave an entire congregation without a minister.

He felt a deep nudge, reminding him that his taking the position permanently wasn't the only answer. Belta's church only had to have someone teaching in the interim. Someone had to lead them until a pastor could be found. Maybe he wasn't meant to be their pastor. Perhaps he was looking at this entirely wrong?

Lord, send me a sign of what I should do. I've never tested You. I've never asked You to show Yourself to me. I've always trusted You. In this, please show me the path I'm supposed to take. I'm confused and worried I'll do the wrong thing.

The door behind him creaked. He didn't have the energy to get up and face Alma or whoever had made their way to the church that morning. If someone was coming by to sit in the sanctuary to pray as some people did, they didn't need him to interrupt them.

Slow and steady steps with the slight swish of skirts alerted him to the fact that a woman was approaching him. In the next instant, the soft scent of roses surrounded him. Olive's scent. He glanced over as she sat down next to him in the pew.

He'd asked for a sign, a clear path, and the very woman who was making him question God's will had come in. Was this God's way of showing him the right path? Was he meant to follow his heart?

But your heart was wrong last time. His own thoughts convicted him. Olive had never shown any interest in him other than as an acquaintance. She'd appreciated him and his efforts as a pastor, but she'd never given him any clue that she would be interested in him as a helpmate.

"You seem troubled, Finch," Olive said quietly.

Her use of his name, without the slightest hesitation, was like the sign he needed. Perhaps she had come to find him because she was as disturbed over this situation as he was. "I am. Are you here to see me through it?"

She bowed her head. "That is what friends do. Is it not?"

He took a deep breath. "It is, and I appreciate it very much. Pray with me?" He reached out for her hand, knowing that the moment he touched her, he would feel that same excitement he had in the past, the excitement that he'd never experienced before with the touch of any other woman.

She reached over and slid her delicate fingers through his, igniting his senses. This woman made the woman of his past fade to nothing. This woman made him want to run far away from the temptation to marry another, even if it meant he could preach in their church. This woman was the one he'd been sent all this way to marry. In that instant, he knew it.

"Lord, thank You for showing me the right path."

Olive's head jerked to look at him, and he almost laughed.

"You've decided? Then I'm too late. I had hoped to come and convince you not to marry Belta." She stood hurriedly. "Please forgive me for disturbing you."

Disturbing him? He turned and caught her swiping at her eyes as she ducked out of the large wooden doors.

Olive was crying. He couldn't have that. She was Olive, the woman he saw as strong and fearless. She was the woman who'd embraced the challenge to introduce him about town and who'd faced the people who didn't want to speak to her, just so he'd know them.

He jogged after her, yanking the door open and making it groan loudly. Olive whipped around at the sound. Her tearstained cheeks tore at his heart.

"Come and talk to me by the tree. You haven't disturbed me at all. On the contrary, I think you've given me my answer." He glanced up at the bright blue sky. When he'd arrived, he'd felt boxed in by the mountains, since the sky seemed close enough to touch. Now he felt free, as if Baker's Nook was home and he'd finally arrived.

Olive strode to him and walked at his side to the large tree where they'd sat after she'd introduced him to everyone. Looking back, he realized he'd started to fall in love with her there.

"What is it?" She sat on the ground, arranging her

skirts over her boots.

"Tell me more about your thoughts. Obviously, something has weighed heavily on you." He tugged a handkerchief from his pocket and gave it to her.

She gently took the fabric square and dabbed her eyes. "I'm sure I have my ideas out of sorts. You know much more than I do." Olive kept her head bowed.

He reached for her hand and laid his atop it. She tensed under his touch and finally looked up at him, confusion clouding her eyes. He prayed for the right words to say and that she felt as he did. This was the moment he'd been waiting for. He had to admit how he felt. He'd tried to hide it, which had led to the turmoil he'd been dealing with all morning. He'd made up excuses for marrying Belta so he could avoid the protestations of his heart. Sometimes the heart was wicked, but sometimes it knew the correct path, if one would only listen.

"I've been afraid that I was doing exactly what I wanted to avoid when I came here." He released her hand and touched her cheek, reveling in its softness. Her little sigh and fluttering lashes as she closed her eyes made his heart race. "I was afraid of the feelings I had for you, Olive. I left Kansas because I'd failed to choose the right bride. I asked God to provide a place for me to teach His Word where I wouldn't ever be in that situation again."

He bowed his head and let his hand fall to his leg. "I'm sorry I hurt you. I was trying to convince myself that I had to marry Belta because my growing regard for you was beginning to terrify me. What if I chose wrong again?"

Olive couldn't touch Finch's cheek the way he'd touched hers. She simply didn't have the courage. She hesitated only a moment then laid her hand on his arm. His head snapped up, and his haunted gaze met hers.

"You didn't. You chose exactly right. When you arrived, I didn't want a husband." She stopped, mortified to be talking so freely right outside the church but close enough to the town to be seen.

"But now you do?" Finch asked, gathering her hand to his once again. "I hope you do."

"I'm not certain I would make a good wife. My father says I'm rather independent." Her spirit rose as Finch relaxed and his face released the pain from a moment before.

"I think you would make a fine wife. Fine indeed." He ran his fingers lightly over hers, sending delicious tingles up her arm.

"I—I believe you would make a superior husband as well." She stuttered over the words, not because they were untrue but because everything that had given her confidence to that point seemed to have vanished. Finch had sounded like he wanted no such relationship. Could they both have been wrong?

Finch glanced over his shoulder and looked toward town. There was no one there. Finally, no one strode down the street or was out for a walk. They were alone. He shifted closer to her, facing her with their knees touching.

"And do you think I would make a superior husband. . . to you?"

The hope in his voice was unmistakable. Her boldness inched back, and she bit her lip for a moment. A negative answer could mean that he would take on the position of pastoring the other church. Her friends would have leadership, but she would not have a husband. And now she knew that Finch was a gift, one she wanted more than she ever realized.

"Yes, for as little as I know about the subject, I'm sure of that." She laughed, unable to keep her nerves hidden a moment longer.

He caressed her cheek again, sending lovely tremors cascading through her. Was this what love felt like? Warmth, happiness, and inexplicable excitement? Perhaps that was God's plan, so that one could recall the joy when hardship came.

Finch cupped her cheeks, softly and steadily leading her closer to him. "I feel like I should ask your father's permission. Then again, I was hired with the hope that this very thing would happen." He laughed as he drew her forehead to his own.

Warmth poured off Finch, and his breath tickled her face. If anyone had asked her before this moment if she'd ever thought of being kissed, she would have rushed away from the conversation. No Christian woman would say that, would she? But here she was, wishing this man would kiss her. Maybe wanting to be kissed by a man who'd spoken of marriage wasn't as scandalous as she'd thought.

"I think Father will be pleasantly surprised when we tell him."

One side of Finch's mouth lifted slightly. "I hadn't planned to share this part with him." He leaned forward and gently brushed his lips across hers. The moment was so brief she was sure she'd imagined it, yet she couldn't deny the rush of warmth.

"I promise you, I will kiss you every day that ends in Y, for the remainder of our days together once I have the proper permission. That comes from you, and then from your father. I don't want to seek a relationship with you if you want no part of it. I've already done that and have no desire to do it again."

Olive gripped his hand in hers and held tightly so he could feel as well as understand her words. "I want that. Very much."

"You will never have to be concerned about not having a friend again. I will be there for you until I take my dying breath."

She hadn't realized how much she needed to hear just that. Belta had been a friend, but not one she could confide in. Her parents were aging. She needed someone to stick closer than a brother, and Finch was that someone. He was the man she loved and the man she wanted to be her closest friend, for the remainder of her days.

"And I will stand by you."

He stood and held out his hand to help her up. "Then I think it's time we go tell your father. Perhaps he can help me figure out what to say to the other church. That's the only part of this situation that feels unfinished."

Her face shone up at him. "We'll pray about it. God will find a way. He always does."

CHAPTER 10

Belta and her father sat across the table from Finch and Olive. Olive heard her parents in the kitchen talking softly, but they wouldn't be entering the room. Father had given his blessing to marry, but he'd said she and Finch needed to handle the delicate situation with the new church together, with God's help.

She laid a hand on Finch's arm under the table. Giving away what was about to be said would only hurt feelings, and that wasn't her intent. She only wanted to give Finch silent support. When she'd laid her head down to fall asleep the night before, she'd marveled at the way the Lord had moved in her life.

"I'm glad you could meet with us today." Finch folded his hands in front of him. "Why don't we start this meeting off with a word of prayer?"

Belta and her father both gave a curt nod and allowed Finch to pray for them. He was kind, offering words of discernment and caring. He truly was concerned for these people, even though Belta's father had tried to manipulate him into marrying his daughter.

Once Finch finished, Mr. Collins started before Finch could even catch his breath. "Reverend, I'm wondering why you have invited Miss Torey to this meeting? It seems like we should've kept this to just the three of us." He indicated his daughter.

Finch smiled at Olive, obviously undeterred. "I've invited Olive because she is a very important part of this conversation. You see, the rumors your daughter spread through town about Olive and me were, at least in part, true. Though we've never done anything untoward, we were growing closer to one another. I can't marry your daughter when I love someone else."

Olive gave him a smile to let him know that she loved him. She couldn't say as much out loud yet, but she felt it all the same. Mr. Collins stared at her with narrowed eyes, like he was trying to read her thoughts.

"You're in love? All of a sudden? You weren't in love when I spoke to you just yesterday about this offer. What changed?" He crossed his arms. "And don't think for a moment that I'll still offer you the job if you won't marry my daughter."

Finch replied, "What changed is my heart. I should be clearer. I care for Olive and will marry her soon. I cared about her yesterday too, but I wasn't sure of her feelings toward me. Your proposal forced both of us to admit what we'd been hiding for quite a while."

"I knew it," Belta said. "I knew she carried a torch for you. Good for you, Olive. I was worried that the nonsense with your parents would keep you from following your heart."

"Quiet. I don't want another word out of you." Mr. Collins scowled at her. He turned his attention back to Finch. "You've left me in a terrible position. It's almost the end of summer now. Fall will only last a short time. We need a preacher."

"Might I suggest you remove the stipulation of marrying your daughter? She has a mind and a heart of her own," Finch said. "I could have easily married her then picked up our little family and moved back to Kansas. Marriage doesn't hold a man in place. Happiness and contentment do. If you want my services, I'm happy to preach for you. If you do not, then I'll be preaching at Olive's church every Sunday morning, promptly at eight thirty. You're welcome to join us."

Mr. Collins scoffed. "Join you? We separated because things were not being done properly. We have our ways." Mr. Collins stood. "This is a waste of my time. Belta, come along."

Belta sat in her chair for a moment. "I don't want to disrespect you, Father, but I won't come with you. I'm old enough now to make my own choice, and I choose Anthony. I'm sorry you don't like the man I love, but I can't keep living a life where you want me to simply do what you say." She closed her eyes for a moment, and the room went completely silent.

"Belta, this isn't the time or the place for this nonsense," Mr. Collins huffed. He turned and left the room.

"Reverend Presly, should my beau ask for my hand, would you marry us?" Belta looked directly at Finch. "As you're the only minister in town, I'm praying you agree. If not, we'll have to take the stage to Custer and marry in front of a judge."

"I wouldn't hear of it!" Mr. Collins strode back into the room. "Married in a courthouse? Never. Not one of my children."

"Which are you more opposed to, Father? Would you rather I marry the man I love in front of a judge, or a preacher? I'm marrying him, either way."

Olive had known Belta was a woman who said what came to mind with little care about how it affected others, but she had thought her relationship was different with her father. He certainly seemed surprised by the turn.

Instead of answering her, he turned on his heel and this time left the house. Belta sighed heavily. "I'll need to go find Anthony straightaway before Father does. I wouldn't put it past Father to threaten him. He doesn't approve in the slightest."

Finch leaned forward. "Is there any reason he feels this way? Should you be concerned?"

Belta chuckled. "No. Anthony is caring and sweet. I don't deserve him, and I want to be better for him. I don't like asking you to go against my parents' wishes, but sometimes they are wrong. They don't see marriage the way I do. Theirs was arranged. They've been passably happy, but they've never publicly shared an embrace or a kindness the way Anthony does with me. I'm sure I could be content with someone they chose, but I prefer happiness."

Olive thanked God for her parents and their support. Every parent she knew in Baker's Nook wanted the best for their child, but what they thought was best wasn't always the right thing. Some people even believed that love was a weakness, believing that a marriage founded on feelings wouldn't last.

"I would like for your father and mother to gently come around to your decision before we talk about a binding wedding. I hope you are able to convince them."

Belta smiled. "I took your advice yesterday and went to everyone I'd spoken to about Olive's parents and asked for forgiveness. Father doesn't know that yet. I'm trying to control my tongue and my desire for the reaction of my peers. If my father sees I can make good decisions, he'll trust me with this one. Thank you, Reverend and Olive, for listening to me when you could've been angry and unforgiving." She stood and adjusted her hat as she headed for the door.

"Olive, I hope I can attend your wedding. I wish you all the happiness in the world." Belta turned and left.

Finch gathered her hands in his. "We need to pray for her and for her father. He's feeling out of control, and he seems to be a man who likes to be in charge of a situation. Having a daughter who is insisting on her own way is going to make for a very stressful time for everyone."

Olive nodded. "And we need to pray for someone to be appointed as their pastor. They need one. If they aren't going to come back to ours, then they need leadership."

"Bless you for thinking of them." He bowed his head.

"Heavenly Father, we ask that You be with Miss Collins as she finds Anthony. Lead them both into being the people You want them to be. If that means they are to be together, please soften her father's heart to Anthony. Let him be looked upon as a son, not an interloper. Reveal Yourself to Mr. Collins and let him know what he needs to do and how to proceed."

Finch continued the prayer, and Olive held his hands, glad he was a man of conviction. He would make a fine leader of their home. When he finished, she added her own words of thanks for bringing a godly man into her life.

Finch released her then cupped her cheeks as he kissed her lips. His tender way was both pleasing and exciting. He was never harsh or demanding. He was simply a man who was sure of his God and so was sure of his own ways. Olive returned his kiss, and Finch leaned in closer, holding her.

Since they were seated, she was not overly close to him, but his kiss ignited an urgency to wed him so they could live their lives as one, together, always.

"I'd like to make you my bride before the snow comes, if that's possible," he whispered softly in her ear.

"I don't see why we couldn't." Now that the idea had come, she wanted it to happen right away.

"Then I'll go down to the newspaper and invite the town."

The only trouble was, there was no other preacher available. Would they have to go somewhere else, just to be married?

"Who will perform the ceremony?"

Finch opened his mouth to answer as someone knocked

on the front door. Mama bustled through the room to answer it. Finch waited as Mama's voice floated down the short hall to where they sat. "Mr. Dogwood, how unexpected. Yes, Finch is just down here. Come in."

Mr. Dogwood entered, and Olive moved away from Finch to make their visitor more comfortable. He took a seat and said, "Reverend, good to see you again. I was walking home from a meeting at work when Mr. Collins met me and told me what happened." He leaned forward. "I want you to know that the other elders in our church do not feel the same way he does. We weren't so sure we wanted to share a pastor with the other church, as that seems like the perfect way to have the same issues we had with the former pastor. To that end, I reached out to a friend in Custer who happened to know of someone they could send to us. I don't see any lack in your ability, but your focus should be on the church who hired you. I hope you understand."

Finch grinned and held out his hand to Mr. Dogwood. "I'm so glad you had the foresight to do that. When he arrives, I'll be asking him to do a wedding service, straightaway."

Mr. Dogwood laughed. "I'm happy to hear it. I'd heard a rumor that you and Miss Torey were seeing quite a bit of each other, but I try not to put too much faith in rumors."

Finch reached for her hand and held it close. "In this case, the rumor is true."

"Blessings to you." Mr. Dogwood stood. "That was all I wanted to share with you. I didn't want you to concern yourself, thinking we wouldn't be able to find someone. And please excuse Mr. Collins. I think he was so concerned with his daughter he couldn't think clearly. I'm sorry to have involved you in this mess."

Finch stood and shook his hand once again. "Think nothing of it. God worked through every part to His glory, and for that I'm incredibly grateful."

Mr. Dogwood put his hat back on and touched the brim before he left.

Finch sat back down and smiled at her. "It appears the Lord is taking care of every issue we can come up with."

She grinned at him. "Then let's pray their minister gets here quickly."

Two months later

Bunting adorned the aisles of the new Immanuel Lutheran church, though Olive couldn't say what else was new, since she'd never set foot in the building before today. Mrs. Collins approached, dabbing her eyes.

"Olive, good to see you. So glad you and your husband could attend." Mrs. Collins kissed her lightly on the cheek. Hearing someone call Finch her husband was still new and thrilling.

"Thank you. I wouldn't miss Belta's wedding." Especially after the change she'd seen over the past months. Belta had worked hard to avoid gossip and situations that would tempt her. Instead, she'd worked to plan for her wedding and the house she would share with Anthony after today.

"I'm so glad. I'm also thankful that Anthony agreed to start attending here. We don't mean to take away your congregation, but Maxwell was beside himself when he thought Belta would be attending the other church."

As much as Olive had wanted her new friend to attend with her, she was happy Belta was being allowed to marry the man she wanted. Anthony still seemed unsure of his place in the whole situation, but he was handling it well.

"Look." Olive nudged Finch in the shoulder and nodded toward the door. There stood Alma with her husband, looking more nervous than a mouse.

"I thought our wedding was the only time he'd set foot in a church?" Finch took her hand as he often did.

"Alma mentioned that she was plying him with sweets and reminding him that if Belta could be forgiven, so could he. The Lord never runs out of mercy."

"Amen." He grinned. "Does that mean we should start expecting him occasionally on Sunday?"

Tears gathered behind Olive's eyes as she recalled the day Alma had helped her. "We keep praying for that."

Anthony nervously walked up the aisle and took his place at the front as the organ played a few notes. Since weddings happened so rarely in Baker's Nook, everyone made a big to-do of the occasion. They all wore their Sunday best and planned to make a day of it.

After the reading of the vows and the presentation of Anthony and Belta to the congregation, everyone headed outside for a picnic. Finch spread out a blanket and anchored each corner with stones he gathered.

A small rig with one horse drove up the street toward the church. Finch shaded his eyes with his hand and squinted at the approaching driver. "Know who that is?"

Olive turned from the task of unpacking their lunch and eyed the man. "I have no idea."

Finch's jaw firmed as the wagon came to a standstill and an older man climbed down. "I know who it is. It's my pa. I don't know why he would've come all this way."

Olive rested what she hoped was a supporting hand on his arm. "I do. Mama and Father sent him a letter. I didn't tell you, because we all hoped he would come but didn't want to give you false hope."

He sighed and gave her a smile then squeezed her hand. "I should go over and meet him. He'll be looking for me." Finch left, and Olive waited by the blanket, since he hadn't asked her to follow him.

Mama appeared at her side. "Is everything all right? Is he pleased?"

She nodded and gave her mother an embrace. Everything would be fine. No matter what Finch's father had to say, they were still a family, and they would support each other. Finch and his father slowly picked their way around the other blankets, stopping and talking to a few people on the way until they finally reached her.

"Olive, this is my father, Alfred Presly. Father, this is my bride, Olive."

The older man looked just as she expected Finch's father to look, an older version of the man she loved. "Pleased to meet you."

He nodded. "And you."

"Ma and Pa got your parents' letter a few weeks ago, and they were getting ready to come when Ma took sick. She's doing better now but staying with her sister."

"I'm so sorry, Mr. Presly. You'll stay for a while, won't you?"

Finch wrapped his strong arm around her waist and kissed her temple.

Finch's father smiled at them. "I was pretty disappointed when you didn't marry Felicia, Finch. Now I'm not. She never would've accepted me. She didn't even come to see your ma when she was ill, and we've known that family for years. It's a shame."

Olive saw the chance to redeem the relationship between Finch and his father. "I welcome you. Stay as long as you'd like."

He looked a little sheepish. "Looks like I arrived in time for a picnic. May I join you?"

Finch crouched and began arranging what they'd brought into three portions instead of two. "There's plenty. Please, sit and join us."

Finch had been very happy the day of their wedding, but one thing had put a damper on his joy. He missed his own family. Now, his father was here with him and would hear him preach.

Being an independent woman didn't mean Olive had to be alone or make every choice on her own. She still found ways to be strong, but now she could be strong beside her husband, loving him and any children they might have. God had shown her steadily and lovingly that she could be who He made her to be and also be Finch's wife, which was the greatest gift of all.

Kari Trumbo is a *USA Today* bestselling author who writes swoony heroes and places that become characters with detail and heart. Her favorite place to write about is the place her heart lives (even if she doesn't)—South Dakota. Kari loves reading, listening to contemporary Christian music, singing when no one's listening, and curling up near the woodstove when winter hits. She makes her home in central Minnesota, land of frigid toes and mosquitoes the size of compact cars, with her husband of over twenty years. They have two daughters, two sons, four cats, and one hungry woodstove.

MORE ROMANCE COLLECTIONS FROM BARBOUR PUBLISHING!

THE LEGACY OF THE ROCKING K RANCH

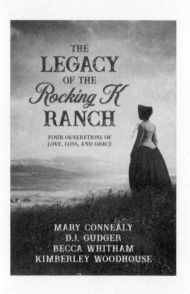

By Mary Connealy, D. J. Gudger, Becca Whitham,
and Kimberley Woodhouse

In 1910, Penelope Cooper, an ambitious writer who has
been commissioned by her publisher to present tales of
the American Wild West, returns to her family's ranch in
Wyoming to interview the women of her family about the
past. As each elder woman tells her story, Penelope discovers
the many facets of her family's legacy—their stories of love,
loss, grace, adoption, struggles with the law, relationships
with natives, and through it all, family bonds.

Paperback / 978-1-63609-739-8

A Louisiana Christmas to Remember

By Betsy St. Amant, Morgan Tarpley Smith, and Lenora Worth

Three heartwarming, interconnected stories of faith, love, and restoration, brought to you by three Louisiana-native authors. Will a rare snowy Louisiana Christmas bring restoration and hope to the hometown and hearts of three women from the town's founding family? Meet Mattie: a passionate visionary who learns to forgive and finds love in unexpected places. . . Meet Jolene: an artist and prodigal daughter who discovers love exists in the very place she once called home. . . Meet Adale: a beautiful widow who finally dares to love again. . . And don't forget Granny, whose feisty spirit, blunt dialogue, and quirky ways play an important and endearing role.

Paperback / 978-1-63609-647-6

MORE ROMANCE COLLECTIONS FROM BARBOUR PUBLISHING!

ACROSS THE SHORES

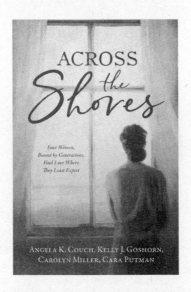

By Angela K Couch, Kelly J. Goshorn,
Carolyn Miller, and Cara Putman

Despite the years and miles that separate them, four women
are linked by a gold pendant and a shared faith in God.
In New South Wales, 1851, Josephine follows her brother
on a hunt for gold. Caroline is determined to start fresh in
Baltimore, 1877, even while hiding the scars of her past. Anna's
wayward brother seeks refuge in Canada, 1906, dragging her
along on the journey. In the Outer Banks, 1942, Lauren is
determined to find her missing brother. Each woman's faith
will be tested even as love meets them on the shores.

Paperback / 978-1-63609-519-6

LUMBERJACKS AND LADIES

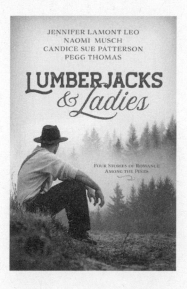

By Jennifer Lamont Leo, Naomi Musch,
Candice Sue Patterson, and Pegg Thomas

Struggling to remain independent in the 1800s,
four women reluctantly open up to help—and love.
Winifred finds herself running the family lobstering
business, stubbornly rejecting help from a local lumberjack.
Eliza Beth cooks for a logging crew, spurning the men's
advances, until reoccurring gifts capture her attention.
Maggie seeks a husband—in name only—from the logging
camps, but the man who answers her letter is a heart-
touching surprise. Carrie will not sell her timberland and
allows the banker's nephew to sign onto her logging crew to
ferret out the reason she is losing money at an alarming rate.

Paperback / 978-1-63609-140-2

JOIN US ONLINE!

Christian Fiction for Women

*Christian Fiction for Women is your online home
for the latest in Christian fiction.*

Check us out online for:

- Giveaways
- Recipes
- Info about Upcoming Releases
- Book Trailers
- News and More!

Find Christian Fiction for Women at Your Favorite Social Media Site:

 Search "Christian Fiction for Women"

 @fictionforwomen